Praise for *Street Corner D*

T0032382

"In this intense multigenerational famny saga, ivraut ionows up her hugely insightful first novel, *How to Make a Life*, with an equally profound and deep exploration into the lives and struggles of early-twentieth-century Jewish immigrants in New York City. With clean, crisp storytelling, we can't help but be as seduced as her characters are lured into the dangerous and seedy world of gangs and the infamous Murder Inc. A great page-turner of a novel."

—Howard Jay Smith, author of
Beethoven in Love; Opus 139 and *Meeting Mozart*

"The 1930s of *Street Corner Dreams* was an extremely challenging time—especially for Jewish immigrants to the US. Florence Reiss Kraut has crafted a compelling family saga with memorable characters swept up in the complexities of life in crowded Brooklyn tenements, impacted by the Great Depression and omnipresent gangs. Kraut raises essential and enduring questions about the nature of love and family responsibility."

—Meryl Ain, author of *Shadows We Carry*
and *The Takeaway Men*

"In this moving and suspenseful novel, an era comes alive. When Gilda sacrifices the independence she came to the US to find, will she find love? Will Ben's pursuit of an honest trade in gangster-ridden New York enable his family to survive? When Morty tangles with gangsters in an effort to save his father's livelihood, will he ever return? I came to care about these characters, to root for them, and to be grateful for the close-knit community that helps them make their way."

—Wendy Sanford, author of *These Walls Between Us:
A Memoir of Friendship Across Race and Class*

"As in her previous novel, Kraut immerses the reader into world of Jewish immigrants. The reader takes the cold plunge in icy waters to navigate the seemingly never-ending obstacles poor, naïve foreigners must swim through. This time, in addition to a well-characterized family drama, the story dives into crime—protection, mobsters, Murder Inc.—and the fearful grip this enterprise held on daily life. As we get deeper into this family story, the trajectory makes this a serious page-turner. This is a must-read for anyone interested in this historic period."

—Jan Marin Tramontano, author of *We've Come Undone*,
The Me I Was with You, and
Standing on the Corner of Lost and Found

"In her new novel, Florence Kraut weaves a dramatic story of family, romance, and suspense set in the Jewish neighborhoods of Brooklyn of the 1930s, where new immigrants are trying desperately to get ahead and pressure from gangs is part of daily life. The enduring power of family is at the heart of this compelling read, proving that sometimes the dreams you give up can lead to something better."

—Virginia Weir, author of *Stay a Friend as Long as You Can*
and *The Two Elizabeths*

Street Corner Dreams

STREET CORNER DREAMS

A NOVEL

FLORENCE REISS KRAUT

SHE WRITES PRESS

Published 2023
Printed in the United States of America
Print ISBN: 978-1-64742-591-3
E-ISBN: 978-1-64742-592-0
Library of Congress Control Number: 2023909295

For information, address:
She Writes Press
1569 Solano Ave #546
Berkeley, CA 94707

Interior Design by Kiran Spees

She Writes Press is a division of SparkPoint Studio, LLC.

For my daughter Ruth, who found the nugget of this story and encouraged me to write it.

And for my husband, Allen, who always has my back.

Contents

Part Three
1940

Part Four
1940-1942

Preface

In the early twentieth century, millions of immigrants came to the United States looking to improve their lives and provide a better future for their children. In the first decade of the century alone, 8.2 million immigrants came to America; by 1910, in New York City, three-quarters of the residents were either children of immigrants or immigrants themselves, and nearly fifteen percent of the country had been born out of the United States.

Unlike prior arrivals from Northern Europe, most of these immigrants came from Southern and Eastern Europe, including Italians, Greeks, Poles, Russians, and Jews. Life was very hard for them as they faced poverty, crowded and dirty tenement living conditions, and enormous prejudice from the established groups who had preceded them. Still, most of these immigrants fashioned new lives, making friends, helping each other, falling in love, creating families. They worked hard, sent their children to school, and saw the next generation better their futures and improve their lives.

But for some of those children of immigrants, the lure of the streets proved too strong. Street gangs ruled neighborhoods by bullying, petty crimes, extortion, and threats. Joining a gang gave boys protection and, more importantly, fast and easy money. Most of the gangs were loosely organized around ethnic groups, and they fought each other for ownership of the criminal businesses in their neighborhoods. That is until Prohibition became the law in 1920.

Arnold Rothstein, born to a wealthy and pious Jewish New York family, was addicted to gambling, but he was so brilliant that he had already earned a fortune by organizing the illegal gambling industry in New York. When Prohibition became law, he again found a way to make a big business from bootleg alcohol by purchasing liquor from England and Canada, smuggling it into America, and selling the alcohol to illegal speakeasies that replaced the legal bars and taverns. Rothstein went on to organize the illegal narcotics trade and was murdered by the time Prohibition was repealed in 1931. But the men he had recruited and trained in the early days of Prohibition—the Jewish and Italian gang bosses like Meyer Lansky, Lucky Luciano, and Bugsy Siegel—had learned how to make big business of a host of criminal enterprises. They went on to develop a more effective organization for illegal activities, which the newspapers called the National Crime Syndicate. Their criminal activities were murder, illegal gambling, prostitution, theft, money laundering, arms trafficking, fraud, fencing, kidnapping, and robbery.

By 1933, with Prohibition behind them, and wanting to distance themselves from the dirty work that was required by their illegal businesses, they had outsourced the worst violence to a group called Murder, Inc., founded in Brownsville and run by Louis Lepke Buchalter and Albert Anastasia. Murder, Inc., was active from 1929 to 1941 and was the enforcement arm of the National Crime Syndicate.

Murder, Inc., was composed of Jewish and Italian American gangsters mainly recruited from neighborhoods in Manhattan (Lower East Side) and Brooklyn (Brownsville, East New York, and Ocean Hill). Murder, Inc., was responsible for hundreds of contract killings until Abe "Kid Twist" Reles, who worked directly with Lepke and Anastasia, turned state's evidence in order to keep himself from jail and possible execution. In the trials that followed, many members of Murder, Inc., were convicted and executed, and Reles himself died, probably murdered, while in police custody.

Today, later generations of Jewish and Italian families, who no longer have any connection with organized crime, are aware of their ancestors' involvement in the gangs of the early twentieth century. In Jewish communities, it is seldom talked about, but well-known, that in the first half of the twentieth century many Jewish immigrant families in New York City had relatives or friends who were involved, tempted, or had to contend with the gangsters who ruled the streets of Brooklyn and the Lower East Side.

Street Corner Dreams is a novel in which one such family is portrayed.

Part One

1914–1921

CHAPTER I

GOLDA

Golda Daneshev walked off the ship with the first- and second-class passengers clutching a blue-blanketed two-day-old baby in one arm and a bundle of quilts and a suitcase in the other. *It was not supposed to be like this,* she thought. Trembling, she swallowed hard over the lump rising in her throat. *Breathe,* she told herself, *breathe. Don't stumble. Keep your mind on your steps. Watch where you walk.*

A uniformed porter approached her and said something in English. She didn't understand the words, but the meaning was plain as he reached to take her suitcase. Golda held tight, shook her head vigorously, and stared straight ahead as she walked down the wooden pier onto Twelfth Avenue. Inside she felt like a frantic animal was racing about the pit of her stomach, running up to her throat, slamming into her heart. Terror, grief, and rage ricocheted around and around her head.

At the sidewalk, Golda stopped in her tracks, peering left and right. The nurse had said the passengers from steerage would be coming off at the next pier after they were examined and approved for immigration on Ellis Island. She could see throngs of people waiting to greet them when they were eventually released, and she'd heard that process took hours.

She was lucky. The doctor who'd delivered the baby she held in her arms had arranged for her to gather with the first- and second-class passengers in the huge, mirrored ballroom. There they were quickly and politely "inspected" by him and one other doctor before being welcomed to step off the ship into the New York City streets, where they were greeted by friends and family or whisked away by taxis.

Golda stood in line holding the baby and glancing every now and then into the mirror as she made her way to the doctor. She knew she looked out of place in her plain navy dress, with a paisley-patterned shawl on her shoulders and a brown cap over her auburn curls. Most of the women in that line wore fashionable tweed city suits and hats with feathers perched at fetching angles on their heads. *I look like someone's maid*, she thought. *Although maybe I look too young to be a maid. Young and scared. And tall and skinny.* Golda took a deep breath. *Why did I let Esther talk me into coming to America now?*

She jiggled the baby in her arms, hoping that would help him sleep, but she needn't have bothered. He was in a deep slumber after having devoured one of the bottles of evaporated milk the nurse had given her. As she got closer to the doctors, the one she knew beckoned her to join his line, and when she was before him, he took her passport, said something she didn't understand, and stamped the book. He nodded his head and motioned her to leave the ship with the woman in front of her. Before she knew it, she was on the street.

She began to make her way to the next pier, pushing through the crowds. That was where Ben Feinstein would be waiting for her, and they would have to find each other. *Do I even remember what he looks like? Will I recognize him?* He would be looking for her sister Esther, his pregnant wife, not Golda and a newborn child. But Esther was never coming off the ship; she lay dead wherever they kept those few unfortunate souls who did not survive the trip across the Atlantic Ocean. A sob caught in her throat. She willed herself to think of something else. *Think of that nurse!*

She'd been so kind to her, that nurse. Before they left the boat, she had instructed Golda, in broken Polish, on how to care for the baby. Somehow Golda had understood her. She wondered how one became a nurse. In her Polish town of Lesko, ruled by the Austro-Hungarian Empire, there were midwives who birthed babies and knew about herbs for healing. And there was a doctor with a clinic for those who were too sick for herbs.

Golda had watched the nurse on the ship help the doctor and tend Esther, and she thought how wonderful it would be to learn to be a nurse, to be independent and care for yourself without consulting others, maybe even to help save lives. She envied her, that nurse.

Then she heard her mother's voice in her head; it was a particular grating sound, always accompanied by a finger wagging in her face as she stood close to Golda, looking up at her daughter who was a head taller. "Don't be jealous of other people. Don't wish for a life other than the one you were given. It's unbecoming." Just the thought of her mother's disapproval made Golda feel ashamed.

Anyway, Golda thought, pushing her mother out of her head, *that nurse had education, something I've never been able to afford.* Golda could read and write, both Yiddish and Polish, but that did not give her an opportunity to get a job, to earn real money. She wondered again what she would do in this new country. Then she looked down at the baby she was carrying and wondered what would happen to him.

It was a blessing to be off the ship, out of steerage, where she and the others too poor to buy second-class tickets had endured a week of what she could only call Gehenna, hell. Her body was still adjusting to the firm earth. She'd become used to swaying with her legs wide apart to keep her balance. Now, though, she swayed holding the baby to keep him from waking. She wanted to keep him sleeping, quiet, for as long as she could.

Golda found a place to wait at the edge of the pier and look out into the city. If the baby woke despite her jiggling and swaying, she would have to feed him. In her bundle was one bottle of evaporated milk, provided by the nurse. She'd given Golda two bottles when they left the infirmary, but Golda used the first one on the ship. The baby was still sleeping, and when he woke up she would use the second one, but after that she did not know what she would do. Her stomach roiled with anxiety. *Where is Ben?*

She looked out into the street. Her eyes scanned each face, each man. She remembered he was tall, Ben Feinstein. That was a blessing, because she could look at the heads of those who stood above the crowd. Golda was very tired, but she braced herself for a long wait. She could not let herself miss him.

She busied herself looking around at the crowds walking on the street. The hum and buzz made her slightly dizzy. Streetcars passed, some still pulled by horses but most motorized. If she were in her town now, she would be on a dirt road, because they lived on the outskirts of Lesko. There would be occasional carts passing by, pulled by a mule or a horse. Most people walked. She rarely saw a motorcar in the village, but when she and Esther had arrived in Hamburg to take the ship to America, they had been all around. And here, in New York, the streets were full of them.

Workingmen wearing rough, well-used clothing, caps on head, pushing carts or carrying burdens, passed her by. Office men wearing suits, looking like they sat behind desks all day, were also in the crowds. And she saw women in ankle-length skirts, with belted jackets and matching hats, or sometimes in fur-trimmed coats.

It was March and still cold, although not as cold as home, where it could still be snowing. A wind blew off the Hudson River, chilling her despite her wool shawl and cap. Golda looked down at her dress. At least it was clean. She'd changed from the dress she had been wearing the day Esther went into labor. It was stained with her sister's blood, and the doctor had ordered her to change before she came back into the infirmary. She'd packed the dress in her suitcase and would try washing it when she arrived wherever she was going. Maybe it could be salvaged. But she couldn't bear to look at it.

What would people see if they looked at her? A young woman holding an infant. And this infant—who was he? She snuggled the baby closer and looked down at him swaddled in the blue blanket. He was beautiful, his face serene in sleep. His features were not red and misshapen like her brothers' had been when they were born. This, she knew, was because he had been taken by surgery from Esther . . . The thought of Esther closed her throat in grief and despair. She knew if Esther had given birth in the village, she would almost certainly have died anyway, and likely the baby too. Golda squeezed her eyes shut. She forced herself to look at the people walking off the pier.

Please, God, help me find Ben. Her back hurt. Her heart hurt.

When she allowed her thoughts to fix on what had happened just two days ago, her throat closed, and she could barely swallow. *What will I tell our parents? What will I tell Ben? Where is he?* She stared here, there, eyes flitting from one tall man to another until they burned. *What if he doesn't come?* Her heart beat hard. She shook her head. *Stop thinking like this!*

After what seemed like hours, she began to give up hope. Her arm and shoulder ached from the weight of the baby. She shifted him to her other arm. Esther had said she was seven months pregnant, but Golda knew that wasn't true. This boy was big. The nurse had noticed and remarked on it. Golda had been embarrassed and wanted to protest and protect Esther's reputation, but she couldn't. Golda's eyes swept across the crowds again, then looked down at the baby. She shifted him to better distribute the weight, glanced up, and focused on the people walking off the ferry that had come from Ellis Island. What had the nurse said? People were examined by doctors to make sure they didn't have any diseases. They were asked questions. Tested. They had to have money too.

The crowds of immigrants disembarking looked exhausted. She wondered where that nice lady was—the one who had helped her on the ship when Esther had gone into labor. Golda wanted to thank her again, and she was still looking for that woman, her eyes darting from face to face in the crowd, when she saw him, a tall man, craning his neck, peering here and there.

"Ben!" she called, "Ben, Ben!" He turned and smiled and came toward her, threading his way through the crowd. She saw the look of confusion and surprise as he recognized her, carrying her suitcase and bundle in one hand and a baby in the other, and saw how he looked behind her, searching for Esther. His mouth gaped open as he struggled to form words for a question.

CHAPTER 2

BEN

Ben had left his cousin Surah's house to meet the ship, filled with anticipation, excitement, and a little dread. What if he didn't remember what Esther looked like? He knew that was ridiculous. Hadn't he married her? Wasn't she expecting his child? But it had all happened very fast, and it had been almost eight months since he'd seen her. Surely, he would be able to pick her out of the crowd. He did have a photograph of her from their wedding day, but it was a small picture, and he couldn't really make out her face.

He had traveled on the subway. It was midmorning, and the subway cars were not crowded, so he sat by the window, peering at the blackness of the tunnels. He wondered what he would say to Esther when he met her. Would they embrace? Surely not in the middle of the throngs of people who would be waiting at the pier where the steerage passengers were let out.

He remembered how bad steerage had been for the women and children. For him it wasn't so bad, he admitted. A single man, alone. He had made out fine. He'd gambled a little with the other boys and men on the ship. And he hadn't minded sleeping on the narrow bunk provided. Why had Esther insisted on leaving before she gave birth? Why had her parents and sister agreed? Her sister was formidable. Golda. She was the one who calmed her parents and made them accept Ben when they found out about Esther's secret marriage to him and their plans to go to America.

That was probably right. Golda was the elder sister. By rights, she should have married first, but Esther had been insistent, and Golda had no prospects. Her family had no money for a dowry. She was strong, that Golda. Ben admired her. She was no beauty like Esther, with her honey-colored hair and blue eyes. Golda was plain—that's what people said. But he remembered he had thought her handsome—that was the word that came to his mind for Golda, with auburn hair that waved off her face. And her eyes were hazel with flecks of gold. He tried to conjure her face, but he couldn't. He knew Esther was petite, where Golda was tall, although not so tall as Ben was. Golda spoke plainly. She said what she was thinking, and Ben liked that. Esther was more circumspect. She talked around things, never saying exactly what she wanted but letting him find out in a circuitous way. At first, he had found it quite charming, but he wondered if, after a while, he would find it tiresome.

The subway train rattled him back and forth, his body rocking with the rhythm of the train speeding down the tracks. His hands were sweaty, and he flexed them nervously, open, close, open, close, the way he always did when he was anxious. They were calloused, and he had rims of oil under his fingernails. Try as he might, he couldn't get the grime out unless he cut his nails. Sometimes he was ashamed of them because they looked dirty.

He was trying to remember how he had first met Esther. She had come into the shop in Lesko where he was apprenticed to a master mechanic, Abe Frankel, and although they mostly fixed machinery for the farms around the small town, they also fixed sewing machines and typewriters, household grinders and hand drills, bicycles and even scissors.

Esther had brought in her mother's meat grinder to be repaired; it had a broken shaft and Ben had promised to fix it. They had flirted a bit, and the next thing he knew, she was hanging around the shop on any pretext. He remembered the day when Golda had seen him kiss Esther. He smiled at the memory. He'd been a little afraid of her—that Golda. Esther told him that Golda had caller her a *courveh* . . . a whore! That had shocked him, all right. That day all he had done was kiss Esther. He wondered if Golda had figured out why Esther had insisted on getting married right away, and why he'd agreed.

The train reached his stop. He got out and walked up the stairs and out of the bowels of the subway, took a streetcar to the piers, and then began to thread through the hordes of people who were, as he was, making their way to the waterfront. When he left Brooklyn, it had been a sunny day. Now there were clouds, and he was afraid it might rain. He wished he had an umbrella. When he reached the pier where the immigrants were making their way off the ferries that brought them from Ellis Island to the city, he craned his neck, looking for a pregnant Esther and her sister Golda.

It's impossible to find anyone in this crowd, he thought. People milled around, calling to each other. *Chaos*, he thought. But suddenly, in front of him, was a tall familiar-looking woman calling his name. He looked behind her but saw no one, and then he noticed what she was carrying. In his bewilderment he couldn't seem to find the words to ask a question.

CHAPTER 3

GOLDA

Golda saw his confusion and, with blunt words, answered his unspoken question. "I'm sorry, Ben. I'm so sorry. She died. She died on the ship in childbirth. This is your son." Golda dropped her valise and the bundle of clothes and quilts and held out the baby to him with both hands, eager to unburden herself. Immediately, she saw that her words had been too harsh and wished she hadn't said them. But they were the truth. How else could she have told him?

Ben stepped back, his hands in front of him, warding her off. He swayed, almost falling, catching himself just in time on the arm of a man standing beside him. The man pushed him away, and Ben stumbled again. This time Golda grabbed him to hold him upright. A sound came out of his throat, a cross between a groan and a scream, a gasp and a cry. It was, next to Esther's screams in childbirth, the worst sound she ever heard. "*Gott! Gott!*" He clutched her arm but did not take the baby from her. He seemed not to have understood her words. He shook his head back and forth, denying her story. People swirled around them, pushed by them, knocked her suitcase over.

Golda needed to take charge. She took a deep breath. "Come," she said, handing him her suitcase and bundle. Taking his arm, she led him down the street to a quieter place overlooking the piers, the water, and the ships. Ben followed her as if sleepwalking. His face was paper white; his bloodless lips moved soundlessly as if in prayer. She propelled him to the curb and pressed him so he sat, weeping, his hands holding his head, and mumbling, "What will I do, what will I do?"

She wanted to shake him. She couldn't bear his blubbering. Didn't she have reason to cry too, to scream? Hadn't she lost her beloved sister just two days ago? But she had wept until she had no tears left;

she felt dried, wizened. She looked at Ben and was ashamed of herself. He was dazed, in shock. She had been given two days to get used to the loss of Esther, but he'd had only minutes.

She lifted her face to the sky. It had begun to drizzle. Her skin drank in the rain, but it was March, and the rain felt cold. Taking pity on him, she waited until his sobs subsided. But she didn't want to wait there forever. "Ben," she said, "we can't sit here any longer. The baby will get wet. We have to go. Where are you taking us?"

Ben looked blank. "Us?"

"Where were you taking Esther when she got off the boat?" She couldn't keep the exasperation from her voice.

"To my room."

"Where is your room? How do we get there?"

As if she were talking to a small child, she got him to speak, to direct them to the streetcar, to the subway. He had been expecting his bride. He must have forgotten Golda was accompanying Esther, that he had promised to find her a job and a place to live. He was in a fog, and Golda realized that right now he was useless at solving the problems they faced just to get through the next few days.

She needed milk for the baby, who was beginning to fuss again. She jounced him against her breast, the way she had seen her mother do with her brothers when they were babies, but she knew this wouldn't work for long. He was hungry again. The last bottle the nurse had given her would have to hold him until she could get more. She needed to be able to boil the bottles as the nurse had instructed her. She needed some diapers. Where would she stay? It would be impossible for Ben to take care of his son. He seemed in such pain and confusion. Golda had no use for him in this state.

Golda wanted to trade places with every woman she saw on the street as she walked behind Ben, carrying the infant. He trudged with the suitcase and the bundle of quilts and clothing. So many of the women looked free, independent. Golda's brain was squirreling with worries, and her throat was tight with tears.

She followed Ben's tall back, his head slumped slightly forward, as if he were looking carefully at each step he took. They walked for two blocks, took a streetcar a short way, and then descended into the underground subway, where they waited in the thicker air for a train that rushed into the station with a great racket. Golda was overwhelmed with the sounds and dirt. The baby began to cry now, startled by the noise of the train coming into the station. "Shush," she whispered, but it didn't quiet him.

They found seats, and Golda fished around in the bundle to find the last bottle of milk. She slipped it into the baby's mouth and prayed there would be help when they got to Ben's room. He lived with a cousin. Maybe she could help.

As the train rocketed through the tunnels, stopping at the stations along the way, they sat silently. People got on and off through the sliding doors. Golda could not imagine how they knew where they were going. She wanted to ask Ben questions, but she could not. To interrupt him while he was so stunned seemed too cruel. He stared straight ahead, his hands between his legs, not looking at anything. The baby finished the bottle and fell asleep. She tucked the empty bottle into the bundle and watched the sleeping infant, wondering why she felt nothing at all when she looked at him, except perhaps anxiety.

She stared at Ben. He was a handsome man. Esther had said he reminded her of the stories of King David in the Bible. He was tall and stood straight, proud of his height. A shock of brown hair fell over his forehead, and he had long lashes—almost like a girl's—shading his warm brown eyes. Golda had noticed he was very quick to smile, as if he enjoyed his life and everything that happened to him.

Not now, Golda thought. *He certainly isn't enjoying life now.* She tore her eyes away from Ben's grief-stricken face and stared at the window on the train. It was grimy and looked out at the black subway tunnel as the train hurtled through.

Eventually they reached their station and got out, although Golda didn't know what the name of the station was because she couldn't read the letters on the signs. They climbed the stairs and emerged on the street again.

It was spitting rain now. The street was awash with people and cars and carts and a few horses. Along the sidewalks in front of the shops, there were hawkers, each one screaming louder than the next. The swirl of bodies pushing against each other, the shopkeepers chanting about their goods assaulted her. Peddlers with pots and pans, clothing, apples, potatoes yelled to passersby. They passed a fishmonger, and the briny smell and the stale smell of fish mingled and assailed her; past the fish was a pushcart with hats and another with dishes. Behind the street vendors were storefronts. A bakery wafted sugary smells, reminding Golda that she was hungry. A butcher shop had cuts of meat hanging. Dress shops and furniture stores, a grocery, a dry goods store followed one after another. Everything was for sale on the street.

They dodged carts pulled by donkeys and horses. They ducked and wove through the crowds. Golda's head was spinning from the color and the smells and the shouts of *Look! Feel! Buy!* She hurried after Ben, wondering what he was thinking. Did he remember he had promised Esther he would take care of Golda if she came as a companion? Was his heart aching? Was he weeping as he walked? She couldn't see his face, only his back.

People pushed against her, shoving her. Once she almost tripped. She held the baby close against her body, shielding him from being touched. *Oh God, when will we be there?* She continued trotting after Ben, trying not to breathe in the stink of horse manure and rotting fish. She stepped around puddles that looked full of garbage, hoping her shoes would not leak.

Think of good things, only pleasant things, Golda thought. She focused on Ben, his broad back a little bent with the weight of his bundles. She had thought him very handsome when she'd met him in the village. That was, no doubt, what had attracted Esther, who'd had a photograph of Ben by her bed that she stared at every morning and every night before she went to sleep. Golda had looked at it too. He was a good-looking man. Tall, with dark eyes and a straight nose. In the picture he had a solemn stare, but when she saw him in person, he smiled a lot, especially at Esther.

Then her mind skipped. *What will I write to my parents? Will they blame me? How could they blame me? The doctor said something went wrong inside Esther.* He had drawn a picture so she could understand, and the nurse, with her broken Polish, had helped explain. The lining of the place where the baby lay inside Esther had peeled off, and that was why she was bleeding. Was that what she said? Now Golda couldn't remember. She swallowed hard against tears and tried to bring her mind back to the questions of the moment. Focus on walking. Make sure she didn't fall.

At last Ben stopped in front of one of the brick apartment buildings. "Here," he said. "I live here."

Golda took a deep breath and clutched the baby closer. They went up the stairs into the dark recesses of the house. Now Golda could barely breathe from the dense, airless staircase. She followed Ben slowly and at the second floor they stopped, and he entered the apartment in front of them.

A tall and buxom woman came to the door and greeted them with a smile. "I'm Cousin Surah," she said to Golda. "You must be Esther."

Golda shook her head and looked at Ben to talk.

"Not Esther," he mumbled. "Her sister, Golda." And he broke down in tears.

This cousin was a wise woman, Golda decided. She did not ask more questions but told Ben to put the rest of their goods into his room and then come out for a cup of tea. Golda followed Ben to his tiny room, saw the one bed, and sat heavily upon it. She wanted to place the baby on the bed and leave. What had she to do with this child? With this man? What would she do with them? But if she left, where would she go? She didn't speak English. She had little money. She was a stranger in a strange land. For the moment, she thought, she was stuck here, in this windowless room, with a man and a baby who did not belong to her. She did not know what she would do.

She looked around the room, taking in its contents. The walls were painted yellow. The bed, covered with a clean threadbare quilt, was pushed against the wall, a rag rug by its side. His clothes were folded neatly in a box in the corner of the room. There were two pegs on the wall to hang a coat or jacket or hat. She saw how tidy the room was and thought that Ben had tried to make it nice for his bride. She was flooded with pity for him.

She shook herself. She could not get stuck thinking sad thoughts. Golda had lists of worries whirling in her head. The doctor on the ship had told her that they needed to claim Esther's body within one day of arrival. That was tomorrow. If not, the body would be disposed of, he said. "Buried in a pauper's grave." That was unthinkable.

But where would they get the money to bury her? How did you get a grave in this big country? And what should she do with this baby, who was now beginning to writhe in hunger, to cry with piteous bleats? Golda had no milk. Where could she get the evaporated milk that the nurse had shown her how to use in a bottle? And the bris, the circumcision? Would that happen on the eighth day, as was required? She stared at Ben, who sat rocking on the floor, his head in his hands.

"Ben," she said. He didn't move. "Ben!" she said more loudly. He jumped. "We have to talk. To decide." He looked up at her, but she wasn't sure he understood what she was saying. "Esther's body. We have to collect it from the ship. Or they will bury her in a pauper's grave." Still, he stared at her. "And your baby, this boy, needs a bris. He was born two days ago." Ben stirred. He seemed to be listening. "He needs food. Or a wet nurse . . ." The words stumbled out of her mouth.

Golda could feel her face getting red. How was she talking of these things? Burial. Bris. A wet nurse. Unseemly. She, a maiden who was supposed to know very little about life, although in truth, as the eldest daughter in the family, she knew plenty, having helped the mid- wife when her mother had given birth to her youngest son. In the village, there were women and men to help with everything. When a man died, there were men who sat with the body. If a woman died, women sat. It was a holy task. They bathed the body and prepared it for burial in a shroud and watched over it until the next day, when it would be buried. At home, when her mother had a baby boy—and there had been three of them—her father had arranged for the bris. If a woman died in childbirth, there were other women who would act as wet nurse, at a price, yes, but not so much. Here, she was alone. And suddenly she was in charge. She knew there was no time for this useless shame.

The questions flew, one after the other, out of her mouth. "Do you have money? What will it cost to bury Esther? Where will I live? Who will take care of your baby?"

Ben stood, his shoulders slumped forward. He finally spoke. "I don't know." His shoulders heaved as he cried. He sat beside Golda on the bed, and for some moments she felt pity for him. He was so broken. But they could not wait.

She patted his hand and said, "Come, we will talk to your cousin. We will find a rabbi. We will get food for this little one." She looked down at the infant. He was squirming and crying in discomfort, in hunger, she knew. She felt pity for him but no love. Just the weight of him in her arms was a burden. She stood and, carrying the baby, said again, "Come."

Ben stood up, took two ragged breaths, and followed her out of the room.

Golda came into the kitchen holding the baby, with Ben trailing behind. "We need help, Cousin Surah," she said. She swallowed hard, not wanting to cry, and sat on a chair at the table, jiggling the squalling baby in her arms. The story spilled out. "I am not his wife. That was my sister. She died on ship giving birth to this son. I can't feed him. He's hungry." Golda's voice broke and she began to weep.

Cousin Surah took charge immediately. "*Oy vay iz mir*, the poor child." She bustled in the kitchen. The heat of the stove had made her round cheeks rosy, and she had half-moons of sweat under her armpits. She picked up the teakettle with its already boiled water, poured it into a little bowl and added sugar, then blew on the too-hot liquid. The ample flesh on her arms swung as she moved through her chores. "Give him here." She took the baby in her arms, and he settled against her bosom. With a spoon, she took a tiny bit of sugar water, blew on it again, tasted it for temperature, and slipped the spoon into the infant's mouth. He swallowed. She followed with another spoonful. A lock of her dark brown hair had slipped out of the bun and hung around her face. She pushed it behind her ears.

Cousin Surah called to her five-year-old daughter, who stood eyes wide with curiosity. "Rochel, go next door and get Mrs. Singer. Ask her to come." She kept feeding the baby sugar water. "Some mothers use evaporated milk, but that costs a lot. Maybe we can find a mother who will feed him too. Mrs. Singer next door has a baby girl who is still at her breast."

Golda began to breathe. Here was help. She looked at Ben, who stood with his head hanging. She nodded toward him. "He's frozen. He can't think straight. He's no help. We need to get the body from the ship by tomorrow, or they'll put Esther in a pauper's grave. We need money for a Jewish burial. Should we sit shiva here? What will he do with this baby? Where will I go? How will I live?" The questions poured out of her mouth.

Cousin Surah, still feeding sugar water to the baby, said, "*Shah*. Only one thing at a time. He is in shock. His wife is dead." She looked at him and said, "Ben, sit down. I will make tea for you. We will get help."

Rochel came in with the neighbor woman, Mrs. Singer, a tiny woman holding a six-month-old baby girl. Golda could see that once she had been pretty, but her face was careworn now, and she was very thin. Cousin Surah explained the problems. First, and most important, was feeding this infant. Mrs. Singer stood and looked at Cousin Surah, who nodded. She handed her baby girl to Golda, took the infant boy in her arms, and went into the back room to nurse him.

Golda's heart was bursting with gratitude. She had never seen such generosity. In the village people helped—of course they did. But usually it was a relative, not a stranger. Here, everyone was a stranger at first and became like a cousin very quickly. She could see it was the only way they could survive. "She's very kind, Mrs. Singer," Golda said.

Cousin Surah nodded. "I helped her when she came." She took

Mrs. Singer's daughter from Golda and sat again with the baby on her lap. "Now, let's see how else I can help." One by one, she talked through the problems, offering choices, solutions, dead ends. Golda's head whirled with it all.

The cost of getting Esther properly buried would be high, but there were benevolent societies that arranged for burials at little or no cost. A rabbi would know about that. There was a rabbi in the little shul nearby. They could sit shiva here. The baby needed a bris. Everything cost money. There was a Hebrew Free Loan Society Cousin Surah knew about. But how much they could loan was a question. They also needed money for a wet nurse for the baby, or evaporated milk and bottles and diapers. Ben's job did not pay that much. Did Golda have a trade? Or maybe she would go back to her village. Or—and here Cousin Surah dropped her voice so perhaps Ben wouldn't hear—maybe they could bring the baby to the orphanage.

Golda sat, heavyhearted. She had not mourned her beautiful sister. How could they not pay for the body to be buried properly? If the lady next door, Mrs. Singer, would just babysit and nurse the baby for a few days, that would be one problem solved. How could they put this baby in an orphanage? Give him away? She thought of Esther and could not imagine putting her child with strangers. And yet, what else could they do? Golda stared at Ben. He was still not speaking. She could not bear it any longer.

"Ben. Ben. He's your baby. You have to decide." She wanted to shake him hard. Make him act.

He stood. Spoke softly, slowly. "This Free Loan Society. Where is it? And the rabbi? Is it the one in the shul down the street? I will try to get the loan; I will make arrangements for the bris."

Cousin Surah asked, "You know when the bris must be?"

"Eight days," he said. Then, almost as an afterthought, he asked, "When was he born?"

Golda shook her head in disbelief. If Cousin Surah hadn't asked, he would have gone to the rabbi without knowing the day the bris must be. "He was born on Tuesday," she said.

Ben nodded and went out the door.

Golda breathed in relief. At least he was alive, acting. All these choices, some hers, some his. They needed to act, but she could not force things. Let him look to get the loan for Esther's burial. Let him talk to the rabbi about the bris. Let Cousin Surah help find food for the baby. Golda would surrender to their decisions for now.

CHAPTER 4

BEN

Ben left the apartment, still walking in a daze. He repeated in his head what he needed to do, so he wouldn't forget anything. Rabbi. Bris. Free loan. Get Esther's remains from the ship. He shook his head to clear it. *Enough tears*, he thought. He remembered Golda's straight back, her square shoulders. *Be like her*, he thought. *I have to be like her; she is so strong.*

Ben made his way to the rabbi's house, which was an apartment above a storefront that served as a shul—a little place for prayer and study. He knocked on the door. A girl answered and walked him up the stairs, where she let him into the parlor and asked him to wait. Ben took in the shabby furniture, the darkness of the room, the sounds in the nearby kitchen of dishes clanking and soft voices speaking. By the time Rabbi Levy came in, Ben had gone over what he had to say several times. About how he had married Esther, and she had come after him on a boat with her older unmarried sister accompanying her.

He took in the rabbi, wondering what he was thinking. Rabbi Levy was a short, stout man with a salt-and-pepper beard, wearing a white shirt and black pants held up by suspenders. He wore small round spectacles, which he kept pushing up on his sharp nose. On his head was a large black yarmulke, and every now and then, he would reach up and set it back in the center of his head.

"She had the baby on the boat," Ben said, "but she died." Here he choked up and began to weep again. "The doctor had to cut her open, or the baby would have died too." The rabbi nodded, began to say some prayers to comfort him. Ben listened but was not comforted. Prayers never comforted him. They seemed to Ben to be just words.

He spoke again. "Her body is at the ship. We have to get it—bring money, I think—otherwise they will bury her in a pauper's grave."

The rabbi shook his head. "We won't let that happen." He bobbed his head. "We will send the burial society, but we will need to pay for a burial plot."

"I have no money."

"We will get it," the rabbi said. "What else?"

"The baby is a boy, born Tuesday."

The rabbi nodded. "Mazel tov. A bris."

Ben nodded.

Now he tried to remember what else he was supposed to ask for. He sat, as if dazed, with his hands holding his brown cap between his legs.

The rabbi got up and went to his sideboard, taking out a black silk yarmulke. "You must wear this."

Ben flushed. He took the head covering and put it on, mumbling, "Sorry."

The rabbi nodded. "Let's have tea, and we will talk and decide how to proceed."

Ben followed the rabbi into the kitchen and sat at the table while the rabbi's wife prepared the tea, placed it and a few cookies in front of them, and then left the room.

They talked quietly about the old country. The rabbi wanted to know about his education, about the rabbi in his town, about his parents' house. Did he have any brothers or sisters? "Two," he said. "A brother and sister. I'm the eldest." Ben's voice had steadied during the conversation. He found himself calmer, remembering where he had come from, describing the fun he'd had with his younger brother and sister. The rabbi asked whether Ben had been in touch with his parents. Ben shook his head. "Once or twice when I was an apprentice in Lesko, and I visited before I left on the ship. They knew I was getting married."

The rabbi nodded. "Perhaps you should write them now and tell them they are grandparents?"

A small smile flitted across Ben's face. "Yes. They'll be pleased about that."

"Do you think they might be planning to come to America? Many of our people are."

Ben thought for a minute. "Perhaps I could encourage them to come?" It was more of a question than a statement.

The rabbi nodded and then asked, "Who will take care of your son?"

Ben shook his head. "I don't know. I have to work."

"Of course," the rabbi said. After a minute he added, "This sister? Can she help you?"

Ben thought about Golda. He knew she could help. She was so competent. But would she? "I think she could help, but I don't know if she would want to."

"Sometimes it is not what we want but what we must do that guides us. We shall see." The rabbi pushed the teacup aside and said, "Come, we will go to *Gemilas Chesed*, the Free Loan Society, and get some money, then the burial society to make arrangements at the ship for the body. And I will contact the mohel for the bris next week. After that we will see."

Ben stood up, feeling like a burden had been lifted from his back. It was strange, he thought, how the prayers had not comforted him at all, but the conversation had made him feel much better. "I am so grateful to you," he said.

The rabbi waved away his thanks. He put on his jacket and put a hat over his yarmulke. Ben removed the yarmulke and offered it to the rabbi before he put his cap on.

"You keep it," the rabbi said. "Put it on under your cap. That way your head is always covered. It is a sign of respect for God."

Ben nodded and followed the rabbi out of the house.

CHAPTER 5

GOLDA

Everything takes so much time, Golda thought. While Ben was out finding a rabbi to see about the burial and the circumcision, she waited in Cousin Surah's kitchen. Soon Mrs. Singer came out, having finished nursing the baby. She handed him to Golda, who whispered, "Thank you." She held the infant as, sated, he fell into a deep sleep, and for the moment she relaxed. But she knew it wouldn't last. In two or three hours he would be up crying again, needing food. It would start with him squirming a little in his sleep, then a few plaintive cries, and soon he would be screaming in hunger. And then what would she do?

She hesitated only a moment and then said, "Mrs. Singer, will you help? For the next few days? Until we can decide what to do with this poor orphan baby?" Her voice choked on the word "orphan." Was he an orphan? He had a father but no mother.

Cousin Surah transferred the baby girl to her mother's arms. She patted Mrs. Singer on the back. "You are very kind," she said. "Can you help a little longer?"

Mrs. Singer hesitated, then sighed. "I will keep him for the next two days, but then you have to decide. It costs money to keep a baby. I have my own little girl. But I will help for now because she asks me." Mrs. Singer nodded at Cousin Surah. "Bring him to me with some clean diapers, some clothes. I'll see you soon." She went to the door, and before she left the apartment, she said to Golda, "This will not be easy for you. Think hard about what you do."

Golda sat holding the baby. She heard the words as a warning and felt she was drowning, foundering in deep water, unable to swim. And the baby was wet. She had not changed his diaper since morning. She wondered what you did to clean diapers here in the city. At home her mother had a big washtub outside the house. She hung clothes on a rope tied between trees. But this was the city. Where did you wash clothes in the city? She looked at Cousin Surah, a kind and sturdy woman who seemed to know how to solve problems. Golda watched her bustle about the kitchen, felt her gentle pat on the shoulder as she passed her. "*Nu?*" Cousin Surah asked. "Are you hungry?"

Golda shook her head. She hadn't had a morsel of food since early morning, but she didn't think she could swallow any now. This was all too much for her. She couldn't answer the questions buzzing in her head or make decisions. "What should I do?" she asked Cousin Surah at last. The question reverberated in her head. It met with silence in the kitchen.

Cousin Surah stirred the tea she had brought to the table. "Your sister's baby?" she asked at last. Golda nodded. After a long while the older woman said, "There are not so many choices for you, I think."

Golda closed her eyes and nodded, but she wondered what Cousin Surah meant. *Not so many choices.* She wanted to hear the choices, and she didn't want to hear them. She was afraid that saying them would close the doors to every dream she had. Cousin Surah did not speak again until Golda opened her eyes and looked straight at her.

"How old are you?" Cousin Surah asked.

"Eighteen."

"Why did you come with your sister? You're a pretty girl. Were there no boys to marry in your town?"

Golda was startled. No one had called her pretty before, except her beloved grandmother, Bubbie Zlata, who would pinch her cheeks and say she had a *shayna punim*, a pretty face. But Golda knew she was not pretty—not when she stood next to Esther, who was so beautiful. She shook her head. "Esther found her own destiny—her *bashert*. My father wanted me to marry this widower I didn't like. He already had two children." She closed her eyes and remembered him . . . a much older man with a large belly and a double chin. Just thinking of him made Golda shiver. His clothes were not so clean. He smelled of sweat. When he looked at Golda, he kept licking his lips, as if he were anticipating a meal. After he left, Golda turned to her parents. "I won't marry him. You can't make me marry him."

"We have no choice," her father said. His voice was stern. "He is the only offer we have, and we have no dowry for you to entice younger men. You cannot be choosy."

"I won't marry him," Golda said. "I'll go to Przemysl and go into service. I can cook and sew. Someone rich will hire me to help."

Her father raised his hand as if to slap her, but her mother caught his arm and begged. "No, Chaim, no."

He'd shaken her arm away and said, "You don't have a choice. Prepare yourself."

Golda shook her head as if ridding herself of the memory. She answered Cousin Surah. "I didn't have a dowry. The only way I could escape was to come with Esther to America. And besides, I didn't want her to go alone, so pregnant. She wasn't supposed to deliver on the ship. She was barely eight months."

Cousin Surah looked skeptical. "The baby looks big. Maybe she was wrong in counting."

Golda nodded. "That's what the nurse on the ship said."

"The nurse, did she help deliver the baby? How did you manage, a maiden?"

Golda closed her eyes, and it came flooding back. The steerage of the ship, a big room with double berths, so many women and children, babies crying. And Esther, her beautiful face contorted in pain.

"At first, I thought it was just a normal birth. I had been around my mother when she gave birth to my three younger brothers. I even helped the midwife with the youngest. So I thought I could help Esther. When her water broke, I ran around the steerage asking if there was a midwife there. But there wasn't. So I held her, I rubbed her back, I breathed with her. At first everything was fine, but then it wasn't. She started to bleed. I never saw that before."

Golda looked behind Cousin Surah's head, as if seeing something that wasn't really there. The quilt had been on the bed when Esther began to labor. It was too soon, she remembered saying to Esther. But

Esther said no, just a little. She had fibbed about when the baby should come, she said. She was eight months, not seven. Her pains were hard, and Golda sat behind her, holding her between her legs, rubbing her back, when the blood came gushing.

Golda closed her eyes, shook her head. "I didn't know what to do. This nice woman had put up a quilt around us so no one would see. I was calling, 'Help me, help me!' I got off the bed, put the quilt—the beautiful quilt she had made—between her legs to stop the bleeding. One of the women ran for the doctor . . . we were lucky there was a real doctor on the ship and a real infirmary . . . and I kept saying a prayer: *the doctor will come, the doctor will come.*

"When he came, he took one look, and next thing Esther was taken to the infirmary, and I was waiting outside the door, sitting on the floor in the hallway." It was in the fancy part of the ship. There was red wallpaper with velvet flowers and blue-and-red carpeting. At first, she could hear Esther screaming, and then quiet that sounded like the end of the world. Golda waited and waited. It was hours, and then a small sound, like a tiny kitten mewing.

"After a while, I heard the baby, and I knocked and went into the room. The doctor was standing by the tall bed where Esther lay covered in a white sheet. Her skin was pale. She seemed to be breathing but faint. A nurse, who by a miracle spoke some Polish as well as English, stood by the doctor's side holding the baby wrapped in a white sheet.

"I asked the nurse if it was alive. She nodded. The doctor told me that he had to do an operation to take the baby. I remembered that there was a woman in the village who had that. 'He cut her open?' I asked.

"'Yes,' the nurse answered. 'It was the only way to save the baby. And hopefully your sister.'"

Golda had felt like she was moving through water. Esther's eyes flickered. Her breaths were shallow. Her skin was white, drained of all color.

"The doctor said we had to wait until she came out of the

anesthetic, and then we would see if she survived. She lost so much blood.

"They let me hold the baby, and the nurse said he was a big healthy boy, ready to be born. He was very pretty, not a scrunched-up face like the babies my mother had." Golda looked down. "Esther had said she was only seven months pregnant, but that wasn't true. I think she was already expecting when she and Ben married."

Cousin Surah nodded. She seemed to understand. Golda was quiet then, remembering how Esther had moved her mouth, but no sound came out. Golda went to her side and bent low to hear what she said, but the words were garbled. Her eyes seemed to be pleading. Golda thought she said, "Take him."

"The doctor said I had to leave the infirmary and come back the next day. He said, 'We'll see if she survives.' He told me to change my clothes and wash." Golda remembered the smell of blood on her hands . . . like metal. "I washed as good as I could, and my dress I saved; I don't know if it will come clean. I only have this dress I'm wearing if it doesn't. I do have Esther's clothes, but she is small, and I am tall. I don't know if they will fit me."

Golda was talking too much, too fast. "I threw away the feather quilt that Esther was lying on. There was no saving it." Golda's heart ached doing it, remembering the countless hours Esther had spent stitching it to bring to America. Thankfully Golda had rescued the quilt cover she herself had embroidered as a wedding present. It was very fine work with sprays of yellow forsythia and purple lilacs, green vines, and pink and red roses. She had sat for hours, stitching flowers and trees on the fabric. The women in the village said Golda's needle-work was beautiful, and many of them asked her to make embroidered blouses and skirts for special occasions.

"I left Esther's suitcase with the nurse. She said when they come for the body, they can take the suitcase too. I couldn't carry it all."

Cousin Surah silently reached out for Golda's hand and patted it. Golda was silent for a long time, remembering. Then she continued, tears choking her voice. "The next morning, when I went back to the infirmary, my sister was gone. The nurse was feeding the baby with a bottle filled with evaporated milk. Two days later, the ship arrived, and I came off alone with the baby. When I walked off that ship, I waited and waited, and then finally came Ben. I don't think he understood when he first saw me, what had happened. I feel very sorry for him."

They sat in silence for a long time. Finally, Cousin Surah sighed. "You poor girl. What do you want to do? Do you want to go back to your village?"

The "No!" was out of Golda's mouth before the question was finished. She knew if she went back, she would have to marry whoever her father picked. And they would blame her for Esther's death; she knew they would, even though it was not her fault. At least she didn't think it was her fault.

"Okay. So, if you stay, you must work. Do you have a skill?"

Golda hesitated, then said, "I sew. I embroider." Golda stumbled over the words. She didn't want to brag. Her mother was always admonishing her, "Don't brag. It isn't becoming." But Golda knew her embroidery was special. Bubbie Zlata had taught her how to embroider, saying she could earn good money with the skill. Bubbie Zlata had been a talented tailor until her arthritic fingers kept her from the work. Like her bubbie, Golda could look at a piece of cloth and see a design on it. Without tracing it first, she could stitch the different colors into patterns or scenes. People said her work on fabric was like a painting. Golda took a deep breath. "I cook too."

She thought she was good at cooking and embroidery, but that was not what she wanted to do. She wanted to have a life of her own, not doing what she had always done in the village. She thought again about the young nurse on the ship. Wouldn't that be a wonderful life? Not that she could ever even think of something like that. A dream.

"You cook good?"

"Yes," Golda said. "I did most of the cooking and baking at home. My mother didn't like cooking."

"I don't either," Cousin Surah said, and smiled. "But I have to cook. I have a husband, a daughter, a son, and two boarders who must eat. If you cook for us and help me clean and wash, you can stay and sleep in the parlor for now."

Golda was so grateful she could barely speak. "Thank you," she whispered. She thought that Cousin Surah was only offering work out of kindness. She had never known anyone so kind before.

"But for the baby, we have to find help. Mrs. Singer said she does not want to nurse him, but I think she will do it for a favor for me if we pay her. Maybe Ben can pay her. If not, maybe we can find someone else, or else we have to find money for canned milk. Either way it will cost money."

"Why are you so kind?"

"Ben is my cousin. My mother is his mother's oldest sister. Didn't you know?"

Golda nodded. "Yes, I know, but still, I think you are kind."

The older woman smiled. "Maybe kind. But not rich." She patted Golda on the arm, took the baby from her, and said, "We will try to work it out. I will bring the baby to Mrs. Singer, and then you and I will go on the avenue, find some things the baby needs and bread for supper. Then Ben will be back, and we will see what he found out about the loan and the funeral and the bris. I hope it will be all right."

Golda hoped so too.

When Ben came back to the apartment, Golda and Cousin Surah were deep in conversation about how Golda would write a letter to her parents to tell them about Esther's death and the birth of their grandson. Then it was Ben's chance to tell how the rabbi was arranging for the *chevra kadisha*, the synagogue burial society, to take care of Esther's burial. They were pious Jews; they would not let Esther go to a pauper's grave. And the rabbi had also arranged for the baby's circumcision. He assured Ben that he would help procure a loan from the Hebrew Free Loan Society to feed the baby. They would loan the money, and Ben would pay it back, but he would not owe any interest. A free loan.

Ben sat in the kitchen while Cousin Surah and Golda cooked

potatoes and carrots and sliced the bread for supper. Tomorrow morning, Ben told them, he and the rabbi would go to the ship and arrange for the burial society to get Esther's body, and they would bury her in a Jewish grave. When he heard that Cousin Surah was going to let Golda sleep in the parlor, Ben said she should take his bed and he would sleep on the floor in the parlor.

"And maybe," Cousin Surah said, "when Mrs. Singer brings the baby back, he should sleep in the bedroom with Golda."

Golda saw Ben look from Cousin Surah to her and back again. What should she say? But after a few minutes it seemed clear to her. She nodded her agreement. She would take her sister's baby in the room with her.

At least Ben is beginning to act like a man again, she thought. A mensch. He even asked to see the baby, who hadn't been named yet. Cousin Surah asked him if he had a name for the baby; he nodded, and they let the subject go. It was customary not to name the child until the circumcision, and even not to tell anyone beforehand what the name would be. A few minutes later, he went next door to Mrs. Singer's apartment, saw his son, and when he came back to his cousin's, his face was drained and tear streaked. He sat at the table and whispered, "I don't know how I'll take care of him."

Cousin Surah patted his back. "It will come to you soon," she said. "Meanwhile, we will get through the next days, one by one."

The conversation lagged, picked up, lagged again. Golda's exhaustion was overwhelming, and she could barely listen to the talk. Surah's husband, Yaacov, came home from his job as a bookkeeper and kindly acknowledged Golda, the new boarder. Cousin Surah took him aside and whispered to him for a few minutes. He nodded, came to the table, and said, "Welcome to our home."

Over supper, they discussed everything, revealing new ideas one after the other. Golda was astonished at the thought that this very morning she had walked off the ship, carrying a famished infant, dreading how she would find her sister's young husband and tell him what had happened. And this evening she had a bed, a meal, a temporary place for the baby, and a way to get her sister an honorable and kosher funeral. It seemed a miracle. *A funeral, a bris, a job, and a place to sleep*, Golda repeated. She dragged herself up, took the dishes off the table, and began to wash them. She needed to prove to Cousin Surah that she hadn't made a mistake taking Golda into her home. And Golda knew that after Esther's graveside funeral, and the seven days of shiva and deep mourning, and the baby's circumcision, Ben would go back to work, and she would start her life as a helper to Cousin Surah and a surrogate parent to the newly named baby Mordechai—Morton.

CHAPTER 6

GOLDA

Cousin Surah was the first friend Golda made in the new country. She confessed to Golda that when she had come to America fifteen years before, she had been, much like Golda, confused and frightened. She spoke no English, had no friends, and barely knew her husband, Yaacov, whom she had married three months before they emigrated.

"How did you manage?" Golda asked, staring at Cousin Surah's round face as if the answer could be found written in the reassurance in her eyes, her cheeks, her mouth.

Cousin Surah sat beside Golda and took her hand. "It was difficult at first. But people spoke Yiddish. We lived with Yaacov's aunt and uncle until Yaacov had work. The first year he sold, in a pushcart, coal in the winter and ice in the summer. And then he sold other things. Potatoes. Men's pants. Once pots and pans." Cousin Surah was quiet for a few minutes, as if remembering. When she spoke again, her words came faster and faster. "Then he went to work for the Free Loan Society as their bookkeeper. He used to bookkeep in the old country. Then others—businesses who came for free loans—began to hire him to do their bookkeeping. By then we got our apartment—two rooms—and I had our first child, Solomon. You'll meet him later." Cousin Surah patted Golda's hand.

"I made friends who took me in hand, showed me where to buy. And my husband, Yaacov, is a good man, and he and I made a partnership. We helped each other. You manage. I learned English from my neighbors and the street. But now we have classes in schools, and there is a settlement house where they teach." Cousin Surah smiled. "Little by little, we made a life," she said. "You'll see, you will too."

Cousin Surah's simple story gave Golda courage, even though she knew that things were never simple. The next weeks were hard—harder than Golda could have imagined. Without thinking about it, and without being asked and consenting, Golda was caring for the baby, washing his diapers, and hanging them on a clothesline out the window, where lines from every apartment crisscrossed the air, the hanging clothes waving in the wind. She boiled the baby's bottles, then filled them with thinned evaporated milk, caring for Morton as if he were her own son.

But he was not. She tried to love him. She peered at him as he lay in her arms feeding from the bottle she had prepared, wondering what Esther would have felt for him if she were alive. She would probably have been lovesick, the way most new mothers were. She remembered how Esther had talked about the baby, thought about what she would do if she had a boy or a girl. Dreamed about holding the baby, rocking the baby. But Golda did not feel that way. She tried, but her heart was closed. She could not let him in because each time she tried, a sliver of resentment would slip in, and the tenderness would disappear.

She wanted her own life, not her sister's, but she was stuck. Here she was in the house of a gentle and kind woman who was not her relative. There he was, Morton, a helpless baby, not hers, whom she could neither love nor leave. And there was Ben, a man who had been waiting for the bride he'd loved when he was in the old country but whose face, he confessed one day to Golda, he could barely remember.

Golda thought about Esther and how she had loved Ben, bragged about him. "Did you know he is a genius with his hands? A mechanic. He's going to have a job when he gets to America. Abe Frankel, the man he apprenticed to in Lesko, went first and promised Ben he would have a place for him in his uncle's business in New York."

Golda wondered, was there any way out for her? What would she do? If she weren't here in this house with Ben and Cousin Surah, where would she go? Each night she thought about it, remembering the young nurse on the ship. Golda wondered how you became a nurse and if she could be one. Could she earn her way? Do something for herself? As she held Morton, sang him the lullabies she had heard her mother sing to her brothers, she daydreamed about being a nurse or a shop girl or a baker in a bakery. She knew it was a dream, not something possible, but she dreamed nevertheless.

One morning, several weeks after the thirty-day mourning period was over, when she was feeding a bottle to the baby and Ben was out at work, Cousin Surah said to her, "So, has he asked you yet?"

"Asked me what?"

Cousin Surah cocked her head, smiled. "To marry?"

Golda's mouth dropped open in shock. "No. He hasn't." She shook her head. Her heart beat hard. She didn't want to marry Ben. He didn't love her; she didn't love him. She had never yearned to be a wife and a mother the way Esther had, but in the old country, what else was there? When she went to Przemysl, the city near her town, she saw women, young women, smartly dressed, going to school, working in offices. She wondered how they had escaped the small-town rules she was bound by. Stay home, help your mother, don't think about school or other ways to live. But now, in this new country, she saw many women in business in the storefronts on the avenue.

She wanted to learn English so she could work like that . . . become an American. But how could she do that? Desert this tiny baby, leave him to Ben. What would he do? Cousin Surah had talked about an orphanage. How could she let her sister's son be taken to an orphanage if she could prevent it? Her heart sank and she shivered.

"Do people really put babies in orphanages?" she whispered.

After a long wait, Cousin Surah said, "Yes. If they can't feed them. Better an orphanage than death by starving." Cousin Surah turned her back on Golda so she couldn't see her face. It was probably full of disapproval, Golda thought. She felt her eyes well up with tears.

Cousin Surah turned and took Golda's hand. "People do desperate things when they see no way out. Men run away and leave their families when they can't feed them. They desert them. Even mothers leave. I know one whose husband died, and she left her ten-year-old son in the care of a neighbor and went west . . . where I don't know. But the boy was ten and deserted, and he turned to crime and was eventually killed. There are more terrible stories in this building than I can talk about. You . . . your story is not so desperate. You have choices."

Golda nodded. The walls seemed to be closing in on her. All the choices came to her, and none, except one, seemed worthy of consideration. She knew that in the village, when a man was widowed with a child, he was expected to marry his dead wife's sister if she was not married. It was a mitzvah, a good deed, for the sister to marry him and raise her sister's child.

"You have choices," Cousin Surah repeated. "But not so very many."

Golda knew what Cousin Surah was saying. She had no trade that made sense. Her embroidery was nice. A side business. All the dreams she'd had as a girl of escaping the life that was laid out before her were just that. Dreams. Make-believe. She closed her eyes, thoughts swirling in her head. *What would Esther want me to do? Would she want me to marry Ben? Did she really tell me to take the baby when she lay dying on the ship?*

"Is he going to ask me to marry?"

"Yes."

"Well, he hasn't yet. Maybe he won't."

"He will soon . . . and what will you say?"

Golda breathed in and out. *If I say no, where will I go? Cousin Surah probably will not let me stay here. If I say yes, I will be married, and my life will no longer be my own. Will I betray my sister if I marry her husband?* A deep sigh escaped her lips. *If Ben asks me, I need an answer.* And with all the scurrying thoughts in her head, there was only one answer that seemed to solve all the problems. And she would have to say it.

"Yes."

They were married as soon as possible, Cousin Surah said Ben could not keep sleeping on the floor in the parlor, and as long as they were going to marry, they should do it soon.

Golda wore a dress that Cousin Surah bought for her on the avenue. They could not waste money on a white wedding dress that would never be worn again, so they settled on a pale blue dress that suited Golda and that she admitted to Surah she liked. She bought some colored thread and stayed up late before the wedding, embroidering delicate flowers along the neckline. Cousin Surah admired the beauty of the workmanship.

"You can get good work—good money—doing that," she said.

"Where?" Golda asked.

"Dress shops. Tailors. We can go on the avenue and bring your work and show it to the tailor shops. I even know someone who works in one."

Golda marveled that perhaps she could earn a wage with her sewing. It would help her to keep some independence.

She had not had a new dress in a very long time and kept looking at herself in the mirror before the wedding. She thought she looked pretty and wondered, if her life had not taken her down this road, whether she would ever have met a man she could truly love. Could she ever love Ben, who still was a stranger to her?

The plan was for Rabbi Levy to marry them in the little storefront shul on the next street, under a chuppah, a wedding canopy, with Cousin Surah and her husband arranging and paying for the wedding and the celebration, which Ben would eventually pay back. There were so many customs related to weddings, decisions that needed to be made, but Cousin Surah did not want to force any of them on Golda.

Did she want to go to the mikvah, the ritual bath, for purification before the wedding ceremony?

Golda thought about it and said yes, she did. So Cousin Surah accompanied her there.

Did she want to cut her hair and wear a sheitel, a wig?

Golda uttered a resounding "No!" and Cousin Surah nodded her head in agreement. After all, Esther, who had married Ben in the village, had absolutely refused to cut her hair and wear a wig, to their mother's horror. She consented only to wear a scarf tied around her curls when she went out into the street. Golda wondered if Ben would care what she did with her hair, but she didn't ask him. If he had a preference, he would have to tell her.

Would she wear a veil at the wedding?

Yes, she would if they could borrow one. Golda did not want to spend money unnecessarily. Cousin Surah arranged to borrow one from a neighbor whose daughter had recently married.

The wedding ceremony was not long, and Golda and Ben were married quietly. After the blessings by the rabbi, Ben stepped on the glass and broke it; there were shouts of "Mazel tov!" and the witnesses and the wedding party celebrated back at Cousin Surah's apartment, where a few neighbors and friends had prepared a dinner for them.

Golda could not eat a bite. She clutched her marriage contract, her ketubah, in her hands and thought that a wedding was supposed to be a happy day, one of the most important days in a girl's life. And here she was, quickly married to a man she had not selected, with a baby to take care of who was not her own. It was not lost on her that her father had wanted her to marry a widower with two small children, and she had refused. It must be her fate, she thought, to marry a widower with a child, because here she was, married to Ben, caring for Morton. It was *bashert*—destined.

After the wedding ceremony, after the dinner, Cousin Surah took the baby for the night and shooed the couple into the tiny bedroom that Golda had been sleeping in since she arrived. Ben followed her into the room, and they sat on opposite sides of the bed, facing away from one another. It was not a big bed. She could not imagine sleeping in it together.

Ben said, "We can wait. I don't want to push you. I know we married for convenience."

Golda felt her body relax. She turned and faced Ben, nodded her head. "Thank you," she whispered.

They closed their eyes without even an embrace.

CHAPTER 7

BEN

Ben lay on his side of the bed, careful not to touch Golda and make her uncomfortable. He could not help but remember how it had been with him and Esther. They had first made love in a field behind the town. Esther had not been shy. In fact, he had been the one who tried to resist, but Esther kept kissing him and pressing herself against him. If he closed his eyes, he remembered the feel of her breasts through her gauzy summer dress, her thighs against his, the taste of her lips, and the warmth of her sun-kissed skin. Then they lay where they were, hidden behind a bush in an open field. He told himself that now she was his wife. When they got up from the grass and he picked twigs out of Esther's coppery hair, he knew he had to marry her. They asked her parents for permission to marry, but her parents would not hear of it. Two weeks later they went to a rabbi in the next town, who, for a fee, married them, with a ketubah and two witnesses.

Esther begged Golda to tell their parents that she and Ben had married. At last, convinced by Golda's arguments that they could not undo the wedding, their parents acknowledged the marriage and Ben moved into their cottage. During the month he lived there, he and Esther could not wait to touch each other when they were alone in the bedroom that Golda and Esther had always shared. Golda was sent to sleep with the three boys in the little room off the kitchen. They held one another, kissing and cuddling, and after they made love, they lay together like spoons until the morning, when Esther shuffled out of the bedroom, shy and blushing, to wash. Golda and her mother went about the business of cooking and cleaning and ignored the couple.

Each morning, Ben went to work with a lunch pail fixed by his wife, and they put together every penny they could so he could book passage to America. They were certain that was where they could make a good life.

But this wedding to Golda was very different from his marriage to Esther. Everyone knew that Golda and Ben were marrying for convenience. Ben overheard one of the guests saying he was only marrying to get a mother for his baby. Well, that was true enough. But Rabbi Levy told him and Golda that it was a mitzvah for a girl to marry the widower of her sister to care for an orphaned niece or nephew. And Ben believed that with all his heart. He was very grateful to Golda, and he believed she would be a good wife, a good mother.

He remembered that when he left for Hamburg, Esther did not yet suspect she was pregnant, and he promised to send money for her passage as soon as he had saved enough. But when he was in New York, a letter came from Esther telling him the good news of her pregnancy and begging him to bring her quickly to America so their baby would be born in the new land. Ben's employer had loaned Ben the money for Esther's passage, and somehow their parents found the money for Golda's ticket, and that was why Golda and Esther had come so quickly. Thinking about how this all happened made Ben's heart gallop in his chest—he had lost so much and, he reminded himself, gained much too.

How did the twists and turns of life happen? He had never meant to marry so young—he was barely twenty, and Esther had just turned seventeen—and yet he had. And he had loved Esther, had he not? He couldn't remember. Just her beauty and her satin skin, the heat of her, the excitement of lying with her night after night the first month they were married.

A fleeting thought occurred to him. Was Esther's death punishment for the sin they had committed lying together in the field under the summer sun? He pushed that thought away. After all, they had married. And so soon after, he had a son to care for, and now he was married again, not quite ready but not knowing what else to do.

He found it hard to look at Golda. She hadn't asked for this either, but here they both were, married, parents to a helpless baby. Would he regret this for the rest of his life? Maybe he should have placed Morton in an orphanage. Cousin Surah had offered him a choice, but he couldn't bear that thought. Perhaps if Golda had refused him, he might have, but he suspected Golda knew that too and couldn't abandon her sister's son either.

So he lay still that night and barely slept, in case he might accidentally touch her. Her breathing told him she, too, did not sleep well. When they awoke, she dressed behind a screen and went into the kitchen for breakfast. And he resolved to let Golda be the one to indicate when she was ready for him to be a true husband, even if it meant waiting for a while.

CHAPTER 8

GOLDA

Cousin Surah, true to her word, had found Golda a job sewing piecework for a tailor on Pitkin Avenue. Each day she left the baby with Cousin Surah for an hour so she could pick up or drop off the garments she was working on. The tailor, Mr. Cohen, was an old man, very nearsighted, who peered at Golda and then examined her work with squinty eyes. Four women worked for him, and Golda did piecework at home. Mr. Cohen had a son about the same age as Ben, who managed the business and the payroll. He was very handsome, and when he took in the money from the customers, he flirted with the women for whom he made bespoke dresses and suits. He even flirted with Golda, flattering her work, telling her she was extremely talented. Golda found herself blushing whenever she was with him. It made her so uncomfortable she hurried out of the shop as quickly as she could. Golda had to keep reminding herself that she was a married woman now, not able to look at a handsome young man and bat her eyelashes the way she had seen Esther do.

But when she walked home, her head was humming with the pretty words he had said. "Your hands fly like birds." "Your stitches are perfection." She tried not to let her head be turned by the flattery, but it was hard. She was starved for appreciation. She felt cheated of her maidenhood, although in truth she still had it. But not really. It had been promised to Ben.

And she was surprised by how much she missed her village. *Where are the trees?* Golda wondered as she walked, remembering the pines and spruces that lined the roads around Lesko, lending their green scents even in winter. Her bubbie, who had learned from the herbalists in the village, had taught her the names of the trees when they would walk to town: the tall oaks and beech trees, sycamore, and maples that colored the woods in the fall and freshened the air. There seemed to be no green in Brooklyn, only grime, gray buildings, and rotten smells.

She pushed her way through the streets of Brownsville, stepping around the dirt and garbage strewn on the road, avoiding the manure and the puddles of dirty water; she wove through the crowds, the horses, cars, pushcarts, and stands. The smells and noise accosted her. Over time, she began to see the same pushcart owners every time she walked by, and she would nod hello to them. They would nod back. *Not so different from home,* she thought.

She saw children running through the streets and wondered why they weren't in school or at home with their parents. It was true that some of the boys were working—even very small children—carrying boxes that were so heavy she didn't know how they could hold them. But others were ruffians, playing tricks whenever they could, stealing from the pushcarts and running away from the owners too fast for the men to catch them. Often, while the pushcart owner was chasing the little thieves, other boys would run up to the unattended carts and take more goods. *This is very different from home,* she thought.

It wasn't that there weren't troublemakers in Lesko—just not so many of them. It seemed that here, everywhere she looked there were boys running and pushing each other and fighting and laughing. After a while she began to recognize some of them.

Once she saw three boys—one she thought lived in her building—lined up in front of a newsstand, harassing the shopkeeper. She shook her head in disapproval; the news seller shrugged his shoulders and turned his back, and in a second the boys had tossed lit matches into the newspapers.

It took a few minutes for Golda to realize what the boys had done. Then she screamed. The news seller turned, saw the fire, started running after the boys, but then turned back as his papers burned, fearing the cart would catch fire. Passersby and nearby tradesmen, who were afraid the fire would spread to their stands, tried to help him smother the flames, but the newspapers were lost, even though he had saved the cart. Golda felt so sorry for the man. She wondered as she walked away, shaking her head, what made boys so destructive. She would ask Cousin Surah about this when she got home. But she thought, *Maybe this isn't such a great country after all.*

She pushed forward, head down, and vowed not to look around so much. That night she asked Cousin Surah, "Why are those boys so cruel? Terrible what they did to the newsman."

The answer shocked her. "They are probably paid pennies by the criminals. The pushcart owner likely refused to pay what they call protection money, and this was a warning."

It was the first time Golda had heard of this protection money. "Protection from what?"

"Ha," Cousin Surah answered. "Protection from them, from the criminals. Pay up or we will burn your business."

"Does that really happen? Fires?" Golda was speechless, but it made her think that maybe this new world she had moved to was not the *goldene medina*—the land of opportunity—she thought it would be.

Through all of April and much of May, Golda went about her business, carrying the garments she finished as a seamstress for the tailor, hurrying past the barren earth strewn with garbage that clung to the twigs of the one scraggly bush that had been planted by the side of an apartment building. She did not even glance at it. But after the first warm days in the beginning of May, she noticed, each day, that the bush was coming to life—first with tiny buds, then with small flowers, and finally with full purple lilacs that hung heavy and spread a fragrance that stopped her heart. Home. It reminded her of home and haunted her with a memory that squeezed her throat and brought tears to her eyes.

Just before the blooms were at their height, she walked to the bush, broke some branches, and buried her nose in the blossoms as she almost ran to her building and up the two flights of stairs to Cousin Surah's apartment. There she found Cousin Surah's glass vase, the only one she had, placed the stalks in water, and stood, breathing in the scent and holding it in the back of her throat.

When Ben came home, the bouquet was right in the middle of the dining table. She watched as he came into the room, paused, looked at the table, and hung his hat and coat on the rack. She waited expectantly, but he never said a word.

"Look, Ben," she said finally, pointing to the flowers. "Lilacs. Like at home."

Ben nodded. "Yes, pretty." And that was all he said. Golda watched Ben carefully until the flowers browned and dried up, looking for a sign that he remembered how Esther had looked that day at the lilac bush. But there was no hint, no hint at all.

Still, Golda could not forget.

When she closed her eyes, she saw Esther, standing before a huge lilac bush in their town, and Ben, the first time Golda had seen him, so tall but hardly more than a boy, gazing at her sister, who had buried her nose in the blossoms. He had moved closer and twisted a lock of Esther's honey-brown hair off her forehead. Esther was such a tiny little thing, slim and pretty, with a shy, sweet smile. What did they have to talk about, her sister and this young man? They were whispering. He kissed her cheek. Esther blushed, pressed her forehead into his chest. He took her hand and held her fingers to his mouth; he bent and kissed her lips and lingered there. The look on his face as he stared at Esther was pure bliss. Golda's first feeling was sadness, jealousy. Would any man ever look at her that way?

Then Golda felt a cold fury in her heart. How could her sister do this? She could not stop herself. "Esther, what are you doing? Come home." Her voice was harsh and loud.

The couple jumped apart and stared at Golda, who stood not ten feet away. Golda glimpsed Ben's face. He was handsome, with even features and dark brown eyes. Golda looked at Esther and saw a look of terror pass over her face. Ben said a few words and disappeared down the road.

Golda ran to Esther, grabbed her shoulders, shook her. "Are you meshuga, crazy? What if someone saw you?"

"Don't tell, Golda. Please don't tell." Esther put her hands together, begging. "Promise me."

"Who would I tell? Do I want to ruin you? Ruin me? Who will marry me if my younger sister goes around kissing boys?" She was almost shouting.

"Shush," Esther said, looking around. "Everyone will hear."

"Well, everyone could have seen you. Who is he? What are you doing with him, kissing a stranger? What are you, a *courveh*?"

"Don't say that. I'm not a whore. Please don't say that." Esther flung herself into Golda's arms. "Oh, Golda, I love him. My heart hurts with love." She started to cry.

Golda felt her shock turn to sorrow, and she began to pat Esther's back. "All right, all right," she said. "What are you crying for, if you love him?"

"He's leaving. He's planning to go to America. If I don't marry him, I'll never see him again."

"Don't be silly, Esther." The words were out of her mouth before she could help herself. "What do you know of love? And besides, what good does it do to love him if he's going away?"

"I can't let him go without marrying him . . . then I can follow when he sends me the money."

Golda was stunned. "How would you marry? Did you ask Mama? Papa? They would never consent. And anyway, I'm older. I should marry first."

"Oh, Golda, you wouldn't stop me from my heart's love. You must help me."

Golda stared at her sister. Something had changed about her. She had not lost her innocent beauty, but she looked determined. Her mouth was set. They argued. Golda thought of everything she could say to Esther: She was too young. She didn't know anything about life. How could she think of marrying this Ben and going off to a strange land where her family would never come? "You'd never see me again," Golda said finally.

"You'll come with me," Esther said.

Golda shook her head. "No, I can't."

For days the arguments went on, in whispered conferences, in tearful pleas. When Golda finally said she was going to tell their mother if Esther didn't stop pestering her, Esther had collapsed against her and whispered, "I will die if I don't marry him."

"What are you talking about, dying?" But somehow, she knew that her sister had found her *bashert*, the soulmate that God had destined to be her husband. Golda felt tears prickle her eyes, and her heart was pounding.

"Please help me," Esther whispered. She looked furtively around. "I have something to tell you." Her voice trembled. "I . . . I have a secret. We are already married. We went to Przemysl . . . and we found a rabbi who married us, with a ketubah and everything. Help me tell Papa and Mama. Please, please, Golda, dear sister. Help me."

The look on Esther's face was so pitiful, Golda could not say no, despite her shock that Esther and Ben had already married. She could not imagine how that had happened.

"How were you so brave?" Golda was dumbfounded. "Weren't you afraid?"

Esther shook her head. Her curls bounced around her face. "I was afraid of not doing it and losing Ben forever . . . and I thought of you. How brave you had been telling Papa no, that you wouldn't marry that fat widower. I watched you stand up to them. I thought, if Golda can do it, I can do it."

That night Golda lay in bed, her head swimming with disbelief. She did not understand where Esther, who never did anything except please their mama and papa, had gotten the courage to go against their parents' wishes. But she was even more surprised that her own actions had served as a model for Esther.

Golda thought about what she could do to convince her parents that Ben was a good man who would provide for Esther. At least he didn't need a dowry, and if she, Golda, were to accompany them to America, she wouldn't need a dowry either. The logic of that argument convinced her parents, and soon they agreed to bless the marriage.

And it was all at the time of the lilacs.

And here, in New York, at the time of lilacs all the way across the ocean, she and Ben waited, married yet still not husband and wife. She wanted to welcome him, but she was afraid. She didn't know how. She was ashamed. She knew that he would not force her, and somewhere, in the back of her mind, foolish as she knew it was, she waited for a sign from Esther, that it would be all right for her to claim Ben as her husband.

How long, she wondered, would she make Ben wait until she let him truly be her husband, until she would truly be his wife?

They waited all through the summer and early fall. It was during the dark days of November that she felt it was time. Lying stiffly beside Ben at first, and then more relaxed as she saw he was not going to force her, Golda became accustomed to the warm body beside her, to the even breath of another human being. It reminded her of the comfort of Esther's body on the cold nights in the village when sometimes their limbs tangled with one another's, and it felt finally like the blessing from Esther that she had been waiting for.

At first Golda and Ben lay back-to-back, each facing outward. Then one night, seven months after their marriage, she felt Ben shift, face her back, and reach out his hand to stroke her hip. She didn't object or move away. The next night his hand moved over to the front of her body, slipped over her breast. Golda's heart beat hard. *He is a good man*, she thought. *He is my husband now. Maybe we can make a life together.* She squeezed her eyes shut tight and then, in one swift movement, turned to face Ben. When she opened them, he was looking at her, a question in his eyes. She nodded her head, not sure what exactly came next. She knew he would somehow come into her body, but she didn't know how.

It was awkward, painful. Ben had lifted her nightshirt and was over her, carrying the weight of his body on his arms. His nakedness was erect, hard. She cried out in terror as he moved to enter her, and he stopped mid-thrust and fell back beside her.

"We can wait," he murmured.

She nodded. She knew that Esther had been a willing partner, and they had coupled often and in joy. How was it she, the elder sister, knew nothing about this part of life?

In the morning, she resolved to speak to Cousin Surah. She came into the kitchen, holding Morton in her arms for courage. He was big now, eight months old, already crawling and pulling himself up on every surface he could grab. But Golda continued to hold him tight, even as he began to protest by squirming and pushing at her to get down. Stumbling over her words, she forced them out. "How . . . does it . . . happen?"

Cousin Surah looked puzzled. "How does what happen?"

Golda breathed, closed her eyes, opened them, and said quickly, "A man and a woman, coupling?" She turned her head and buried it in Morton's curly hair, hiding her embarrassment.

Cousin Surah's mouth dropped open. "You haven't come together yet? Almost a year?"

Golda nodded. She could feel the blood rush to her face in shame. Tears prickled her eyes. "I asked Esther after she and Ben got married, but she was so vague. She said it was good, I shouldn't worry. And my mother said I would understand when I married . . . I've never had a boyfriend."

Cousin Surah embraced her, patted her back, and said, "Shush, don't cry. How could you know if no one told you? Shame on me. I thought because you said how you helped at the birth of your brothers that you knew." Golda buried her head in Cousin Surah's breast. She smelled of sweat and honey and onions.

"I know how babies come out. But not how they get in to grow in their mother's belly."

Cousin Surah patted Golda's back. "I should have asked before if you knew. Many women are shocked the first time." She sat Golda down at the table, gave her some tea, and brought a cookie for Morton to chew on as he sat contentedly on Golda's lap. "It will be all right," she went on. "You will see. I'll explain what to do." Cousin Surah explained to Golda how she could make it less painful, how eventually she and Ben would fit together nicely and she would even get pleasure from the act.

Golda was reassured. It took two more tries, two more nights when Golda lay, her legs spread, her nakedness open to Ben's eyes, and then he finally entered her and pushed and thrust until he collapsed upon her with a great sigh and rolled off her and patted her hand. Then he leaned on his elbow and reached over to kiss her on her cheek. She did not look at him, but she closed her eyes in gratitude. *He is not a bad man*, she thought. *I am lucky.*

She felt wet. Was there blood? She got up and used the commode in their room behind a curtain, wiping herself with the water she had prepared as Cousin Surah had instructed her. Then she crept back to bed and pulled the covers over her. Ben was already asleep. She looked over at him. His face was serene. He was so handsome she felt her heart jump. Was it true? Was it possible that this man now belonged to her and she to him?

When that thought came to her, she shivered. Had he imagined she was Esther when they lay together that night? What was he thinking of when he leaned over and kissed her cheek afterward? Maybe someday he would tell her.

Over the next months, they got into a rhythm, and she began— almost—to look forward to the times when he reached for her. She never turned him away.

CHAPTER 9

Ben

From the first days he was in New York, Ben noticed the men, standing on street corners near small diners and candy stores. They hung out, laughing and talking, making remarks to the women who walked by, smoking cigarettes and flicking the butts into the streets, playing craps and shooting dice in raucous circles.

When he asked his boss about them, Abe shrugged. "Gangsters," he said. "They own the streets. Stay away from them. Act respectful. Then they leave you alone—except for the protection money. You pay, and you're protected . . . from them."

"They're Jews?" Ben asked.

"Yes. Some are Jews. Some Italians. Some Irish. Big shots. Don't mess with them."

Ben decided not to worry about it. It was Abe's worry, not his. He would watch and learn from Abe. It would be all right.

The first time Ben saw the man who collected money come to Abe's shop, Abe hurried to the front of the store and almost shoved Ben away from the cash register. Ben stood behind him, his heart pounding. The man stood silently, slightly stoop shouldered, waiting. He was tall and thin, wearing a gray striped suit and a red tie; his shoes were polished. He didn't remove his hat. Abe opened the register, counted out some bills—try as he might, Ben couldn't tell how much he counted—and handed them into the man's outstretched hand. Ben saw a pinky ring flash as the man pocketed the money, tipped his hat, said, "See you next time," and walked out of the store.

Abe turned to Ben. "Don't say anything. I know what I'm doing. This is how you do business around here. Otherwise, there is no business."

Ben nodded. He took his place behind the register again and filed away the information. It was clear that Abe was successful despite the hoodlums who appeared regularly, hands out for a sum they collected each week. It seemed all the shops on the street paid some sort of protection money. The dry goods store owner down the street had refused the collector one time, and there had been a fire in his shop the next week. After that he paid up.

Ben wondered if there was anything different Abe or his brother could do to fight this kind of robbery but decided not to ask. It seemed everyone paid protection money. He repeated what Abe had said, and he didn't ask any questions. "That's how you have to do business."

Ben knew he was fortunate. He had a good trade, a promising position, and a plan for the future. He worked hard for his boss. He was, he knew, a valuable employee. The customers liked him. He was learning to be a master mechanic, and he did everything he could to help make his employer successful. His dream was to have his own shop one day, close to his house. His employer's shop was in the neighborhood of East New York, in Brooklyn, and Ben was eyeing a storefront in Brownsville, his own Brooklyn neighborhood.

Ben was not unhappy at work, and his happiness spread to his home life.

It was true his first wife had been taken from him in a terrible, untimely death, but from that he had his son, whom everyone now called Morty. Ben never thought that he could love a child so fiercely, that he could find such joy in each remarkable milestone of this beautiful boy, so it shocked him the way his heart swelled when he entered Cousin Surah's apartment and Morty toddled to him, shouting, "Papa, Papa!" Each time he would pick up the boy and swing him around, Morty chortled in glee, and then even Golda would smile looking at them.

Morty had the honey-gold curls that had framed Esther's beautiful face and the large, startling blue eyes that had captured Ben's heart. Even as a toddler, Morty promised to be tall, as his father was. And he was exceptionally smart. Cousin Surah said she'd never seen a baby speak so early and so well! Ben thought Morty could become anything he wanted in this wonderful new country of America.

Sometimes Ben noticed that Golda didn't seem to take the same delight in Morty as he did, as even Cousin Surah and her husband, Yaacov, did. He tucked those negative ideas out of his mind to be dealt with at another time and told himself that when Golda had her own baby, perhaps she would make room in her heart for her sister's.

Ben liked to watch Golda when she wasn't looking. A wash of warmth spread over him. He tried not to stare at her unless he was sure she wouldn't see him. It was hard to read her mind, to see what she thought. He wanted to ask her so many questions, but he was always afraid. He felt such gratitude toward her for all the sacrifices she had made for him—from getting her parents to accept his marriage to Esther, to accompanying her pregnant sister on the steamship to America, to marrying him so that his son could have a mother, and to accepting him in their bed. Once they had finally made love, she never turned him away, and he enjoyed her body.

They fit together perfectly; sometimes he thought it was better than it had been with Esther, whose body had been so small, almost childlike, that he'd been half afraid he would hurt her. Golda was strong; he loved to feel her arms about his back, and he liked to watch her face when her eyes were closed but she was letting her body feel the warmth of his hands moving over her skin. She satisfied him, and he thought she felt the same way about him. Sometimes afterward, they would stay entwined in each other's arms, and Golda would fall asleep that way. They slept close to one another, letting their skin touch, except in the summer when the apartment sweltered in heat.

But still Ben worried about how Golda felt. There was often a look of dissatisfaction on her face, and her mouth was drawn down in a frown. He was afraid to ask her why. The answer might rake his heart.

Over the months, he began to use Rabbi Levy as a guide, a consultant, finding that talking to him was very helpful. Every so often he would knock on the door of the rabbi's apartment and ask to speak to him. He always made sure to be wearing his yarmulke under his cap so that when he removed his hat, his head was still covered. He noticed that the rabbi's eyes always flicked up to his head and that he seemed to smile when he saw the yarmulke there. They would go into the parlor and sit to talk.

"I think Golda isn't happy," Ben said this day. "She feels I'm comparing her to Esther."

"Are you?"

"No," Ben said, but too fast. Then he added, "I don't think I am."

"It is not fair to compare one to another," the rabbi said thoughtfully. "Each woman is a separate person, a soul all her own to be loved for herself." Rabbi Levy stroked his beard, in the characteristic way he always did. "Do you show her how you appreciate her? Thank her for the things she does? Bring her something nice to show you are thinking of her?"

"Like what?" he asked.

"Flowers maybe," the rabbi said. "My wife loves flowers. And sweets."

Ben thought for a minute. "I haven't. I am shy of doing that, afraid she will question why I am doing it."

"Why would she question that? Have you ever been untruthful?"

Ben shook his head. "No."

"Well then. What stops you from showing her appreciation? Do you feel it is untrue?"

"Oh no. I appreciate her so much. I'm very grateful to her."

"Don't you think she wants more than gratitude? Do you not yet love her?"

Ben felt his heart was pierced. Was that it? Was he afraid to say anything lest she think he loved her, or lest she not believe he did? "I think I do love her," he admitted, "but I'm not sure. I don't feel like I did with Esther. Or how I feel about Morty."

"Of course you love your son differently. A child is a precious gift from God and needs all your care. And Esther. Perhaps she was maybe an illusion? You were with her for two months and then gone. How can you measure that kind of infatuation with true love? Did you even know her?"

"Maybe not really." He thought for a minute. "She was very pretty," he said.

Rabbi Levy held his hands up, empty. "Pretty disappears with life's travails." Ben sat silently as the rabbi went on. "I don't mean to say that Esther would not have become a good wife. Only that you don't know what she would have become. And you do know Golda."

Ben thanked Rabbi Levy. As always, he felt better having spoken to him.

When he left the rabbi's apartment, he decided he would start with flowers. The next day, when he came home from work, he bought a bunch of daisies, a little fearful that Golda would chide him for wasting money. After he'd reunited with Morty, swung him around and around, he went to Golda and touched her shoulder, kissed her on the cheek. He handed her the flowers.

She was startled, stared at him, held his eyes. "Why?" she asked.

"To say thank you. I appreciate everything you do."

Golda's face softened. A small smile flitted across her lips. She nodded her head, said, "Thank you," and went to put the flowers in water.

After that Ben made it a habit to touch her shoulder or kiss her cheek when he came home from work. He bought flowers for her and for Cousin Surah, who was so kind to them, every Friday to grace the Shabbat table. And it seemed to him that things were better between him and Golda. She even looked different.

Is she getting prettier? he wondered. Her face was not as gaunt as it had been; her breasts, when he touched them, were fuller. And then one day in late 1916, he knew that Golda was going to have his baby. He touched her stomach and looked questioningly at her. She nodded, and he smiled.

CHAPTER 10

GOLDA

Golda was afraid to show Ben how she felt, her secret desires and dreams and most of all the stirrings of love in her heart. What if Ben did not feel them too? Sometimes, when they lay together after making love, she thought she saw a softness in his face. He would smile at her and even reach down to kiss her shoulder or her neck. It was a caress that made her heart pound.

Then, just as she was ready to say something to him, to open her heart, she would think, *No, he will think me foolish. He never promised to love me. What if he doesn't?* And she would swallow the words she was about to say. *Perhaps,* she thought, *he will love me if I become pregnant, and then we will truly be wed.*

Each month she prayed that she would not bleed, but each month there would be the brown spots on her underwear and then the gush of red blood, and her heart would sink. For a few days she was heart-sick, and then she squared her shoulders and told herself, *Next month. It will happen next month.*

Then came the month she did not bleed. She could not let herself believe. She did not tell Ben or Cousin Surah but kept it to herself, checking frequently to see if she was imagining things. Then her breasts became tender, and she went to Cousin Surah, and even before Golda said anything, Cousin Surah smiled and hugged her. "*Du bist shvanger?* You're pregnant?"

Golda looked at her, shocked. "How did you know?"

"You have a glow. A glow of pregnancy. I am so happy for you. Mazel tov. Good luck to you and Ben."

And that night Ben had touched her stomach in a silent question, and she had smiled and nodded. In bed that night they held each other, and she thought she heard him whisper, "You are a good woman, Golda. I am a lucky man that you married me." It was not exactly a declaration of love, but Golda thought it was a very close thing.

Golda often had thought about luck. How lucky she had been to leave the old country when she did. March 1914. A few months later the war broke out in Europe, and it was harder and harder for immigrants to come to America.

She thought how lucky she had been to have a friend like Cousin Surah, strong and wise and loving. A place to stay. Food to eat. Even piecework, stitching bespoke dresses and embroidering shirtwaists for a tailor in the neighborhood where she could earn money and help pay their expenses. Cousin Surah had helped her find the language class she needed so she could learn English. She attended classes at the nearby public school once a week at night until she felt her English was proficient enough to get along.

She watched the other students in the class, wondering what they would do with this strange new language, in this strange new country. Most of them were serious, working to learn so they could get ahead. Golda was adept at languages and learned quickly. She was able to use her English with the women who came to the tailor to have her embroider their clothing. She began to feel useful, as if maybe she could make a good life for herself in this country.

She had decided on her dream. Of course, she would not be a nurse, but she could be a dressmaker; someday she would open her own shop and make her own money. Ben was earning enough at the mechanic's shop where he was an assistant, no longer an apprentice, and with the extra money Golda earned, she and Ben were able to move to their own two-bedroom apartment a few blocks from Cousin Surah.

As the date of her baby's birth came closer, she was more and more frightened, thinking about what had happened to Esther. But she didn't dare put words to it. Maybe saying it out loud would make it happen.

Cousin Surah promised that she would tend her with the midwife who lived in the building. And in August, Golda went into labor. She was terrified, but Surah had said to her, "You are you, not your sister. You will be fine." And Golda believed her, looking into her friend's eyes each time a labor pain came, breathing through it, and finally pushing through the last hour until the baby was born.

"See?" Cousin Surah said. "I said it would be normal, and it was." When it was over, the memory was a blur that Golda barely recalled. The baby was born, and Golda and Ben had another boy.

They named him Isaac. For a few weeks she nursed him, feeling his rosebud mouth latch on her nipple and gulp the nourishment her body provided him, loving how he sucked until he was sated and then dropped off to sleep. She could not help but remember how she had held Morton in her arms and prayed she would feel love for him. With Isaac, she did not need to pray for love. It was there, full blown in her heart.

She could not take her eyes off his face as he slept peacefully in her arms. She even found that having Isaac to love allowed her to acknowledge her love for Morton, whom she began to call Morty. She thought with amazement, *There is always room to love more.* And she took Morty into her heart.

He would stand at her knee, his normal three-year-old energy stilled as he looked at his young brother and asked question after question about him.

"Did I drink from you?" he asked, his blue eyes wide with curiosity.

"Yes," Golda lied.

"I guess I liked it. He likes it, doesn't he?"

"Yes, that is what babies like."

Morty reached out a finger and touched Isaac's silken cheek. Then he touched his own. "He's soft," he said.

"Yes," Golda said. "Babies are soft, and then they grow up like you, big and strong," and she smiled at Morty as he watched Isaac suck on her breast.

But then Golda developed a sore on her nipple, and the abscess made it too painful for her to allow Isaac to nurse. Her breast ached, her abscess leaked, and she developed a fever. She consulted the midwife who had attended Isaac's birth. The midwife told her to put a salve on it, but that did not help. She did not know what to do, but in desperation began to feed Isaac with evaporated milk and bottles, the way she had when Morty was an infant. Hoping her abscess would clear up, she only nursed him on the other breast, but that nipple began to hurt, and then her milk was not enough for him. He cried and cried until finally she gave up, afraid to let him nurse at all lest the abscess return. Eventually her breast milk became so scarce that Isaac fed completely on canned milk.

Isaac seemed not to take well to cow's milk. He developed diarrhea and began pushing the bottle out of his mouth. He lost weight. He developed a rash on his arms and his belly. Golda was beside herself, not knowing what to do. Cousin Surah told her to make a thin gruel of rice cereal and feed that to him, which she did. Over time, Golda believed that because she fed him evaporated milk, which did not agree with him, Isaac was not strong. He became a sickly baby, with a perpetually runny nose and chest colds all winter. He suffered from fevers. She fussed over him, worried about his scrawny arms and legs, his pitiful cries. She held him constantly, and although that seemed to comfort him, Isaac did not gain weight the way Morty had until he started to eat the mashed-up food she made for the family. Then she breathed with relief as he became the plump toddler she had prayed for.

Golda worked from home, embroidering beautiful designs on the linen, cotton, and wool clothing of wealthy women. With two little boys to take care of, she no longer did piecework for the tailors that had started her employment in America, but now she was making more money with her custom embroidery. After Isaac and Morty were asleep, she would work until late at night, uninterrupted.

She hardly had to plan her embroidery. She could just look at the garment and see the design. After first drawing her designs on paper and getting the approval of her customers, she copied them on thin tracing paper that she had bought in an art store on the avenue. She gradually purchased silk threads, colored with every hue of the rainbow, until she had a collection that allowed her to paint pictures on the bodices and collars and plackets of shirts and blouses and dresses. One day a week, she would drop the boys at Cousin Surah's for her to take care of them, take the subway train into lower Manhattan, and sit at a bespoke tailor's store where women came to have their clothing made.

This tailor, Mr. Herzog, printed a sign, Hand Embroidery Done Here, which he placed in his window beside Bespoke Clothing. Golda, sitting in the corner with her own treadle sewing machine and a box of colored threads, could observe the patrons who came in to be measured and to select the fabrics for their suits and dresses. Hanging beside the dressing room was a blouse and a dress, each decorated with Golda's embroidery.

One young woman, her hair cut in the latest gamine look, held the blouse up against her, preening in front of the mirror. "I only came to this tailor because my friend told me about the lady who embroiders. She did a whole design with bugle beads on a silk dress. But this is really special. Like a painting."

Golda could feel her face heating up. She loved the compliments, but they always made her blush. By this time, Golda's language was good enough to be able to converse with the customers in heavily accented English, and when Mr. Herzog came to her to introduce her to the customer, she stood shyly and asked, "What you like me to sew on dress?"

"Flowers maybe? Gold thread?"

Golda sketched on a piece of paper, changing her design to meet the suggestions of the young woman. This was her favorite time, when she let her creative mind fly and drew on paper what they wished to have embroidered on their clothing; then she colored it with pencils. The tailor was glad to give her space because she began to bring in business as word of her beautiful handiwork spread from woman to woman and friend to friend.

Golda's earnings helped her family's livelihood, and she began to tuck away money in a drawer in her clothing cupboard. She wanted to send money to her family, but the war, raging now in Europe, made her fearful of sending money by post. Golda's father wrote to her of the terrible siege in Przemysl and said that the Jews were constantly being set upon by both armies. Golda was very worried about her family, but there was nothing she could do for them.

Finally, in April 1917, America, enraged at the unrestrained use of submarine warfare by Germany and the loss of merchant ships and civilian lives, declared war on the side of the Allies and against Germany. In New York, doughboys were all over the streets, showing off in their uniforms, flirting with the shopgirls, and having a last fling before they were sent overseas. They loaded the troop ships for the fields of France, the trenches, the mud, the death, and the disease, and over the next year, with the draft established, hundreds of thousands of soldiers traveled through New York and across the Atlantic.

Then in March of 1918, while the war was still raging, the first cases of influenza were detected in an army camp in Kansas, and over the next six months there were flu outbreaks all over Europe and Asia. By August, what came to be called the Spanish flu had come to New York City.

New York was a cauldron, boiling in the summer heat. Crowds pushed on the subways during the rush hours, people breathing in each other's faces. In Manhattan theaters, people sat close to one another. Tenements and apartment buildings were places where the disease flourished. And soon, coughing and sneezing were heard in the apartment building stairways. It seemed the flu was everywhere.

You could hear it in the hallways as you walked the stairs to leave the building for the streets outside. You could hear it in the shops, on the avenues, and quickly, often so fast that close friends and neighbors did not even know the individual was sick, the cough and fever killed, sometimes within twenty-four hours. The very young and the very old were not especially vulnerable. It was strong, healthy young adults who more often fell victim to the flu.

Golda stopped going to the tailor in Manhattan, afraid to ride the subway. Her neighbor, a twenty-four-year-old laborer, came home with a sniffle and was dead the next morning. Soon signs were posted on doors where individuals had the flu, warning the house was quarantined.

One of her neighbors described to Golda what the victims of the Spanish flu looked like in their last hours, and it seemed unreal to her. She told Cousin Surah what her neighbor said. "They turn lavender, like the color of lilacs. They call it 'the purple death.'" She couldn't picture it. Golda watched each member of her family carefully every day. She boiled the silverware the way she boiled the bottles and nipples for Isaac's milk, hoping she was killing the flu before it attacked her family. They seemed well enough, and then, just as she was beginning to breathe with relief, they weren't.

Ben came home one day in December with a cold, complaining that his throat was closing up. Golda made a sick room of their bedroom, pulling in a cot for Morty and Isaac's little crib beside it. She knew she was supposed to quarantine the sick, but how could she care for Ben and the children if they were not all together? Besides, she told herself, babies and children were not as susceptible to the flu as young people like her and Ben. She made soup and tea for her family and fed Ben and Morty. Ben lay in bed, his breathing labored. First he sweated heavily, throwing off the blankets; then he shivered so with cold that he begged her for more blankets.

Golda rushed to pile another blanket on the bed, and then he was sweating again, and she had to pick the blanket up off the floor when he tossed it off his body. She made chicken soup and tried to feed it to him and to Morty. She sat on the edge of the bed and held the spoon to Ben's lips. He tried to grasp the spoon, but his hand shook so hard he spilled the soup all over the blanket. He pushed her hand away. He sat up and said, "The room is moving." He closed his eyes tight.

"What do you mean the room is moving?" Golda asked. She swiveled her head around as if looking to see a moving picture.

"In and out," he said. "The walls are moving."

"No, they aren't," Golda said. "It's the fever."

Ben was gasping for breath. "It hurts to breathe," he whispered.

Golda was terrified. "Please, God, please, God," she said, over and over, not able to even say the words for what she was praying for. "Let him live. Don't take him too." She looked hard for the telltale lavender color, but she didn't see it. He was pale but not purplish. She patted his arm. "Try to sleep," she said.

She went to Morty. He had a fever, but it didn't seem to be so high. She fed him soup and tea. His eyes fluttered. She felt his forehead. Not too hot. Her heart swelled with relief. Thank God he was not too sick. She could not bear it if anything happened to him. She turned away, a new feeling in her heart. She turned back to him, saw his sweet face quiet and sleeping on the pillow. She went back to him, kissed his brow, and smoothed his hair. She wept silently as she prayed over and over, "Please, God, please, God."

Then she hovered over Ben again. He was hallucinating, thrashing in bed. She dragged herself to the bathroom to wet towels to cool his fever and then had to cover him with blankets again as he began to shiver. She was exhausted but pushed on. She began to feel ill, but she thought it was mild. Not like Ben. She feared for Ben. She bargained with God. If he let Ben live, she would devote herself to Ben and Morty. She would love them forever. She vowed she would not allow him to get sicker. Soon, Morty just seemed fretful and listless. He slept a great deal. When she looked at Isaac, she thought he was impervious, standing in his crib, happy, it seemed, just to be in the company of all of them. She left him in his crib to observe them and rested as much as she could, secure in the knowledge that babies and small children seemed not to get sick. She herself seemed to be strong.

Gradually Ben's fever broke, and he stopped shivering and sweating. He was weak and could barely walk, but she was convinced he had survived the illness. Then, when she and Ben were getting stronger and Morty had begun complaining that he was hungry, she noticed that two-year-old Isaac's nose had begun to run. She could feel her heart speeding up, her anxiety mounting as she scurried about trying to ward off what she was afraid she would not be able to stop. Praying, she told herself that babies didn't get as sick as young people with this flu, that Ben and Morty were fine and Isaac would be too. But somehow, she didn't really believe it. He had been so sickly for so long. She took Isaac into her bed, covered him with her quilt, sang to him, rocked him. But nothing she did—not compresses, not steam, not hot baths or cool wet towels—stopped the unstoppable virus. Within forty-eight hours, Isaac's skin had turned a cyanotic purple, and Golda knew she had lost the battle for him.

Her heart pounding, she began to cry and scream, "No, no, no! They said babies don't die from it. Why? Why?" She held Isaac, but he stared sightlessly at the ceiling, and as Golda held him to her breast, sobbing, Ben extracted his son from her arms and placed him back in his crib with a blanket over his face. Then he went out to arrange for his burial with Rabbi Levy. There had been so much death in the community that they did not sit shiva. There was no visiting, lest people transmit the disease or become sick themselves.

After Isaac died, Golda could not function. She glanced at Ben, pale and thin, who sat at the table sipping his tea, and then looked away. She could not pay attention to Morty, the way she should have, making certain he ate and got stronger. Golda just could not bear to look at them. Where was Isaac? She was confused, conflicted. The tiny love feelings she had felt for Morty began to fade. *If I was not so focused on Morty and Ben, I would have been able to see that Isaac was ill. I would have been able to care for him earlier. It was their fault that I neglected Isaac.*

No. It was my fault. I'm to blame. Golda lay in bed, her eyes open but staring at nothing. Ben went to Cousin Surah's and asked her to come to their apartment. Having survived the flu herself, she came. Golda did not appear to notice her. When Cousin Surah spoke to her, she didn't answer. Cousin Surah straightened the apartment and tried to put clean linens on the bed, but Golda wouldn't stir.

Cousin Surah conferred with Ben. "She won't even bathe," she said. "Should I force her?"

Ben stirred, got up, shuffled into the bedroom. "Golda, you must get up. You have to take care of yourself."

Golda turned her head. Barely moving her lips, she said, "I have nothing to live for."

Ben shook her. "Nothing? Nothing? I need you. Morty needs you."

"Isaac," she whispered. She turned her head away; she closed her eyes.

Finally, between the two of them, Ben and Cousin Surah got Golda to sit up in bed. Cousin Surah gave her a sponge bath, washing Golda's limp arms and legs. She dressed her in clean underwear, pulled her up, and invited her to the table to eat with them. Golda sat staring at the plate but not picking up her spoon or fork. Cousin Surah spoon-fed her tea, then soup. She obediently opened her mouth, sipped the liquid, swallowed.

Cousin Surah said to Ben, "I can't stay any longer. I have to get back to my family, but I will take Morty with me. And when you are ready to go back to work, if she is still like this, bring her to me, and I will keep her too."

That is what they did. Golda went, compliant, to Cousin Surah's house and sat silently in her kitchen. Normal life swirled around Golda. She began to talk, gradually, then offered to cook for Cousin Surah, knowing that the older woman did not like to make food. Cousin Surah cared for Morty, and Golda did not interfere. Golda did not talk about Isaac. She did not ask about Ben. She just did the tasks Cousin Surah asked of her and moved through the days, pale and ghostly.

Gradually she began to care for Morty as well, feeding him and telling him stories before he went to sleep. Ben came to visit often, staying for supper and spending time with Morty. The color came back into Golda's cheeks.

One afternoon, before dinner, Cousin Surah sat Golda down and said, "Golda, we have to talk. I have something to say to you."

Golda listened.

"You and Morty should go home with Ben now. He is your husband, and he needs you."

Golda nodded. She knew what Cousin Surah said was right. But Cousin Surah's next words shocked her. "You and Ben should have another baby."

Golda gasped. It was like Cousin Surah had punched her. Her stomach churned with nausea. She looked away. As if a new baby could replace Isaac. She couldn't find words to express what she felt. She sat mute. She couldn't breathe. The walls were closing in on her. She pulled her sweater close to her and stared at her feet.

When Cousin Surah went into the bedroom for something, Golda fled the apartment and walked like a ghost out the door and down the street.

She walked. She walked fast. The first thing she noticed was that it was cold out. January. The wind whistled down the street, and she had only her thin sweater for warmth. Her breath made puffs of smoke in the air. She had not noticed that she was crying at first, but the tears became frost on her cheek.

She walked toward Mr. Cohen's, the first shop she'd worked at, as if her feet remembered something her mind did not. At the shop, the window was dark, a sign posted on the door: Closed for Death in the Family. Golda wondered if it was Mr. Cohen the elder or Mr. Cohen the younger. That handsome young man. He had been drafted into the army, and she didn't know if he had come back from Europe. She wondered if he was still alive. She wondered if the tailor shop would open again after the flu epidemic subsided. Would she have a place to work again? She shook her head, dislodging unwanted thoughts. Then she turned and kept walking, the heat of the exercise warming her. There were people on the street, some wearing masks. She had none, but she had recovered from the flu. She would not get it again, she thought. Cousin Surah had said fewer people were getting sick now. It was as if the epidemic was abating. *Too late, too late.* The words thrummed in her head.

Her strides grew longer. Where was she going? Where could she go? She reached the end of the block and stopped to lean against the corner of the building, a little dizzy. She wished she could go crazy like the lady in Cousin Surah's building who had lost most of her family. But Golda knew she had already had her moments when she had withdrawn from the world, sightless, speechless. She was not going to be graced with the oblivion of madness again. Just despair and sadness.

She could end it all and be done. That thought had occurred to her many times, but she knew she could not act on it. Or she could go on with a miserable life. And she knew what her choice would be. She was too sensible . . . wasn't that what everyone had always called her? Sensible Golda. And she always did the sensible thing. Dreams aside, that was the way she would live out her life.

She turned and walked back the way she had come, keenly aware now of how cold she was and how foolish she had been to run out of the house without her coat. When she returned to Cousin Surah's house and opened the door to the apartment, the warmth engulfed her, the smell of soup on the stove, the sound of Morty chattering.

Cousin Surah looked at her. "Where did you go? Without a coat? You could freeze to death." She stared at Golda for a long time. There were questions in her eyes, but she didn't ask them. She nodded. "But you are back now."

"I'm back," Golda said and took a deep breath as she sat at the table, aware that she could breathe now, and that many things could be said without words.

Cousin Surah nodded. "Come have some soup to warm you."

Golda ate the soup, told Morty his bedtime story, put him to bed, and came back into the kitchen. "You are right, Cousin Surah. It is time for us to go home."

The next day she packed up her few belongings, and when she came out with a small satchel in her hand, she said, "Cousin Surah, you have been an angel to me. I am grateful to you for all your help."

"Please don't be angry at me for what I said about a baby," Cousin Surah said. "I just feel you must go on with life. You cannot live in this half life you have been in. It is enough."

Golda did not look at her. She stretched out her hand to Morty. "Come, Morty. We will go home."

Morty looked from Golda to Cousin Surah, seemingly unsure what to do, but then he walked to his mother, who turned at the door. "Thank you, Cousin Surah. I am going home now."

They walked the three blocks to their apartment, Golda holding her satchel in one hand and Morty's hand in the other. Morty had to almost run to keep up with her, she was walking so fast. When she entered the apartment, she dropped the satchel, let go of Morty's hand, and sat, leaden, on the sofa. She wondered when Ben would come home. Would he go first to Cousin Surah's and then come running here when he discovered what had happened? Or would it be one of the nights when he would not turn up at his cousin's apartment but would instead just go . . . where? Golda realized she had no idea where Ben went on those nights when he didn't come to check on her and Morty. She was suddenly very curious. She would have to ask him.

Sitting in her own apartment, surrounded by the familiar furniture, the familiar smells, brought back memories. The last time she had been here, Isaac had just died.

Golda could not forgive God. Why had Morty survived and not Isaac? Then she was pierced with the agony of guilt. Was she wishing Morty dead? Esther's only child? She despaired of ever getting over her grief or forgiving little Morty for living, but she knew it was right that she had gone home to her apartment. It was time to start to work again.

Her needlework had always been a great comfort to her. She picked it up now whenever her grief or anger overtook her. While she pushed the needle with colored thread through the bodice of an ecru linen shirtwaist, she had daydreams. Up the needle went, trailing blue thread; pull and tug just so, then down, a puncture in the linen beside the earlier stitch. As she sewed, pictures came to her, and she remembered. She remembered her childhood, her mother's soft bosom, sitting on her mother's lap and she, Golda, comforting her mother.

Her mother was crying. Esther was a toddler, walking about with her thumb in her mouth, sucking, sucking. The cradle beside her mother's chair was empty. Golda thrust the needle down through the next stitch, just so, spaced evenly, and then up again, the blue thread making a pattern along the placket.

Her mother's sobs were soft. Golda knew why. The baby in the cradle was gone—fast—in the night; carried for nine months, birthed in anguish, suckled for a week, and then still. Lost.

Golda knew what that loss was. While she was embroidering, she often thought about Isaac. He had been gone for several months now. But loss was forever. The needle went into the linen and up again, making a zigzag line beneath which she would place pink and red roses in a chain, like the pattern on china she had seen in the store on the avenue. Expensive bone china, the same color as the ecru shirtwaist.

Sometimes Golda copied decorations she had seen on china and on wallpaper. They would have to be delicate enough to be adapted to embroidery. Her patrons loved the patterns. She changed the color of the silk fibers she was using, threading three needles with shades of rose, red, and pink, and began a small rosebud just beginning to unfurl. The designs were in her head. She did not need to sketch them on the garment anymore, so exact was her eye.

Her mother sobbed quietly for two days and then put the cradle aside. Golda soon learned there would be another baby in the cradle the next year. But sometimes as her mother rocked the new baby, she would weep in silence. And Golda knew, even as a child without the words to express it, that the new baby did not replace the old one. That loss was forever.

Accept loss forever, she told herself, like a mantra. *Accept.*

After the horrors of the Great War and the ravages of the Spanish flu came catastrophic pogroms in Eastern Europe. Letters from their families had thankfully resumed, but they told of murders in Ukrainian and Polish towns and cities. Even the major newspapers in New York City had stories, buried on page two or four, about thousands of Jews being murdered, raped, buried in mass graves. The populations began fleeing west, but there were movements to close the borders to immigrants from the east. And antisemitism, always present as an underlying thrum in Europe and even America, began to rise.

Golda and Ben tried to save money to send to their families so they could emigrate, but by the time they had almost enough for Golda's family, the laws had changed, and America was limiting the numbers of immigrants from Eastern Europe. By 1924 the Immigration Act had been passed, making quotas stricter and more permanent, and Golda's and Ben's families, never really anxious to emigrate, had decided to stay in Europe.

Golda and Ben resumed their lives. Golda let Ben hold and comfort her, and they made love, but not with the joy she had experienced at first. She wanted so much to become pregnant that she felt she needed to try and try. She began to pray again for pregnancy, but again she didn't conceive, and she thought, *I will be childless myself and have only Morty, my sister's son, for solace.*

"Why do some women get pregnant so easily, and I don't?" she asked Cousin Surah one day.

Cousin Surah shrugged. "I don't know. Even the doctors don't know. There's a lady I knew who got pregnant every time she even looked at her husband. She had so many children she had to go ask the rabbi if she and her husband could stay apart for a while, just so she could take care of the ones she had." Cousin Surah shook her head. "And this rabbi, he said no. God would provide. She was so desperate she tried to get rid of a pregnancy, and it didn't work."

"What did she do?" Golda asked.

"She had another baby. She's up to fourteen now."

Golda's head was swimming. Fourteen babies? Even her mother had only had six.

Golda tried so hard to settle in, to settle down and live a calm and happy life. But she could not stop her feelings, and sometimes Golda would erupt with anger at the way her life had been determined by events over which she had no control. To her great shame, she blamed Morty for things that had happened.

Sometimes Golda's rage was like a pile of combustible paper and sticks, dry as desert tumbleweed, just waiting for a spark to ignite it into a conflagration. It sat in the center of her heart, always ready to burst into flame and consume her. But it was, to her great shame, especially sensitive to whatever Morty did, or even what he did not do.

There was no way to know when the anger would explode. It could be a comment he made at dinner that reminded her of the many ways in which she had given her life to him, although she owed him nothing. It could be a look on his face that reminded her of Ben as a young man, or even of her long-gone sister Esther. Sometimes Morty would sing tunelessly under his breath, and to Golda it was an irritant, like the off-key scratches on an old violin. She would grit her teeth and will herself not to say anything, not to give in to an angry outburst.

She knew he sensed it. And she knew he was befuddled by her anger. She hated herself for feeling this way. Once, in a moment of quiet, sitting alone at the kitchen table, waiting for the tea with honey she was preparing to help soothe his slight sniffle, he whispered in his plaintive six-year-old voice, "Why don't you like me, Mama?"

She felt as if a knife had sliced through her heart. She closed her eyes, breathed. She looked at Morty, sitting quietly, his sweet mouth like a rosebud, his beautiful blue eyes focused on her face. Blue eyes. Like Esther's blue eyes. She saw in him her sister when she was little, looking up at her with such complete adoration. He had such a lovely face, such beautiful blue eyes. His soft brown hair fell over his forehead.

Golda felt her throat close over tears. "Of course I like you. Don't be ridiculous . . ." Her voice stumbled. "I love you," she said, and she turned her back. She wondered. Did she in fact love him? Even like him? She placed the tea in front of him and then, as an afterthought, went back to the kitchen to bring him a cookie. She put it down and sat at the table watching him sip the tea and nibble on the cookie. It was hard to be near him and feel his distrust and think that she had failed them all . . . Ben, Morty, Esther, even herself. She thought, *Maybe if I say it again and again, it will be true. I love you, I love you, Morty, I love you, Ben.* She practiced and practiced, hoping to fill her heart.

Ben had begun to attend Rabbi Levy's shul on most Shabbat mornings, sometimes taking seven-year-old Morty with him. They both seemed to enjoy it and came home for lunch afterward in a good mood. Golda also noticed that occasionally Ben would come home late from work and, when asked, tell Golda he had stopped off for a talk with the rabbi. Often, after these meetings with Rabbi Levy, there would be something lighter about him. He would smile and say something kind to her. Why?

One day she asked him if he wanted some tea. Morty was in his room reading. They were alone. As she went into the little kitchen, she asked Ben, "What is it that the rabbi says to you that makes you feel better?"

Ben thought for a moment. "I think he just listens, so I'm not talking to myself and saying things that make me unhappy."

"Like what?" She put a glass of tea with a spoon in it before Ben. He liked to drink his tea in a glass, the way his parents had when he was growing up. He would sip the tea through a sugar cube that melted in his mouth.

Ben waited a minute, taking a sip of the hot liquid. Then he took a breath and said, "I sometimes wonder why I cannot seem to make you happy. I told him that."

"And what does he say?"

"Different things. He told me to bring you flowers or sweets."

Golda nodded, remembering when he had begun to bring her flowers on Friday night. She had liked that, but it hadn't really made her happy.

Ben hesitated and then said, "He also said that I cannot make you happy. Only you can do that."

She looked down at her hands. They were careworn, rough, the cuticles of her nails ragged. She closed her eyes, letting his words sink in. "You like him," she said, more a statement than a question.

"Yes. He is very pious, but he never tells me what to do." He chuckled a little. "I never spoke to the rabbi in my village at home. He was always telling everyone to daven. 'Pray to God,' he told me. When I said I didn't like to pray, he cuffed my head."

Golda smiled, thinking that Ben might have been a bit of a troublemaker as a young boy. She had a question buzzing in the back of her head, but it was hard for her to ask it. She took a breath and said, "Does he talk to women?"

"Of course he does. They come to him all the time, with all kinds of questions."

"Maybe I could talk to him." Golda looked into Ben's deep brown eyes and held them for a long time. Her heart lurched.

Ben nodded. "Yes, he suggested that several times. I didn't want to ask you to do it. But I think it would be a good thing to try."

Golda went to Rabbi Levy's one afternoon when she was coming home from delivering her embroidered shirtwaists to the tailor on Pitkin Avenue. As she came home, she passed the little shul on the corner. She hesitated, thinking she would go and ring the bell. *Maybe he won't be home*, she thought. *Maybe he will.*

With a deep breath, she went to the side door and pushed the buzzer. After a few minutes a clatter of feet ran down the stairs, and the door opened to a young girl about ten years old. "Is Rabbi Levy in?" Golda asked.

"He's at evening prayers," the girl said.

Golda was embarrassed. "I'll come back," she said and turned quickly to walk away even before the girl nodded.

I should have known, she thought. *Of course he is at prayers. Look at the time.* Her father used to go to prayers each night. Golda felt her cheeks redden, and she walked quickly to let the breeze cool them. That night she did not tell Ben about her failed attempt to see the rabbi. Neither of them would know. She hadn't given her name.

But the idea of going to see the rabbi persisted in her head, and a week later she went out again just before she started to shop for lunch. This time when she rang the buzzer, the teenage girl who answered took her upstairs to the parlor and asked her to sit. Golda thought the other girl must be in school. As she waited and looked around the room, she tried to quiet her beating heart. Would he remember her? After all, he had buried Esther and had married Golda to Ben. But that was a long time ago . . . seven years. Should she remind him of that? She wasn't sure what she would say to him. She would start with her name. Maybe then he would know why she was there.

When the rabbi came into the room, Golda stood, surprised at how short Rabbi Levy was. She stood a head taller than he. "R . . . Rabbi Levy, I . . ." Her voice felt thick, like she was going to cry. "I am Golda Feinstein," she stammered.

The rabbi nodded. "Ben's wife," he said. "Please sit. I am glad to see you again."

Golda clutched her pocketbook. So he did remember her.

"How can I help you?"

"I don't know. I am not sure anyone can help me." And she burst into tears. How would she tell him all that was eating at her heart? *There is such a long list of sins . . . a catalog of betrayals*, she thought. *I betrayed my sister. I did not save her on the ship.* Even as she thought it, she knew it was not true. She was not a doctor. Still, she felt she had failed Esther. Hadn't she suspected that Esther was already pregnant when she married Ben? Why hadn't she said something? She should never have let Esther convince everyone to let her sail when she was so pregnant. She knew better.

But if she had stopped Esther from sailing, her sister would have had the baby at home and would probably have died anyway, Morty as well. And then where would she, Golda, be? She would most likely still be in Lesko.

Morty, Golda's second sin. She had not loved him wholly. She had cared for him with cold resignation. She felt sick when she thought of that. Did it matter that she had realized how much she cared about him when he was sick with the flu? That she had saved him and Ben? She pushed that out of her mind. But then she had not been able to save Isaac. She was not God.

Isaac she had loved with all her heart, but she couldn't save him anyway. God, if there was a God, was punishing her . . . for her jealousy of her sister, for her neglect of Morty, and that was why he had taken Isaac from her.

And she did not embrace Ben or love him as a wife should.

In the ensuing time, after the rabbi let her cry without trying to stop her, and then just listened as she poured out her pain and her sins and her fears and her anger, Golda felt a little better. He didn't say much, which surprised Golda, but even so, just unburdening herself was helpful.

At the end of about a half hour, the rabbi said, "Now that I think I know what your situation is, is there something particular you want to ask me?"

Golda thought, *I've told him everything. I've admitted why I'm angry, why I'm ashamed of myself when I'm not kind to Morty, why I'm bereft of my own children. What can I ask for help with?* She stared ahead silently. "I don't know if you can help me, Rabbi. I'm just so unhappy."

"Is there something that you know would make you happy that you don't have?"

"How many children do you have, Rabbi?"

"*Baruch Hashem*, seven," he answered.

"I have Morty, and he isn't even mine."

"Whose is he, then, if he is not yours? You have held him since his birth."

She didn't answer that but simply murmured, "I want my Isaac."

"Isaac?" He nodded, stroked his beard. "A lost lamb. May his memory be a blessing. God took him, we don't know why."

Golda closed her eyes, and the words came out before she knew what she would say. "I want a child again. But I don't deserve one. It's because of me that Isaac died."

"No, no. How can you say that?"

Golda had hardly allowed herself to think that, but somehow, in the rabbi's presence, the words came pouring out, mixed with sobs. How she had tended Ben so carefully, and Morty too. How she had been sick and could barely pay attention to her own boy. And then when he started to sniffle and cough, it was too late . . . too late.

"No, dear woman. You are not to blame. You did everything, everything right, and God made his decision . . ." After a moment the rabbi said, "I myself lost my oldest son. No one escaped untouched."

Golda's eyes widened. She shook her head. "I didn't know. How do you bear it?"

Rabbi Levy did not answer. The two sat silently for a while.

Then Rabbi Levy said, "Do you want a child?"

Golda was still. "Yes. But I can't . . . I don't get pregnant. And there is no joy." Golda shook her head, not able to speak. She was filled with shame. She couldn't look at the rabbi, couldn't say anything else.

He was silent for a while. Then he said, "If you deny yourself the joy of your husband's love, then perhaps you deny yourself the possibility of a child again." It was a simple statement, but Golda didn't think it was true. By now she knew how women became pregnant. It was not through joy.

"God helps us to make a path in life, but we each make our own way. Think hard about what you want your path to be and how you will walk it." The rabbi stood. "Come back in a few days. We will talk again."

Golda stood. "I'm sorry I have taken so much time . . . with my woman's foolishness," she said. She didn't really think she was foolish, but it was something she had heard her mother and father talk about—women's foolishness.

"It is not foolishness to want a child, to be jealous, to yearn for happiness. Only human." Rabbi Levy walked out of the parlor, and Golda followed him. As she walked down the stairs, he said again, "Come back in a few days. Maybe you will have a thought in between. Be well. You are a good woman, you know. Better than you think."

Golda walked home, forgetting that she had been on her way to the market before she stopped at Rabbi Levy's house. Just as she was about to enter the apartment, she remembered her errand and turned back to the street once more. She was a good cook. She would make a nice dinner for Morty and Ben. She would bake a cake for dessert. Cooking made her feel better, and eating good food put everyone in a better frame of mind. She headed back down the street again.

Golda saw Rabbi Levy a few more times. He never told her what to do, but he would give her a prayer to say. He always left her with "Be well. You are a good woman, better than you think." She left him feeling lighter, although when she said the prayer he gave her, it did not mean much to her.

She pondered the things she had told the rabbi, about Esther and how envious she had been of her beauty; about Morty and how he reminded her of her failure to save her sister; of her own lost choices; and of Ben and how she never felt he could love her. She told the rabbi her secret dream to escape the prison that she felt her life was now, how she longed to get rid of the bitterness. Some of the things the rabbi told her made good sense to her. Some of them did not. He was, after all, just a man, and although he was a wise man, he didn't know the answers to everything. But one thing Rabbi Levy said that she came to believe was "If you keep thinking back, you will never leave the prison of the past. Think about the rest of your life."

She wondered, *Can I do that? How can I do that?* And then she found that each day the past faded a little bit more, and each day it was more possible to just live that day. One morning Golda woke to sunshine spilling in through the room's curtains. She opened the window, and the air felt soft and fresh. At breakfast, when she served Ben his tea and oatmeal, she touched his shoulder as she leaned over to put the dishes before him. The solidity of his back sent a tingle through her fingers. He looked up at her, and she couldn't stop the small smile that flitted across her face before she turned away.

All day she felt a thrill of anticipation. She would welcome Ben back and try to make the best she could out of what had been given to her in life. Her life maybe was not so bad, she thought. And if Ben could not love her as he had loved Esther, he was kind and good to her. She would have to settle for that. Maybe God would give her another chance to be a mother. But she had a son, Morty. He was hers and she cared for him. The thought lifted her heart. Golda dreamed of another child—a girl, she hoped. She would name her Zlata, Sylvia, after her beloved grandmother.

PART TWO

1928–1939

CHAPTER 11

MORTY

Morty and Ben were not watching where they walked that bitter cold February noon when they almost bumped into Abe Reles and his men. Both father and son were hunched in their coats, hands crammed in pockets. Morty had a gray wool hat with earmuffs jammed on his head. He was staring down at his feet, walking carefully around the slushy puddles on the sidewalk because he had discovered there was a small hole in the sole of his left shoe, and he was trying to avoid water seeping in and wetting his thin socks.

He wondered what his friends had been doing that morning while he was spending his time in synagogue. When he was little, he had loved going to synagogue with his father, and they would walk home talking about what the rabbi had said in his weekly sermon, or even the Torah portion they had read that morning. Ben would try to explain it in detail to Morty, whose face shone with delight at the grown-up conversation he was having, even though Ben himself was not so learned that he could really understand it all.

But now that he was fourteen, Morty thought he had better things to do with his weekend days off than spend them in synagogue with lots of old men *shuckling*, bending their bodies back and forth as they prayed. He noticed things now that he had never thought about when he was little—the fusty, sometimes unwashed smells that came off the men crowded together in the tightly packed room, their beaten looks as they prayed out loud, their bent bodies, as if they had forgotten how to stand up straight. And he was bored. He wondered if he would ever be able to tell his father, whom he loved very much, that he was through with going to shul. He glanced at Ben, who was now just an inch or so taller than he was.

Ben was also looking down. He walked, head bowed, hands behind his back, ruminating about something—but what? Morty wondered. He didn't think his father was very religious. He knew he didn't strictly keep all the commandments, and although he observed the Sabbath by going to synagogue in the morning, eating a nice Sabbath lunch, and taking a Sabbath rest, he was not very observant otherwise. He turned the electric lights on and off at will and sometimes even listened to the radio on Saturday afternoon. They had just bought their radio in the last year when they seemed to have more money to spend.

Ben and Golda went out to the avenue after their naps and shopped for items they needed in the stores that were owned by gentiles, which were open on Saturdays and closed, like all the stores were, on Sundays. Morty had asked his father why he went to synagogue so regularly on Saturday when he clearly didn't believe in all the rules of a strict Jewish life. Ben simply said that he went out of respect and gratitude to Rabbi Levy, who had helped him and Morty's mother in so many ways when they had first come to America. When Morty asked how the rabbi had helped, Ben did not explain further. He just reiterated that Rabbi Levy was a wise, kind, and very helpful man.

So Morty was either staring at his father or looking at the puddles on the street that Saturday, walking home from synagogue. Neither father nor son was paying much attention to the crowds on the street, and they were about to crash into a man walking toward them when Ben grabbed his son's shoulder to stop him from walking any farther.

Startled, Morty looked up and met the eyes of the man they had almost collided with. He knew immediately who it was. Abe Reles, known as "Kid Twist." The man was not big. He was short, shorter than Morty, but brawny, and although he was young, in his twenties, his face was already scarred from all the fights he had been in since he was eight years old. He had thick rubbery lips and a mashed-up nose, and his eyes bulged with anger as he stared. He was dressed in a double-breasted striped silk suit, with sharp creases in his trousers.

His overcoat was a gray tweed, and his shoes were polished, shimmering up at Morty. He held a lit cigarette in his pudgy fingers. Reles put his cigarette between his lips and dangled it out of the corner of his mouth, and the smoke swirled around his eyes, causing him to partially close them so they were menacing slits, barely visible under the brim of his black fedora. He did not move from the middle of the sidewalk. Two other men, much taller, stood on either side of the short man, blocking the way entirely.

Morty's father was looking down at his shoes. Morty's stomach dropped. He stared at his father, not sure what to do. Ben, taller and slimmer than Reles, seemed to shrink into his overcoat. He took off his hat, and Morty saw the black skullcap that he wore beneath it. Morty also had one on beneath his wool hat, but he didn't like to show it. To religious Jews, it was a symbol of honor and respect for God, but to Morty, it was an embarrassment, a sign of difference from the rest of the world.

Ben bowed his head, then, white-faced, whispered, "*Shuldich mir*," falling into Yiddish, as he always did when he was nervous.

"What did you say?" the man asked, putting his face close to Ben's. There were white bubbles of spittle at the corners of his mouth. Morty's heart was hammering.

"Excuse me." Ben's voice shook.

"Watch where you're walking . . . *sir*," the man said with an emphasis on the *sir*. And he stepped aside, sweeping his hand before him in an exaggerated way, as if bowing to royalty. He did not take off his hat to Ben. He let them by, but you could tell which of them was the boss. Abe Reles and his friends were laughing.

Ben whispered, "Thank you," took Morty's arm, and hurried him along, staring straight ahead, never letting go of Morty's arm, and saying nothing.

They reached their apartment house, a six-story brick building. Morty took a last deep breath of the clean cold air as his father pushed the door open into the crowded tenement and began to climb the four floors to their flat. It was dark in the stairway. The air was fetid, thick. Each floor landing had four doors opening to tiny apartments, crowded with occupants; some of the doors were open a crack, as if somehow the air in the hallway would be fresher than the air inside the apartment, and Morty could hear loud voices and babies crying, smell cooking odors of cabbage and soup.

On the fourth-floor landing, Ben stopped in the hallway before their apartment, his key in his hand. He said, "Those are bad men, Morty. Stay away from them."

Morty was irritated. "I know that," he said. "Do you think I don't know that? I heard he just got out of jail, and he's back in business."

Ben stared at him. "How do you know so much about it? Where did you hear that?"

"People talk. Everyone in the neighborhood knows about Kid Twist."

"Just stay far away from them. Walk across the street if you see them. Don't talk to them. They're trouble." He slipped his key in the lock and opened the door to their apartment as the warm smell of chicken soup engulfed them.

Morty and Ben took off their wet shoes and hung their coats on the hooks on the back of the door as they stepped into the crowded dining-sitting room. The table against one wall was set for lunch, the gas stove had a pot of soup bubbling on its burner, and Morty's mother, Golda, sat on the worn sofa beneath the one window in the room, embroidering something on a blouse for one of her rich private customers—proof positive that their family did not really observe the Sabbath. Sewing, like most other activities, was prohibited on the Sabbath for true observers. Seven-year-old Sylvia sat at the table reading a book from the library. Golda stood to greet her husband and Morty and to serve lunch. Ben leaned over Sylvia and kissed her forehead. "It's good to be home."

On that, father and son agreed. It was good to be home. If Morty didn't like going to synagogue on Saturday, he liked the Sabbath meals. They ate chicken soup with some shredded chicken and slivers of carrot left in the stock, lots of potatoes fried in chicken fat, and more boiled carrots with the tiniest bit of honey to enhance their sweetness. There was challah that his mother had baked on Friday, and for dessert, applesauce, honey cake, and tea. Saturday meals were the best meals of the week.

Morty slurped his soup, dipping the crust of the bread into it. When he had drained his bowl, he looked up at his mother and then his father. "We met Kid Twist when we were walking home," he said.

Golda looked from Ben to Morty and back to her husband again.

Sylvia looked from one to another, her soup spoon poised, as if she did not want to miss a word they were saying. "That's a funny name, Kid Twist," she said.

Golda ignored her. "Who? Who did you meet?"

Ben took a deep breath. "The kid, Abe. Abe Reles."

"The one with the pushed-in face? Who comes to your work?"

Ben nodded.

"What did he say?"

Ben didn't answer her.

Golda turned to Morty and repeated, "What did he say?"

Morty looked from his mother to his father, trying to remember what he had said. He shrugged. "Nothing," he answered finally. "He just said we should watch where we were walking. He called Papa 'sir.'"

"Yes," Ben said tiredly. "But he didn't mean it. Stay away from him, Morty. Stay away."

"Do you think he knew you?" Golda asked her husband.

Ben shrugged. "I don't know." There was silence at the table.

Morty watched his parents carefully. He knew that, among other illegal businesses, Abe Reles ran a gang of thugs who collected money from the shopkeepers and businesses in Brownsville. Protection money. If you didn't give it to them, they had various methods of making you see the error of your ways. Like setting a fire. Or having kids throw rocks through the windows. Morty wondered why Reles would recognize his father, although he thought he knew the answer. He asked anyway. "Why would Kid Twist know you?"

Sylvia sat swinging her legs back and forth. "Who's Kid Twist?" she asked.

"He's a mean man. He'll twist your neck off if you cross him," Morty said.

"Stop that," Golda said. "You'll frighten your sister." She frowned at him.

"I know why he might recognize you," Morty said to his father. "You pay him off."

His father was silent, looking down at his plate. Morty took this for consent.

Sylvia looked at her brother. "Does Kid Twist really twist people's necks? How does he do that?"

Morty leaned over and gently put his hands around Sylvia's neck and pretended to twist her throat. "Like this."

"Ow," she said. And then she laughed so her parents knew she was joking. Morty patted her head. They ate the rest of their lunch in silence.

After lunch, Golda resumed her embroidering on the sofa—she was not willing to lose any time from her embroidery, which earned her good money from the wealthy women who custom ordered her extraordinary work. Ben took a nap, and Sylvia sat at the table reading. When Morty's friend Rudy Schmidt came over to play checkers, they tiptoed through his parents' room into his and Sylvia's bedroom, a tiny square right behind his parents' room.

Rudy's family, German Jews, lived in the same apartment building, and Morty and Rudy had been best friends—inseparable—since first grade.

Sitting cross-legged on Morty's bed, the two boys played checkers. Morty would have preferred to play chess, but Rudy never could get the hang of it, so they played game after game of checkers, splitting their wins and losses. Morty told Rudy about meeting Abe Reles.

"You mean Kid Twist?" Rudy asked.

"The same. We almost bumped into him."

"You're lucky he didn't slit your throat. He didn't get his rep for nothing."

"Ha. We're small potatoes to him. Why would he bother with us?"

"I heard he'd shoot a guy or cut his throat if they looked crosswise at him. He's a mean son of a bitch."

"He was dressed really beautiful," Morty said. "He must make a lot off the protection racket. I wonder how much he makes?"

"A lot," Rudy said. "If I could get into his business, I would."

"No, you wouldn't."

"Yeah, I would. Where else are we going to make money? Peddling on the street?"

Morty was quiet for a minute. "King me," he said, pushing his red checker to the end of the board.

Rudy groaned and put one of his checkers on top of Morty's. "You're too good. I'm finished." Then he swung his hand and swept all the checkers off the board. "Next time we play gin rummy. At least with cards I got a chance to win."

"Not much," Morty said and laughed. He was a much better card player than Rudy. Morty leaned back and looked at Rudy. He thought about making money. "How much do they make, the guys in the gangs?"

"A lot more than our fathers," Rudy answered. "You want to be poor all your life?"

Morty shook his head.

"Then you gotta do something else than work for someone or peddle stuff on the street like most of the Jews around here. Kid Twist is some other kind of Jew."

"Yeah, a murdering kind. Anyway, I won't end up like our fathers. I'm going to school. I'll be an engineer."

"That's better than what they make, but it's not gonna be a lot of money. And college costs a fortune. Where are you gonna get the money? You're nuts if you think those nickels and dimes your folks put in a jar are gonna be enough to pay for college. There's probably not more than half a year's worth of the cost. Not to mention how long it takes to go to school for it. Years and years."

"Maybe, but it's what I want to do."

"We'll see if that's what you do. Meanwhile, watch what I do."

"What are you going to do?" Morty wasn't sure he wanted to know the answer to that question.

"I'm about ready to ditch school," he said. "There's a big world out there, and I want a piece of it. I got plans."

"You can't get anywhere without school," Morty said. "We're lucky. Our high school is a good one. We can get somewhere from there."

"Yeah? Where? Where are you going to get to?" Rudy swung his legs off the bed and stood up. "I hate school. I'm not good at it. And there's more than one way not to be poor. All the guys on the corner are rich, and I'm gonna be too. Watch and see."

Rudy faced Morty and hesitated a minute. They were standing eye to eye, the exact same height, both tall for their age, but the red-headed, freckled Rudy was beefy, with broad, muscular shoulders. Morty was slimmer and was working hard at the Boys' Club to develop his muscles. He was already one of the best boxers in his weight class because he was so quick on his feet. Privately they called themselves the "Tough Twosome," because it made them feel unbeatable. That was important in their neighborhood, where weakness was dangerous and sometimes deadly.

"Look, Morty," Rudy said after a minute. "You and me have it better than some of the other guys. Think of where Paulie lives. Him and his brothers all sharing a bed. And Davy, living on the street half the time because his parents never have enough money to pay the rent. That's a crappy way to live, and I'm not doing it. Anyway, I'm going home. I'll see you tomorrow."

Morty followed Rudy to the door and let him out of the apartment, thinking about their conversation. Morty couldn't argue with Rudy. He was right about Paulie and Davy and lots of his friends. Everyone he knew was poor. They all lived in the tenements around him, in crowded walk-up apartments warmed by coal in the winter and suffocating with heat in the summer, when they sweltered in windowless rooms with the sweat pouring down their faces, stinging their eyes. Morty and Rudy lived a little better than most of them, but not the way he wanted to live.

Morty knew his ticket out of the slums would be education. He thought about the jar Rudy mentioned. When he was seven, his father began putting coins in a big covered jar for his college fund. Every week his father would pull the jar down and deposit coins in it. It was heavy now with money. Morty had no idea how much was in the jar, but he suspected that Rudy was right—it wouldn't even be enough for half a year of college.

What else had Rudy said? The guys on the corner were rich. He had plans—big plans. Sometimes Morty was very much afraid of Rudy's plans. Rudy cut school often and spent his time hanging around Solly's Corner Candy Store in Brownsville, rubbing elbows with the young hoodlums who worked for Mickey Adler, a local street boss. He said he'd heard how they made money and how easy it was. Rudy kept bothering Morty . . . telling him how they could get a piece of the action. But the truth was Morty was afraid.

His parents were proud of Morty, even to the point of bragging about him every chance they got. Morty was known in his family and at school as one of the smartest of the boys. He was particularly advanced in math, being able to do all the sums and multiplication in his head. Golda said he got that from her father, who, in the old country, had been a bookkeeper for several of the local shopkeepers. Ben wanted him to be an engineer and go to Brooklyn Polytechnic College.

Morty remembered how Golda had laughed at that at first, but then it seemed she began to believe in it too. That was why she put away a share of her embroidery earnings for Morty's education. It cost a fortune to go to college, but Morty's math teacher had told him that he might be able to get a scholarship. Morty wondered. It seemed like a pipe dream that he could go to college, but Ben was insistent. "You aren't going to be a tailor or bookkeeper, or a mechanic like me. You're going to be an engineer."

Maybe he would be an engineer, Morty thought. But he would have to save too. It was time for him to get a job after school and start giving money to his parents for his college education. He was fourteen now. Old enough to work.

Morty applied for every job he could think of and took whatever job he could get—stacking groceries, unloading trucks, cleaning stores. At Hansen's Grocery Store, where he first worked unloading supplies off the trucks and stacking them on the shelves, his boss, Mr. Hansen, took a liking to Morty. Mr. Hansen walked with a pronounced limp, caused by a broken leg in childhood that had been improperly set. Because Morty was hardworking and reliable, as well as good at math, the shopkeeper sometimes trusted him at the cash register. This was a plum job, paying a little better than the money he earned stocking the shelves and sweeping the aisles.

And that was when he saw firsthand how the Adler gang took money off the top of the grocer's earnings. The collector, a silent hoodlum, stood, hat perched on his head, snowy white shirt blazing against his gray striped suit, waiting. Mr. Hansen counted out some bills and handed them to the man, who pocketed the money, tipped his hat, smiled, said, "See you next time," and walked out of the store. Morty noticed his crooked teeth when he smiled.

Mr. Hansen turned to Morty. "Don't say anything. This is how you have to do business around here. Or else there is no business."

Morty nodded. He wondered if there was anything the store owners could do to fight the mob, but decided not to ask. He remembered his father telling him how he had seen Abe Frankel, his boss, give money to the Italian mob. *That's how you have to do business*, he repeated to himself. And didn't ask any questions.

The next week when the collector came, he called Mr. Hansen over and stepped aside, letting the owner open the cash register again and pay the protection money. Then he quietly resumed his work. And he never mentioned this to anyone—not his father or mother and certainly not Rudy.

CHAPTER 12

SYLVIA

There were only the two of them. Sylvia knew there had been one more child, a boy, born between her and Morty, but no one talked about him. Sylvia was curious. She only knew about this baby because she had seen a picture of the family before she was born, and there were two children in it: Morty and a baby, about two years younger, who, Morty told her, had died of Spanish flu. Sylvia was born when Morty was seven, and they were the only children in the family.

Sylvia's first distinct memory was of her fourth birthday, July 4, 1925, when Morty carried her on his shoulders to see the parade go down Fifth Avenue in New York City. She remembered the hot subway ride from Brooklyn on the BMT, with her parents and Morty. Her father kept wiping the sweat off his face until his handkerchief was damp and wrinkled. Sylvia didn't mind the heat because she was so excited. They had seats on the train, and she sat next to her mother, swaying with her as the train swept through the tunnels. Her mother smelled of lavender, and her skin was soft.

The crowds on the sidewalk were three deep, and they found a place on the street to watch the parade, but not in the front of the sidewalk. That was when Morty, tall for his age at eleven years old, lifted Sylvia onto his shoulders so she could see the marching bands sweep down the avenue. And she remembered flags waving and noise and laughter. Morty told her it was for her birthday.

Sylvia was a little beauty. Golda said that when she saw her daughter, she thought about her sister, Esther; it was as if she had been reborn. Sylvia had the same honey-colored curls and blue eyes that Esther had. She was a smiley baby and a lively toddler whom everyone loved, but Sylvia loved Morty best of all.

Sylvia and Morty shared a small bedroom behind their parents' room. Two single cots, one on either side of the room. There was one tiny window over Morty's bed, and sometimes he would let Sylvia kneel on his cot and peek out to see the street below. Whenever Sylvia and Morty played card games together, he never let her win. He said she had to learn how to beat him fair and square.

One morning, shortly after Morty and Ben met Abe Reles, there was a big snowstorm. Sylvia awoke, and she could see from her bed that the window framed the fat flakes falling so thickly that the whole window was white. Morty wasn't there, so she went to his bed, climbed up, and peered outside. The streets were silent, all the sounds muffled by the snow that already lay in white pillows along the street and sidewalks. A few cars plowed through the snow, and the streetcar was running.

Sylvia ran out of her room into the parlor and shouted in excitement. Morty was sitting at the table eating oatmeal. She started begging even before she sat down. "I want to build a snowman! Please, please will you help me build a snowman, Morty?"

With urging from Golda, Morty finally agreed. They would go to the street after they both finished breakfast.

Sylvia could hardly wait. By the time she went downstairs, the weather had turned just a tiny bit warmer. The snowflakes were wetter and spaced farther apart. The snow on the sidewalk was pristine white. The smoke and dirt had not yet mixed with the snow to create the brown slush that would come later in the day. Outside, the boys were having snowball fights, pummeling each other with wet round balls, perfect for throwing.

Sylvia picked the spot to build, right beside the building's doorway, where anyone coming in or out could see her snowman. She jumped up and down, trying to stay warm while she waited for Morty. She wore a red wool coat and hat and a brown scarf, which her mother had wound around her neck to keep her warm. Her mother had insisted she wear galoshes, floppy rubber boots that fit over her shoes. The ones Sylvia wore were too big—hand-me-downs from a neighbor—and Sylvia hadn't grown into them yet. Her feet slid up and down when she walked, and several times she almost fell. She thought maybe she should take them off, even if her feet got soaked.

Morty came out of the building, her handsome brother with his blue eyes and a wide smiling mouth. To Sylvia he looked like a movie star.

They began to build the snowman. Sylvia rolled the ball in the snow, packing it around until her wool mittens were so wet that she stripped them off. Morty wasn't wearing his either. They had just seated the head of the snowman on the middle ball when Joey Simpson, a boy who lived in the next building, came up to them. He was three years older than Sylvia but so big he was almost as tall as Morty. She could not say why, but she didn't like him.

"Can I help?" His voice was whiny.

"No," she shouted. "Go 'way. He's my brother, and he's making *me* a snowman. Not you."

Morty looked at her, surprised, but didn't say anything.

Joey said, "You're mean."

"I don't like you either," Sylvia said, a deep frown on her face.

Joey shoved her. Sylvia fell hard on the sidewalk, scraping her cheek. She reached her hand up and touched her face. She began to cry.

"Hey," Morty said. "You had no call to do that." He gave Joey a small push, more to get him away than to hurt him. He was turning to see how badly Sylvia was hurt when Joey punched Morty in the stomach.

"Stop it," Morty said. He took hold of Joey's shoulder and held him at arm's length. Joey twisted away and rushed the snowman, knocking the head off. Then he took his metal shovel and swung it at Morty, hitting his forehead and cutting the skin. It began to drip blood, freezing into red drops on the slush. Morty was furious. He wrenched the shovel from Joey's hand and threw it down and began to pummel Joey until the kid was sobbing, his nose bleeding.

Sylvia was jumping up and down in excitement and fear. She wanted Morty to hit Joey hard, but as they fought, she became afraid that he would get too hurt. She pulled at Morty's arm, and he stopped himself from punching Joey again, and finally Joey jumped up and ran off to his house. Morty stood, staring after Joey, breathing hard. Then he wiped the blood from the cut on his forehead and fixed the snowman for Sylvia. But Sylvia couldn't stop looking at the droplets of red blood that were scattered on the snow.

Golda and Ben were both in the apartment when Sylvia came upstairs, glowing after the completion of the snowman and showing it off to her friends and neighbors. Her hands were beet red, her mittens soaked through, the too-big galoshes falling off her feet. There was no mistaking her glorious delight in her morning. She had almost forgotten Morty's fight with Joey Simpson, and she chattered away while Golda dried her with a towel, made her change her clothes for dry ones, urged hot soup on her.

Then she cuddled in her bed under the blanket with a book and only came out when she heard her father's cries of "*Gutenyu*. What happened to you, Morteleh? What happened?"

By the time Sylvia rushed into the living room, Morty was sitting at the table holding a kitchen towel, which blossomed red with blood as he held it to his nose.

"Press on it, press on it," Mama kept saying.

"Put your head back," Papa ordered.

Sylvia gaped at the scene. Morty's right eye was closed and puffy, already turning purple. His lip was split and leaking blood.

"*Gutenyu, gutenyu*," Ben kept saying.

Golda brought a pot full of warm water with another clean towel, and she wiped his face as gently as she could. All the while Morty winced and yelled, "*Ow*, that hurts!"

"Of course it hurts," Golda said. "Who told you to get into a fight?" She turned to Ben. "I knew he shouldn't be fighting at that Boys' Club place. Why does he need to know how to fight? What good does it do? What's the fight about that's worth getting beat up for?"

Ben said, "Shush, Golda. Who did this to you, Morty? What boy is so big he can beat you like this?"

Morty's eyes drifted to Sylvia, who was hovering close by. He shook his head, the words barely audible as they came out of his swollen mouth. "No boy," he said.

"No boy?" Ben repeated. "Then who?"

"Joey Simpson's father."

Sylvia's face went white. It was her fault if Joey Simpson's father, a big man with a beefy face and a lumbering walk, had attacked her brother.

"Joey Simpson?" Golda asked. "The boy in the next house? He beat you?"

"No. His father," Morty said louder. Then he winced because, Sylvia could see, his split lip hurt.

"His father? That big man? With the funny walk? With the big friends?"

Sylvia stifled a laugh. Funny walk? Joey's father walked like a duck, waddling along. He was fat, but not so fat he couldn't move. And strong. Sylvia had seen him once help a neighbor lift the back of his wagon so he could fix a broken wheel. Also, Sylvia thought, he had a bump in his nose. Obviously broken in a fight. She hoped he hadn't broken Morty's nose. Morty's nose was beautiful. Straight and clean.

"Why? Why?" Golda said. "Why would a grown man hit a boy?"

Morty didn't answer. Sylvia thought it hurt him too much to talk.

"I know why," she said finally. "It's because Joey wanted to help and I said no, so he pushed me, and Morty pushed him back, so Joey banged him on the head with a shovel, so Morty and him fought, and Joey ran home crying with a bloody nose."

Golda looked shocked. "With a bloody nose? You gave that child a bloody nose? What are you, meshuga? Are you a gangster, to give a little boy a bloody nose?"

Again, Morty didn't answer. He shook his head. Sylvia saw a tear slide down his cheek.

Sylvia took a quick breath. She had to help. She knew what should happen now. If Joey's father beat up her brother, then their father had to defend Morty. Her father had to go talk to Joey's father. But somehow, and she didn't know why, she didn't think her father would do that. She said instead, in a loud voice, "You should complain. Maybe get a policeman."

Her father stared at her. He shook his head. "Better let it go. Don't start a war with the neighbors."

"But you can't *not* do anything," Sylvia said. "He started it."

"Be quiet," her mother said. "What do you know? A seven-year-old?"

The apartment was still. Mama finished cleaning Morty's face, gave him a cold compress for his eye, and sent him to bed.

After a while, Sylvia crept into their bedroom and saw Morty lying prone on his bed, facing the window. She stood beside the bed and touched her brother's shoulder just with her forefinger.

Morty shifted and looked at her with his good eye.

"I'm sorry," Sylvia whispered. "It was my fault. I should have let him help." Morty turned back to the wall. "Papa should go to him and yell at him," she said. Morty still didn't answer. Sylvia started crying. "I'm sorry, Morty. I hope you don't hurt too much."

Morty turned to face her. He patted her arm. "I'll be okay," he said. "But that'll never happen to me again. And if I ever have a kid, no one will hurt them."

She nodded to Morty. "You're right, Morty. You're a good guy. Papa should do something, but he won't. You're a good guy," she repeated.

Morty tried to smile, but Sylvia could see it hurt too much. "Go to sleep," she said. Then she remembered what her mother always told her. "It will be better in the morning."

Morty nodded, rolled back to the window, and was still.

CHAPTER 13

BEN

The night after the snowstorm, Ben couldn't sleep. Each time he closed his eyes, he saw Morty's bruised face, his swollen lip. Joey Simpson's father, Big Al Simpson, had beaten up his son, and Ben would not defend him. Somehow, he had to let Morty know that Big Al Simpson and his son Joey were people to stay away from. His head was swimming. There were so many people to avoid in the poverty-stricken tenements of Brooklyn.

The next morning, Ben got up after a sleepless night. Golda, too, he thought, had been tossing and turning, and she was up and sitting in the kitchen long before her accustomed six thirty waking time. She had boiled the water for tea and was sipping a cup.

"You didn't sleep good?" Ben asked.

She shook her head. "I'm scared, Ben. Who is this man who beats up boys?"

"He's a mobster. He's called Big Al. He runs alcohol, and he's a loan shark."

"What if he comes after Morty again?"

"He won't," Ben said. "Why would he? He already beat him."

Golda seemed to shiver. "Don't they sometimes just kill you if they are mad? How could Morty get mixed up with that? I thought he was such a good boy."

"He is, he is. It was a mistake. He didn't know who the kid was."

Golda looked at Ben and appeared to hesitate. "Maybe you should go talk to him? To Big Al? Find out if everything is okay?"

Ben shook his head. "Better leave it be. If I go to him, I'll only be opening the wound again, and maybe he'll make me do something bad. Or beat me up or worse . . . Better leave it be." Ben looked at

Golda. She had turned her face away, and he recognized a look of disappointment. He had seen it many times on her face when she saw someone do something she didn't approve of. "What?" he asked. "Do you think I'm a coward?"

Golda didn't move.

"I'm not. I'm being practical. This is the best way to protect us. These gangs are all over—everywhere. You pay them to let you stay in business, you pay them to get you a job, you pay them if you're in a union, you pay, you pay, you pay." Ben's voice rose. He was part pleading and part angry with Golda. "Doesn't your tailor boss, Mr. Cohen, pay protection?"

"Maybe." Golda got up, poured a cup of tea, and put it in front of Ben. "I never saw him do it. And I don't think Morty will agree."

"I'll talk to him. I'll explain."

When Morty awoke, he sat at the kitchen table with his head in his hands. If it were possible, Ben thought when he saw him, Morty looked worse today than he had the day before. His eye was swollen shut and turning purple; his lip was so puffed he could barely open it. He had a gash on the side of his cheek.

Ben sat beside his son. "Does it hurt much?" he asked.

Morty couldn't answer. He just nodded.

Ben took a breath. "Do you want something? Some tea?"

Morty shook his head. He breathed hard.

"Do you know who he is? Joey Simpson's father?"

Morty shook his head again. He evidently couldn't speak, Ben thought. He was looking at his father through his one good eye.

"He's Big Al Simpson, and he's got his own gang here. Not as big as Kid Reles's, but maybe as brutal. He smuggles alcohol, he loans money." Ben waited. "You know what I'm saying, Morty? I can't cross him."

Morty nodded. He mumbled, trying to talk without moving his mouth too much because it hurt him. "I didn't know that. I never saw Joey before." He glanced at his father.

Ben could barely understand Morty. He patted his son on the back. "It's hard to talk?"

Morty nodded. Ben felt ashamed. He wished he were brave. If he were a brave man, he would go face Al Simpson and at least make a protest. But he was afraid.

Ben never did complain to Joey Simpson's father. Morty's eye turned black and purple and yellow, and eventually the color faded, and he looked normal again, but Ben thought Morty would never feel confident in him again. He had deserted his son because of his fear, and it made Ben ashamed. Afraid and ashamed. A bad combination.

CHAPTER 14

MORTY

The first time Morty saw Rudy after the big snowstorm, he still had black and blue marks on his face.

"What the hell happened to you?" Rudy stared at Morty and frowned. "You walk into a door or something?"

Morty considered lying, but Rudy was his best friend, so he told him the truth.

"Geez, Morty. If you had told me and Paulie, we would've got the gang together and gone after that Joey's father."

"Are you kidding?" Morty said. "You know who he is? Big Al Simpson's a big shot in the gangs. My father said he'd as soon kill you as kiss you."

Rudy thought for a minute. "That's why you gotta be in a gang. That way you always have backup, and guys like Big Al don't go after you so fast. You could have justice."

Morty considered this. "Maybe, but what they call 'justice' is killing. They kill each other. One gang does something the other doesn't like, and bam, they're shooting each other and turning up dead bodies in alleyways." Morty wasn't making this up. Brownsville, like other Brooklyn neighborhoods, was full of hoods vying for top of the block. Sometimes Morty heard shots late at night, if he was out on the street with his friends, and once he had seen a dead body, or just the legs and feet of the man, sticking out from a narrow alley between two stores.

"Yeah, but you gotta be smart too. Otherwise, you might turn up dead." Rudy shrugged, like he didn't care if he turned up dead.

Morty stared at him. "Doesn't it scare you?

"Nah. If you're dead, you're dead. You don't even know it."

Morty shook his head. He didn't know if Rudy was cool and smart

or just a dumb fifteen-year-old. He seemed to enjoy fighting and bullying boys who were frightened of him. Morty had seen how excited
Rudy got when he was pushing around smaller kids, laughing at them
when they stuttered in fear. Morty would never admit it to anyone, but
for the first time he understood the elation that came with dominance.
He had felt it when he was pummeling Joey Simpson, shocked at the
momentary pride that swelled his head. Afterward, even before Big
Al Simpson had come after him, Morty felt ashamed of himself. He
almost thought he deserved the beating Joey's father had given him.
He wondered if a man became more callous the more he lorded over
another person. Morty did not want to become like that. He thought
he would just stick to his own plan. School, work, school. Repeat.

But still, as Morty watched Rudy inching his way into Mickey Adler's
gang of hoodlums, he felt a little envious. Rudy acted like he was
having more fun than anyone else. Daytimes, when they cut school,
Rudy and Paulie hung around Solly's Corner Candy Store, where the
street corner was owned by Mickey Adler's gang, who could be found
sitting in the back booths of the candy store. If you hung out on their
corner, you were beholden to them.

"I don't get it," Morty said to Rudy on one of the rare days when
his friend came to school. They were eating lunch in the cafeteria.
"What's the big attraction to standing around on the corner all the
time?"

"You're kidding, right? Where else am I gonna make the kind of
dough I want? Last week I made fifteen bucks. And it's not for standing around the corner."

"If it's so great, why aren't you there now?"

"Are you nuts? Have you looked out the window? It's raining cats
and dogs out."

Morty looked out the big window on the side of the room. It was
streaked with rainwater, the drops sluicing down the grimy glass. "So
go inside Solly's."

Rudy shook his head. "Can't do that yet. Have to be invited to hang out in the booths with them. They talk there, and you gotta be invited, or you might hear something you shouldn't. When they're back there, no one else is."

Morty thought about it and realized it was true. Although he had often been inside Solly's, he'd never been there when Adler's gang was. If he walked into the candy store and saw them in the back booths, he either sat at the counter in the front or left the store entirely. He stared at his friend. Now he noticed that Rudy was dressing better than he used to. None of his shirts were mended, and he wore nice leather shoes. If he'd made fifteen dollars, Morty guessed he could afford to buy himself some clothes. But he wondered what he'd been paid to do. "What'd you have to do to make fifteen bucks?"

"I'm a runner for Adler's boys. You know—messages, packages. I'll do anything they ask. When I started, they were tossing me and Paulie quarters and fifty cents. Now it's dollar bills. One time I made ten dollars just for delivering a package to someone's apartment three blocks away."

"What was in the package?" Morty asked.

"No idea. You don't ask questions like that. Questions like that could get you killed."

Morty stared at Rudy. "Just to ask a question? How do you know what was in the package? Maybe a gun. Maybe someone's finger. I read once they cut off someone's finger just to prove that they could do it."

Rudy shrugged. It seemed to Morty that nothing he said to Rudy could dissuade him from hanging out at Solly's and mixing in the business of the gangs.

"You're a patsy," Rudy told him. "Why work so hard all the time? You can make twice, three times the dough you make at Hansen's with some smarts and a little muscle."

"The smarts I got," Morty said. "It's the muscle part I don't like."

"Why not? You're a better boxer than me. You're one of the stars at the Boys' Club."

"That's different. There're rules there. You can't jump anybody. Or bully them. There's a ref to make sure. They match you with guys the same size. It's a fair fight."

Rudy shrugged. "The stronger guys get ahead. The weak ones don't."

"Yeah, well, when a big guy beats a small one, it's no contest. I'm not gonna be like Big Al and pick on someone half his size like me."

"Maybe someday you'll have to. You never know."

Morty shook his head. "Not me." He looked at his friend. "Would you really do it? Beat up little guys?" He stared at Rudy. His friend was changing. He walked with a swagger now. Once Morty had seen him almost push aside a man walking with his daughter because Rudy wouldn't step aside. The man and his daughter had moved out of the way just in time. It reminded Morty of when he and his father had met Abe Reles two years before.

Rudy glared at Morty. "You don't have to beat them up if they do what you say."

Morty didn't answer. For a minute the memory of his shameful elation when he was punching Joey Simpson came to him, but he pushed the memory away. He didn't want to think of himself like that. But it helped him to understand Rudy's behavior a little better. Sometimes Morty thought the gang members were glamorous too. They dressed so well and had beautiful women hanging on their arms. But mostly the gangs scared him, and he didn't like the way they acted, even around each other. Morty didn't know what was happening to his best friend, but he was pretty sure that whatever it was, he wished it wasn't happening.

CHAPTER 15

BEN

In 1928, when Ben's boss, Abe, had decided to expand and open a repair shop in Brooklyn, he had asked Ben to run it. Ben was excited. As Abe always said, "Success is a lot about timing and good luck, a little *mazel*." And it was clear that he felt he had had the luck and the timing on his side.

Abe was flush that year. For him the stock market was a money machine, and his bank account was flourishing. So was his body. He was living high, and he had developed a round belly and a double chin from eating good, rich food. His hair was thinning as he got older, and he dressed, Ben told Golda, like a banker, not a mechanic. He hardly ever got his hands dirty with oil anymore. He left that to his apprentices and assistants.

"I was right about America and making a fortune. That's what I've done. Some people call it gambling, but to me it's a pretty sure bet," Abe explained to Ben one day. "If you give the stockbroker ten or twenty percent of the cost of the stock, he lets you borrow the rest from him, and then, when the stock goes up, you sell, pay back the broker what you owe, and pocket the profits."

Always a little fearful, Ben asked, "What if it doesn't go up?"

"It always goes up," Abe said.

"And the broker gives you the money? Just like that?"

"Well, he charges interest, of course. But the way the stock market goes up and up, it's easy to pay everything back." Abe insisted it was a surefire way to make money. And flush with money from his investments in the stock market, Abe decided to buy the building for the new business in Brooklyn with a down payment and a loan from the bank. He used his stock as collateral. Because Ben had been with him almost from the start, he offered him a piece of the property. Ben could put in $500 of the $4,000 building cost, and then he would have a percentage of the profits and not just a salary.

"A piece of the profits," Golda said, her voice wary when Ben consulted her. They were sitting over tea at the dining table, as they always did to talk about important things. "That sounds good, but we don't have $500 to buy, except what we saved for Morty's school. So how could we buy into the building? Where would we get the money?"

"Borrow?"

"From who? Who lends us money?"

Ben admitted that it was unlikely any bank would lend him money. But he said, "Golda, it seems everyone is making money now. Buying stock and making money."

Golda shook her head, disagreeing. "I don't understand what a stock is. What are you buying, this stock?"

Ben hesitated. He wasn't sure he understood it either.

Golda went on, pressing her point. "We can't buy when we don't understand how it works. We can't."

Ben reached out and patted her hands. "I know you are right," he said. "But I wish you weren't." He held her hands for a long time, rubbing the fingertips. They were rough from pushing the needles through fabric when she embroidered. Once or twice he had seen her prick herself and draw blood. She would suck her finger and then wipe it on her skirt. He hoped it didn't hurt too much. Now, he was relieved to have her make the decision. "If we don't understand how it works, we shouldn't do it," he said.

She smiled at him, kissed his cheek, and said, "Thank God you agree, Ben. You are a good, hard worker. It will be all right."

Ben told Abe he couldn't invest.

Ben went on running the Brooklyn store. The economy was booming, and the family was living better. Golda's needlework had earned her a reputation among the wealthy matrons in Brooklyn and their daughters, and between that and the work from the dressmakers, tailors, and dress shops on the avenue, she had earned enough to buy herself a sewing machine. She and Ben even talked about renting part of a storefront so she could launch a business where she was the sole proprietor. She was thinking about embroidering fancy tablecloths and bedlinen. That would bring a nice amount from wealthy patrons.

And they talked of a new, bigger apartment, but again, Golda was cautious. Ben urged her on. "Come," he said. "Sylvia is getting older. She shouldn't be sharing a room with Morty. We should have another bedroom, or at least room for Morty to sleep in the parlor."

And this time Ben persuaded Golda. They moved into a new apartment just a few blocks from their old one. This one had its own bathroom. It had two bedrooms with windows, a parlor, and a kitchen with a big dining area. It felt like the ultimate in luxury. Even though Morty now slept on a cot in a corner of the parlor, everyone was happy.

Meanwhile, at Abe's repair shop in Brooklyn, Ben fixed all kinds of mechanical items: radios and toasters, lamps and irons, and the newly popular vacuum cleaners. Soon there was an opportunity to rent the storefront next to the repair shop, and Ben took it, turning it into a hardware store, selling new merchandise. People could buy items like nails and lightbulbs and hammers and other tools. He was able to fill the store with merchandise, buying on credit, and since times were good, Ben's business flourished. In fact, the whole economy was booming. They had even fit Golda's embroidering and dressmaking business into a small corner of the new store. She was doing well. She dreamed of hiring a helper so she could take in more work.

They really didn't understand what happened next. The newspapers talked of a stock market crash. Of the prices of the stocks falling drastically. Of margin calls and bankruptcies and banks failing and closing their doors. Gradually, in the fall of 1929 and the spring of 1930, the newspapers talked of a Great Depression. And then, as businesses failed and people lost their jobs, no one was buying the way they had been before.

Ben and Golda sat on the sofa and held hands like two lost children. They tried to understand why so many people had lost all their money. How did the stock market work? What happened, and what did it mean that a bank would fail?

"Abe lost everything," Ben said.

"But where did it go?" Golda asked. "How could all that money disappear?"

"I don't know," Ben said. "I never understood the stock market."

"I'm so glad we didn't buy."

Ben nodded. "No one is buying anything now. The store isn't doing so good anymore."

Golda's eyes were wide. "What will we do?"

"I don't know," Ben admitted. "The building that the repair shop is in Abe doesn't own anymore. The bank owns it. I will pay rent to the bank from now on. But the hardware store, I don't know if we can keep it. If business stays bad, I think we won't be able to afford the rent. You'll have to move your sewing machine back to the apartment."

Golda nodded. "I could do that, but I really don't want to. Try to keep it a little longer. I'll work harder. We'll just both work harder."

Ben nodded. "Thank God we didn't buy."

CHAPTER 16

MORTY

One afternoon in late January 1930, Morty, late to meet Rudy, ran down the stairs to the street and out into the world. Their new apartment was on a street lined with brick buildings and small front courtyards where the women clustered to gossip in the hot summer nights and the little kids played ball and jump rope until bedtime. Around the corner was the main street, Pitkin Avenue, where life opened up. It was one of Brooklyn's shopping avenues, with grocery stores and butcher shops and dairy shops selling cheese and bagels and lox, and bakeries with their smells of sugar and cinnamon drifting out the doorways. Even with the hard times, some people could still buy what they wanted.

Rudy was waiting for him at Solly's corner, a look of excitement on his face. "You're late. I thought you wasn't coming," he said.

"Sorry. Just finishing my homework."

Rudy gave him a disgusted look. "I'm done with all that stuff. I got better business now." He grabbed Morty's arm and walked him away from the corner where some of the other boys were hanging out. "I got big news," he said. "Adler asked me if I wanted to collect for him."

Morty stared. "Collect? Collect what?"

"Don't be a dumbass. Collect from the shops. For protection. He's been watching me. He gave me and Paulie little jobs at first, and now he thinks I'm ready for bigger stuff. He told me I should go with Little Jiggy, who's collecting the money for him, so I could see how he does it, and then Adler would give me a chance to do it too. It's easy money. Just go to the clients' shops, pick up what they owe, and deliver it to Adler. They pay good."

Morty was shaking his head. "What do you mean, owe? They don't owe Mickey. For what? It's robbery."

"Don't be such a schmuck, Morty. They owe money, the collectors pick it up. That's all." Rudy's voice was harsh.

Morty hated this business—protection money. When he thought about going into the stores and businesses and demanding payments, he felt his insides clench. He knew that when his father had worked as an apprentice in Manhattan, one of the Italian gangs would collect money from them. And now that Ben had his own store in Brooklyn, Morty knew that first Abe Reles and then Mickey Adler's boys were picking up protection money from Ben's storefront the way they had at Mr. Hansen's store. There didn't seem to be any way to get around it.

"It's awful business, Rudy. Don't get into it. It's always hard times for people like us. People are out of work; stores are fighting to stay in business. And what if they refuse? Are you going to have to beat them up?"

"Nah," Rudy said. "They don't refuse us. If they do, we bring in the big guys. They're the ones that beat them up." He laughed. There was a trickle of hysteria in the laugh, and Morty felt his heart freeze.

Rudy kept looking at Morty. "Come on, Morty. I'm just watching. I'm not doing anything wrong. I'm going to follow Little Jiggy and see what he does. You know Little Jiggy? The guy who's always jiggling his legs when he sits?"

Morty knew who Little Jiggy was, a tall, skinny guy who couldn't keep still. Morty had never seen him smile. He nodded.

"Maybe later I can get you a job too."

Morty shook his head. "I don't want that kind of a job."

"Well, I'm going with him Friday night," Rudy said. "We meet at four o'clock when the stores start shutting down."

Morty didn't say anything.

"Aren't you going to wish me luck?"

"Good luck," Morty mumbled. "I hope you don't get caught."

Rudy stared him down. "Don't come begging to me later, when

you're all poor and need some money," he said. And he turned and walked away.

Friday afternoon, while Morty did his homework, he kept thinking about Rudy, wondering what he was doing and feeling a little sick to his stomach with worry for his friend. He kept thinking about what his father had said at the dinner table the night before. The newspapers were calling it the Great Depression. They wrote about the businessmen, the giants of industry, who moaned about the huge losses for their businesses. Some had lost everything and committed suicide.

It was true it didn't mean much to Morty and his friends. They had been poor before, and they were still poor. They certainly didn't know anything about the stock market. They didn't have savings in the banks; they kept their money in the house, in safe places, like the jar in the kitchen cabinet where the Feinsteins had been saving for Morty's college fund. But the world was changing. Everyone was scared about money, and Morty didn't like what his friends were doing. He had made up his mind. This was one activity where he wouldn't be following Rudy. He was very glad to be off the street.

At supper that night, after his mother lit the Sabbath candles and his father blessed the wine, they sat at the dinner table eating soup. Morty, very hungry, shoveled food into his mouth. He knew his mother prided herself on her cooking and liked it if they savored the food and complimented her on it. "This is good, Mama," he said, his mouth full of food.

"Don't talk with your mouth full," she said to him. But she smiled, and he knew she was pleased.

His mother sat at one end of the table, his father at the other. She ate carefully, spooning the soup away from her. Papa sipped his, tipping the bowl toward him. Eight-year-old Sylvia clattered her spoon in her bowl and sometimes lifted it and slurped the soup without the spoon.

Morty looked at his mother, feeling sorry for her for a minute. She tried so hard to dress nicely, but there was no money for clothes for her even though she made beautiful clothes for rich women. Like today she was wearing the same old blue flowered dress she wore most days, neatly washed and ironed but tired looking. He had seen her scrubbing their clothing on a washboard in the bathroom and hanging them on a clothesline out the window. She tried hard to be proper, but it wasn't easy. Their apartment was bigger, but everything else was the same.

After dinner, after the dishes were washed and put away, Golda worked on her embroidery, pulling a basket of linen and cotton and wool and spools of colored thread beside her easy chair. Morty watched his father walk by, touch her shoulder, and smile. She looked up at him and smiled back before returning to her needlework. Morty wondered if this was what love looked like when you got old. Did they love each other? Sometimes, Golda would hum as she stitched. Sometimes he thought he saw tears in her eyes. Morty watched her and wondered what she was thinking.

CHAPTER 17

BEN

The one thing that Ben and Golda argued about was money. Ben did not know how to manage it. He was good with his hands and mechanically apt. He could fix anything broken. But he did not know how to charge for his work to make a profit. He bought parts for fifteen cents each and charged twenty cents, figuring that included his labor. But he didn't compute the rent on his store, or the heat in the winter and the lights, or the time and value of Morty's work when he helped him in the store.

Golda said to him, "If Morty works for you, he isn't working at the grocery store. So we aren't getting help from his money."

"If Morty doesn't help me at the store, I'd have to pay someone else, and it would cost more."

They argued, and their voices carried into the bedroom, where one afternoon Ben found Sylvia hiding with her bed quilt covering her ears. He sat on the bed beside her and patted her back.

"I hate when you and Mama fight," Sylvia said.

"It doesn't mean anything," Ben said. "Everybody argues sometimes. You shouldn't worry about it."

But Ben worried—not about his occasional fights with Golda but about the money problems he was having. He was struggling to pay the rent on both his repair shop and the hardware store. He tried to pay the bank first, because they threatened to evict him if he was late more than a few months, and of course they charged interest. The man who owned the building where the hardware store was located let him slide for a while on the rent. He said that no one else would rent it now, and he trusted that Ben would eventually pay him, but he, too, put interest on the amount Ben owed. The debt accumulated as Ben tried to keep his promise to Golda to keep the store where she had her small business and to pay enough of what he owed the bank so that he wouldn't be evicted.

When he had taken the storefront for the sale of hardware, he had hired a man he knew as a clerk. Now he thought he would have to let him go, although the man had a family and it would be hard for him to find other work. He could only manage that if Golda was also the shopkeeper, but then she would not be able to continue to work for the tailor, Mr. Cohen. Another thought he had was maybe he could consolidate the two shops. Put his workshop in the back and sell in the front. But then there wouldn't be room for Golda's sewing machine and embroidery business. He went over and over all the possibilities, deciding on one and then the other, but he never spoke to Golda about his worries. And he did nothing.

One Sunday afternoon he sat in the parlor, pretending to read the newspaper. Both of his stores and the tailor shop where Golda also worked were closed because the law required it, but he saw Golda carrying a package and getting ready to leave the house.

"Where are you going?"

"Delivering to some ladies I embroider for."

He nodded. Of course. Every evening Golda would work for ladies who engaged her privately to embroider on their dresses and jackets. As she walked out the door, he wondered, for the first time, where she kept the money she earned from this work. Her pay from the tailor shop she used for food and household expenses, but this was extra.

Ben pondered. The money they put away for Morton's school was in a jar in the kitchen cupboard. He knew how much was in there. But her money—where was it?

The house was empty. He thought there weren't so many places she could put her money. Drawers? Cupboards? A box in the closet? He began to walk about the apartment. He started in the kitchen, opening drawers and cabinets. He found nothing. He looked around their parlor. There was nowhere he could see where money could be kept. He went into their bedroom. He and Golda shared a bureau for their clothes. She had the top two drawers. He had the bottom. The bureau was old, secondhand from the street. The wood was scratched, and the drawers stuck, especially in the heat. Ben pulled hard and opened the first drawer, which contained her undergarments. His hand burrowed among her cotton pants and brassieres. He felt his face flush. Stupid. Was he embarrassed because he was touching her private underwear? He had touched more private things. He found nothing.

The second drawer had two blouses, one white and one yellow, and a dark blue sweater. As he touched the sweater, his hand found a bulge in the sleeve. His heart beat a little faster. He removed the sweater and shook the sleeve. Into his hand fell a roll of bills held with a rubber band. It was big. How much? he wondered. He removed the rubber band and unrolled the bills. He counted. There was over one hundred dollars. How much did she earn each month? And how was it he did not know how much she earned? Had he never asked her? This embroidery business was a good one.

Carefully he rerolled the money, secured it with the rubber band, and placed it in the sleeve of the sweater again. He wanted to be sure to leave it in the same place he had found it. Was it folded or laid flat? He couldn't remember. He looked at the way the blouses were folded and copied it with the sweater, hoping it was right.

He closed the drawer and went back into the parlor, where he sat and thought. It was good to know the money was there. He wouldn't take it, but he could ask for it if it became necessary. What would Golda say if he approached her about it? Maybe he would try it out.

When Golda came back home, she went straight into the bedroom. Now he knew she would be adding to the roll of money in her sweater. One day, when she was in a good mood, maybe he would broach the subject. Or maybe he would borrow a little from the roll of money, or maybe even bet the money and win. He would see. Just knowing it was there was comforting. He could breathe a little easier, even though the worst of the Great Depression was just beginning.

CHAPTER 18

SYLVIA

Sylvia's best friend was Frieda Lichtenstein, who lived a block away and was in her class at school. Frieda was one of five children, and Sylvia envied her. She loved going to her friend's apartment. Even though it was crowded, the atmosphere was lighter somehow. Frieda's mother was often smiling and hugging her children, especially her daughters. Sylvia couldn't remember when Golda had hugged her, but she knew that it wasn't very often. When she stayed for supper at the Lichtenstein's house, the conversations were loud and full of jests and teasing, gossip about the neighbors, and sometimes even stories about the people back in the old country.

When Frieda's grandmother, who lived with the Lichtenstein's, told stories of life in the old country, Sylvia was absolutely enchanted. She'd never met any of her grandparents, who all still lived in Europe. Her mother and father sent money to them whenever they could. Her grandparents were foreign, shadowy figures. She could only imagine what they were like from grainy sepia photos her parents had on the living room table.

Sylvia was jealous of Frieda's siblings. There were two brothers and two sisters, and Frieda, like Sylvia, had been the youngest until baby Jacob was born. He was now just a few weeks old. When Sylvia and Frieda were alone, she would ask her friend about what it felt like to have all these brothers and sisters, and Frieda would say, "I don't know, it's just normal." Sylvia felt like telling her what normal was in her house, and it was nothing like the normal in the Lichtenstein's apartment.

Sylvia remembered when she had discovered that Mrs. Lichtenstein was expecting a baby. It was early in November, and Sylvia was with Frieda in her kitchen with her oldest sister, Mollie, and her mother. "Mama, sit down," Mollie kept saying to her mother. "You shouldn't be on your feet so much."

Frieda's mother sighed and sat down on a wooden chair at the table. But in only a few minutes she was up again, bustling about, pulling out a dish from the cupboard and milk from the icebox, checking the oven to make sure the temperature was not too hot. Again, Mollie would say, "Sit! Tell me what to do and I'll do it." And Frieda's mother would sit and then jump up again. It made Sylvia and Frieda laugh out loud.

Later, when Sylvia and Frieda went into the girls' bedroom, Sylvia asked why her mother had to sit all the time. Frieda said, "She's expecting. In a few more months we're going to have a new baby in the house. Mama said it was a big surprise."

Over the next months, Sylvia watched as Mrs. Lichtenstein's belly got bigger and bigger, and she almost waddled around the apartment. All during that time Sylvia wondered how the baby got into Mrs. Lichtenstein's belly, and why it was a surprise.

In March 1932 Mrs. Lichtenstein's baby was born, and the next week Sylvia's family celebrated Morty's eighteenth birthday. Sylvia had saved up some of the money she had earned for helping a neighbor with a new baby. She bought Morty a birthday present of a deck of brand-new playing cards, since he loved card games. She made homemade wrapping paper, coloring newsprint with pictures of birds and flowers and trees, the way her mother embroidered them on clothing. She wrote him a poem on a sheet of paper, about his being born on the ship in 1914 just when Golda had arrived in New York.

In America you were born in nineteen fourteen
To your mama, Golda, it was like a dream
And soon you will study to be an engineer,
And about having enough money you'll never have to fear.

As she was writing, she paused, thinking, *No, that surely isn't possible.* She remembered Cousin Surah talking to her mother about birth on a ship. *Who was born on a ship?* When and where had her parents married? Her mother had once told her that she and Ben got married a few months after she arrived in New York.

But how could that be? Sylvia thought. That meant that Morty was born before she got married. The thought made Sylvia blush. She didn't know how she could ever ask her mother about that. She pushed these ideas away. *Not now, later.*

When Morty came home to dinner, Sylvia looked at him carefully. He didn't seem to be wondering about his birthday. Why should she? But she was still confused, still doing the arithmetic in her head, still finding it did not come out correctly, still not understanding what had happened.

Sylvia did not like secrets. This was one she would have to unravel herself.

The week after Morty's birthday, Sylvia decided to confide in Frieda and tell her about her confusion about Morty's birth. Sylvia's long auburn hair was braided every morning to keep it neat, but when she was nervous, she had a habit of chewing the end of one of her braids. She was doing that now. She and Frieda were sitting on swings at the playground near their school, and Sylvia said, "Frieda, I want to ask you something."

Frieda stopped swinging and said, "What?"

Sylvia stopped swinging too. Her heart was pounding. Maybe she shouldn't say anything. She felt like she was betraying her family, telling something she shouldn't. Sylvia took a deep breath. She still could decide not to tell Frieda what she was worried about. It wasn't too late.

"Yes?" Frieda prompted.

Sylvia took another breath. "Never mind," she said. "It's nothing."

"Sylvia, come on. You can tell me. I won't tell anyone."

"Okay . . . when I was wrapping Morty's birthday present last week, I started thinking about the stories I'd heard about when my mother and father got married and where Morty was born. I'm not sure . . . maybe I'm making it up. But my parents were married in April 1914 . . ." Sylvia hesitated and then pushed ahead. "And Morty was born in March of 1914."

Frieda swung slowly back and forth. "Well, that's only a month. Maybe there was a mistake."

"But it takes nine months to make a baby," Sylvia said. "We watched your mother's belly get bigger and bigger. It doesn't make sense. If they weren't married, how did they have a baby?" Sylvia was not sure of the exact way babies were made, but she knew you had to be married. She looked at her brown oxford shoes and white socks. Her shoes were scuffed. They needed polishing.

Frieda stared at Sylvia. "What are you thinking?"

"I don't know. I don't understand how my mother was expecting on the ship when she came to America if she wasn't married."

Frieda sat silently swinging. Then she turned again and said, "Well, maybe they did it before? In the old country."

"Did what?" Sylvia asked.

"You know. What a man and woman do when they make a baby."

Sylvia was suddenly very nervous. She shook her head. "I don't know what you're talking about. Tell me."

Frieda looked at her for a long time. She stopped swinging. "Mollie told me how. The man puts his . . . his thing . . . into the woman's hole . . . down there . . ." Frieda was blushing. Sylvia's mouth was wide open, and she shook her head back and forth. Frieda stopped speaking.

"Are you making that up?"

"No. Mollie told me. That's how you make a baby." Then in a rush, Frieda said, "But look, maybe they got married twice. So it's okay. Maybe they got married in the old country and then came here and got married by a rabbi and everything. So it's all right."

Sylvia thought very highly of Frieda's opinions. Hearing her say it was all right was comforting to Sylvia. She did not understand what Frieda had said about the man's thing and the woman's hole, and she vowed to find out more about it. But meanwhile, she liked the idea of them marrying twice. Then the fact that the dates didn't match was not somehow shameful. "You think so?" she asked.

"Yes," Frieda said. "I do. But if you are still worried, you can always ask your cousin . . . the one that you like so much."

"Cousin Surah?"

Frieda nodded. "Yeah, she'd know all about it."

Sylvia considered this and decided it was a good thought. Cousin Surah's, after all, was where her parents had lived when they first came to America. She certainly would know. It took a long time for Sylvia to get the courage to visit Cousin Surah and ask her about it. Several weeks went by, and then, one Friday, Sylvia found herself alone with Cousin Surah when Golda sent her there with a fresh-baked challah. Golda had never given up providing some of her delicious baked goods to her husband's cousin who had been so kind to her when she came to this country.

Usually, Sylvia would just drop the food off and leave the house, but this day she stood fidgeting by the doorway.

"Something else?" Cousin Surah asked.

Sylvia pushed a stray hair behind her ears. She took a deep breath. "I wanted to ask you something."

"So ask."

Sylvia walked back to the table and sat down, hoping Cousin Surah would offer her a glass of tea or lemonade, but Cousin Surah was too busy, and she stood, waiting, her hands on her ample hips.

"My mother and father got married here, right?"

"Here? No. Not in my apartment, in the rabbi's house."

"Yeah. In the rabbi's house . . . just after Mama arrived on the boat. But the dates . . . it seems Morty was born first, in March, and then they got married."

Cousin Surah licked her lips. Sylvia thought she looked startled, and her face got white. "You know, I don't really remember. It was so long ago. You know, I'll check with your father and get the right dates, and then we can talk, okay?" She seemed to be hurrying Sylvia out of the house. Sylvia nodded, but she didn't understand why Cousin Surah had to check dates with her father. She left reluctantly, sure somehow that Cousin Surah was not telling her the truth. Sylvia thought Cousin Surah knew something and didn't want to tell. And Sylvia didn't like it.

CHAPTER 19

BEN

"Cousin Surah," Ben said when she entered his store on Monday morning. She had only been there once before that he could remember—when she had brought him a broken lamp to fix. "I'm surprised to see you here. Of course, you are most welcome. Do you have something for me to fix?"

Cousin Surah didn't smile but said, "I would like to talk to you in private, Ben."

Ben felt his heart bump. It seemed very serious, whatever Cousin Surah wanted to talk about. He nodded and took her to the back workroom. Where would she sit? he wondered. The workbench was piled with small appliances waiting for him to repair them. A box of nails had spilled over onto the bench. He moved all the pieces to the table he worked on and then wiped the bench of dust. But there were smears of oil on the seat, so he said, "Wait, wait," and found a relatively clean apron to spread across the bench. "Sit here," he said and patted the bench, then sat beside her. "What is it, Surah? Is there a problem?"

"Yes," she said. "On Friday, Sylvia came to me to ask why Morty was born before you and Golda married. I was shocked. Do they not know that your first wife died on the ship giving birth?"

Ben's mouth dropped open. "She asked you that? How did she even know to ask that?"

Cousin Surah shook her head. Her voice was exasperated when she answered. "The dates. She knows the dates. Morty was born in March. You were married in April. That's why she asked me."

Ben looked at his hands. He had not had time to wash them before bringing Cousin Surah into the workroom. They were stained with oil. He was embarrassed by them. He got up and took a rag from the table and wiped them carefully. He did not know what to answer her. Why hadn't he and Golda told Morty that Esther had died on the ship? It had not seemed important. Golda had taken care of Morty from the day he was born. And if they hadn't told Morty, they certainly hadn't told Sylvia. Ben felt now that they had done the wrong thing by keeping this secret.

"We just never thought to tell him. It didn't seem important."

"Of course it's important. If only because some people know, and if one person knows, then Morty can find out and feel that you hid something from him."

Ben looked down at his shoes, then up at Cousin Surah. "Should we tell him now?"

"Of course you should tell him. He has a right to know. And Sylvia is so smart she figured out something was wrong. And I don't think she even knows how babies are made, but she thinks you have to be married to have one."

Ben stood, his head bowed. He felt stupid somehow, like he should have known this would happen, he should have been prepared for this. Golda too. She was so smart, so organized. She always figured out what to do before they did it. Why hadn't Golda thought to tell Morty about his real mother? They never even discussed it.

"I will talk to Golda. We will decide what to do."

"And what will I tell Sylvia when she comes back to me? I told her I would ask you."

"Tell her to talk to me."

Cousin Surah got up and turned away. "You will do the right thing if you tell them. They should know." And she walked out of the store.

Ben thought maybe he should talk to Rabbi Levy for advice, but he spoke to Golda first. She was as shocked as he had been with the news that Sylvia had been asking about when they were married and when Morty was born. She sat heavily at the kitchen table. "What should we do, then? Tell him now? He will be so angry."

"But if we don't tell him, it will come out somehow. And won't Sylvia keep asking?"

Ben couldn't think which was worse—not telling Morty the truth of his parentage or telling him and facing his anger that they had never told him before. Together Ben and Golda decided to consult Rabbi Levy.

They hadn't seen him privately in several years. Life had been going on so smoothly that they had not felt the need to confer with him. It felt awkward, sitting in his parlor, Golda clutching her pocketbook on her lap, Ben sitting with his hands clasped together, opening and closing them in his old nervous habit.

The rabbi came in and sat before them. Ben thought he looked older than he had the last time he had seen him. His hair was streaked with gray, his beard completely white. He had put on weight, and his face, always ample, was now round like a full moon. The rabbi waited quietly until Ben finally blurted out, "We have a terrible problem, Rabbi. We never told Morton that Golda is not his real mother, and now our little Sylvia is asking questions because she somehow figured out that we were married after Morton was born."

The rabbi remained quiet for a time. "Golda is his real mother. He knows no other one."

"Yes, but you know what I mean . . . she didn't give birth to him."

The rabbi shrugged his shoulders. "Motherhood is more than birth. It is tending and feeding and loving and worrying and caring."

"We are afraid he will be angry at us."

The rabbi was thinking. He kept stroking his beard. When he said nothing, Golda asked, "So we should just tell him? Tell him the story?"

"The story is a good one, is it not?"

Ben thought of the story, remembering Golda standing by the ship holding his infant son, with nowhere to go but home with him. How she had married him so he could keep his child. It was a good story, he thought. There was certainly nothing to be ashamed of in the story. Maybe they could share it with Morty, and he wouldn't be angry at them for keeping it from him.

Ben looked at Golda. He could see she was thinking the same thing. And when they went home, they agreed they would tell Morty together. They would explain. Now that he was eighteen, they felt he should know, and that was why they hadn't told him before. And then they would talk to Sylvia.

CHAPTER 20

MORTY

Morty was impatient on Saturday night when his father said they had something to tell him. He was itchy to leave. He only had one night a week when he was free—no work and no school—and he was eager to get outside with his friends.

Golda sat opposite him, Ben beside him. "Do you want some tea?" Golda asked.

"No," Morty said. "What's up? What do you want to talk about?" He wanted to urge them forward. It was unusual for his parents to want to talk to him, especially without Sylvia. They wanted to talk to Morty alone and had asked her to go to her bedroom.

His father looked at his mother. She nodded to him. "You talk," she said.

Ben cleared his throat. "I want to tell you about something you don't know. It concerns you." He stopped.

Morty looked from his mother to his father. He suddenly had a feeling of dread. What could this be about? As his father's pause dragged on, Morty said, "What? What is this about? Is it bad?" His voice cracked.

"Okay, no, it's not bad, just something you don't know." He took a deep breath. "In Europe, in the old country, I was apprenticed to a mechanic in the town of Lesko."

"Yes, I know. Mr. Frankel . . ."

"I met there a young girl, a young woman named Esther, and we loved each other." Ben looked at Golda and patted her hand.

Morty saw his mother look away, then down at her hands, which were pressed flat against a photograph on the table. He couldn't see what it was. Golda swallowed and pressed her lips together.

Ben kept talking. "Esther was your mother's—Golda's—sister."

Morty was confused. His father had loved this Esther, his mother's sister. Then why had he married Golda? He asked, "Why didn't you marry Esther if you loved her?" He looked at his mother, who was sitting still as marble.

There was a long silence, and Ben said, "I did. I married Esther." He was talking very fast now, not looking at Morty. "Your mother, Golda, helped me convince their parents that it would be okay for me to marry Esther even though she was very young. Seventeen. And I was going to America to follow Mr. Frankel, who was going to give me a job in New York. I was going to save my money and send for Esther to join me. When I got to America—after only a few months—I got a letter from Esther saying she was expecting a baby, and couldn't I send the money for her ticket sooner? She begged me and said her sister Golda would come with her. So I borrowed the money from Mr. Frankel, and I sent it to Esther, and, because she was expecting, Golda came with her. Their parents gave the money for Golda's ticket. I promised her I would help her settle in America." Ben stopped speaking. His face looked mottled, full of pain as he turned toward Golda. He seemed to be silently begging her to speak.

Golda nodded. "We came on the boat, and while we were at sea, Esther began to labor . . ." She stumbled on the next words. "It was very hard and was not going well, and we had to call the ship's doctor and nurse, and they took her to the ship's hospital and delivered her of a boy. You, Morton. You were born, my sister's son. But she did not survive."

The room was silent. Morty's heart was pounding so hard he thought they could hear it. There was a loud rushing in his ears. He swallowed, but he couldn't get any words out. His mother was not his mother. She was . . . what . . . his aunt? He looked at her, at Golda's stern face, the downturned mouth. He knew, when he was a very little boy, that he was not sure if his mother . . . his aunt, he corrected himself . . . loved him. But then, when the baby, Isaac, was born, she seemed to be able to take care of them both. He had been the big brother. And when he was sick with the flu, she had cared for him and his father, even ignoring herself. Morty shook his head as if pushing cobwebs out. Then he thought, *What did she look like, my mother, Esther? Is that why my eyes are blue?*

"Why didn't you tell me?"

"We didn't think to tell you," Ben said. "Your mother—Golda—cared for you from the day you were born. You knew no one else. We married the month after she came. It didn't seem like there was a time that was right. But now you are eighteen, and it seemed you should know."

Morty thought about that, but he couldn't take it in right at that moment, so he asked, "Do you have a picture?"

Golda took the picture she was holding and handed it to Morty. It was a group photograph. "That's my parents, my three brothers, and Esther and me."

Morty stared. Golda looked young. But this Esther—she was a beauty; he could see that. He pointed. "My mother?"

Golda hesitated a minute and then nodded. She looked away.

Morty fingered the photo. "Did she have blue eyes?" he asked. Again, Golda nodded. "So, what is the rest of the story? How did you become my mother?" Although he thought he knew the answer to that.

Ben said, "She was waiting with you at the ship when it docked. I came to meet Esther and her sister, and I found only the sister—Golda—and you. She had you in her arms, and she told me Esther had passed on the ship. We went to Cousin Surah's house, and she helped us. We buried Esther at the cemetery, Golda took care of you, and soon it became clear that the best solution was for us to marry. And we did. Your mother, Golda, gave up everything to marry me and take care of you."

Morty looked from one to the other of his parents . . . now his aunt and his father. He observed them carefully, wondering if they had ever loved each other then and if they loved each other now. He examined his feelings. Would it have made a difference if he had known from the beginning? He didn't feel anything. He didn't think he felt angry or upset, but he wasn't sure. The only thought he had right then was *This is interesting. Life throws you curveballs.* And then he had a funny thought. He almost chuckled to himself.

"What? What's funny?" Ben asked.

"Sylvia is my cousin . . . and my sister."

"You aren't mad?" Golda asked. "That we didn't tell you before?"

"I don't know what I feel," Morty said, honestly. "But it's good to know. Maybe you can tell me about her—my mother . . . your sister—sometime. Right now, I need to go. I have an appointment to meet my friends." Morty got up and went to the door. "I guess there's a lot to think about here, but I don't want to do it now. Maybe tomorrow. Or next week." He turned and went out the door. *Or the week after that,* he thought. *Or never.*

CHAPTER 21

GOLDA

"He didn't seem mad," Golda said. She was relieved. She had expected him to burst with anger, to rage against them, but he hadn't. He seemed to accept it. Almost not to care.

Ben said, "He's a grown man. What do we expect?" He breathed hard. "I am very happy he knows. Now there is no secret."

"Except Sylvia," Golda said. "We have to tell her now." Ben nodded.

Golda got up to call her into the kitchen. When she came in, she didn't sit. She stood beside the table staring at them both.

"You don't want to sit?"

Sylvia shook her head.

"We just spoke to your brother. Now we will tell you," Golda said. She looked at Ben, he nodded to her, so she went on. The story poured out again, longer this time, with more details. Golda told her about Esther, how she and Ben had married in secret and then begged Golda to convince thier parents to accept the marriage. Sylvia stood until halfway through, when Golda got to the part about the birth on the ship. Then Sylvia sat down on the chair, as if her legs could not hold her. Golda spoke her feelings of guilt and sorrow, the terror she'd felt. The waiting until she found out her beloved sister had died.

"When I came off the ship with the baby in my arms, I had to wait so long for your father to come. Finally, when he did, I had to tell him Esther had passed giving birth to the baby. We went to Cousin Surah, and she helped us so much. And in the end, it seemed better for your father and me to marry so Morty would have a mother to care for him, and your father could work." Then Golda was silent.

Ben got up. "I will leave you both to keep talking," he said. "I am going to lie down."

After he was gone, Sylvia said, "I knew there was a reason that you got married after Morty was born."

Golda thought this was a good time to make tea. Sylvia sat at the table and waited. When Golda put the tea in front of her, Sylvia asked, "I knew that you couldn't have been Morty's real mother, because you didn't marry Papa until after Morty was born. And it takes nine months to make a baby in your belly. I watched Mrs. Lichtenstein when she was expecting little Jacob." Sylvia fidgeted with her skirt.

Golda nodded. Her stomach clenched. This was what Sylvia had asked Cousin Surah. Was she too young to be told about how babies were made? Golda remembered how she had not really known, even after she was a grown woman. She had known how babies came out of their mothers. She had seen her own mother delivered by a midwife of her younger brothers. But she didn't know then how babies got into their mothers' bodies. She had to ask Cousin Surah about that. But here was Sylvia, just eleven years old, about to ask her.

Sylvia said, "Mama, Frieda told me that the man puts his . . . his thing into the lady's hole . . ."

"You are a smart girl," Golda interrupted. "But you are very young. You don't have to learn everything all at once."

"But, Mama, she already told me. I'm just asking if it is true."

Golda turned her back. She would not speak any more about it. Sylvia finally got up and went to bed.

CHAPTER 22

MORTY

It wasn't true that Morty was okay with the new information. As the story sank in, he felt sick to his stomach, but he didn't want his parents to know, especially his mother. His mother . . . not his mother. He did not know who to talk to about this. Rudy? He would laugh at him . . . make some stupid remark about how this explained how screwed up Morty was. Who else could he go to? The only person he could think of was Cousin Surah. And hadn't the whole story begun in her apartment?

Morty went, nervously, because he had never gone to Cousin Surah for help with anything. He knew his parents often consulted her, and even Sylvia would go to her to talk over her problems. Cousin Surah seemed more approachable than his mother . . . than Golda. So he went to her apartment the day after his parents told him the truth of his parentage.

When Cousin Surah opened the door, she did not seem surprised to see him, but she asked him, "Morton? To what do I owe this visit?"

Morty had not known exactly what he was going to say when he came up the stairs to her apartment, so he blurted out, "I want to know about my mother. And how my father married my . . . my aunt."

Cousin Surah opened the door wider and said, "Come in. Come in. I wondered if you would come to me to ask." She went into the kitchen, where everything of any importance was always discussed. "Sit down. I'll make you tea and you can ask whatever you want. What I know I will tell you. And what I don't know, you will have to ask your parents."

Morty sat down in the kitchen. The tea was served. Cousin Surah sat opposite him and said, "So ask."

Morty hesitated. What did he want to know? He knew the bones of the story. This happened, then that happened, then this . . . but he did not know about the feelings. The love. The pain. The loss. So the question that came out of his mouth was "Did they love each other? My mother—I mean Golda—and my father."

Cousin Surah put her large hands on Morty's. "Morton, Golda *is* your mother. She was with you on the ship when you were born, and she brought you here when you were two days old. And she has been your mother ever since then."

Morty nodded. "But did she love him? My father? Did he love her? And me? Did she love me?"

Cousin Surah was silent for a few minutes. "There are many kinds of love, Morton," she said at last. "I hardly knew my husband when we were married. It was a *shiduch*. A match made by a matchmaker. We didn't know from love. We got married, and we grew to love each other. He is very dear to me and me to him.

"I think that is the same with your parents. Your father was a romantic fool with Golda's sister, Esther. That's what he told me. But he had such gratitude to your mother for caring for you, for marrying him, for putting her dreams aside. And they grew to love each other. You can tell. They are kind to each other. They help each other. Is that not true?"

Morty thought about it and nodded. He guessed it was true. "Do you think she loved me?"

"You? Everyone loved you. You were so bright and beautiful. And when you and Ben were sick with the flu, she devoted herself to you both. In fact, it's very sad, but she blames herself that she was taking so much care of you and your father that she didn't catch Isaac's sickness fast enough. But he was a sickly baby. And I think that was why he died. It was a huge blow to her. She was so sad, so depressed, she couldn't take care of you or Ben. I brought you here. Do you remember?"

A vague image came to Morty. He was four or five, and he was living at Cousin Surah's with his mother. But she was hardly able to do anything. She stayed in bed a lot. "I think I remember," he said, nodding his head.

"She is so proud of you, Morty. Of how smart you are. How you will be an engineer, she says. She puts her money aside from her beautiful embroidery to pay for your school. She loves you. Ask her. She'll tell you herself."

Morty fiddled with his teacup. He thought to himself that he didn't much like tea, but it was a comfort to sit and drink it at Cousin Surah's table. He liked to put honey in it. Talking to Cousin Surah was comforting. So he sat and sipped his tea. After he finished, he said, "So you think I should ask her? Talk to her?"

"Yes. And your father too. You should ask them both what they can tell you."

Morty felt peaceful. The jumpiness and the nervousness were gone for now. Maybe they would come back when he went to talk to his mother and father. But for now, he felt gratitude. He stood up to thank Cousin Surah. He bent and kissed her cheek. "You have helped me a lot," he said.

She stood up too and looked up at him. "You are a fine young man, Morty. We are all proud of you." She walked with him to the door, and before he left, she hugged him again. "Be well," she said. "Be well."

It took a few days before Morty got up the courage to talk to his father. On day four after the big announcement, Morty walked into his father's shop and sat down on the bench in the workroom. The shop was quiet, because in the first year after the Great Depression began, Ben, with great sadness, had let his assistant go. He was a one-man shop now and was working harder than ever. Morty's appearance seemed to surprise him.

Even more surprising were Morty's opening words. "Do you love my mother? Golda?"

Ben stood, mouth agape. "What do you mean, do I love her? Of course I do."

"But what about my real mother, Esther? I thought you loved her."

Ben was silent for a while. He sat on the bench and finally answered. "First of all, Golda *is* your real mother. She took care of you your whole life. She gave up many things for you and for me. And as for love, it is different at different times in your life."

Morty thought to himself that Cousin Surah and his father had probably conferred, their answers were so similar. "Then what was it like with Esther?" He found it hard to call Esther his mother.

"I was young," Ben said. "I was crazy with love. You know how it is when you are young . . . the physical feeling, the . . . the wanting to touch." Ben couldn't look at Morty when he said this, stammering.

Morty said, "Yeah, I know." He remembered a girl he had met last year who had big breasts and a narrow waist and red hair that swung around her face, like Rita Hayworth. He had lain in bed and felt himself get hard just thinking about her. Just thinking about it shamed him—what he had done then, at night in his bed. He'd never even kissed her in real life. Just in his daydreams. "Tell me how you met," he said to his father.

Morty could see his father struggling. "I want you to understand that we were like children. When we met, all we thought about was touching each other. She was beautiful, but like a child. She did not have many responsibilities at home. I remember how she begged Golda to speak to her parents. To make them approve of the marriage. The good thing was I didn't ask a dowry—they had no money. And when we first asked and they said no, we ran away to the next town and found a rabbi who married us. I had to pay him. I don't think I really knew what I was doing.

"After we were married, they let us stay together in the house. And later Esther asked if Golda could come with her to America. And I said yes. Golda was very excited. She had all these dreams. She didn't want to marry the man her father picked for her. He was a widower with two children, and much older. So it suited everyone the way it was. And I went to America, and right away, Esther wrote that she was expecting. She begged me to send the money for them to come soon. For her and Golda, because she couldn't make the voyage alone." Ben stopped. "So that's what I did. And you must ask your mother what happened on the ship. I wasn't there." Ben went back to his work, not looking at Morty.

"But when she came off the ship with a baby, and Esther wasn't there, what did you do?"

"Do? What could I do? I was shocked. To be honest, I hardly remembered what Esther looked like, except that she was pretty. We were so young. We didn't really know anything about each other. And Golda came off the ship, carrying you, and she took me in hand. We went together to Cousin Surah's, and she helped, and Rabbi Levy helped, and we did the only thing we could to make sure we took care of you. Golda, she was strong and smart. And in truth, I was afraid she wouldn't marry me, because that was not her dream. We should all thank God that she did."

After a while Morty said, "So she married you out of duty."

Ben bobbed his head in agreement. "Maybe at first. But then we came to care for each other. She is a very good woman." Ben looked at Morty. He was silent for a long time. Then he said, "She kept you from an orphanage. Or she kept me from marrying someone I never even met. Either way, she would not let a stranger raise Esther's child."

Morty could see how that could be.

There didn't seem to be anything more to say. Morty nodded, thanked his father, and left the store. He wandered down the street, and after about an hour, he resolved to finish his questions with Golda and try to put this new information about himself to rest.

Golda was not home when he arrived. He sat at the table, took out his homework books, and tried to concentrate on his trigonometry. Usually, he could lose himself in the equations, but this afternoon his mind went round and round with the pictures he had in his head from Cousin Surah's stories and his father's account. At last Golda came home.

At first she seemed startled to see him. She paused, and then, walking by him, she patted his shoulder. "I am glad to see you are studying."

"Trying to study," Morty said. "I keep going over the questions in my head. From the other night."

Golda took a deep breath. She took off her jacket, hung it on the hook beside the door, and sat at the table. "You can ask."

"I want to know why you wanted to come to America and what you hoped would happen when you got here. And what happened. What happened on the ship. And when you came to Cousin Surah's. And with Papa." Morty stopped talking.

"That's a lot to know," Golda said. After a while she said, "I had dreams about coming to America. I thought I could escape the little town and make a different life for me, not like my mother's life.

"And my sister, Esther, she wanted a life like my mother had. A husband and babies. And she fell in love with your father. It was shocking really, but she knew what she wanted, and when my parents said no, she couldn't marry Ben, they ran away and got married by a rabbi in the next town. I didn't know about it until later." Golda sighed. "She was spoiled, Esther. She was so pretty everyone let her do what she wanted. This time was no different. I helped her like always. She could always get from me what she wanted.

"So she and Ben married, and I made it all right with our parents. I told them how now they wouldn't have to make a dowry for her. And I said I would go to America with her, and Ben would help me settle there, so they wouldn't have a problem marrying me off. In truth I was eager to go to America. I had so many big dreams." She was silent for a few moments. "So, they listened, and they said yes. And after a month Ben went on a ship to America, and then a month later, Esther realized she was expecting you, and then she insisted on taking the ship before you were born."

Golda got up, went into the kitchen, put on an apron, and began to slice onions. Morty followed her and stood in the kitchen door, watching. He thought how Golda's hands often smelled of onions because she used them in everything she cooked. He smiled. It was like a perfume of his childhood. He waited, but Golda didn't say anything, so he urged her. "What happened on the boat?"

Golda stopped cutting the onions and put down the knife. "She started to labor early. It was bad. She was bleeding. There was a doctor and nurse on the ship, and they came and took her to the infirmary. They couldn't save Esther. But they saved you." Golda's face was white. "The doctor and nurse said something was wrong inside her, and that was why she bled so much. She would probably have died even if she didn't come on the ship so early." Golda turned away but kept speaking. "The nurse was so kind. She was smart too." Golda stopped talking and looked up, as though remembering something. "It's funny. I thought then maybe I could be a nurse. That would have been a good life. But of course, it was a ridiculous idea."

Morty remembered how she had nursed him and his father through the flu. "You could have been a nurse. You were a good nurse to us when we were sick," he said.

Golda looked at him. "Not so good I could save Isaac," she said. She picked up a spoon and stirred the onions in the pan. "It was a crazy dream anyway. When I came off the ship with you and met your father, I realized how crazy it was. You were this helpless baby in need of a mother. Ben didn't know what to do. So I stayed and married him." Her voice sounded thick.

Morty could see how hard it was for Golda to talk about this, and he didn't want to push her now, but he still had questions. He said, "You must have hated me for making you get married when you didn't want to. Did you ever love me?"

"Yes, of course I did," Golda said. "I never hated you. How could you hate a tiny baby?"

He hesitated but then said, "I remember you seemed angry at me a lot when I was little."

Golda bent and lifted her apron to wipe the corners of her eyes. Her voice cracked, but she seemed to want to speak. "I was—mixed up," she admitted. "I would hold you, and you were so helpless and beautiful, I would feel the stirrings of love, but then this awful selfish thing would poke its head up. I was mad because I thought my choice had been taken away. I was so foolish, Morty. Because when you were sick with the flu, I was desperate to save you. And I prayed and prayed, and if there is a God, he answered me. You lived." Golda breathed in. "It is hard to talk of this. I realized then how much I loved you . . . you are my fine boy."

Morty's eyes filled with tears, but he wouldn't let himself cry. He nodded and said, "I know. I'm not mad at you. I think I understand. I know you saved me from the orphanage."

Golda's eyes opened wide. "Who told you that?"

"Papa. He said how much you gave up for us. And how grateful he is." As an afterthought he said, "And how he loves you." *Maybe he didn't exactly say that, but that's what he meant*, Morty thought.

Golda nodded. "Yes. I remember that Cousin Surah told me it was one of the choices I had. If I didn't marry Ben, you might have to go to an orphanage. I couldn't bear that. And Ben's been a good husband to me."

"Do you love him?" Morty didn't know why, but this seemed an important question to him.

"I do. I love him."

"And I know you love Sylvia. I can see it in your face when you talk to her."

"Yes, I love Sylvia." She took the edge of her apron and wiped her eyes again. "And I love you too." She gave a little laugh. "I'm not used to talking like this . . . about love. Now I have to go back to cooking. And you need to do your homework."

Morty smiled. This was the old Golda. "Okay, I'll do my work. Make you proud."

Golda smiled back. "You always make me proud, Morton."

They stared at one another for a minute, and Morty went to her, grabbed her, and hugged her. He thought with wonder that Golda fit under his chin. Had she shrunk, or had he grown taller? He expected her to push him away, but she didn't. She stood and let him hold her. "I love you too, Mama," he said finally. Then, with a laugh, he added, "Now you cook dinner." But when he turned to his books, he said, "Mama, can you tell me more about Esther? Not today maybe, but another time, when you aren't so busy. Tell me what she was like. Maybe some stories about her."

Golda stood quietly. She seemed to be thinking. She nodded. "I will tell you about her, about Esther. I have many stories to tell you. We will sit and talk about her . . . my sister. Esther." She turned back to the kitchen and Morty went to his books. But he kept looking up at Golda, wanting to ask questions, and he wondered if they ever would have that conversation.

Later, Morty went into Sylvia's bedroom. He sat on the bed and asked her, "Did Mama and Papa tell you about my real mother?"

Sylvia nodded. "I'm the reason they even told you. Because I asked how come they married one month after you were born. Because if they weren't married, how did she have you? Frieda said how, but I don't know if I believe her."

"What did she tell you?"

Sylvia blushed. "It sounds awful."

"Tell me anyway."

Sylvia took a deep breath. "The man puts his thing in her hole . . ." She stopped talking. Morty was laughing. "What's so funny? That's what she told me. Stop laughing." Sylvia pushed him, and he fell on the bed. "Is it true?"

"Yes. It's true. But I think it isn't so horrible as it sounds."

"It sure sounds horrible. I'm never going to get married and have a baby then."

"We'll see about that. You might change your mind." He turned to leave the bedroom.

"Morty, wait a minute," Sylvia said. Morty stopped. "Does this mean we're not full brother and sister? We're only half?"

"Are you kidding? Half what?" Morty said. "We're not half anything. We're double. We're brother and sister, *and* we're cousins. We're double."

Sylvia smiled. She nodded. "Double. That's even better than full."

CHAPTER 23

Morty

Morty's graduation from high school was a grand event for the family. Morty had graduated with honors and was going to college in the fall. He was surprised at how excited he felt.

Golda had pressed his slacks that morning, and he wore a freshly laundered white shirt with a tie under his black graduation gown. Golda and Sylvia had new dresses that Golda had sewn herself, and his father was dressed in his best suit. The day, Wednesday, June 16, 1932, was, up until then, the happiest day of Morty's life.

Golda gave him a party at their apartment, the first time Morty could ever remember having one. Cousin Surah and her husband and daughter, Ruchel, were there. Golda had invited their neighbors, and Frieda also came. Ben had invited Abe, his old boss, and his wife. Morty had invited his friends Rudy and Paulie and Davy and Len, but Davy and Len, who both had graduated with Morty, had their own celebrations with their families. Rudy and Paulie, who had dropped out of school the year before, came but didn't stay too long. Rudy said he had business and left with Paulie after eating a plateful of Golda's delectable food. Everyone brought a small gift for the graduate.

Golda had cooked and baked for two days for the party. Golda had saved for weeks from her household money to buy the food. She had a spread of cheeses and breads and herring in cream sauce. There were pickles and a fluffy noodle kugel and crisp potato pancakes with applesauce. She baked a chocolate cake with icing that spelled out "Congratulations, Morton!" Morty wished it said "Congratulations, Morty!" but didn't say anything. Ben had bought a bottle of schnapps for toasts, and Golda had made lemonade and tea and coffee. Morty felt rewarded with respect from both his parents, and he was very happy.

Because of the Depression, and because he knew his father's repair shop was not doing as well as it had before, Morty had decided he needed to keep his job at the grocery store and enroll in his college classes at night. This would mean that he would not graduate from Polytech in four years, but, he thought, even if it took six or seven years, at the end he would be an engineer. His heart swelled with pride at the thought.

Morty worked hard. He swept the store, stacked the shelves, bagged groceries for patrons, and sometimes made deliveries to the homes of favored customers. Meanwhile, Rudy and Paulie hung around at the corner where Mickey Adler's gang owned the street. They seemed to be accumulating more and more money. Sometimes Morty wondered what they did for the gang that they got paid so much. Was it all collecting protection money? Or did they have to do more? In a way, he didn't entirely blame Rudy. Good jobs were very hard to get; Rudy was obviously picking up money and not working hard for it. Morty didn't ask too many questions.

One day in the fall after Morty graduated, he was walking home from his job when a smooth-looking automobile pulled up beside him, the driver tooting the horn. Morty peered into the car, a dark blue Plymouth sedan, and saw Rudy leaning nonchalantly on the wheel. He was dressed in a blue suit that matched the Plymouth, and he wore a brown fedora tilted back on his head. He looked sharp.

Morty whistled. "Wow. Where'd you get it?"

"Oh, I need a car for business. Want to come for a ride?"

Morty jumped into the passenger seat, stroking the dashboard with admiration. "It's a beauty. How much did it cost?"

"About three hundred dollars. Adler fronted the money."

"You're lucky," he said. "I didn't know you could drive."

"It's easy. I'll teach you if you want."

Morty was thrilled. "I want," he said, knowing that being able to drive would be a benefit to him for his whole life.

He picked it up easily. Rudy took him to the big parking lot at Coney Island, where he taught him to shift the car and put it in reverse.

Soon he was able to drive down the side streets near the beach, and Rudy declared he was good enough to pass the test for his license. Morty didn't think he was—parking was a little problem for him, and he was nervous when he had to make a left turn against traffic—but Rudy insisted he was ready. "You're fine," Rudy said. "Everybody really learns how to drive after they get their license."

Morty shrugged. He figured if he failed the test, he could take it again.

They made the appointment for the road test, and Rudy drove him. When they pulled up for the test, Rudy told Morty to wait in the car while he spoke to the examiner. He slicked back his hair and swaggered over to a tall, skinny man who was facing him. Morty only saw Rudy's back, and although he couldn't hear the conversation, he could watch the examiner's face as he responded to whatever Rudy was saying. The examiner was shaking his head, talking with his hands. Morty watched him finally hold his hands up, a surrender.

The next thing Morty knew, the examiner came up to the car window and said, "Congratulations, you passed." With a sour look on his face, he handed Morty an official-looking piece of paper. "Turn that into the Driver's License Bureau," he said and walked away.

Morty gave Rudy, who slipped into the car beside him, a befuddled look. "But I didn't even take the test."

"Ah, you didn't need to. I vouched for you."

Morty stared at Rudy, who was grinning at him. "What? Did you bribe him?" Morty asked.

"Nah. I just told him who I was. He didn't want to mess with me."

Morty wondered what Rudy had said to the man if he hadn't bribed him. He looked down at his hands, flexing his fist and opening it again. He took a deep breath, swallowed, and tried to relieve the itchy feeling in his throat. It just proved the power of the mob, he thought.

Rudy stared at him. "What? No thank-you?" he asked. Morty was silent. Rudy looked irritated. "You're a schmuck, Morty. Don't look a gift horse in the mouth." He waited a minute and then said, "Are you going to give me a hard time about this?"

He pulled out a cigarette from his pocket, lit it, and blew the smoke in Morty's face.

"Cut it out, Rudy. That's not funny."

Rudy laughed. "Aw, come on. I'll buy you an egg cream at Solly's." He threw his arm around Morty and patted his back. "We still friends?" he asked.

"Yeah, sure," Morty said. "I'm only sorry I didn't get to pass the test myself."

"Well, you might not have. You know you don't park so good."

Morty nodded in agreement, and Rudy put the car into gear and drove away.

When Morty went to the bureau and handed in the piece of paper, the clerk stamped it and made out an official-looking document, handing it to Morty. "Go get your picture taken. This is a temporary license. They'll mail you the real license in a couple of weeks."

Two weeks later the license came in the mail. If Morty still felt guilty about not having really passed the test, he pushed the feelings away. He figured he'd get better at driving with practice, so it would be all right.

Morty worked full time the following summer and all through the next year, feeling lucky to have a job. Rudy and his friends didn't seem to be hurting. They weren't working, but they always had money. They were often at Solly's hanging around inside, doing the bidding of the big shots in the gang or playing cards at a back booth. On nice days they stood outside, watching the people come and go in and out of the candy store. And once in a while when he had free time, Morty would hang out there with Rudy. It seemed strange to be hanging out at a candy store when he had so many other things to do, but sometimes he went just to see his old friends.

If Morty had any thought that crime didn't pay, watching the way Rudy was living convinced him otherwise. Rudy had enough money to move his parents and brother into a large two-bedroom apartment on Ocean Parkway, a nice neighborhood of Flatbush. He also moved himself, but to Brooklyn Heights into an apartment overlooking the

East River and Manhattan. He drove a snazzy new car and wore expensive suits and shoes. When they were together, he regaled Morty with stories about the dinners at fancy supper clubs like the Stork Club in Manhattan, where he sometimes saw movie stars and often brought beautiful showgirls he was dating. To Morty, Rudy seemed to be living in a dream world or a Hollywood film.

Once in a while Rudy invited Morty to go with him to clubs or restaurants. "Hey, Morty, I'm going to the Rainbow Room at Rockefeller Center." Morty had read about the Rainbow Room, which had just opened in September 1934. "Wanna come?" Morty couldn't imagine having enough money to go to a nightclub. And he didn't have the kind of dinner clothes you needed to go to clubs, so he always declined. But Rudy, on his twenty-first birthday, treated Morty to dinner at The Palm, a restaurant that was one of the finest steakhouses in New York. Morty ordered a porterhouse steak, mashed potatoes, and creamed spinach. Rudy ordered a bottle of smooth red wine. Morty told him it was the best meal he had ever eaten.

Rudy often threw parties in his new apartment, with the neighborhood gang and lots of pretty girls who fawned all over him. They seemed to go for Morty too, who was handsome in an innocent, boyish way, and the girls loved sitting on his lap and ruffling his honey-brown curls. "You have such beautiful blue eyes," they would say as they planted big lipstick kisses on his mouth.

Rudy loved to gamble and play cards, and he thought he was a pretty good card player. He had big card games at his apartment, opening his dining room table and hiring a showgirl in skimpy clothing to serve liquor and sandwiches. The room was foggy with cigarette and cigar smoke, and the betting got wild. He invited Morty many times, knowing how much Morty loved playing cards and how good he was, but Morty didn't have the money for the kind of wild betting that went on at Rudy's table. He came once or twice but only watched from the sidelines. He could pick up the "tells" of the better card players and see how the poorer ones lost and then borrowed money from Rudy or the other winners at exorbitant interest rates. It made Morty's head swim.

When Rudy had a small game, Morty played. He was a good enough card player that he would often win, and the boys started calling him Shark, with some admiration, and that became his nickname. One day, Paulie, Rudy's second-oldest friend, lost a bundle on a bet and was determined to recoup his loss.

"Lend me, Rudy," he said. "You know I'm good for it."

"You'll only lose it," Rudy said, dealing the cards around the table but cutting Paulie out of the game.

"I won't," Paulie said. "And if I do, it's on me."

Rudy gauged Paulie, who was chewing his lip and staring hard. "The interest rate's twenty."

Paulie hesitated. "Yeah, okay."

Morty felt his heart pounding. He wanted to say, *Don't do it. You'll lose, and then you'll owe forever*, but Morty knew he couldn't say anything. He had been winning and had a pile of chips in front of him. He wanted to drop out, but winners didn't drop in these games . . . even the small ones. Observing Rudy taking such advantage of Paulie's shortcomings made Morty wonder what had happened to his old friend.

Rudy continued dealing. "Okay, you'll be in the next round. Meanwhile, get me a drink." Rudy picked up his cards, fanned them out, and waited while Paulie trotted over to the bar, mixed a highball, and brought it back to Rudy. Morty felt sick to his stomach.

Rudy would often disappear for weeks at a time, and Morty had no idea where he had gone. When he returned, Morty would ask him, "Where were you?"

"A business trip," he'd say. "Just taking care of business."

Morty wanted to ask him what kind of business it was, but somehow, he didn't think Rudy would tell him. Once he dropped that he had been in Chicago, and another time he said he was in a little Podunk town in Ohio. Morty knew it wasn't smuggling alcohol the way it had been in the first years of the Depression. Prohibition had been over for two years, and selling liquor was legal.

But most of the time, Morty caught up with Rudy at Solly's. One afternoon, Rudy told him a new face had appeared at Solly's, a pretty girl on the arm of Frenchy LaPointe. She wasn't from the neighborhood, and Frenchy was clearly smitten with her, almost puffing his chest out as he walked her inside Solly's to the back booths, where the gang sat. At least that was what Morty had heard from Rudy.

Morty saw her the next Saturday afternoon when he was hanging out on the sidewalk at Solly's with his friends. Morty leaned against the building, his left knee bent with the foot flat against the wall, and he was smoking, casually blowing smoke rings into the air.

It was a windy day, and the girl's long black hair blew in the wind as she walked down the street.

Rudy, standing nearby, poked Morty. "That's her," he whispered. "The one who was with Frenchy last week. Her name's Anna."

This time she was alone, and Morty caught her eye as she approached. He was jolted with surprise. Her eyes were a violet blue— he had never seen a color like that—and they lingered on him as she passed. She looked to Morty like she was about his age, maybe a year younger or older. She was slim and wore a blue dress with a white cardigan sweater draped over her shoulders and a small blue-and-white scarf knotted around her neck. He could barely breathe looking at her.

His eyes followed her, bored into her back, willing her to turn around, and she did, just as she got to the doorway of Solly's. Their eyes met, and she hesitated for a second but then pushed into the store and disappeared.

"She's probably meeting Frenchy," Rudy said.

Morty took a deep breath. "Wow. She's something." His heart was pounding. *Stupid*, he thought. *She's just a girl*. What chance did he have with her?

"Want to go in?" Rudy asked.

Morty swallowed, hung back, then pushed down his reluctance and said, "Sure."

Inside, the back booths were empty except for the girl, who was looking in a mirror and carefully applying a slick of lipstick. Morty approached her and stood beside the booth, silent, because he did not know what to say. She glanced up, and again he felt the visceral punch—like his insides were roiling in his stomach. Those violet eyes. She smiled slightly.

Morty looked around the store. No Frenchy, if that was who she was waiting for. He nodded his head at her, signaling toward the door, wondering if she would understand. He didn't think he could speak. He felt Rudy standing behind him and heard him whisper, "Go on, get out of here with her."

"Let's take a walk," he said to her. His voice sounded strange, hoarse. She slid out of the booth and followed him outside. Still no Frenchy. Morty breathed more easily. Side by side, they walked quickly down the street until they turned the corner and were out of sight of Solly's. Then he felt her hand brush his, and moments later he intertwined his fingers with hers. They still did not talk but walked staring straight ahead, holding hands the whole way.

When they got to the playground near the elementary school, it was empty except for two boys shooting marbles in a corner. Morty paused. "Were you waiting for Frenchy?" he asked.

"It's okay," she said. "I only told him maybe I'd come."

Morty nodded. "Okay then," he said. "I'm Morty Feinstein. And I know you're Anna. What's your last name?"

"DeMaio. Anna DeMaio."

"Italian?"

She nodded.

"I'm Jewish."

Did she hesitate for a second? Morty wondered. But then she said, "I don't care."

"Me either."

She followed Morty to the swings, where he pushed her higher and higher until she squealed for him to stop, and he did, deliberately slowing the swing by holding the chains back. When she was down on the ground, she said, "I'm scared of going so high."

"Why didn't you say so?"

"I was embarrassed."

"Don't be scared to say things to me," Morty said. He stared into her eyes until she nodded and looked away. A long slow flush came up her face. His heart was pounding, and a warmth came into his own face. *She likes me*, he thought, and he was full of joy.

He searched for something to say to her, but he couldn't think of anything. "How old are you?" he blurted.

"Twenty."

That's good, Morty thought. *Just the right age.* "Yeah, me too," he said. "I'm going to Brooklyn Polytech College part-time. To be an engineer." Did he sound like he was bragging? Was it too much?

Anna nodded. "That's great. I'm working at my uncle's deli."

"Want to see something?" he asked, walking away from the swings and going to the jungle gym. He climbed quickly to the top and then did flips over and under the bar. He could hear her below saying, "Stop, stop! You'll fall." But he kept on and finally did one last flip and jumped to the ground.

"Ta-dah!" he said as if he were finishing a performance. He stood facing her, and not sure what possessed him, he grabbed her in a bear hug.

"Stop," she said, pushing him away.

"I'm sorry," Morty said. "I just couldn't help myself. I won't do it again." *Jeez, what am I doing? I heard Italian girls are fast, but maybe they aren't.*

"No, it's okay," Anna said. "Just a little too fast for me."

"Okay," he said. *I better slow down.* "We'll go as slow as you want. I don't want to scare you. I want you to be okay with me. I don't want you to be afraid."

She breathed in and out, in and out, and looked straight into Morty's eyes. "I won't," she said. "I won't be afraid."

Morty loved being with Anna because she made him laugh. There was a brazenness about her, a surety that he thought maybe was because she was Italian and twenty already—the same age as he was. He didn't know any other Italian girls. They would walk together, sometimes holding hands, sometimes not, and she would look sideways at him and blink her violet eyes, and his insides would turn over.

"Where'd you get those eyes?" Morty said to her the second time they were together. "I never saw eyes that color."

"I ate grapes. I especially love the purple ones." She was smiling, and Morty noticed that she had a dimple.

"Stop. You're pulling my leg," Morty said.

"No. That's what my ma told me."

Morty threw his head back and laughed.

"Of course, she also told me my hair was black because I loved to eat licorice. And I don't like licorice."

Morty laughed again. "What else do you like to eat?"

"Oranges," she said promptly. "I love oranges."

"Ha, I think I only had a few in my whole life. My mother says they cost too much. Where do you get them?" They resumed their walk.

"My uncle Mario Amato gets us whatever we want. My mother's his favorite sister."

"What does your uncle do?"

"Oh, the usual."

Morty looked at her sideways. "What usual? My father is a mechanic. He works in a shop fixing all kinds of things. What does your uncle do? And where's your father?"

Anna hesitated. "Well, my father worked with my uncle Mario, until my father died. He had an accident. My uncle Mario has a lot of money, and he gives me an allowance for clothes and stuff. He likes me to look pretty."

"He's right about that. You do look pretty." Morty noticed that today she was wearing a new dress. This one was green striped with orange, and the skirt swung around her legs when she moved. He wondered where this Uncle Mario worked. Probably gang business. Those were the only jobs, he had noticed, that made any money during these hard Depression days. There were gangs all over the Lower East

Side and Brooklyn. Italian gangs, Irish gangs, American gangs, Jewish gangs. Sometimes they fought each other, and sometimes they worked together. But they all made money.

"You're lucky about your uncle. That he can take care of you." Morty hesitated and then asked the question again. "What does he do, your uncle?"

Anna shrugged. "I don't know. He works for some other guys, and I don't know what he does exactly. But something." She looked away. "He owns the house we all live in. It's a two-family. My other uncle, my father's brother Tony DeMaio, lives in the downstairs, and he owns a deli. That's where I work. Tony's Deli in Ocean Hill."

Morty slipped the information into the back of his mind. He figured he'd check it out one day, see what kind of deli it was. "We live in an apartment," he said. "All my friends and my parents' friends and families live in apartments. We got nothing. I used to share a bedroom with my sister, Sylvia, but now I sleep in the living room. I'm getting out as soon as I can."

Anna took his arm. "I know I'm lucky to live where I do. But you're doing good in school, aren't you? You said last time you were going to college."

Morty nodded. "Yeah, I finished one year, even though it took me two. I'm going part-time, so it'll take me longer, but I'm going to be an engineer. I go at night because we don't have enough money, and I have to work." Morty thought about the money his father had put away every Saturday night. He knew a lot of it was gone now . . . he had used it for the store in the first days of the Depression, but he didn't understand why his father had needed it. It was supposed to have been for him. For Polytech, so he could be an engineer. He couldn't begrudge his father if he'd needed it, but it sure made things harder for him. "I hope I can make it all the way through."

"I think you should finish college. That has a future." Anna was quiet for a few minutes. "The streets here have no future. My father was only twenty-eight when he died. I hardly remember him at all. I was five. Fast lives. Fast death."

Anna and Morty stood and looked at each other. A lot passed between them. Morty wanted to ask her how her father had died, but he knew it hadn't been an accident. He could imagine. They both knew stories. They both knew what she was talking about. There were gang fights on the side streets. Dead bodies turned up in alleyways. They could sometimes hear popping sounds that they knew were gunshots.

Not too long before, Morty had passed a dirty white concrete wall that was splattered in blood. He stood and stared, his heart pounding hard. He couldn't look away. "That's Murder, Inc.," a passerby murmured. "I guess the police got rid of the body."

It wasn't the first time Morty had heard those words—Murder, Inc. They were all over the paper describing the gang responsible for the random killings all over Brooklyn. It made Morty's skin crawl.

And no one scrubbed the wall clean, Morty thought. *It's like the police left it as a warning.* He wondered who was dead. Someone like him? Another gangster? Suddenly he wondered about Rudy. Had he ever seen murders done? Had he done any murders? He hoped not, but he wasn't sure. He thought about what the scene must have looked like in the dead of night. Men with shotguns, one or two victims standing against the wall, bullets flying, cutting through the men, and leaving a pattern against the wall, like a red decoration.

Morty agreed with Anna. A fast way to die young. They turned and kept walking.

Walking was the way they saw each other. Neither one could bring the other to their home. The Italian Catholic Anna would be most unwelcome at Morty's house. And Morty was, he acknowledged to himself, a little ashamed of his family . . . of his parents' accented English, his father's stooped posture, the way he spoke so hesitantly and quietly you almost had to bend over to hear him.

Anna told Morty she couldn't bring him to her house. "Mama would kill me if I brought a Jew home with me," she said and glanced at him and then away.

Morty's mouth dropped open. To him, when people called him

"a Jew," it was like a curse. Not that he thought there was anything wrong with the word *Jew*, but it was used to put you down . . . it was like a punch, like the other swear words people used, and it was often combined with the word *dirty*. His stomach turned, but he decided he would let the word go . . . this time.

"I'm sorry, but I can't help the way she is. They're already pushing me to find a nice Italian boy and get married. And you wouldn't like my house anyway. My aunt and uncle live downstairs with my four cousins, and my nonna lives upstairs with me and my mother. And everyone is always in everyone else's house. There's so much yelling, even I don't like it."

He nodded. "Yeah, we probably can't go to either of our houses. We'll have to figure out other ways to see each other."

They agreed that they would walk, or sit in the local public-school playground, or take the train to the Botanical Gardens and walk there. That was all fine now because it was still warm—early fall. Morty wondered what they would do in the winter. Then the thought popped into his head, *Wow, I really like her. I'm thinking I'm going to be seeing her in the winter.*

"Let's stop at Solly's," Morty said. "I'll buy you an egg cream."

Anna almost clapped her hands in delight. "I love egg creams," she said. "They are so . . . creamy and rich."

Morty laughed. "You know there are no eggs in egg creams. Do you know how to make them? Just chocolate syrup, a little milk, and seltzer."

"Yeah," she said, "I do know. But I like to think they're made different. With real cream and melted chocolate bars. Like they do in Paris."

"What do you know about Paris?"

"I read about it. They drink wine and they have great food and a wonderful dessert called *pot de crème*. That's what I dream about. Going to Paris and having *pot de crème*. And sleeping on silk sheets."

Morty looked down at her. He allowed himself to think about the silk sheets and Anna stretched out on them. Her violet eyes were feathered with black lashes. He couldn't believe how beautiful she was. "I'll take you there," he said. "I'll take you to Paris one day."

Anna laughed.

"No, don't laugh. I'm serious. I will take you there. We'll go together on an ocean liner, like in the movies. With silk sheets." He grinned.

"And how will you get the money for that? You're just dreaming. I know how people make money in Brooklyn. And you shouldn't go anywhere near that stuff." Anna was standing still now, her eyes blazing. "The kind of money we're talking about boys like you never have."

"I will have it," Morty said. "I'll get it."

They walked in silence and soon were in front of Solly's. But the mood had changed. Anna pulled back before they went in. "I got to go home," she said. "I'll see you." She turned.

"When?"

"The day after tomorrow. I'll meet you then, after church."

Morty nodded and watched her leave. *Church*, he thought. *I wonder what that's like.* There was sure a lot about Anna he didn't know.

Morty saw Anna as often as he could. Sometimes he would buy her an ice popsicle at a candy store nearby; sometimes they shared an egg cream. While the weather was nice, they would go to the Botanical Gardens and walk through the paths and plots of flowers, and after a while they would choose a bench and sit and talk. They talked nonstop. Morty told her about how he had found out his mother wasn't his mother, and how he felt about it. Anna told him the truth about how her father had died, and it wasn't an accident.

"It was during Prohibition," she said. "My father stole some of the crates of whiskey and sold them on the side to make money. He thought he wouldn't get caught. My uncle told me he was pretty stupid to do that. You never get away with that kind of stuff in the mob."

The first time Morty kissed Anna, they were sitting at the Botanical Gardens, and he was holding her hand, moving his finger

gently around on her palm. They had walked through the park sucking on popsicles they'd bought just before entering the gardens. She
leaned against him, her head tilted toward his shoulder and her long
silky hair brushing his cheek. His breathing hitched slightly, and he
turned his head, stared at her eyes, and leaned in and kissed her full
lips, still red from the cherry popsicle she had just finished sucking.
Lingering there, he tasted her mouth, the sweetness, the coldness. His
tongue roamed over her lips, and she pushed him away.

"Don't eat my mouth," she said and laughed.

"I want to," Morty said. His arms moved around her, and he pulled
her close, nuzzling her neck.

"Not here," she said, pushing him away.

"Where then?" he asked. He felt his heart plummet. Where could
they go? Where could he take her to be alone? He knew some of his
friends went to cellar clubs they belonged to, places they could hang
out in, furnished with finds from the storefronts in the neighborhoods.
Some of them had been cheap speakeasies from Prohibition, and now
that liquor was available all over, some of the local guys were paying
a small rent to have a clubhouse. Morty had never taken a girl there
before, never wanted to. He wondered how Anna would feel about
that. "Would you come with me to this cellar club I know about? My
friend told me about it."

"Maybe," she said. "What is it like?"

"I haven't been there. I'll check it out and let you know." They
got up from the bench and walked slowly out of the park and to the
subway so they could both get home in time for supper. Morty wanted
to walk Anna back to her house, but she didn't want him to. When
they parted, he leaned down, kissed her cheek, and watched her walk
away, wondering if anything would ever come of this. A voice in his
head told him that if she wouldn't let him walk her home, for fear of
her family, how could he ever really be her boyfriend?

She had mentioned that she worked at her uncle's business in an
Italian deli. One day Morty decided to visit the shop, Tony's Deli in

Ocean Hill. He walked into the store and immediately saw Anna at the cash register. Glass cases lined the sides of the aisles displaying meats and cheeses. There were salamis hanging from the ceiling, and shelves opposite with cans of tomatoes and boxes of pasta. Another case held Italian cookies and pastries and bread. Everything smelled delicious.

Morty ordered a sandwich and went up to the cashier, pretending he did not know Anna. She paid little attention to him, acting as if she had never met him either, but she was blushing, and her eyes darted around the deli. Morty tried to chat to her, but she answered him in monosyllables. "See ya," he said as, feeling chastened, he walked out of the store to eat his sandwich alone when he got to a local park.

Morty had a date with Anna the next night. She was waiting for him at Solly's, and her eyes were blazing with anger as he walked toward her. "Are you crazy, coming into my uncle's store like that? What were you thinking?"

"Nothing. I just wanted to see where you work."

"Well, don't do that again. They'd kill me if they knew I was seeing a Jew."

Morty's chest constricted. There was that word again. He felt like he had been punched in the chest. This was the second time she'd called him that. *Did I tell her I hated it when she said that?* He didn't think he had made an issue of it. He was upset with himself. *I'm a coward*, he thought. Now he said, "A Jew? It sounds like a curse word. Is that how you feel about me? That's the most important thing about me? That I'm a Jew?"

Morty turned and walked away from the candy store. Anna followed him, trying to catch up. He felt sick to his stomach. He had read in the paper about what was going on in Germany. Adolf Hitler was always talking about the Jews, and he made life miserable for the Jewish citizens. His parents were always saying how happy they were that their families didn't live in Germany. Morty knew there were many people in America who were antisemitic.

He looked at Anna, who was almost trotting beside him to keep up. Antisemitism was everywhere. He thought about the German

American Bund, which was really nothing more than American Nazis; they called President Franklin Roosevelt "Frankel D. Rosenfeld," and his New Deal was the "Jew Deal." Charles Lindbergh, who was beloved by most Americans and who defended Hitler in all his speeches, was a Nazi sympathizer. And then there was Father Charles Coughlin, the Catholic priest from Detroit, who had these radio broadcasts that were very popular. He was always spewing all this antisemitic crap. Morty's father had talked about him just the other night. Millions of people listened to his poison.

"I suppose your family listens to that priest, Father Coughlin, and his lies? He's a priest, so everyone thinks he's so holy. But he's not. He's disgusting. A disgusting man."

"No," Anna said. "Of course not. We don't listen to that." But she turned away, and Morty didn't believe her.

Anna grabbed his arm. "I'm sorry, Morty. I didn't mean anything bad about that . . . calling you a Jew. It's just what they think—my family. And I don't want to get them all riled up. My uncle's mad enough about me not dating the Italian boys he keeps bringing to meet me. They want me to get married."

"Look, Anna. We've both got it hard enough. Don't make it worse." He touched her cheek. "I don't want you to marry someone else, but I sure can't marry you now." Just saying it made his breath stop. He thought, *Do I love her? I think I love her.* "No one's getting married now," he said. "It's the Great Depression. I know all my money is going to help my folks and to my tuition."

"I know," Anna said. "Don't worry. I'm holding them off. I'm not marrying anyone now either." She wound her arm through his, and they walked down the street.

They dated often. As it got cold, in December and then January, it became harder and harder to hang out together. Morty told her he wanted to take her to New York, to Manhattan, where there were big movie theaters and the Automat, where for nickels you could get a delicious dinner and sit all night. The Automats were glamorous places with marble floors and tables and glass windows with brass knobs on the side walls. "Have you ever been to the Automat?"

Anna shook her head. "We only eat in Italian places."

Morty laughed. "Yeah. And we eat at home. But you'd love the Automat," Morty said. "The food's great. Macaroni and cheese. Baked beans. Salisbury steak. And more kinds of pies than you know. And the best coffee in the world for a nickel. It comes out of a brass dragon spout!" Morty had only been to the Automat once, but he made it sound as if he went there all the time.

They went to Manhattan by subway, walked around Broadway looking at the shows they couldn't afford to go to, and then ate dinner at the Automat on Broadway and Forty-Second Street. Anna was completely enchanted. The walls were lined with gleaming glass-and-brass windows. Morty laughed when he saw how she giggled when she inserted her nickels and opened the glass door to take out her purchase—a slice of lemon meringue or apple pie or a dish of Salisbury steak swimming in gravy with a side of mashed potatoes. There was deliciously creamy macaroni and cheese and plain sandwiches too. And best of all was the coffee, which, as Morty had said, came from a brass spigot shaped like a dragon's head. It was, Anna agreed, all wonderful.

Once in a great while, they went to the movies to see a romantic comedy or a thriller. They saw *It Happened One Night* with Claudette Colbert and Clark Gable and months later *Mutiny on the Bounty*. He had his arm around Anna's shoulder in the movie theater, and sometimes she put her head on his shoulder. He wondered again where he could go with her to be alone. He still hadn't checked out the cellar club in his neighborhood, and although Rudy had twice offered his apartment if Morty wanted to take Anna there, Morty couldn't bring himself to ask her. It remained a tantalizing possibility but one he didn't think he would ever use.

CHAPTER 24

GOLDA

There was something wrong, Golda knew it. Ben was so withdrawn, silent, sitting on the sofa in the parlor, staring straight ahead. Often, he fell asleep like that, his head lolling heavily forward, chin on his chest. A small snore would escape his mouth, and sometimes he would jerk his head up, waking himself. Then gradually his head would sink again, and he would sleep.

Golda sat beside him, staring at his face. He was still a handsome man, she thought. His hair had streaks of gray, but he hadn't lost any of it. She felt a softness within her, and she put her hand over his, but he didn't stir. She had been so afraid he would never love her, but she knew now that he did.

There was a certain way he brushed her shoulder when she sat in her "embroidery" chair, the tufted chair she had bought herself with some of her earnings from her sewing. She would look up at him as if to ask what he wanted and see there was nothing in particular he wanted to say except, *I'm here. I'm glad you are too.*

And at night, in their bed, he still reached for her in the dark, and she always turned to him and melted into the warmth of his embrace. His hands, work worn and cracked from his labors, still felt gentle on her bare skin, still brought a surprising response from her, even after all these years. Yes, she knew he loved her. It was obvious. The way he looked at her over the supper table when he was enjoying her food and smiled at her with satisfaction; the way he came to her with work problems and questions; the way he shared his worries about the children and their future. It all made her feel their closeness and their partnership in life.

But now something was wrong, and it worried her. Ben wasn't

confiding in her. There was a shiftiness about him, as if he was hiding something. She asked him, "Ben, is everything all right? Is there something I can help with? I know things are hard. But you know I can help. I'm making pretty good money on the embroidery. I'll help."

He shook his head. "No. Don't worry. I'm fine. Just figuring out things."

"Tell me and I'll help you figure," Golda said. She felt like the air was thick in the room. The daylight was waning, and one long shadow came through the window and onto the sofa.

"I will, I will. But first I want to think it through, what I want to say. I'll tell you then."

But he never came to her and told her anything. They each worried alone, in silence.

CHAPTER 25

MORTY

Rudy was having his twenty-second birthday party. "Come. Bring that doll you're going with—Anna. There'll be booze, food."

Morty hesitated. "I don't know. I don't know any of the guys there anymore."

"Sure you do. Lenny, Paulie. It'll be fun."

Morty took a deep breath. "I'll see if Anna wants to come. I'll ask her."

Anna's first answer was "I don't think so. I won't know anyone there."

"Me. You know me. And you met Rudy before."

"Yeah. And I didn't much like him."

Morty stared straight ahead, wondering how much he should push Anna. "He's my oldest friend in the world. You know that. It's his birthday. Please. We won't stay long. A drink, maybe. A sandwich. Then we can go." Reluctant, Anna agreed.

Morty spent considerable time picking out a necktie for a present, and he had it professionally wrapped at the store. He spent more money than he could really afford, but he knew it was important to Rudy that the present be nice and expensive enough to show respect.

The apartment was crowded and noisy. Morty held Anna's hand the entire time they were there, remembering his promise that they wouldn't stay long. It was winter, cold outside, and coats were piled so high on the bed Morty couldn't see the bedspread. There were even women's furs lying there, fox and beaver.

"Wow, expensive," Anna whispered. "Must be gangsters' girlfriends."

"Didn't you say your uncle's a gangster? He buys you pretty clothes."

Morty watched as the color mounted on Anna's face and he regretted his words. "I'm sorry, I shouldn't have said that. It's just that you're always saying to stay away from them, and you and your mother live off one."

Anna shrugged. "He's my uncle. He's her brother. They love each other."

Morty sighed. "It's complicated." She nodded and gave him her hand. They threaded their way through to the kitchen, where the drinks and food were.

Rudy spotted them and came over to say hello. He gave Morty a one-armed hug around his shoulder and leaned down to kiss Anna on her cheek. "Great that you came, Morty, Anna. Get a drink, a sandwich." He led Morty, who still clasped Anna's hand in his own sweaty one, to the table where platters of sandwiches and bowls of potato salad and coleslaw were laid out. "Then come in the living room. I want to introduce you around."

Anna accepted a drink but shook her head to a sandwich. "I don't want to stay long," she whispered to Morty.

Morty nodded, already wishing he hadn't brought her. With their drinks in hand, they joined the crowd in the living room and followed Rudy's beckoning arm to the man on the sofa. Morty knew who he was immediately. Mickey Adler.

Adler wasn't a big man, but he sprawled on the middle of the sofa, taking up the largest part of it. His arms were draped along the back, and he relaxed into them. Every now and then he leaned forward and took a sip of an icy drink.

"Mickey," Rudy said. "I want you to meet Morty Feinstein, my oldest friend. Since kindergarten."

Adler didn't get up. "I didn't think you even graduated from kindergarten."

Rudy laughed. "Yeah, just."

Adler reached out and shook Morty's hand. "Who's the doll? Aren't you going to introduce me?"

"Sure." Morty almost scrambled to answer. "This is my girlfriend, Anna DeMaio."

Adler eyed her. "DeMaio?" His eyes lingered a little, appraising her. "Sounds familiar." After a long pause, he nodded. "Yeah, I think I heard about this guy—maybe your cousin, or your uncle or something? Got into a bit of trouble or something . . ." Anna didn't say anything. Adler turned back to Morty. "I heard you're a card shark. Everyone says you're unbeatable."

"I don't know about that," Morty said. "Everyone loses sometimes."

"Maybe. Not if they've got a great memory and are able to do math." There was a long pause, and he said, "I heard you have talent. Why don't you come to Solly's sometime and we can talk."

"Yeah, sure," Morty said. He wondered what Mickey Adler would want to talk to him about, but he knew he didn't want to get involved with him. Adler turned to the guy next to him on the sofa, and, knowing he'd been dismissed, he and Anna wandered away toward the picture window that looked out at the cold East River and across to the lights of Manhattan. The skyline glittered in the dark, and the river shimmered with lights.

They gazed silently for a few minutes before Anna whispered, "I want to get out of here."

"So soon?"

"Yes, I don't like those men. That Adler, he gives me the creeps. And he knows my family. What he said . . . about my father."

"How do you know it was about your father? He was just talking."

"Morty, he's a gangster. He never just talks. Everything is a threat. And he invited you to join him."

"I don't think so."

Anna raised an eyebrow. "Sometimes I think you're just too innocent to be believed."

Morty felt his face flush, but he ignored the remark. He pointed to the lights of the Chrysler and Empire State Buildings. Then he said, "Five years ago that skyline would have looked completely different. The Chrysler and Empire State weren't built then."

"How do you know that?" Anna asked.

"I'm in engineering school, you know. We study buildings and bridges. And those two beauties were finished in 1930 and 1931."

Anna smiled up at him. "Smart aleck," she said.

Morty laughed. "Okay, let's get a sandwich, and then we'll go. Might as well eat the free food."

Morty and Anna went back into the kitchen, filled their plates with food, and ate standing around the table. They left before the birthday cake was served. They rode the subway home in silence, and when Morty said goodnight to Anna, he could see that she was unhappy. They wouldn't go to Rudy's again, Morty thought. Certainly not if it meant Morty would owe him. That meant he couldn't take Rudy up on his offer to use his apartment if he wanted to be alone with Anna. Morty pushed that out of his head.

But he did check out the cellar club that his friends had for socials and dancing, and he thought he could use it if he joined the group. They all worked and chipped in a few dollars a month to rent the basement of the small apartment building that Paulie lived in. They had outfitted it with a few easy chairs, two old couches, some rugs, lamps, and a table with a gramophone, some records, and a radio. Mostly they had gatherings where they could bring their girlfriends, dance, share stories, and have parties. Sometimes all the guys played poker or gin rummy. Rudy would even come down and hang out with them for friendly card games. But late at night, there were usually one or two couples necking on a sofa, a radio playing big band music very softly in the background.

Morty thought that by now Anna would have made up her mind about him. They'd been dating long enough. He was sure about her. When he awoke in the morning, the first thing he saw in his mind was her face: her high cheekbones, the small slope of her nose, her piercing eyes—blue, then violet, then blue again—and the smile that flashed one small dimple on the left side of her mouth. He loved to kiss that dimple. Immediately Morty would close his eyes tight and shake his head as if to rid it of the picture of her. Sometimes it worked, but not always.

They'd sit on a bench in the park where they'd begun to go to meet as the days grew longer and more temperate. Leafy green trees shaded them; city pigeons waddled down the path, pushing their heads forward; and yellow dandelions speckled the grass. Anna told him about how her grandmother, her nonna, would gather the first green dandelion leaves in the spring for her bitter salads and how she would feed them to Anna and her other grandchildren because, she said, "It will make you *forte. Robusto.*"

As they sat, Morty would play with her hand, rubbing his finger up and down her palm; she said it made her arms shiver. It tied up his insides in knots, made him desperate to make love to her.

Morty didn't want to push her because he loved her too much for that. Anna had to be a willing participant to his lovemaking. "You want to come to the cellar club?" Morty finally asked her one day. "I've looked it over. It's okay. It's a place we can be alone." She didn't answer immediately but kept walking with him, and it didn't seem that she was hesitating at all. Morty took her silence as a yes.

"Okay then. It's around the corner." He guided her around the corner to Paulie's apartment building, which they could tell just by looking was crammed with people and smells of food and sounds of noisy conversations and arguments. But they didn't go into the building. Instead, they went through a side door and then down a set of dark stairs that smelled of damp and dirt. The cellar door opened with a high-pitched squeal. A bare light bulb hung in the middle of the room, spreading a dim circle of yellow on the floor.

"It's okay," he said, feeling her hesitation, the tension of her arm holding her back. "You don't have to come if you don't want to." He waited. "We can go back."

"No. That's okay. I just couldn't see for a minute." She followed him into the room.

It was a big cellar. On one side were old couches with heaps of blankets. Even in the summer heat, the room was cool. Morty heard some sounds—whispers and soft groans and sometimes a giggle—across from them, but he couldn't see into the dim recesses. He wondered which of the guys was there.

Morty and Anna went to a couch in a corner, where they necked until Morty could not stand it, and Anna, realizing where things were going, said she wanted to go home. Then one rainy night, a week later, Anna suggested going to the cellar club again. Morty hung back and said, "I'm not sure I can do it. It's too hard to stop."

"I know," she said. "Let's not stop, then."

Morty looked at her, eyes wide. "You sure?"

She nodded, held his eyes, and they walked, holding hands, down the stairs to the club.

Downstairs, Morty nestled with her, kissing her long and gently, and soon he felt the familiar stir below his belly and the tightness inside. He let his hands drift gently over her breasts and then down under her skirts. "It's okay, Anna. We don't have to do anything. But if you want . . . I got a skin." Morty always was prepared.

She had her eyes open, and she nodded. "It's okay," she whispered. "Don't stop." And in the end, it happened so quickly it surprised him. When it was over, she lay on her back, his weight on her. As his breath, ragged at first, became more even, she whispered, "I belong to you now. You know that, right?"

"And I'm yours too, Anna. We'll be all right together. I know we will."

Her body was a vivid picture in his mind. The long slope of her neck that he kissed gently and then let his mouth drift to the fullness of her breasts. Her stomach was so flat he could trace her hip bones with his fingers. Her long legs would intertwine with his, and they felt like silk when his fingers moved down her thighs. At night, when he slept in his own bed, he would go over the memory of those moments spent with her.

Later, when he reflected on what had happened, he realized that their relationship had gone sour sometime after they had first made love. They had been dating for almost two years, and at first, it seemed she was just reluctant to go to the club with him again. He thought, *She probably regrets having sex. Okay, I won't press her for it. Or maybe I should have taken her to Rudy's apartment. Much classier.* But somehow Morty felt that wasn't it. Their dates became further and further apart. When he asked her what was wrong, she wouldn't say.

It was late spring, and Anna was even harder to pin down about when they could meet. Finally, Morty couldn't stand it anymore. He was determined to find out what was wrong. He pressed her to go out with him to dinner, and she finally agreed. He took her to a small restaurant in downtown Brooklyn where no one knew them. The restaurant wasn't too crowded, and they took a secluded table where Morty was sure they could talk unnoticed.

Anna looked beautiful. Her hair waved down her shoulders, and her dress was a brilliant blue that made her eyes shine. She kept licking her lips, which were slicked with a bright red lipstick that matched her polished nails. They ordered the special—chicken pot pie—and while they were waiting for the waiter to bring their meals, Morty ate a roll. He made rings on the Formica top with his water glass as they sat in awkward silence. She let him take her hand.

"What's wrong, Anna?" Morty asked in a rush. "Did I do something wrong?"

"No, no," she said. "It isn't you. You're wonderful. You didn't do anything wrong . . . but I don't know. It's us . . . I . . . think we probably should stop seeing each other."

Morty slumped back against the chair. He wasn't sure he could speak, but he finally got out the word "Why?"

"I don't know, Morty. I don't know. But I don't think this can go anywhere."

"Why?" *I know why*, he thought. *But let her say it.*

The waiter brought their pot pies, browned and steaming.

"Let's eat first," Anna said. She picked up her fork and dug into the crust, letting the filling ooze out. She took a forkful and blew on it.

Morty picked up his fork, stuck it into the pie, but then put it down. He took a breath. "I can't eat."

Anna sighed. "Okay." The next words were rushed. "We got to stop seeing each other. It can't go anywhere."

"Tell me what happened. Did your uncle or your mother say something? Find out about us?"

"No, no," she said very fast. "They don't know anything about us. But they're pressing me to get married. I'm going to be twenty-two soon. My uncle wants me to marry this guy . . ." Her voice drifted off.

"What guy?"

"Someone he knows. From home."

"What home? Where?"

"Italy." She sounded exasperated.

"What are you, chattel or something?"

Anna stared at him. "Don't be mean, Morty. They wouldn't understand about us. My uncle doesn't like Jews . . . I mean Jewish people."

Morty ignored the antisemitism of her family. He knew about it. "So what? You're going to marry who he wants you to marry? Even if you don't love him?"

"Well, didn't your parents do that? Marry because it was convenient. Because of you and family?"

Morty sighed. "Yes. But that was different. A long time ago. They had no choice."

"Well, maybe I don't either."

"Of course you do. If I wasn't Jewish, you would have brought me home a long time ago. You're afraid of him—your uncle."

"I'm not afraid for me . . . but maybe I'm afraid he might do something to you."

"What?" Morty said. "Are you kidding?"

"No. I'm not kidding. I don't think I could ever marry you. My family's from Sicily."

Morty stared at her. He didn't know what that was supposed to mean, that her family was from Sicily. He shook his head, picked up his fork, ate a little bit. "Can we talk about this another time?" he asked.

She nodded very fast. *She's relieved.* They both bent their heads and finished their pies.

He took her home, almost to her house, but she stopped him two blocks away. "I can make it the rest of the way." She stood on tiptoe, kissed his cheek, and started to walk. Then she turned. "I'll see you," she said, and she was gone.

Two days later, he came to her uncle's deli again, at five o'clock, when she got off work. It was a beautiful evening, a light breeze blowing, and this time he waited for her across the street so her uncle wouldn't notice him loitering to the side of the deli entrance, where there were already three other young guys standing.

When Anna came out, she walked straight to the three men, and one of them peeled off and immediately took her arm. He was taller than her, handsome in a classic Italian way, with black hair slicked back, and he was smiling at her. She smiled up at him.

Morty's heart dropped. He stood like stone and stared, hoping his gaze would feel like a hot poker on her. *So that's it,* he thought. *That's why she's been so hard to see.* He walked along the street, parallel to Anna and her new boyfriend, thinking about whether to call her name and see what she would do. But he didn't have to. Halfway down the block Anna and the man turned to cross the street, and suddenly she was facing him. He stopped, looked straight at her, and cocked his head as if to say, *What's up?* He thought maybe she would say hello, but she looked at him, shook her head very faintly, and when they reached him, walked right by. He smelled her perfume, watched her back disappear, and knew it was over.

CHAPTER 26

BEN

They thought the Depression was ending, but it still hung on. In the southern Plains region of the United States, from Texas to Nebraska, where the farms had once been fertile and lush, there had been almost a decade of drought, and the earth had dried up and blown away in huge dust storms. Farmers, unable to grow crops or keep their animals alive, had deserted their land and gone west, where they hoped there were jobs.

In the cities, it was hard times for everyone. There were fewer and fewer customers in Ben's shop, and he owed more and more on his rent. Now the bank was threatening him with eviction by the end of the month, and the debt to his landlord had accumulated too.

When Golda came home from delivering the garments she had worked on for the tailor on the avenue and found Ben sitting at the kitchen table with his head in his hands, she came to him, put her hand on his back, and spoke gently. "What's wrong, Ben? Are you feeling ill?"

Ben swung his head up as if swimming through deep water. "No, no. I'm fine," he said.

"You don't seem fine." She put her hand on his forehead, as if testing to see if he had a fever, the way she used to with the children when they were young.

He brushed her hand away, irritated. "I said I'm fine. I'm fine." He looked up at her, standing behind him, saw how her face had fallen, and realized he had hurt her. "I'm sorry," he said quickly. "I'm worried a little about money, that's all. I don't have enough this month."

Golda sat down beside him. "Tell me," she said. "We can figure out what to do."

Ben looked at her. She was as tired as he was, he could tell. He put his hand on hers and patted it. "I didn't want to worry you, Golda. You work so hard."

"We both work hard. How much more do you need? I have some put away from my embroidery."

Ben almost said, "I know," but then realized that she had no idea he had found her savings wrapped up in a sweater. He told her how much he needed, and she went immediately to their bedroom and came out with the bills in her hand.

"Next time don't keep things from me," she said. "We have to work together."

Ben stood up and embraced her. "Thank you," he whispered into her hair. "I pray things will be better next month."

But they were not. Ben did not want to go to Golda again, so he borrowed some money from Cousin Surah, enough to tide him over. After he had shared his fears with Golda, she began to work twice the hours she had worked before. She stayed up late doing embroidery and complained that her eyes were hurting her; Ben noticed she squinted when she read, but when he told her to go to the doctor to get new glasses, she refused. She didn't say why, but Ben was sure she didn't want to spend the money.

He worried more and more, tossing in bed at night, getting up to sit at the kitchen table, and then going back to bed. He tried not to wake Golda or Morty in his nighttime walks, but he knew he was disturbing their sleep. Each month he took small amounts of money from the jar where they had saved Morty's college fund. First it was only a few dollars, but then when that wasn't enough, he snuck into their bedroom and opened the drawer in the bureau where Golda kept her sweaters and blouses, and he took money from the roll of bills in Golda's sweater sleeve, knowing she would eventually notice but hoping she wouldn't say anything about it.

With no hope, he went to the bank for a loan, but they refused him, as he knew they would. Without consulting Golda, he did the only thing he could think of. He went to a local money lender. He reasoned that if he could keep up the interest, the loan shark wouldn't bother him. And for a short while, that worked, but then it all collapsed.

CHAPTER 27

MORTY

Morty was despondent, sick to his soul. He had lost Anna. She was with another guy now, an Italian her mother and uncle approved of. She'd probably marry him. Morty knew he had to get on with his life and not think about her, but she was always there in the back of his mind. When he woke in the morning, she was the first thing he thought about. When he went to sleep, she was the last thing he thought about. He told himself to go out with other girls, but he never met anyone who could compare to Anna, and he dreamed of her all the time.

He struggled through his classes and his work. Each morning when he awoke and opened his eyes, a black dread would wash over him, and he would remember. Then one morning, he awoke, and she wasn't the first thing he thought of. *It's over*, he thought. *Thank God.* Anna was gone. He got out of bed and started his day. It was February 1938. It had taken him almost a year. He was almost twenty-four years old, but he had finally shaken her out of his head and could get on with his life.

Until the day he walked out of his night class, and there was Anna, standing at the door of the school, waiting. His heart almost stopped. They stared at one another, and she walked so close to him that he could not stop his arms from encircling her and pulling her close.

"I'm sorry, Morty. So sorry," she whispered. "I'm done with him. I couldn't make myself do it. I love you."

Part of Morty wanted to just take her at her word. Part of him yearned to understand. "Let's walk," he said, breathing into her hair. It smelled of lemons.

He walked so fast she had to run to keep up with him. "Slow down, Morty. Please. I'll tell you everything."

Purposefully, Morty slowed his pace. It was dark out. Cold. His hands felt like ice. "All right. Tell me. We'll get a cup of coffee. There's a little place a block away I sometimes go to."

They ducked into the local restaurant and took a booth. They sat quietly until Morty ordered coffee and pie, and the waiter brought it. Morty couldn't take his eyes off her. She was more beautiful than ever, but her face was pale. She wasn't even wearing lipstick, he noticed, and it didn't matter. She was perfect. She gripped her fingers together on top of the table. She took a big breath, sighed.

"My uncle wanted me to marry him."

"Yeah. So why didn't you?"

She shook her head. "I knew deep down he was connected. He was part of my uncle's business. Not the deli business. The protection business. I told you how I feel about that. I told him too. I told him I'm not going to stand by and live my life in the shadows. I couldn't marry him unless he got out of that life. He said he would, but then he didn't. I found out, so I broke it off."

Morty touched her hands. She let go of her own fingers and took his.

"To tell you the truth, I was relieved. Believe me, Morty, I never wanted to marry him. I still love you."

They drank their coffee in silence. Morty's head was buzzing. *So,* he thought, *we can go back to what was before . . . hiding from our families.* He didn't want to go back to the way it was. "Will you bring me home to your mother? Introduce me?"

Anna hesitated for a minute. "I will," she said. "Will you?"

Morty nodded. "Okay then," he said. He picked up her hand and drank his coffee while he held it. Then he paid the check, they walked out together, and Morty took her home. They went up to her front door, and he kissed her goodbye right there. *Next time I'll get inside.*

Morty came to Anna's house a week later when he picked her up for a date. He rang the doorbell and heard her footsteps on the stairs in the hallway, and the door opened, framing her in the light behind her.

His breath caught in his throat; she looked so lovely. They had decided she would invite him in and introduce him to her mother, so Morty followed her into the hallway and up the stairs.

The upstairs was a large apartment, and Anna brought him into her living room and told him to sit down. He tried to still his heartbeat. *No need to be so nervous*, he thought. *It's just her mother.*

Anna came back with an older version of herself trailing behind. Morty jumped up to greet them.

"Morty, this is my mother, Patricia DeMaio. Ma, I want you to meet my . . . my friend. Morty Feinstein." She emphasized his last name, making sure her mother heard it.

"How do you do, Mrs. DeMaio," Morty said, with his best manners.

Mrs. DeMaio stood, appraised him for a while, and said, "Feinstein?"

"Yes, ma'am."

"Where are you from?"

"From? I was born in Brooklyn," Morty answered, knowing that wasn't what she was asking.

She nodded. "Your people? Were they born here too?"

"Oh, no. They came from Europe. Poland."

"So . . . Jews?"

"Ma," Anna said, a warning in her voice.

"It's okay, Anna," Morty said and turned back to Mrs. DeMaio. "Yes, we're Jewish. And I know you're Italian." The sentence hung in the air.

Mrs. DeMaio nodded. "Glad to meet you," she said. "Don't come home too late," she said to Anna, and left the room.

Morty and Anna faced each other in silence. Then she shrugged and said, "I told you."

"You did. But we broke the ice. I met her. The first time is the hardest."

Anna nodded. "Now you can call me. She knows who you are." Anna wrote their phone number on a piece of paper. Morty knew that Anna's family had a phone in the house, courtesy of her uncle, and it gave Morty a sense of security to know that he could get in touch with Anna if he wanted to. He folded the paper and put it in his pocket, took Anna's hand, and said, "Let's go."

A few evenings later Morty came home after his classes at Polytech were over, dropped his books on the table, and saw his father sitting across from him, staring into space. Ben looked up at his son and took a breath. "I've been waiting for you," he said.

Morty was surprised. His father had never waited up for him. It was late, after ten o'clock, and Morty knew his father usually would be long asleep, as was his mother. Sylvia was probably reading in bed, or maybe asleep. "Is there something you need?" he asked.

Ben looked at his son. His eyes were bleary, red. He shook his head slowly and whispered, "You have to help me." His father's eyes shifted away, looked behind him, to the side of him.

"With what?"

"I'm in trouble, Morton."

Morty felt his legs giving out. The panic he saw in his father's face, heard in his voice, frightened him as never before. He pulled a chair from the kitchen table and put it opposite his father with the seat facing out. He sat legs astraddle, leaning on the back of the chair. "Papa, what's the matter? How can I help?"

There was a long beat of silence. Then, "I don't know how you can help, but maybe . . ."

"Tell me."

"I owe money—a lot," Ben said.

"For what?"

Ben sighed. His shoulders seemed to collapse. He put his head in his hands. "When Abe owned the building of the repair shop, he paid me a salary. But he lost the building when the stock market fell, and the bank took it. Then there was no salary, and I had to start paying the bank rent. Otherwise, they would have evicted me. And there was rent on the other store too and debt from all the merchandise I had bought. It all added up, and I had to use some of Mama's money from the embroidery." Ben looked sideways at his son. "And a little of your school money."

Morty looked alarmed.

"Not all," Ben said. "Not all of it. I borrowed where I could. I went to the *Gemilas Chesed* to borrow, but they had none. Nothing. The banks don't lend either—not to me anyway. I even went to my cousin Surah, and she gave me a little, but then she didn't have any more to give me . . . so I did something stupid. I borrowed."

"Why didn't you tell me, Papa? From who did you borrow?" Morty asked, but he knew. He felt a hard knot in his stomach. On every street corner there were loan sharks ready to lend anyone money, at high interest. And if you were late paying . . . at least the interest . . . there were consequences.

Ben closed his eyes. "From them. On the street. That's the only place you can get money now. I thought I would get another job," he repeated. "But no one is hiring. So the loan, the money, each month is more and more. I can't even pay all the interest now. Can you help me?" he asked. He was begging.

"I have no money, Papa. I could quit school and work full time . . ."

"No." Ben's voice was sharp. "You won't quit school . . ." They were silent for a few minutes.

"What about what you saved for me for next year? You could use that."

Ben whispered, "I already did. I spent it."

Morty was stunned. He thought. "Mama's money? That she puts in her drawer?"

His father shook his head. "I took most of it."

"And you still need more?" Ben nodded. "How much do you owe?"

"Fi . . . five hundred forty-seven dollars," Ben stuttered.

Morty couldn't believe it. He had no idea how his father had come to this, and after he had used the money for his school, and his mother's savings. He sat silently, hearing the clock ticking on the wall and the traffic in the street. He said, "I don't have any money to give you, Papa. Maybe we can ask the school for a refund for next term's tuition. I'll take a break."

"I don't want you to do that. Anyway, they won't give it back."

"We could ask."

Ben shook his head. "I already asked," he whispered.

Morty's heart was beating so hard he thought his father could hear it. His father had stolen from his mother. Tried to get his tuition back. All without telling them. His stomach was in knots, acid rising in his throat as he thought of his next question. "Who gave you the money, Papa?"

"Not a good man, Morty. Not a good man." Ben shook his head. "Georgie Lieber."

"Georgie the Gonif?" Morty could barely say his name. He knew who Georgie was. He worked for Mickey Adler and was known as a great enforcer. No one stiffed Georgie Lieber. "He's one of Mickey Adler's guys."

Ben looked shocked. "How do you know about Mickey Adler?"

Morty sighed. "Rudy works for him. I met him at a birthday party Rudy had."

Ben looked up. "Rudy? He works for him?" Ben's voice had changed. It sounded hopeful. "Maybe you could talk to Rudy . . . you think you could?"

"What would I say to him? What would I ask?" Was his father begging him? It was such an enormous sum of money. "We're hardly friends anymore, Papa, since he started working for Adler, and I started college. We grew apart. I don't think he'd listen to me."

"You were such good friends, Morton. I remember how he came here and played checkers with you . . ."

Morty was silent. Finally, he said, "I'll think what I can do. I'll see." He got up from the table, bone tired now. "I think I'll go to bed now. Maybe I'll look for him tomorrow. I'll see." He could not think of another thing to say, and he couldn't bear to look at his father's face. Morty felt a shiver of disgust; his father looked full of pure hope. He patted his father on the back, feeling that somehow their roles had been reversed. He went to the cot he now slept on in the living room, while his father got up slowly and went to his bedroom. He looked broken, his body stooped, his steps faltering.

Morty lay on his bed, his arm covering his eyes, struggling with his feelings. He had never in a million years expected to hear words like he had from his father's mouth. He did not know what to do with the information. What could Rudy do? Could Rudy do anything? Morty had never asked him for that kind of a favor before. Could he get the loan delayed? Forgiven? Even as the thought came, he knew it would never happen. Georgie Lieber didn't forgive loans. What would Rudy say when he went to him?

Morty was furious with his father. As he lay on his bed and thought about it, he knew that if he asked Rudy to help and Rudy agreed, he would owe Rudy. He didn't know exactly how, but he would owe him somehow. And that could be big trouble for Morty.

He and Rudy had been so close as kids. And hadn't he flirted with joining the group of young teens that hung out on the corners and at Solly's, waiting to run errands for the big-shot gang members who gathered in the back room? It had only been his father's encouragement, his complete belief in Morty's ability to do something better, that had kept Morty studying. That and his own natural ability at math and science.

Rudy had been angry when Morty refused to join him with Mickey Adler's gang. He didn't understand why Morty wouldn't want to get in on the good life that Rudy was living. He thought Morty was nuts. And Morty hadn't even taken him up on the favor of using his apartment to be alone with Anna.

Now, he wondered, if he couldn't get help from Rudy without some kind of payback, what would he do? How could he leave his father, never a fighter, to deal with the gangsters and loan sharks who ran the street business? Morty remembered how his father hadn't even been able to defend him when Joey Simpson's father had beaten him up. He touched his nose. There was still a slight bump from a small break in it. Thinking of it, a sliver of resentment entered Morty's heart.

Morty wanted to walk away from the whole thing. But what would happen to his father if he didn't pay the money back? How could he turn his father away?

His parents had sacrificed so much to send him to school. Morty didn't think he could live with himself if he didn't help his father. It didn't matter what he had to do to help, he would do it. He closed his eyes. He would go see Rudy. Then he would decide what to do.

The next day he went to look for Rudy. He found him in the back booth of Solly's—the same booth where Morty had first seen Anna. He was sitting with two other gang members; Morty only knew them by sight. He realized how far apart he and Rudy had grown if he didn't even know the names of Rudy's friends. Rudy told the two men to leave, and they scooted out of the booth without a word, showing that he was their boss.

Morty slid into the empty seats opposite Rudy and looked at his old friend. Rudy looked sharp. He wore a gray striped suit with a blazing white shirt and a red-and-blue tie. His red hair, darker now than it had been when they were kids, was slicked back with pomade, and he had grown a thin mustache. His nails, Morty noticed, were manicured and buffed to a shine, and on his pinky was a gold ring with a red stone. Morty wondered if it was real.

Morty took a deep breath and forced himself to speak. "I need your help, Rudy. My father's in trouble. He owes Georgie Lieber a loan payback."

Rudy blew out a breath and shook his head. "Georgie Lieber. He's a tough one." He waited, and then said, "Why should I help your father?"

"Come on, Rudy," Morty said. "He's my father. If you help him, you help me."

"Yeah, how? And why should I help your father? When did he ever give me anything but fishy eyes when I was at your house? And your mother. She always disapproved of me."

Morty felt slightly nauseous. What Rudy said was true. His

parents had never thought much of Rudy; they had only tolerated him because Morty liked him. But Morty knew that if Rudy didn't help him, there was nowhere else for him to turn. These were hard times. Everyone was looking for extra money.

"Listen, Rudy, maybe I can do this? Take on the loan? You give me the money to pay Georgie Lieber back, and I'll be your runner. I'll work for you until I pay you back."

Rudy was quiet, playing with the soda glass he had in front of him, making rings on the Formica table. Morty took Rudy's silence for a good thing. He pressed his point. "I'll do whatever you tell me."

"Whatever I say?"

The air in the store seemed to get heavy. Morty took a breath. "As long as I don't have to hurt anybody."

Rudy shrugged. "I can't promise that."

Morty didn't say anything.

"I'll try for that," Rudy said after a while. "I can't promise, but I'll try."

Morty's breath slowed. He nodded, smiled, stuck out his hand, and shook Rudy's. He figured they could always work that out.

"How much do you need?"

Morty told him.

Rudy shook his head. "He really screwed himself, didn't he?" Rudy said. He reached into his pocket, took out a wad of bills, and peeled off enough to pay Georgie back and a little extra. "There's twenty bucks more there for you. Make sure your father don't get into any more trouble."

Morty nodded. "Thank you, Rudy. You won't regret this."

"I better not," he said. "Go pay your father, and then he should pay back Georgie. He shouldn't let on where he got the dough. I'll get in touch with you."

Morty stood up and slipped out of the booth. He hesitated, but there didn't seem to be anything more to say, so he left the store.

There was a part of Morty that wanted to make his father wait to get the money, but then he felt ashamed. Every second that his father didn't know whether Morty could help him was torture. Holding the money in his pocket, he went home as fast as he could. He found Ben sitting in his chair in the living room, a prayer book open on his lap, but he didn't seem to be praying. He looked up at his son, who stood in front of him, staring.

"I got it," Morty said. He reached into his pocket and took out the money, leaving the extra twenty dollars tucked away. His father's hands were icy and trembling when he took the bills. He counted them and looked up at his son. "How did you get it so fast?" he asked, bewildered.

"You don't need to know that."

Ben nodded. "Th . . . thank you," he stammered.

It hurt Morty to see his father so diminished. He was afraid his father would begin to cry, so he said, "You pay Georgie back, but don't tell him where you got the money. Don't mention my name. Don't mention Rudy's name. That's important."

Ben nodded. "I'll go and find him now and pay him back. I am so grateful," he said.

"And, Pop," Morty said, "don't borrow from them again. You need money, ask me. I'll get it for you."

Ben stood up and reached over to touch his son's shoulder. "You're a good son," he said. "A very good boy." Morty didn't feel like such a good boy. He felt tarnished. Like he had done something shameful. But he didn't know what he had done. All he was trying to do was help his father.

There was a lot to learn, working with Rudy. So much of his time he was learning the ropes, hanging back, slightly afraid of the gang members. Rudy urged him on. "Stop being such a patsy," he said. "You can't act afraid."

All through the winter, Morty struggled with his feelings. He knew he wasn't made for this life. Petty thieving. Guilty feelings. Conflicted feelings. But this was a way to get rich, working for Adler. He had never had so much money at his disposal before.

He kept going to school but often cut his night classes to do something for Rudy. Then he would have to work extra hard to make up the work he'd missed. He was working for Rudy, at his beck and call, but increasingly their meetings together were fewer and fewer. Rudy had gradually climbed the ladder of Mickey Adler's Brownsville gang, and as one of the more reliable senior members, he had less and less time for Morty.

Rudy had put him to work, first as a gofer, a small-timer who could be counted on to run errands, keep his mouth shut, and not demand too much money. But more recently, Morty had gotten a reputation as a card shark. If he got into penny gambling games with small-time bettors, he always won, and that had drawn the attention of the gang members. He picked up most of his extra money gambling. He liked the extra money, he liked the card games, and he liked winning. His card acumen made him famous in the neighborhood. He had a terrific memory, keeping the cards that had been played in his mind so that he knew the possible combinations that were left. The gambling added a little bit of excitement to what he was doing.

He spent the money on clothes, so he didn't look shabby anymore. He bought himself two good pairs of shoes and a soft brown leather jacket. At the store, they sewed a label in it with his name embroidered on it. He bought a brown leather wallet. Wearing the jacket and using the wallet made him feel like a king. He had deliberately not bought one of the silk suits that the other guys in the gang wore. He didn't want people to see him and associate him with gangs. But he bought a fedora and some nice shirts. His parents noticed.

Ben said nothing, but Golda was a different story.

"Where did you get that shirt?" Golda asked him one morning.

"Why?" Morty felt defensive. "What's wrong with it?"

"Nothing," Golda said, "but it's the third new shirt I've noticed. You have so much money?"

For a minute Morty wasn't sure how to answer. *The truth. Say the truth.* "I won some money at cards."

"Cards? You have money to bet at cards? And your papa is working so hard."

Morty could see the look of disapproval on his mother's face. "I usually win, Mama. I'm good at cards," he said.

Morty saw the familiar downturned mouth, the furrowed brow. "Don't be a big shot. You can lose as well as win. And then where will you be?" she said and went into the kitchen.

Morty had built up a cache of money from his card games. Soon he had enough to pay the last of his debt to Rudy. When he gave him the money, they were sitting in the back booth at Solly's where they usually met. Morty felt this was a great day. He was going to pay Rudy the last of his debt.

He laid the money on the table between them. "Are we even now?"

Rudy picked up the bills, counted them, fingered them. "Yeah, for the money for your father."

Morty breathed deep. "Okay, now I want out. I got to get back to school. I don't want to run errands for you anymore."

Rudy didn't answer at first. Then he said, "It's not so easy as that, Morty. You don't get to come in and go out when you please."

"What do you mean?" Morty didn't like the sound of Rudy's voice or the way he was staring above Morty's head.

"Maybe you know a little too much, Morty. Adler won't like it if you just stop like that." He shook his head. "You know once you're in . . ." His voice drifted off into silence.

Morty shook his head. He didn't trust his voice. His throat felt tight. Finally, he said, "That wasn't what you told me when I asked you for help."

Rudy shrugged. "I sort of did. I told you that you had to do what I said. And now I'm saying . . ."

Morty's heart was pounding, but he made his voice calm. "I want out. I never signed on for life. You got to get me out." Morty stared into Rudy's eyes, which were hard, glinting. It was a look that Morty didn't like.

Rudy waited a while before he answered. "Look, I'll talk to Mickey. We'll see what he says. Until then, you're still on the payroll."

The next time Morty saw Rudy, he got his answer. Mickey Adler wanted Morty to go up to Sullivan County and take charge of the slots that were more and more being set out in the casinos, hotels, and bars. "He sweetened the deal for you too. Because I asked him to. He knows what a card shark you are, so he said you can also set up card games—gambling, craps—and you keep half the profits."

But Morty wasn't interested. "Didn't you tell him I wanted out? That's what we agreed." He could hear Anna in the back of his head. She was more and more insistent that he get free of the gangs.

"I told him. Yeah, I told him. But Adler wants you upstate," Rudy said. "And he doesn't like to hear no."

"Why would he care?" Morty asked. "I'm just a penny-ante messenger. What does it matter if I stay in Brooklyn?"

Rudy sighed. Rolled his glass round and round on the table. Sighed again. "Look, Morty," he said. "He trusts you, for some reason. I think he likes the way you play cards. You always were a good player."

"What would he do to me for saying no? I don't want to leave the city. Anna's here."

"So what? Up there is money to be made. Big money."

"I don't need big money."

Rudy's mouth dropped open. "What? Are you going to live on nothing like your folks do? Scrimp and save and mumble prayers for better times?"

"Look, I don't need a lot for Anna and me. We just got back together. I can't leave her now. I want to marry her."

"Forget Anna," Rudy said. His voice was hard. "The last guy Adler had up in the Catskills, Al Satella, did something stupid."

Morty's heart stopped. "What did he do?"

"He got married. He's no good married, always pining for his wife. Adler dumped him."

"D . . . dumped him?" He could hardly get the words out. "Had him killed?"

Rudy stared at him for a long minute. Morty thought he was evaluating what to say. Then he laughed. "Don't get nervous. He's not into that. Nah, he just fired him."

Morty evaluated what Rudy said. He breathed a little more easily, but he wasn't sure. Something made him doubt what Rudy said. Morty thought maybe they had gotten rid of Al Satella, but he couldn't prove it. He didn't even know who this Al Satella was.

Rudy was saying, "I told you, forget Anna. She's nothing. You don't need her. Listen to me. Do what I tell you."

Morty looked Rudy straight in the eye. "Since when do I have to do what you say?"

Rudy breathed deep. "If you want to stay healthy."

Morty couldn't speak he was so stunned. His eyes began to wander. He looked behind Rudy and saw some of Mickey's crowd sitting at another booth. He shivered. One of them was a guy he had played cards with many times; he'd usually beaten him. He looked away.

"Look, Morty." Rudy's voice had taken on a more reasonable tone. "I don't mean to push, but there's a lot of rumbling around. Adler says there may be a war down here. He needs you up in the Catskills, in Liberty, and you'll be better off—safer—up there. And make more money. There's definitely going to be trouble down here."

"Why don't you go up there, then?"

"I have important business here."

"And I don't?"

"No, you don't. All you have is a girlfriend who's turning your brain to mush."

"I don't want to go," Morty said. He was afraid to say an absolute no . . . Rudy didn't seem to be willing to take a hard-stop no. "How about I think about it a little bit. Maybe I'll go just for the summer. Then I go back to school in the fall."

Rudy shrugged. "You really don't get to think about it too much. Mickey decides for you. But maybe he'll be okay with the summer. Once you get things established, he might let you come back to Brooklyn. One week. I give you one week to go. Otherwise . . ." His voice drifted off in menace. Morty did not like the tone of Rudy's voice. Rudy stood up and walked out of the store.

The next time he saw Anna, Morty told her about what Rudy had said. It was late May, and the days were long again. He had picked up Anna when she finished working at the deli, and they were walking in the Botanical Garden along paths lined with pink and red peonies. Anna would lean over and smell the flowers, gently brush her hands over the blossoms. "These are so gorgeous," she said. "I think they may be my favorite flowers."

Morty didn't respond to her.

"Are you listening to me?" Anna asked. She pushed her long black hair back off her face. When she worked at the deli, she had to pin her hair up. As soon as she left work, she would pull out the pins and let her hair flow down her back. Now she had stopped walking and was facing Morty.

He reached out and took a lock of her hair and smoothed it behind her. He hesitated, then said, "He wants me to go up to Liberty, in the Catskills. Set up the slots. I don't want to, but Rudy acts as if I have no choice, so I said I'd go for the summer." When he said that, his heart bumped in his chest.

"Rudy's crazy," Anna said. "Why do you listen to him? Of course you have a choice. There are always choices."

Morty stared at Anna. He was a little surprised. It seemed as if there were things she didn't know about the gangs and how they worked. He realized that she also didn't know that he had gotten involved because Rudy had given him the money to get his father out of debt, and Morty had taken on the debt himself. Even though he had paid it back, that hadn't freed him.

He'd once heard that if you were in a gang, you were in it for life. They didn't trust you if you left, because even if you swore you would never betray them, they didn't believe you. There was always someone who could bribe you for information.

The thing was, Morty didn't really know if he was in so far with the gang that he couldn't get out. If he was, the big guys wouldn't ever trust him not to turn on them if they let him walk away, and if he did it anyway . . . well, they'd get rid of him . . . maybe not right away, but eventually.

Now Anna looked carefully at Morty. "You have only one more year to graduate as an engineer. Why would you stop now?" she asked. "You almost have your ticket out."

Morty nodded his head. She was right, and she was wrong. He wanted to tell Rudy he wasn't going upstate, but if Rudy insisted . . . he probably would have to go anyway. Morty gave a half promise to Anna that he wouldn't leave Brooklyn. He wondered if he could keep it. He didn't want an argument with Rudy, but he also didn't want to be pushed around.

When the week was up, he came to meet Rudy again. He sat in a booth at Solly's pushing around a Coke, unable to drink it. His insides were gnashing. He was not looking forward to the upcoming meeting. He sat, jiggling his leg, glancing out the door again and again. No Rudy. It was midafternoon, and the store was quiet—too early for the schoolkids to stop by for penny candy. Too early for Adler's boys to be gathering, playing cards, filling the back booths.

"Shark?" A short boy, his acne-pocked face puffed with self-importance, approached him. He was using the name Adler had dubbed him . . . Shark for card shark. Morty turned to look at the boy. "They sent me to tell you in case ya didn't hear."

"Hear what?"

Morty could see the boy was just hanging on to the information, not wanting to give away his importance and be left with his ordinary presence. He shifted his weight from foot to foot. Opened his mouth. Closed it.

"What? Tell me. What?"

"Rudy bought it."

Morty's throat closed. He could feel his heart pounding. He stared at the boy, certain he was making this up and at the same time certain he was telling the truth. All he could muster were the words "Tell me."

Filled with self-importance, the boy puffed out his chest and spoke in a rush. Morty concentrated on a big pimple on his chin, trying to slow his heartbeat. "He was standing on Pitkin. Some guy comes up, sticks a shiv in his side, twists it, and walks away. No one even knew who he was or could give a description."

The picture began filling out. He could see Rudy standing there, maybe lighting a cigarette so he wasn't looking around with his usual watchful eyes. Caught unaware, the look of surprise flashed over his face, then horror, pain, and the awful knowledge. *Bought it. Bought it.*

The boy made a sound, like a cough. Morty noticed he was fingering an envelope. He stuck his hand out and gave it to Morty, who held it without opening it. "What's this?"

"Adler gave it to me. To give to you."

"Okay."

The boy didn't move. He seemed to be waiting for something. Morty couldn't still his mind. What did this pipsqueak want anyway? Why was he waiting? Then knowledge flooded him. *A tip. This little pisser wants a tip.* He should give him a tip for telling him that Rudy was dead.

"Get the hell out of here," Morty said, as clearly as he could, with his throat closing over tears. He couldn't let the kid see that. "Don't let me see your fucking face again."

The boy hesitated at first, then turned and walked out of the candy store. Morty watched the boy's back disappear and then sat staring at the envelope without seeing it. He knew, even before he opened it, what the note inside would say.

Morty let his mind linger. He wondered what happened to the men wiped off the face of the city by the violence around them. Where were Lucky Pete and Big Nosey? No one talked afterward. If they didn't see their friend fall, if they weren't there watching, it was as if it hadn't happened. As if they had not existed. Would that be the way it would be for Rudy? Gone. Forgotten. Morty swallowed hard. He took a breath and opened the envelope.

It said he had to leave Brooklyn for Liberty. He'd have to go that night.

First Morty had to see Anna—at least to tell her he was leaving. It was Monday, and Anna had the day off, so he'd have to go to her house. He walked quickly down the streets, all his senses humming. His eyes darted, left and right. He swiveled his head in each direction, turning backward to see if anyone was following him. As he passed each group, he strained his ears. What were they talking about? The weather was warm, the evening coming on them, the streetlights shimmering. He could smell all the familiar odors as he passed the restaurants and stores; the greengrocer was throwing out the rotten vegetables, there were three men smoking cigars on a corner, the open bar door let out a boozy smell of old beer. He hurried along and turned down the street where Anna lived, and stood, hesitating in front of her two-family house.

The house had a stone facade. Two pillars of brick, each topped with a cement sphere, stood on either side of the stairs that went up to the front door. Morty had only been inside the house once. Before that, he had brought her home and watched while she entered safely before he quickly left the block. He took a deep breath, walked up the stairs, and rang the doorbell on the right, praying that Anna would come. There was no answer, even after he rang a second time. He moved over and rang the bell on the left side. Her aunt and uncle lived there with their four kids.

It was an eternity before the door opened. A girl of about twelve stood peering out at him, not saying anything.

"I'm looking for Anna."

"She's not here. She lives upstairs."

"I know, but no one answers there. Do you know where she is? When she'll be back?"

"Who's asking?"

"I'm her friend, Morty. Do you know where she is?" he repeated.

"Yeah."

"Could you get her for me? It's important."

The girl stood appraising him. She was short and pretty, with the slight pudginess that adolescent girls sometimes get when they start developing breasts. He could see small buds under her shirt and immediately thought she wasn't wearing a bra. Her hair and eyes were intensely black, and he felt her gaze boring into him.

"I know who you are," she said.

Was that a warning? Morty wondered. He swallowed hard, nervous, and looked around him. There was no one else there. "So, will you get Anna for me?" he asked.

The girl smiled, a flash of brilliant white teeth. She put her finger to her mouth, warning him not to say anything more, turned her head, and yelled, "Ma, I'm going over to Angie's. I'll be back soon." Closing the door behind her, she signaled for him to follow her across the street, where she told him to wait while she went inside.

Morty waited, watching as two men walked down the street and passed by, hardly noticing him. Why was he so nervous? He wasn't a target like Rudy had been. He hadn't done anything with the gang except run errands and play cards. Why would anyone be after him?

The door to Angie's house opened, and Anna ran down the steps to greet him. As always, the sight of her took his breath away. She took his hand and paused thoughtfully. "What's wrong, Morty? Is everything all right?" she asked. She stood close, looking into his eyes. He could smell the perfume she used. It was all he could do not to lean over and kiss her. She twined her hands in his.

"Let's walk," he said.

They turned the corner. "What's wrong?" she asked again.

Morty stared straight ahead, afraid if he looked at her, he couldn't get the words out. He noticed the street traffic, cars and buses rumbling down the avenue. He saw a vagrant, a man down on his luck, rummaging through the trash can on the side of a bakery. He forced himself to look at Anna. "Remember I told you Rudy said I should leave Brooklyn, go upstate?"

"Yeah. But you said you weren't going."

"I know." He took a deep breath, swallowed the lump. "Things are different now. Rudy, he . . . he's dead."

Anna pulled him to a standstill and stared, mouth agape. "What happened?"

Morty shook his head. "I'm not sure. A kid came to tell me. He said it happened on the street." Morty felt his eyes fill up. He looked past Anna. "Someone knifed him and walked away. And now I have to go away, at least for a while. That's what Adler says, so that's what I better do. It's like they're threatening me or something."

They kept walking, silent, somehow knowing where they were going without saying anything. One last time they would go down to the cellar club. There, at least, they could hold each other, whisper plans they could not guarantee would come true. Morty gripped Anna's icy hand. What would he do without her? What if he never saw her again? What would happen after he left, he didn't know. But one last time he would hold her and tell her he loved her, and then he would take her back home, pack, and leave for Sullivan County, New York, wherever the hell that was.

After he took Anna home, Morty went to his father's shop. It was late, but he knew his father would be there. Morty found him in the back room working on a broken vacuum cleaner. Since Morty had saved his father from financial and personal disaster, Ben paid Morty respect. He saw his son, put down his tools, and wiped his hands with a nearby rag.

"Morty," he said, "is everything all right?"

"No," Morty answered. He took a deep breath. "I've been ordered to go up to Liberty."

"What do you mean, ordered? By who?"

Morty looked at his father, annoyed at the question. "Who do you think? Adler. Mickey Adler." His voice cracked. "Rudy was just murdered."

Ben was speechless. He sat hard on his bench. "Why? Who did it?"

"No information. I just know I have to leave."

Ben could barely control his voice. "Are you in danger too?"

"Anyone who works for Adler is in danger. You know that, don't you? You knew when we started this business of getting Rudy to help with the money." Ben was silent. He looked down at his feet. The irritation Morty felt toward his father was palpable. "I'm only telling you so you know I'm all right. For now. But don't tell Mama where I am. Just say I had to go away."

Ben nodded. "But what will you do there? How will you live? What about your schooling?"

"What do you think? I'll do whatever Mickey Adler tells me to do. I'll quit school. I have no choice. Unless I want to end up like Rudy."

"Do you think Mickey had Rudy killed?" There was shock and disbelief in Ben's voice.

"I have no idea, Papa. I only know Rudy's dead, and if I don't follow Mickey's orders, I'm in trouble." He looked at his father's face. He had aged a lot in the last months. He had been such a kind and sweet man for most of Morty's childhood and youth. Now he seemed broken. "I'm sorry, Papa. I got to go. Tell Mama I love her. Beyond that, tell her whatever you want about why I had to leave." He reached out and embraced his father, and then, afraid his father would start to cry, he turned and left the store.

Morty went next to the apartment. Sylvia was in the living room, curled up on the sofa, reading. She jumped when he came in. Morty did not usually appear in the middle of the day. She followed him into the bedroom, watched with alarm as he gathered his clothing into a pile on the bed and then went rummaging in his parents' room for the one valise they owned. He came back to the bedroom with it, brown-leather-colored cardboard, bent on the side. The latch didn't work, and after he loaded his clothes in it and added one book, he slammed it shut and tied it around with the rope that had been inside it. He picked it up and brushed by her, his face set in a grimace.

"Where are you going?" She pointed to the suitcase.

"Away," Morty snapped. "Upstate." Then, after a minute, his voice softened, and he added, "I just have to go, Sylvia. Don't ask me any questions."

"But why?" Sylvia asked. "Why do you have to leave? What should I tell Mama and Papa?"

"I have to go," Morty said. "I don't want to, but I have to. Tell them I went upstate. I already told Papa." Morty swung the valise, battered and crushed, over his shoulder. "I'll see you." He turned, ruffled her hair, and bent to give her an awkward hug and a peck on the cheek. Then he was out the door, almost running down the staircase.

"Wait, Morty, wait," she called, following him. But he didn't.

CHAPTER 28

SYLVIA

Sylvia reached up and touched her cheek. She wasn't crying, but she felt like she could. She sat on the sofa and picked up her book again, but she couldn't read. Why did Morty have to go away? What was upstate? She was confused and upset. She kept going over the same things again and again, but there were no answers that she could find.

An hour later, Golda came home, carrying parcels wrapped in a bulging string bag that hung on one shoulder. A bunch of celery stuck out to one side and a loaf of bread to the other.

Sylvia hovered around her mother. Should she tell her about Morty? Morty had said that Papa already knew. Should she wait until her father came home and let him tell Golda?

Golda was busy unpacking her groceries, taking out an onion and the frying pan, getting ready to make supper. Sylvia knew her mother wouldn't ask about Morty. Many nights he didn't come home for supper. Some nights he didn't even come home to sleep. They had begun to ignore his comings and goings. He was enrolled in the Brooklyn Polytechnic College, and school had just ended for the term. He had only one more year of night classes to go, but who knew what would happen now? It had seemed to Sylvia that his interest in school had fallen off this last year; he seemed so busy with other things. But still, she often would see him hunched over his textbooks, scribbling in a notebook. Sylvia didn't know what to think.

But now she couldn't keep the news to herself. Her insides were jumping. She felt the words bubbling up. "He went away. He took a valise."

"Who went away?" Golda asked. Her words were sharp, clipped.

"Morty. He packed a valise and left. He said to tell you he went . . ." She paused. "Away."

"Where away? Where does he know to go away?"

"Upstate."

"Where upstate?" Golda asked.

"That's all he said. Upstate." Sylvia looked at her mother, who was standing perfectly still, staring at her daughter. "Papa knows. He told me he told Papa."

Golda went on preparing dinner. "Then I'll wait until Papa comes home and tells me." She was silent for a long time. She was cutting onions to fry when she turned and asked, "What about his school? Did he say about that?"

Sylvia shook her head. "No. He didn't say anything about school."

Golda put down her knife. "All that scrimping and saving so he could go to school. It was wasted."

Sylvia felt her heart hammering. She didn't know what to say. Then her mother was crying. She sat down at the table, put her head on her arms, and sobbed. Sylvia patted her mother's back, made shushing sounds, and, when her mother's sobs subsided, sat down next to her.

"I have been so worried," Golda said. "I don't know what happened to him. He was such a good boy, but now, he's changed. We scrimped and saved, and he throws it all away."

Sylvia shook her head.

"Such a waste. Such a waste," Golda said, her voice choking. She sat quietly for a minute. Her fingers twisted around themselves. "You make a choice, or you have no choice, so you go with it, and you think your choice is the best one, but then . . . it turns out like this. Burned bridges. Dreams in ashes. Maybe I should never have married your father." She seemed to be talking to herself.

But if you hadn't married Papa, I wouldn't be here, Sylvia thought, then said it. "I wouldn't have been born if you hadn't married Papa." She held her mother's eyes. She could see her mother's eyes fill up with tears again.

Golda wiped her eyes and stood up. She breathed in and out. "You are right. I wouldn't have wanted that. You are my jewel." Just before she turned and went back into the kitchen, she said, "Never mind. It's not your worry. It's mine." She would not say another word.

When Ben came home, he seemed to be dragging. He sat silently at the table, saying nothing about Morty leaving. Sylvia couldn't stand it anymore. "I told Mama about Morty. He came home to pack a valise, and he left. He said he told you already. Upstate."

It was quiet in the kitchen. Ben fidgeted with his knife. "He came, he told me. He had to go."

"Do you know why?" Sylvia asked. "He didn't tell me why."

"I don't know why," Ben said. He wouldn't look at her or at Golda.

Golda glared at him. "How is that possible? Your son tells you he's going away, upstate, and you don't ask why?"

"I asked. I asked. But he just said he had to go. He kissed me good-bye and said for me to tell you that he loves you."

Sylvia looked at her father. And she did not believe him. She looked at the table, at the mashed potatoes and the green beans and the crumbs of the rye bread. She looked down at her plate. She didn't think she could eat anything. But when she looked at her mother, she thought at least she would have to try.

"Eat," Ben said. "We won't talk of it anymore."

And they ate the rest of their dinner in silence.

PART THREE

1939–1940

CHAPTER 29

MORTY

Morty took the bus from Penn Station to Liberty. He found a window seat in the back, put his small, battered valise on the shelf above, and sat staring out the dirty glass. His leg jiggled nervously. He kept glancing at the front of the bus, watching the men coming in and taking seats. He didn't watch the women. They wouldn't be looking for him.

There was a man, young like him, his hooded eyes glancing around, but he swung into a seat in the front of the bus and didn't look back again. Maybe he wasn't anybody Morty should be afraid of. A little girl and her father walked to the back and took the seat in front of Morty. The girl was chattering away, and she reminded him of Sylvia. He wondered when he would see her again. He wondered when he would see any of his family or friends again. Or Anna. He missed her already.

He leaned his head against the glass, closed his eyes, but then reminded himself that he needed to be vigilant. He opened his eyes again and kept them moving around the bus . . . right, left, right, left. Until finally the doors closed, and the bus pulled out. Then he allowed himself to breathe.

He took the note the boy had given him out of his pocket and read it for the fourth time. The note had been folded and refolded. It was grimy and sweaty from his hands gripping it, putting it in his pocket, and removing it again. It said simply: *Leave Brooklyn. Take the bus to Liberty. Go to Frank's bar on Main Street. Talk to Frank there. He'll set you up. Go now.* Tucked inside the envelope was a $50 bill. It was signed M. A. for Mickey Adler.

Morty had broken the bill to buy his bus ticket and now had

$47.36. He had his wallet with the bills, and the change was loose, jingling in his pocket. He had no idea what was waiting for him in Liberty. He'd never been there. He was confused. He was excited. But mostly he was frightened. He felt that he had taken a pathway that would not let him go back home. What had happened? He'd been on the road to becoming an engineer. He still could be an engineer, get a good job, and marry Anna as he'd hoped to do. Now he was moving in another direction, a road he really didn't want to go down but was going down anyway.

He stared out the window, mesmerized by the green of the trees along the road, the small-town bus stops, the scenery that gradually turned into hills and then mountains. He began to feel the tightness in his chest loosening, and he was breathing more easily. The bus stopped for twenty minutes at a rest stop, a big diner-cafeteria on Route 7 called Red Apple Rest, where he bought a hot dog and a Coke. When the bus started again, he relaxed, and gradually the vibrations of the bus lulled him to sleep, his head leaning against the grimy window. When the bus stopped in Liberty, he jumped up, terrified he had missed his stop. He was the last one off and walked quickly down the aisle and off the bus, clutching his valise.

He looked around the depot, uncertain where he was going. Finally, he read the note again, made sure he had the name of the meeting place, and asked at the ticket window for Frank's Bar. He walked the two blocks to the bar and went inside.

Frank's Bar looked like a lot of neighborhood joints in Brooklyn, and Morty had no trouble identifying the owner, who, big and burly, stood behind the bar occasionally swiping at the gleaming wood in front of him.

It was early evening, the first week of June, and still light out. Morty walked up to the bartender and said, "Frank?"

"You Morty?"

Morty nodded.

"Yeah, Adler said you'd be coming today. I'm going to get you set up with a place to sleep and some dinner, and then we'll talk."

Morty nodded. He figured he'd just let this man, Frank, take care of the way his life was going to go for the next few days. Then he would see.

It turned out it was for more than a few days. Frank fixed Morty up with a room in a boarding house down the road. It was clean and comfortable. A woman named Delia Stein ran the house and provided him with breakfast every morning, usually oatmeal and a cup of coffee, and dinner at night. She was a good cook. During the summer, Mrs. Stein rented out her rooms to people who were looking for a week away in the country and couldn't afford to stay in the nicer hotels and boarding houses. Mrs. Stein took a liking to Morty and would sit with him in the morning, having breakfast and telling him how hard it had been in the early days of the Depression. Things seemed better now. She had reservations through all of July and a few weeks in August. Morty thought that boded well for the businesses in the mountains.

Adler's orders were for Morty to pick up the slot business that Al Satella had started before he went back to Brooklyn. The main job was to collect the money from the hotel owners who had slot machines on their premises and make sure they paid every penny they owed.

The work was easy, Morty knew, because the hotel and restaurant owners had put in the slot machines several years earlier. All Morty had to do was collect the money. Morty was good at math. It was easy to keep track of what they owed. There was a meter on the back of each machine that totaled the money collected, and a percentage—a large percentage—of the take was owed to Mickey Adler. Morty showed the managers of the properties that he could calculate what they owed in his head. He knew how many machines they had—in their game rooms, in the hallways to the ballrooms where people could mingle, in the lobbies. If they tried to short him on the money, he would know it right away and would have to lean on them in some way.

Morty was not good at bullying, but he was good at presenting the slots as a business proposition. Most of the hotels already had them in their lobbies or social halls. If they had not placed them yet, Morty could talk to the managers about the competition from the other hotels, and then they willingly acceded. If they didn't, Morty would mention his boss's name. They were afraid of the name, Mickey Adler, and mostly came around.

Morty quickly developed a reputation for being good with the owners and not ruffling too many feathers as he collected from some and signed the few who were new to the business. But Morty felt the tension building every Monday morning when he woke to start his day. He tried stretching, breathing, doing some easy calisthenics. Nothing worked. His back and his neck would feel stiff and tight, and he knew it was pure nerves. He didn't like this business.

He would dress in the morning, and to his surprise and horror, he would find his hand shaking as he buttoned his shirt. He knew he had to look sharp to do the work he was doing. He slicked back his hair with pomade, gave himself a close shave. He was thinking of growing a mustache and wondered how Anna would like it if he did. He imagined she would say it tickled when he kissed her, and just thinking about it, he would feel his heart speed up, and he had to shake the image away.

He went down to Mrs. Stein's kitchen and sat at the table, eating his oatmeal, drinking one cup of coffee, and exchanging pleasantries with his landlady and, later, the other boarder in the house. He had been instructed by Frank, the bartender, to keep himself under the radar, not to do anything that would attract attention, so he didn't have much conversation with the man. He didn't want to have to answer any questions that might give his "business" away. He said, when asked, that he was a salesman.

The June mornings were sunny and warm in the mountains. If he was free, in the afternoons he would enjoy the weather, even go for a hike along some of the trails outside of town. He had never experienced outdoors in the country before, and he liked it.

He'd never been surrounded by so much green. The concrete of the city streets, the bits and pieces of trash blowing in the spring air, gray puddles of rainwater along the gutters—that was June in the city. He knew all the smells too. Rotten food spilling out of garbage pails, stacks of old unsold newspapers at the doorways of the candy stores, the sweetness of the bakeries with their breads and cakes and cookies, and the metallic smell of blood at the doorways of the butchers. There were only a few places where green showed or flowery weeds grew in the city: an open lot—unbuilt, waiting—and the beauty of the large expanses like the Brooklyn Botanical Gardens and Prospect Park.

Here in Liberty, you could move through the small town and out to the country lanes. The houses were spread out, surrounded by green lawns and flower gardens. There was a lake not too far away. He imagined swimming there on hot summer days if he was still here during July or August. He hoped he wouldn't be. But he knew he had to take care of business first.

On Monday morning, he would make his rounds. The job was easy. Just go from one to the other of the hotels, restaurants, and bars where the slots were. The Grossman Hotel. The Merryman Bar. The Western Steakhouse. They all had slot machines placed in their lobbies, or in the vestibules and hallways—some even in the main dining rooms. Slots were good business, both for the proprietor and for the guys like Adler who placed the machines. Morty liked to go in the morning because there weren't many customers around, and he could deal with the manager quietly in the back room. He remembered his first job with Mr. Hansen and how he had watched the collector from the mob picking up money each week . . . *protection money*, he called it. Mr. Hansen had paid willingly, because he said he was afraid if he didn't, they would burn his shop down like they had the tailor's shop on the next block. And now, here Morty was, the very one doing the threatening, the collecting. It made him sick to his stomach. He calmed himself by saying, *All I have to do is collect.*

In the beginning, he didn't want to get into a discussion with the owner or manager. He just wanted to check the slots to see how much had been collected, pick up the envelope with the cash, and count the money to make sure it was the right percentage. His quick math skills helped him make short work of the arithmetic, and only once, so far, had one of the managers tried to short him. That had been a trial for him. To walk up close, put his face next to the manager's, and say, "I think you made a mistake in your addition." He wasn't sure what the man would do, but to his relief, the guy pulled out the additional bills. Morty had tipped his hat and said, "I trust there won't be any more arithmetic errors in the future."

When he left the hotel, he felt the tension lift from his shoulders. Maybe this wasn't so hard after all. It was not what he had thought he would be doing this summer, but maybe it would be okay.

The second time he noticed that the math didn't add up, he had to confront the manager of the hotel, a burly man half a head shorter than Morty who denied he had made a mistake. Morty left the hotel and walked. His stomach was in knots. He knew what had to be done, and he wondered if he could get Adler to send up one of his hoodlums to strong-arm the manager, but when he called, Adler just laughed. "What do you think your job is? You better get it done or everyone else up there will be cheating us."

His heart pounding so hard he was sure Adler could hear it over the phone, he said, "Okay," and hung up the phone.

Thankful that he had spent so many hours at the Boys' Club learning to box, he went back to the hotel and waited in the shadows until the manager left to go home. He was not such a big guy or a young guy either. Morty thought, *I'm stronger and taller*, and he stepped out of the shadows and caught the man by surprise, landing a few good punches. He stood over the man, who lay on the road with a bruise on his cheek and a split lip. "I'll be back tomorrow," he said. Then he walked away.

His heart was going a mile a minute. *I'm not cut out for this*, he thought. He walked quickly down the road into the darkness. He was sweating, almost gagging. How was he going to keep this up? To his enormous relief, when he showed up the next day, the manager, sporting a purple bruise on his cheek and a fat lip, was sitting in his office, and he sent a bellhop out with the money. The envelope he delivered was fat and full.

Morty was relieved. Adler was right. Once this manager paid up, word got around not to mess with Morty. After that, Morty was in good shape. He thought he wouldn't have to get physical with any of the other owners once the word got out, and he was right. But he was flooded with shame.

At night he lay in his bed and wondered how he had ever gotten into this dilemma. He was going to be an engineer, marry Anna. Now he was caught up in the underworld workings of gambling and slot machines and graft. Each time he tried to figure out how he had arrived at this place, he came to the same conclusion: his father's pleading had pushed him here. To save his father, he had made a bargain with Rudy, taken the route to crime, and now found himself even more connected to gangs than he had been when Rudy was alive. At least when he was reporting to Rudy, he could argue about what he was asked to do. Now he had no one to argue with. Sometimes he thought about the guy who had been up here before him, Al Satella. Had he really gone back home? He hoped it was true, because if it was, maybe Morty could go back to Brooklyn too.

Every week through June and early July, one of Adler's men would come up to Liberty and collect the money Morty had for him, counting it carefully before he got into his car. Morty made him sign for how much was in the envelope, just to make sure that none of it was missing when the envelope was delivered to Adler. It had to be correct to the penny. Adler wouldn't tolerate one of his boys cheating him. He remembered Rudy telling him that if you cheated, you would wind up floating in the river.

After he had been there for three weeks, Adler came up to check things out. Little Jiggy was sitting beside him in the passenger seat. He nodded to Morty as he moved from the front seat into the back. Morty took his place. Adler was a good ten years older than Morty and had once been slim and handsome. Now, after years of good living, he'd put on weight, and his face was round with a double chin. Somehow the softness of his face was more menacing than if he were still young and good looking.

It was unnerving to Morty, knowing that Little Jiggy was behind him, silently listening and watching, all the while bouncing his leg against Morty's seat back. After they had taken a drive around the town, they sat parked in front of Mrs. Stein's boarding house. Morty still wanted to know if he had to stay in Liberty beyond the summer. He thought he would start by asking Adler if he could go home to Brooklyn for a visit.

Adler eyed him. "I like you here," he said. "You're good for business. I'm going to get you a car."

Morty was surprised. He remembered that Adler had bought Rudy his first car. He said, "I don't need a car."

"Yeah, you do. Too much space here. You need a car. I got plans for you. We're going to spread out some. Otherwise, we'll lose the business to some other gang. And I don't want to lose the business to another gang. You understand?" Morty nodded. "You know how to drive?" Morty nodded again. "I'll get you a car."

Morty figured a car would be all right. "But after the summer . . . then I can go back to Brooklyn? I need to go back to school."

"You don't need to go to school . . . you'll make a lot more money if you stick with me."

Morty's hands were sweating. "It's not about the money. I've always wanted to be an engineer. I only got into this business because Rudy did my father a big favor. And then Rudy got killed."

"Yeah, that was unfortunate. I liked Rudy." He reached into his pocket, took out a pack of Lucky Strike cigarettes, and lit one, blowing the smoke toward the open window at his side.

Morty hesitated for a minute, and then he asked the question that had been on his mind since he heard about Rudy's murder. "What happened? Who killed him?"

Adler shrugged. He stared out the window. "Well, I don't know. There are lots of guys on the street." He turned and eyed Morty. "You know Rudy didn't only work with me. He sometimes worked with Lepke and Reles." Adler paused. "You know who they are?"

Morty took a deep breath and nodded. This explained a lot.

Everybody in Brooklyn knew who they were. Louis Lepke and Abe Reles were the bosses of Murder, Inc. To Morty it was suddenly very clear why Rudy was always taking those trips out of New York—to Chicago and Detroit and little Podunk towns around the country. He would always say he was "taking care of business," but he never explained what the business was. Now Morty knew what he had been doing on those out-of-town trips. It wasn't called Murder, Inc., for nothing. He could feel his heart racing at the thought of his old friend as a cold-blooded murderer. "You think they had him murdered?"

Adler didn't answer. They sat in silence while Adler smoked. Morty felt his heart pound. The vibrations of Little Jiggy's leg seemed to pick up speed. Morty stared out the window at the green trees, the flower beds in Mrs. Stein's front yard. It was peaceful and pretty, and it was hard to believe he was sitting in a car with two gang members talking about murder.

Adler flicked his cigarette out the window. "Which reminds me, you also need this," he said. He reached over Morty, opened the glove compartment of the car, and pulled out a gun, which he offered to Morty.

Morty shook his head and put up his hands. "I don't want that. I wouldn't even know what to do with it."

"You might need it. Take it."

Morty's heart was pounding. He was shaking his head. "I don't want it. I'll take the car, but no gun. I don't want a gun." He worked hard to make his voice convincing, strong.

Adler stared at him. He put the gun back in the glove compartment. "There'll be a car for you in a few days. Don't ask any questions. Just take it. Jiggy here will bring it up with one of the other guys."

Morty breathed with relief. He nodded. Morty took the car Jiggy brought him, a black 1936 Chevrolet that looked almost new. He was glad it wasn't a Ford, but he knew none of the Jewish gangs would buy Ford cars. Henry Ford was a notorious Jew hater, and Morty didn't know a single Jew who would buy a car from Ford.

Before he started driving the car, he looked at the glove

compartment several times, wondering if there was anything in it. He finally opened it. There, on top of the registration, was a small black handgun. He slammed the glove box closed and sat, staring straight ahead. *The bastard. I told him I didn't want a gun, and Adler left it anyway.* He wouldn't touch it. Never. If he did, he was doomed. His stomach was churning in rage. He shuddered. *What if Adler is setting me up? What if the gun was used for a murder, and Adler expects me to touch it and put my prints on it? He's a bastard*, Morty thought again. *Breathe*, he told himself. *Just take it to the bedroom and think it through. I don't know where the gun was before, and I just need to get rid of it. But not anywhere it can be found.*

That night, Morty took a paper bag, went to the car, and opened the glove box. Careful not to leave any fingerprints, he picked up the gun with his handkerchief, placed it in the bag, and put it on the seat beside him. What would he do with it now? He could bury it. He could throw it in one of the big garbage bins outside the bar on Main Street. Or at a hotel. Even if someone found it, they couldn't trace it to him.

He went to his room with the bag and put it in the back of his closet. *I'll think about it later.* Later took longer and longer.

He hated to admit it, but he loved having the car. He began to drive around the back roads of Sullivan County, enjoying the green grass everywhere, the dairy farms with cows grazing in the fields. It was some compensation for not being able to go home, but not enough. He still missed Anna. He wondered how his family was doing. Now he wanted to check in with them. He wrote a letter to his parents, telling them he was okay, and he'd hopefully come home for a visit later in the summer. By return post he received three letters, from his mother, his father, and Sylvia. All of them begged him to come home as soon as he could. The letters made him more homesick and sadder than he had been before.

He had already written to Anna and received a letter back from her. Now he wanted to ask her to come up to Liberty, but he knew that would mean an overnight because the trip was too far for one day. He wondered how she would manage that and wasn't sure she'd be up for it. He wrote to Anna, enclosing enough money for her to come up by bus and visit him.

Anna wrote back. She wouldn't come for an overnight. It would cause too much of a commotion in her house. Couldn't he come into the city for a visit? For the first time Morty used the telephone number she had given him. Anna picked up on the first ring. Hearing her voice on the phone made Morty want to see her even more. He told her his backup plan. If staying overnight wouldn't work, he would meet her halfway. It took between three and four hours for the trip from New York City to Liberty. Halfway up to Liberty was the Red Apple Rest, the way station where the bus had stopped when he first came up to Liberty. He knew that Anna would be able to get off and spend a few hours with him before she had to turn around and go back to Brooklyn. She agreed, and they made a date to meet in two days.

When Morty drove down to the Red Apple, the sun was shining, the air balmy. He waited anxiously where the buses stopped to let the passengers out. At least one bus came and went, and Anna was not on it. He paced around the parking lot until the next bus arrived.

Morty craned his neck as the travelers disembarked. And there she was. He could barely swallow. She stood on the step of the bus, looking around until she finally saw him, and a small smile lit her face. She flipped her hair back and showed her ivory neck over her yellow V-necked dress. They stood motionless, staring at each other, until the person behind Anna impatiently tapped her on the shoulder, and she jumped and quickly came down the last steps. Morty felt as if he were moving through a fog. They stood facing one another, and, unable to resist, he reached out and embraced her.

Anna buried her head in his neck. He rocked her back and forth. "Oh God, I missed you so much! So much."

When she looked up at him, he saw that her violet eyes were glistening. "I feel like crying," she said.

He took her hand, and they walked away from the bus, toward the crowds at the restaurant.

"Are you hungry?" he asked.

She shook her head. "Maybe a Coke?" She smiled at him shyly. "Or an egg cream?"

Morty laughed. "I don't know if they make egg creams out here in the country. For sure I can get you a milkshake."

Morty went into the cafeteria, and after waiting in line, he came back to Anna with two hot dogs, a cardboard square of french fries, and two milkshakes. He walked Anna back to where his car was parked and suggested they could eat at one of the rustic picnic tables around the parking lot.

"You got a car?" Anna asked in disbelief.

Morty smiled. "Yeah, I need it for my work." He led her to a table, spread out his handkerchief on the wooden surface, and put the food on it. Each of them picked up a hot dog and bit into it.

"This is good," Anna said. "It reminds me of Coney Island . . . Nathan's, you know?"

"Yeah," Morty agreed. He sucked his milkshake through a straw. "This is good too."

Anna nodded. She took another bite of her hot dog and chewed slowly. Then she said, "What are you doing here, Morty? What kind of work?"

Morty hesitated for a minute. "I'm in business, sort of. I place slot machines in hotels and restaurants, and we share the profits."

Anna stopped eating. "I was afraid it was something like that."

"What? Why?" Morty asked.

"Don't play me, Morty," Anna said. "Remember the guy my uncle wanted me to marry? Did I say no to him because he's in the business, and not to you? The business with the gangs isn't safe. Stay out of it."

Morty stared at her. "Look, Anna. Maybe it's a little dangerous. But only a little. Nobody else is up here doing the business. It's good for the owners of the hotels too. They get a cut."

"It won't last. Sooner or later, there'll be some other gang wanting to have their slot machines in the hotels. And you'll be fighting for your life. Please, Morty, get out of this."

Morty sat quietly. He didn't know what to tell her. He remembered his conversation with Adler. He knew he couldn't get out of the business so easily. He was trying to figure out how he could escape, but he felt helpless. Maybe he knew too much, and they would never let him leave. He could run away, but then maybe they would find him. Rudy had told him that the bosses didn't ever forget if someone left them. They always settled their scores. The men who tried to get out were always a threat. Better they be silenced for good. Morty was afraid. He didn't know what else he could do but play along and keep his head down. Give them every penny they were supposed to get and look for an opportunity to get out.

"Could we talk about something else?" he asked. He reached out and took her hand, rubbed his finger against her palm.

She pulled her hand away. "You're giving me shivers."

He laughed. "Me too. Come here," he said. She slid closer to him and put her head on his shoulder, and he reached over and kissed her, lingering on her mouth. "Let's take a drive," he said. "It's really pretty around here on the back roads. I'll show you."

They got up and threw the remains of their lunch in the garbage pail. It was full to overflowing now. Then they got into the car.

Morty turned the ignition, looked at Anna out of the corner of his eye, and said, "Nice, isn't it?"

She nodded. He drove out of the parking lot and took the first turnoff from the highway, and they were on a road lined with fields and farms. There were tall silos beside barns, and houses with shaded front porches stood near the road. The pavement stopped, and the road turned to dirt, winding along fields lined with trees that were leafed out in their brightest greenery. Morty pulled off under one of the trees and turned the motor off. There were no houses around them, only empty fields, an empty road, and the quiet of the countryside.

He reached for her, and she came into his arms willingly. "I missed you so much, Anna. I can't stand not being around you." His lips slipped along her cheek and into her neck. His hands moved slowly down her shoulder and covered her breast.

She grabbed his hand as if to stop him. He ached with wanting. "Please, baby," he said. "We won't do anything you don't want. I promise. But I love you, Anna. I've loved you from the minute I first saw you at Solly's, remember?"

She nodded. "I love you too," she whispered. "Oh, Morty, what are we going to do?"

Without thinking, he said, "We'll get married. I want to marry you."

Anna sat back. "Marry me? You're serious?"

They stared at each other, laughing at the audacity of this. Morty nodded. "I love you, and I'm going to marry you."

She looked straight into his eyes. "Listen, Morty. I love you too. And I'll marry you. But you got to get out of this business. I told you I won't marry someone in the business."

Morty was quiet for a minute. His heart was pounding. Suddenly he believed with all his heart that if he got married, Adler would let him go. Why not? Hadn't Adler let the other guy leave? Al Satella? If he let him leave, why not Morty?

Morty pushed away the contradiction in the information Rudy had given him . . . that the gangs didn't let anyone leave them and that Adler had let Satella go. He figured there was a good reason, and Rudy wasn't around to ask anymore. "Okay, I'll leave. I want to get out anyway." He pulled Anna into his arms.

She leaned her head on Morty's shoulder, and soon they had climbed into the back seat of the car to make love. Afterward they began to plan. He would come down to Brooklyn next time, and he'd stay for good.

Morty went to Brooklyn the day after he collected the money from all the hotels and bars and restaurants. He drove straight down, three and a half hours, right at the speed limit so that no cops would stop him, and directly to Solly's, where he hoped he'd find Mickey Adler. If not, someone would get a message to him that Morty had a package. But he was in luck.

Adler was sitting in the back of Solly's, dealing cards with three of his men, smoke curling from the cigarettes dangling from the corners of their mouths.

Adler was surprised to see Morty but pleased when Morty gave him the envelope that was flush with summer gains from the vacationing guests at the hotels. This was the most lucrative season for slots and gambling in the Catskills.

The card game had paused. All three of the other players sat still, looking at Adler. Morty saw Little Jiggy, who sat opposite Adler, jouncing his leg up and down. And Frenchy LaPointe was there too. He glared at Morty.

Ah, Morty thought, *Frenchy never got over Anna's standing him up and going out with me.*

"You didn't have to come down," Adler said. "Fatty Frank was coming up tomorrow."

Morty nodded. "I know. But I need to see my mother. She isn't feeling so well."

Adler smiled. "I hope she feels better," he said. "But you can't stay down here and leave a hole in Liberty. There're people wanting to fill it."

"Yeah, I get it," Morty said. "I was just wondering if you could find someone else to be in Liberty."

"I thought we talked about this before," Adler said. "Why would I find someone else? You're doing a good job."

"My folks need me."

"For what?" Adler's cards were steady in his hand, fanned out perfectly. Now the three other players were looking at Morty.

"Help in the store." Morty could feel his voice faltering.

"You can give them money. Then they won't need help in the store."

Morty took a deep breath. "And I want to marry my girl."

Adler looked at his men. "Oh, the boy wants to get *married*." He drew out the word so that the other men laughed.

This was not going well, Morty knew. His face was flushed from the neck up. He felt hot, embarrassed.

"You got a wedding date or something?" Adler said finally.

This was a way out for the moment, Morty realized. "No. Nothing like that. I haven't even asked her yet," he lied.

"Oh well. Then we can talk about it when I come up to see you in Liberty." Adler took a card from his hand and threw it on the table. Then he said to the boys he was playing with, "You remember Al Satella? The guy that was up in Liberty before this one?" He nodded his head in Morty's direction.

"Oh, yeah. Whatever happened to him?" Little Jiggy asked.

"He's gone," Adler said. "He was married and wanted to go home for good, and no one ever saw him afterward. Wonder what happened to him." The card game resumed, the players mumbling something about how none of them had seen Al either. Morty knew he had been dismissed, and his stomach dropped as he thought about what had happened to Al Satella. As Morty started to walk away, Adler turned to him. "By the way, give my regards to your folks. Your father's store is on Pitkin, isn't it? I remember that one. He's doing better now than he did before—since you've been working with us. Say hello for me."

Morty's heart sank. This was bad. Mickey Adler did not trust him anymore. He knew where Ben's store was. It was a flat-out threat, and Morty was in trouble. He was going to have to figure out a way to get back in Adler's good graces—or run away.

Morty didn't go visit his family. He went straight to Tony's Deli, where he was sure Anna would be working. When he entered the store, he signaled her to meet him outside. He waited on the sidewalk, his stomach tight, his heart beating.

When Anna came outside, she took one look at Morty's face and said with alarm in her voice, "What's wrong?"

Morty took a big breath and, in a rush of words, told her what had happened at Solly's when he'd gone to talk to Mickey Adler. He was pacing up and down the sidewalk, and Anna took his arm and walked him around the block.

"I don't want my uncle to see us," she said. She didn't add that the rest of her family still didn't know anything about him, only her mother. Morty knew that was on her mind.

"It isn't going to work, my walking away from them. He even threatened me. Rudy told me that Adler let Al Satella walk away and go back to his wife, but now I know he was lying. Adler all but said Al was dead." Morty shivered.

"What did he say, exactly? They don't usually tell you someone is dead. They use other language."

"Yeah. Adler asked the guys if they remembered Al Satella, who was in Liberty before me. One of them asked what happened to him, and Adler said he was married and wanted to go home to his wife, but no one ever saw him again. And he wondered what happened to him." To Morty, as he repeated the words, they seemed even more ominous than they had the first time.

"I told you not to get mixed up with them. Why'd you ever get mixed up with them?"

Morty had never told Anna why he was working for Mickey Adler. Now he said, "I didn't want to do this. I did it to save my father and his store."

Anna stared at Morty; her mouth was open as Morty told her the whole story. "Why didn't you tell me? Maybe my uncle would have helped."

Morty shook his head. "I believed Rudy would help me. I thought I could rely on him. I never thought he would be killed."

"What are you going to do?"

"Go back upstate. And hope that Adler doesn't get it into his head that he can't trust me anymore."

Anna shook her head. "Oh, Morty. I don't know if I can do this. Be with you, marry you, worry all the time if you're going to be arrested or killed. I can't live like that. My mother did, and it almost killed her too. She's a nervous wreck."

Morty thought, *She breaks up with me, she gets back with me, she breaks up with me again. What is this?* But he said, "Anna, please. You can't break up with me now. I won't have anything."

She started walking, turned back to him, and said, "I love you, Morty. I'm not breaking up with you, but I need to think."

Morty started to walk after her, but she was already around the corner, and although he followed fast, by the time he caught up to her, she was almost at the deli, where her uncle Tony stood in the doorway looking in both directions. "Where the hell did you go?" Morty heard him exclaim as Anna walked inside. He didn't hear what excuse she gave.

Morty didn't know what to do. He walked around Brownsville and debated going to see his parents but knew there would only be grief as a result. He could wait until Anna was out of work, but he was afraid that she would give him a final no if he did. Instead, he got in his car and drove back to Liberty.

During the next week, Morty called Anna twice. Once her mother answered the phone, and Morty hung up. The next time Anna answered, and she agreed to meet him again at the Red Apple Rest the following Wednesday. When she came up this time, things were different. The mood was dark. Even the sky was cloudy and looked like it would rain.

She stepped off the bus but didn't walk into his arms the way she had the last time. She let him lean down and kiss her cheek but then began to walk to the car park.

"Let's take a drive," she said.

They drove in silence to the same road they had gone down last time, and Morty parked under the same tree. When he turned to face her, she wasn't looking at him. She was staring out the window.

"Do you have something you want to say to me?" he asked finally, breaking the silence.

"I can't do it, Morty. I remember too much. I loved my father. I was five years old when he was murdered. He was *murdered*, Morty." She kept talking and staring out the window. "He used to play with me when he was home. He'd toss me in the air when I was little, and when I got too big for that, he would dance with me to music on the gramophone. I would stand on his feet, and we would move around the living room in time to the songs that were playing. My mother would sit on the sofa and laugh at us. I don't think she really knew what was going on with him. Not then."

"Tell me again what happened to him."

"I don't know exactly," she said. "He used to run errands for my uncle and the Santoros—they're important in the neighborhood. They live down the block. But he wanted more . . . bigger stuff. Finally, my uncle got Harold Santoro to give him more work, and—it was during Prohibition, you know—he stole a couple of crates of whiskey and sold them on the side. The Santoros found out about it, and next thing he was found in an alleyway on Ebbets Avenue. Shot dead." Anna's voice was shaky. She couldn't look Morty in the eye. "We don't talk about it in my house, but I learned my lesson. It never ends well with the gangs. The guys all die young. It doesn't really matter what you do. A lot of things get you killed when you work for the mob. And you don't always know why. Sometimes you just do the wrong thing. Why was Rudy killed?"

Morty remembered what Adler had told him, but he thought it was better not to disclose Rudy's connections to Murder, Inc. He shrugged.

Anna nodded. "See, you don't even know. I remember how it was for my mother after my father was killed. She was like a zombie, and I don't want to be like that." Anna still wasn't looking at Morty.

Morty touched her shoulder. "Are you really going to leave me?"

Now she turned to face him. "I will if you don't leave them." Her eyes held his.

Morty moved toward her, took her shoulders, and pulled her into his arms. He began to kiss her, gently at first and then more passionately. Anna kissed him back, and there was a desperation in both of their mouths, in their bodies as they climbed over the front seat and fell into the back, in the way they tore off their clothes, in their moans and whispers, in their final coupling. Morty felt the satin of her skin, her perfume on his face. He moved his hands over her limbs, her breasts, her stomach, as if memorizing the geography of her body. He thought he must remember it forever.

Afterward, Anna sat up. She put on her panties and her bra and slipped her dress over her head—the yellow dress, now crumpled and creased. She took out a comb from her purse and pulled it through the tangles of her black hair. She took out a lipstick and slicked red on her mouth. Then she opened the door and walked to the front of the car. She leaned against it while Morty got dressed.

It was starting to rain when they drove back to the bus. He waited with her in silence for half an hour until the southbound bus arrived. He was surprised that they were both dry-eyed. Somehow, he thought they would be crying. When the bus pulled up, they got out of the car, and Morty walked her to the door. He was glad it was raining. They couldn't linger, or they would get soaked. He watched her climb the steps, walk to the back, and take a seat. She didn't look out the window. When the bus pulled out, he felt the wetness on his cheeks, and he wasn't sure if it was raindrops or tears.

Morty passed the time in a fog in the days after he left Anna. He bought some stationery and stamps and wrote her several letters, begging her not to leave him. Each day he searched frantically for a letter from her, but none came. He did his job, played in poker games that some of the hotels offered, and usually won. He began to hear rumors about gang violence in Brooklyn. Dead bodies in the streets of Brownsville.

One day in mid-August, Morty came home to Mrs. Stein's boarding house in time for the supper she served her boarders. He could smell delicious roast potatoes and sweet carrots and a thick soup bubbling on the stovetop. He wondered if there would be any meat tonight. The table was set with cutlery and plates for Morty and the other boarder, who worked at the desk of the Liberty Hotel and who was already sitting and eating. Morty nodded to him and was about to take his chair when Mrs. Stein said, "There's a man waiting for you in the parlor."

Morty felt his stomach tighten, his heart bump. "Who?" he asked.

"He didn't say. Go talk to him. I'll keep your food warm."

Morty nodded and walked into the parlor. It was a small room, filled with big stuffed furniture, and the curtains were always drawn, because Mrs. Stein said the sunlight faded the material on her chairs. She was very proud of the furniture in the parlor and didn't let the boarders use it except on special occasions. Morty figured this must be special. A small lamp in the corner shed a bloom of light around its base, casting everything else in shadows. On the sofa a very tall, lanky man sat, dressed in a suit and tie. He held his brown fedora in his lap. He unfolded himself and stood when Morty walked into the room.

"Morton Feinstein?" The man's voice was deep and resonant. He sounded like a professor or something, Morty thought.

"Yeah, that's me. Who are you?"

"Patrick Hanrahan, federal officer." He flashed a badge and slipped it back into his pocket.

The badge had come and gone so fast Morty could barely see it. "Let me see that again," he said. Hanrahan took the badge out of his pocket and held it steady for Morty to look at it.

Morty could see the initials, the name. It looked real enough, but he couldn't be sure. It could be fake. "What do you want?"

"Do you know Mickey Adler or Rudy Schmidt?"

Morty hesitated. "Why do you care?"

Hanrahan put his hat on the table beside the sofa and sat down. "Sit," he said.

Without thinking, Morty sat down, then immediately felt ashamed of himself. Who was this guy to tell him what to do? He felt like jumping up again, but he didn't. He clamped his mouth shut and vowed not to say anything else.

But it wasn't so easy to be quiet. The questions started easily enough, and Morty couldn't see the harm in answering them. Questions like where did he live in New York, was he a student at Polytech, did his father own a repair shop? Each time a question came, Morty nodded or shook his head. Soon, though, the questions got too complicated for Morty to answer with a shake or nod of his head.

"What are you doing up here, Mr. Feinstein?"

Morty swallowed. "Working."

"At what?"

Morty jumped up. "Look, mister, I don't have to answer all these questions, and I'm not going to answer them."

"Calm down and sit down. I'll explain."

Morty sat again. Hanrahan began talking in a slow, deliberate voice. He knew, he said, about the slot machines, about the money the owners of the businesses that housed them paid to Morty, and he knew the money went to the gang run by Mickey Adler. He held his hand up to quiet Morty when he seemed about to speak. Everything was illegal, he said.

"You read the papers?" he asked. "You know there's a gang war in Brownsville. Dead bodies around every corner. There are rumors that Benjy Molino's gang is coming up here. Mickey Adler has competition. You're going to be in trouble." Hanrahan was silent for a time.

Morty thought of what Anna had told him, the warning she'd given him that there would be fights between the gangs. Everyone wanted in on the money.

Hanrahan finally spoke. "We're going to be shutting down everything up here. Arresting everyone . . . unless they work with us. We figured you're one of the smart ones—a college boy. Work with us, and we'll protect you."

"I don't think so," he said. "No one gets protection from the gangs." He rose from his seat and turned to leave the room.

"You're wrong. We can protect you. Give you cover, a new identity," Hanrahan said. "I'll be back next week. You should think about what I said. Work with us, and we'll keep you out of jail and alive." He took out his wallet and held out a card. "Take this. It has my number on it. You can call me if you change your mind."

Morty pocketed the card, turned, and started to walk out of the parlor when he thought of something. He faced Hanrahan. "Wait a minute. I want to ask you something. Do you know the name Al Satella?"

Hanrahan was quiet and looked hard at Morty. "I do. Why?"

"What happened to him?"

"We found his body a few months ago, riddled with bullets. Under the El on Avenue J."

Morty stood still. He could hear his heart thudding in his ears. Al Satella dead under the El. Riddled with bullets. He felt his body sway. "Would you wait here a minute?" he asked, his voice shaky.

"Sure," Hanrahan said.

Morty ran upstairs to his bedroom, opened the closet, and took out the paper bag on the top shelf behind his suitcase. The bag felt heavy. He hadn't touched it since he had put it in the closet at the beginning of the summer.

Hanrahan was standing just where Morty left him.

"I don't know if I should be doing this," Morty said. "It may be a mistake."

Hanrahan shrugged. "You won't know until you do it."

Morty nodded and handed the paper bag to Hanrahan. "I never touched it. He left it in the glove compartment of the car he gave me. I took it out with my handkerchief and put it in the paper bag and hid it."

Hanrahan opened the bag, glanced inside, and nodded. "Who gave it to you?"

"Mickey Adler."

"Did he say anything else?"

"Ha," Morty said. "He didn't even tell me that he left it for me in the glove compartment. He offered it to me before he brought the car, but I wouldn't take it. Then when he left me the car, I checked the glove box and there it was. I just want to get rid of it. And I never touched it."

Hanrahan nodded. "It's probably wiped clean of prints anyway. But maybe we can tie it to some crime. We'll see. It's good that you gave me this. It shows me you're smart. That you want out. I'm telling you I can help."

Morty shook his head. "Listen," he said. "Just take that package. That's all I got to say." He didn't even say goodbye. He left the parlor, went into the kitchen, and sat down to supper. He had no appetite, but he picked up his soup spoon anyway. His brain was racing. He had a week to decide. What was he going to do? The future was waiting for Morty to choose. Hanrahan had held out one future to him. Safety, a new identity, a way out of the tight spot he was in. He wondered if they would give a new identity to Anna if he could persuade her to come with him. He knew that if he didn't choose, life would choose for him. It always did. The way he saw it, he still had time to decide. And maybe giving the gun to Hanrahan had sealed his fate anyway.

He could run. He had the car. He could drive it to another big city, like Chicago. Sell it. Take the money and hightail it to California or Mexico. Somewhere far away. For a minute he let himself drift on a daydream of warm sunny skies, endless summers. But it felt too big and lonely. All his life he'd been surrounded by people, and sometimes he'd felt suffocated, but he didn't know if he could stand being alone. And was anything far enough away for him to escape the network of snitches and hangers-on who populated the reach of the gang's businesses?

He knew one thing. He couldn't go back to Brooklyn, tell Adler what he'd learned from Hanrahan, and throw himself on the mercy of Adler and his boys. He didn't trust Adler anymore. To Adler, Morty was expendable, a nothing. And Morty didn't owe Adler anything.

Or he could join the army. The posters were everywhere. Lots of people were saying there would be war in Europe soon. Morty thought that might be a way out. If he drove far away, joined up, used another name, he would be safe. He was sure of that. None of Adler's boys would join up. They would never find him.

But then, if the gangs couldn't find him, there was no chance Anna, or his family, would ever find him either. Could he bear it if he left the gangs but never saw them again?

Each choice would take him, he knew, to a different future. And not choosing would take him someplace else. Nothing was clear.

Morty went about his business for a few days after Hanrahan came to see him. He was collecting, going from hotel to restaurant to hotel to pick up the cash the managers owed. When he got to Albie's

Diner, the owner, Albie himself, pulled Morty aside and took him into the kitchen.

"You got competition," he said. He sounded casual, like he was talking about the weather.

"What do you mean?" Morty tried to make his voice hard.

"A guy came. His name is Jake Gold. He's going around to all the other restaurants and hotels too."

Morty tried to look calm. His palms were sweaty. His heart was beating hard. "Who does he work for?"

"He said the message was from Benjy Molino."

Morty knew the name, Benjy Molino. That Hanrahan guy had mentioned it when they'd talked three days before. Molino came from over on the Italian side of Bushwick. He wondered if Anna knew him, who he was. "Okay," Morty said. "Thanks for the heads-up."

He took the cash Albie offered him and walked out of the diner. Suddenly, the sunshine and the quiet of the streets seemed menacing. He found himself glancing around and looking for Jake Gold, but of course, he didn't know who Jake was.

He walked in a daze. So, the rumors were true. Hanrahan had been right, and Anna. Did Adler know about Benjy Molino, about this Jake Gold, whoever he was, coming up to Liberty and starting a competing business? Well, there was no room for competition up here. Only one slots business could operate in such a small place. Which meant—what? Tell Hanrahan what he knew? Call Adler?

If he called Adler, he would be up here in a flash with a couple of his guys, and there would, for sure, be war. The competition would be dead in the water. And maybe if he called Adler, he would be dead too—killed by this Jake Gold or someone else like him.

But if he called Hanrahan and told him he had heard the Molino gang was already up in the Catskills, about the likelihood of a gang war, he would be a snitch . . . the absolute worst person in the world of the rackets. He would have a target on his back, and he could never come home.

Morty ducked into his car and drove around thinking. Finally, he drove to Loch Sheldrake, where he found a telephone booth on an empty corner and called Adler to give him the news.

"Shit," Adler said. "They're butting in around here too. You lie low. Don't do anything to call attention to yourself. I'm coming up this afternoon with a few guys, and we'll deal with him."

After he hung up, Morty took out the card from his pocket with Patrick Hanrahan's phone number on it and stared at it for a long time. Was there any harm in calling him? What would he want from Morty—what could Morty tell him that would be of value to the law? And if he did tell him anything, could Hanrahan help him get away from the gangs, get to Anna, his parents?

He stared at the card in his hand and thought about making that one more call. He did want to know something that only Hanrahan could tell him. Had the gun planted in his car by Mickey Adler been used in any other crimes? He made the call.

Hanrahan seemed happy to hear from Morty. "I'm glad you called. Did you change your mind?"

Morty hesitated. "I wanted to know if that gun I gave you was— you know—associated with any other crimes."

"Yes. It was used in at least two other murders besides Al Satella's. I was going to come up and tell you about it."

"Don't bother. The word is that the Molino gang is already up here. I don't know what I'm going to do."

"Come in. I'll protect you. We can make all that illegal activity you're involved with up there go away. Otherwise you're on our wanted list." Hanrahan's voice drifted off.

"Wanted for what?"

"Racketeering. Illegal gambling. Extortion. Not to mention that the gun you had in your possession was a murder weapon. We can arrest you on all those charges, or you can come in and work with us."

Morty was tied up in knots. The gun was dirty. There was a list of crimes they could pin on him. And Mickey Adler would be up here today. There was nothing more to say. He hung up the phone, put the card back in his wallet, and drove away. He knew what he had to do.

In his room, from the drawer that held his underwear and socks, he pulled out the wad of money he had collected that morning. What should he do with it? If he took it with him, he'd be a mark for Mickey. A thief. He took an envelope and a piece of stationery, then wrote the date and the names of the businesses he'd collected from and the amounts of money in a list. He wrapped the bills in the paper, put it in an envelope, and addressed it to Mickey Adler, c/o Solly's Corner Candy Store. He stamped the letter and put it in his pocket. He took another sheet of stationery and wrote a brief letter to his father, stuck it in an envelope addressed to his store on Pitkin Avenue, and stamped it. He would just catch the morning mail pickup if he got to the post office now. He left his room and went out to mail both letters.

It was a beautiful day, mid-September, still sunny and warm and light, when he went to the town center and dropped the letters at the post office. Then he went to Albie's Diner and ordered a turkey sandwich and a Coke. He sat at the counter and made his plans. He hadn't taken more than two bites when Albie cleared his throat and pointed with his chin to the door. Morty looked up. But it was too late.

Behind him stood two thugs, one on each side of him. One put his hand on Morty's shoulder, pressing down hard. "Hiya," he said. "Morty, isn't it?"

Morty's heart jumped. "Yeah," he said, turning his head to look up. "You are?"

"I'm Jake. Let's go for a walk, okay?"

Morty looked up and tried to catch Albie's eye, but Albie had turned his back; he was drying some glasses and putting them away, showing only his burly back to Morty, so Morty rose and walked out with the two men, propelled by their grips on his arm.

Outside, they marched him around the corner to an empty lot and pushed him against the back wall of the building. Jake frisked him, but since Morty never had a gun or a knife, he said, "I'm not carrying."

"Yeah, that's a good thing." He patted Morty's pockets and lifted out the billfold that Morty had bought when he first started to work with Rudy. He took out the money, put it in his pocket, and seemed about to toss the billfold when he looked at it again. "Nice leather," he said. Morty looked regretfully at the wallet. When he bought it, he had his name stamped on the inside.

Easy come, easy go, he thought. "Keep it," Morty said. "A present." He hoped his bravado sounded real. "But could I have my driver's license?"

"Sure thing," Jake said. He opened the wallet and rummaged through it.

Morty saw the identification card with his name and address under a piece of plastic. His license was in the billfold part of the wallet. "It's in with the money," Morty said. Jake found it and gave it to him.

"Thanks," Morty said and looked directly into Jake's eyes. They were almost the same height.

Jake put the billfold in his jacket pocket and continued patting Morty down. The car keys bulged in Morty's pocket. "Nice," Jake said. "Where's the car parked? What kind of car?"

Morty hesitated. It wasn't his car, it was Adler's. Morty took a breath and answered. "Around the corner, in front of Mrs. Stein's boarding house—a Chevy, black," he said as fast as he could.

"That's good," Jake said. "Now you can go home, pack up your bags, and get the hell outta here. If I see you around tomorrow . . ." He let his voice fade. "Got it?"

Morty nodded. He pulled away from the man who was holding his arm and walked down the street. Trying to project strength, he walked fast, hoping to push down the panic. He glanced at his watch. If Adler had left even an hour after he spoke to Morty, he could be up here in another two hours. By two thirty.

In his room at Mrs. Stein's, he threw some of his clothes in a rucksack he had bought for hiking on the trails, and he left the battered suitcase he had used when he left Brooklyn along with some of his clothes in the closet and drawers—as if he were coming back soon. With regret, he remembered that his favorite leather jacket, a sharp one that he had bought and wore constantly, was in his car. That was gone. Probably Jake would be wearing it from now on. They were about the same size.

He took fifty dollars that he had kept in a pair of black socks and two days' worth of underwear and socks. He owed Mrs. Stein five dollars, but he didn't have the change. He stuffed all the money in his pocket, took an old jacket and the rucksack, and almost ran down the stairs and out the front door. The car was already gone.

It was now about one o'clock. Morty hoped he could grab a bus before Adler arrived. Let him deal with Jake Gold and Benji Molino. He walked fast to the bus depot, trying not to be noticed by any of the passersby. But just as he was nearing the bus depot, Bob Roth, the guy who owned the candy store and who sold him cigarettes, saw him and came up to him.

"Hi, Morty. Where you off to?"

Morty thought fast. "Got to drop this rucksack here with the ticket guy. Friend of mine is picking it up. I'll be in later to get some cigarettes. I'm almost out."

Bob looked at him for a long minute. "Okay. See you later." Bob walked on, and Morty hurried into the small depot, where he bought a ticket on the next bus out, leaving at two o'clock for Cincinnati. He took a deep breath. That was cutting it close. Adler could be here by then if he had left right after their phone call.

He sat down in the waiting room and jiggled his leg. Kept looking at his watch. At two thirty the bus hadn't arrived. Morty went up to the booth. "Is the bus usually on time?"

The guy in the ticket booth shrugged. "Sometimes yes, sometimes no. Depends on traffic, weather. Looks like the Cincinnati bus is a little late. Usually not much more than half an hour."

Morty nodded and went back to the bench—and prayed the bus came before Mickey Adler did.

PART FOUR

1940–1942

CHAPTER 30

SYLVIA

In early September, Sylvia found a letter in a lavender envelope, addressed to her and stuck in the mailbox. It was from someone called Anna DeMaio, who asked her to meet her downstairs on Saturday morning. Sylvia was not sure who this Anna was, and she waited outside early that day in front of her apartment building until she came down the block.

As soon as Anna walked toward her, Sylvia remembered seeing her with Morty in the spring. Now she stared at the tall woman with long black hair and deep-set violet eyes. She looked like the movie star Hedy Lamarr, Sylvia thought. Beautiful, like a model.

Anna stopped in front of Sylvia, then stepped closer and said, "Are you Sylvia?"

Sylvia nodded.

"I'm Anna DeMaio. I'm looking for Morty Feinstein. Do you know where he is?"

Sylvia squinted. Her heart hammered. "He's gone. He went upstate at the beginning of the summer, but I haven't seen him. I had one letter in July, but nothing since."

"He's not upstate anymore," Anna said. "His landlady said he was gone." She hesitated. "If you see him or hear from him, would you tell him Anna came by?"

Sylvia stood, heart beating. She wondered what Anna was to Morty. Maybe she should ask her what she wanted to tell him? She took in the girl, admired the blue striped skirt she wore, the white blouse and flat black patent leather slippers. Her skirt had pockets, and her right hand was tucked in one of them.

"I have a note here for him," Anna said. From her pocket she took out a small lavender envelope, like the one she had left in the mailbox for Sylvia. "Will you give it to him?"

Sylvia nodded and stretched out her hand. "If I see him, I will." She took the envelope and looked at it. "Morty Feinstein" was printed in capital letters on the front of the envelope. In the corner was a return address: 138 Hull Street, Ocean Hill, Brooklyn, New York.

"Okay. Okay then," Anna said and turned to go. "Thank you. I'll see you. Don't forget to give it to him. It's important." She walked a few steps down the block and turned. "Could you tell me when you give it to him? We have a phone. Our telephone number is in the phone book under P. DeMaio. Could you call when he gets it?"

Sylvia was impressed that Anna's family had their own phone in the house. *They must be rich*, she thought. She nodded again and said she would call if she was able to give the note to Morty. She watched Anna walk to the end of the block. At the corner Anna turned toward her and waved, then went around the block so Sylvia couldn't see her anymore.

Sylvia held the envelope in her hand. She wished she knew where Morty was. The whole family had received letters from Morty in July. They'd all written back, but none of them had heard from him again.

Golda had been complaining about it all summer. "Why doesn't he answer our letters?" she asked many times.

"He said he couldn't tell us where he was or what he was doing," Ben answered.

"Why not? What is he doing he can't tell us? And he left school. All our hard work and money and he just leaves it." Golda was angry. Sylvia could see she was working herself up as she talked. "I scrimped, put away money, didn't buy clothes for me or Sylvia. Why? Why did I do that? A waste." Her face was red. "He said in the letter he's in business. What kind of business can he be in in Liberty? What's in Liberty?"

"Hotels," Ben said. "Nice hotels where people go for vacation. Shows, entertainment, gambling."

Golda whirled and stared at Ben. "So that's it. He's gambling. He always loved to play cards, him and that Rudy. I can't believe it. I knew Rudy would get him in trouble. No wonder he was killed."

Ben said nothing, just shook his head.

After a minute Golda said, through clenched teeth, "I don't care if I ever see him again."

Sylvia's mouth dropped open. "What? How can you say that, Mama?"

"How?" Her words came out clipped and angry. "He ruined my life, that's how." And that was all she would say.

Ben looked at her with bleak eyes and said nothing.

After that, there was a stillness in the house, as if a curtain had fallen between her mother and father. They barely spoke to one another. Their conversations consisted of requests to pass the salt at dinner and questions about when Ben would be home.

Now, holding the lavender envelope in her hand, Sylvia wondered if she should open it and find out what was so important that Anna DeMaio had left this for him. But it was his letter. Sylvia didn't think she should open it. When she went up to the apartment, she put the letter carefully in her bureau drawer, tucked under her socks, and prayed she would hear from Morty so she could give it to him.

In mid-October, Sylvia was sitting at the kitchen table doing homework. As a college English major, she had a lot of reading to do. Her father was at work. Her mother was in the kitchen making supper. The doorbell rang.

Golda said, "Go, look and see who is there."

Sylvia went to the door and looked out the peephole. "It's a man, Mama," she said. "I don't know who he is." The man was tall, wearing a dark suit and tie and a brown fedora. "Should I open it?"

Her mother came out of the kitchen, wiping her hands on a dishtowel. She smoothed her hair, moved Sylvia aside, and opened the door but kept the chain on. "Yes?"

"Mrs. Feinstein?" The man's voice was deep. "I'm Patrick Hanrahan, a federal officer. May I speak with you?"

Golda hesitated. Her face was drained of color. "What about?"

"Please open the door, Mrs. Feinstein. I have to speak with you."

Golda took a breath, unfastened the chain, and opened the door, but she blocked the way with her sturdy body. She had been making dinner when the man knocked, and she wore an apron that covered her weekday brown dress. Even though it was October, it was a very warm fall day, and it was hot in the apartment; the short-sleeved dress left her upper arms bare.

The man removed his hat. "May I come in?"

Golda did not move. "What is this about?"

"I'm afraid I have bad news . . ." He waited. Golda said nothing. "It's about your son."

Golda still said nothing.

"Morton. Your son, Morton Feinstein."

There was a long silence, and then Golda said, "What son?"

"I'm speaking of Morton Feinstein," the detective said. "I believe he is your son. I am sorry to report his death, but we only recently identified him. Now we can release his body to you for burial."

Golda was shaking her head. There was a long silence. The man waited. Golda finally said, her voice choking, "How did this Morton Feinstein die?"

"It seems he was involved with illegal activity. Gangs."

"Gangs? My son was not involved with gangs. If this boy was killed by gangs, he's not my son. Do what you want with the body."

Sylvia's mouth was open. She could hardly stand. She leaned against the wall and tried to catch her breath. What did her mother mean, he was not her son? Of course he was. But Golda was rigid, her mouth set in a tight line. Her eyes were bright, and she stared into the distance at the hallway behind Detective Hanrahan. Sylvia thought there were tears brimming in her mother's eyes, and if she blinked, they would roll down her cheeks. She reached out to touch her mother's arm, to comfort her, but Golda shrugged Sylvia's hand away.

"Please, Mrs. Feinstein," the man said. The whole time they were speaking, the man remained in the hallway. "Let me come in and talk to you. Don't you want to know . . . ?"

"No!" Golda shouted. "I don't want to know." She slammed the door shut, took two ragged breaths, straightened up, and walked into the kitchen. Sylvia heard the pots clanking. She ran into the kitchen and said, "Mama, why didn't you let him come in and tell us what happened to Morty?"

Golda said through clenched teeth, "I don't want to know what happened to this gangster. He can't be Morty. He can't be. Don't speak of him to me again."

Sylvia's insides were churning. "What's the matter with you?"

Golda did not turn around, did not answer her. Sylvia turned and ran out of the apartment, dashing down the stairs to find Detective Hanrahan.

She caught up with him on the street. "Detective Hanrahan," she called. He turned. "I'm Sylvia Feinstein, Morty's sister. I don't know why my mother said that. Please tell me what happened."

Hanrahan faced her. "How old are you?" he asked.

Sylvia knew she looked young for her age. She was short and she seldom wore makeup, except when she and Frieda went out to the movies or to one of the dances in the gym at Brooklyn College. She supposed he wanted to make sure she was old enough to hear what he was going to tell her. "I'm nineteen. I go to Brooklyn College."

He nodded. "Okay. Then you must know your brother was involved with the rackets upstate."

Sylvia kept quiet. She didn't really know what Morty was involved in, but she nodded as if she did.

"Slot machines and gambling. Another gang wanted to come up and take over the business, and we believe he was killed in a gang fight. His body was dumped in the woods. It was found almost two months later, and I'm afraid it was in bad shape. Decomposed."

Sylvia felt faint. She could barely stand. "How can you be sure it's him? Are you sure it's him?"

"He was wearing a leather jacket with his name in it. His billfold with an identity card was in his pocket. His car keys were there too. We're sure. I'm sorry."

Sylvia swallowed the bile that had come up her throat. "My father will be home soon. I'm sure he'll want to talk to you. How can he reach you? He'll feel differently from my mother. I know he'll want to get the body."

Detective Hanrahan rummaged in his pocket and handed her his card as he thanked her. He seemed about to leave, but he paused. "There's a lot of local interest in this from the papers. The *Brooklyn Eagle* and the *Daily News* particularly. Don't be surprised if they come for an interview."

Sylvia nodded, turned, and walked back home.

When Ben came home from work, Sylvia waited a few minutes for her mother to tell him about Detective Hanrahan, but Golda said nothing. Sylvia stood up. "Mama, you have to tell Papa about the detective."

"What detective?" Ben asked.

Golda glared at Sylvia but didn't answer.

"What detective, Sylvia?" Ben asked again.

"Detective Hanrahan," Sylvia answered. "He came to tell us Morty was dead. He said, 'Morton Feinstein.'"

The room was silent. Papa stared with his mouth open. "When?"

"This afternoon," Sylvia whispered. Sylvia handed her father Detective Hanrahan's card. "Mama said she had no son."

Golda stared ahead, not looking at either of them. "I said if he was a gangster, he wasn't my son. They offered his body. I said no."

Ben stood, and the chair fell backward. "How could you say that? How?" His face grew red, his eyes bulged in rage, and his voice shook. "Morty is your son, your boy. You raised him from an infant. How could you deny him like that? You wouldn't let your sister's body be in a pauper's grave, but your son . . ."

"Not my son! Gangs! He was involved in gangs."

"Yes, your son!"

Golda was weeping. "He's not my son! He disgraced us. Fooled us. A gangster. Wasted our hopes and all the money we scrimped and saved. I gave up my life for him. And for what? For him to be a big-shot gangster?" Her sobs interrupted her words. "How will I face my neighbors?"

"You're worried about that? About what people say? What do we care? When our son, our only son, is dead." He went to the door.

"Where are you going?" Golda asked.

"I'm going to call this detective and bring my boy's body home."

Golda remained at the table, shaking her head back and forth, repeating over and over, "He's not my son. My son wouldn't be involved in gangs. Not my son." Sylvia did not know what to do, so she sat there quietly. Somehow, the more Golda said it, the more Sylvia believed her mother loved Morty beyond anything in the world.

CHAPTER 31

GOLDA

Ben didn't come home that night. Golda thought that he must have gone up to Liberty to collect Morty's body. All the while her mind was in turmoil; memories crowded her brain. Morty as an infant, his sweet milk breath, the blue of his eyes that fixed on her face, just like Esther's. She had not loved him at first. He had been the cause of her sister's death and the reason she had given up her dream of an independent life. But he had been irresistible. His brilliance, the sweetness of his smile, the way he reached for her when he woke from his nap and nestled his head on her chest. Despite herself, she knew she had loved him.

When he was so sick with the flu, she had hovered over him, even neglecting Isaac, who had seemed fine until the last day of his life. Morty had made her proud with his accomplishments in school, with the way he treated his sister. And now this. What had turned him? She couldn't fathom it, and she couldn't forgive him for it.

The next day she sat in the parlor with Sylvia, waiting for Ben to return. They didn't speak. Sylvia tried to read. Golda held her embroidery in her lap but didn't make a stitch.

Late in the afternoon, the doorbell rang. Golda got up and answered the door. This time she opened it without the chain. A man wearing a jacket and a hat and holding a camera stood behind a young woman wearing a green dress and a matching hat. She held a pad. The woman spoke first and very quickly.

"Mrs. Feinstein, my name is Edith Sperling. I'm a reporter with the *Brooklyn Eagle*, and we'd like to interview you about your son, whose body was found upstate—"

Golda interrupted her. "He's not my son."

"What do you mean? Isn't your son Morton Feinstein?" she persisted.

"My son wouldn't be in a gang. He was a good boy. And then this? You think he let us scrimp and save to send him to Polytech College so he could be an engineer, and then he left school and became a criminal? No, not my boy. That's not my son." The words poured out of her, as if she had prepared a speech. They surprised even Golda.

The reporter wanted to ask her more questions, but Golda became very agitated. "That's all I have to say. Nothing else. No picture," she insisted as the photographer raised his camera. She slammed the door in their faces. She walked back to the sofa, sat down, and began to cry. Sylvia took her in her arms and tried to comfort her.

Golda kept murmuring, "It can't be Morty. It can't be." There were pictures in her head, things she would have thought she had forgotten, but they bubbled up and filled her with longing and sorrow. The first time she looked down at the newborn baby, his face calm and beautiful in sleep. His first smile. His first toddling steps. How quickly he learned to speak. All the milestones in his life. How he cared for Isaac and then Sylvia. Golda shook her head, walked around the living room, sat down again.

Still Ben did not come home. Golda wondered if there would be a story in the newspaper. The next day, she sent Sylvia down to buy the *Brooklyn Eagle*. Sylvia brought the newspaper upstairs and handed it to her mother. On page three was a small story with no photo. Golda read it quickly.

Date: October 12, 1940

MOTHER SPURNS RACKETEER SON SLAIN IN GANG WAR
by Edith Sperling
SLOT MACHINE WAR

A boy's best friend may be his mother, but even she is justified in forsaking him when he takes up a life of crime. This was the attitude of Mrs. Benjamin Feinstein when police asked her if she wished to claim the body of Morton Feinstein, slain racketeer whom they believe is her son, from its temporary resting place in a Liberty, New York morgue.

Feinstein, a slot machine manipulator who made thousands weekly for the syndicate, was murdered in a gang war feud in which others were also wounded.

Mrs. Feinstein said, "If this boy was a gangster, he was not my son. I don't know who this body is, but I don't care. I don't consider him my son." Mrs. Feinstein has no interest in claiming the body of Morton Feinstein.

Golda held the paper, limp in her shaking hands. The story shamed her. How could she have said that to the reporter? Had she really said that? Where was Ben? Would he ever forgive her? How had their lives turned out like this? She sat on the sofa, staring at nothing, and waited for her husband to come home.

CHAPTER 32

BEN

When Ben left the apartment after hearing of the visit of Detective Hanrahan, he went directly to a pay phone, called the number on the card Sylvia had given him, and asked for the detective. After a brief conversation, they agreed to meet the next day and drive together to Liberty to arrange for the retrieval of Morton's body.

After he hung up the phone, Ben stood outside the phone booth almost paralyzed with indecision. Where should he go? His stomach clenched, and his heart hammered with the thought of going back to his apartment and listening to Golda. Her words reverberated in his head even now: "He's not my son, not my son." Ben did not think he could face her right now.

He could go to Rabbi Levy's house. Perhaps that would calm him. He could ask for advice, but then he would have to tell the rabbi how his poor Morty had been forced to work for the hoodlums because of Ben's own mistakes and actions . . . his stupidity in getting into debt with the wrong people, and then his inability to get himself out of debt without Morty involving himself with Rudy, who was a criminal. The shame of that washed over him. Ben felt directly responsible for Morty's death.

The only place he could think of as a refuge was Cousin Surah's apartment. He turned and trudged there through the twilight of the October evening. He walked up the familiar stairs in her apartment building, smelling the familiar smells, remembering how, when Golda first came to America, he had brought her and his newborn son from the boat to Cousin Surah's house, and how she had helped him.

When he knocked on the door, Cousin Surah answered, greeting him warmly. The smells of supper cooking, soup and bread, enveloped him. He had been hungry when he went to his apartment, anticipating supper with Golda and Sylvia, but now the smell of food nauseated him. He could not put a morsel in his mouth. He could not help himself; as soon as he looked at her welcoming face, he began to cry.

"What is it, Ben?" she asked. She reached out and took him in her arms. Ben was crying so hard he could not speak. She walked with him to the parlor and sat him on the sofa. She brought him a glass of water. She sat beside him and held his hand while he tried to compose himself.

When he caught his breath, she repeated her question. "What is the matter, Ben?"

"It's Morty. A detective came to the house when I was at work and told Golda and Sylvia that . . . that Morty . . . is dead." He stuttered over the words, reluctant to allow them to be heard.

Cousin Surah gasped. "What happened?"

Ben did not know where to begin, but he thought he could only begin at the beginning, when he had needed money and made the mistake of going to the loan shark. The story spilled out. Ben stumbled in the telling; in fits and starts, he went from event to event. Morty borrowing from Rudy, promising to work for him. Rudy's murder. The demand from Rudy's boss that Morty go to Liberty to work for him. Morty's fear that he couldn't say no. How they had not heard from him for months until this detective came to tell them that Morty was dead.

Ben was silent then. It was not exactly true that they hadn't heard from Morty. He had heard from him, just two months before. A brief letter had come to his store, saying only that Morty was leaving Liberty and going someplace no one could find him—not the gangs, not the law, no one. Ben had not known what to make of the letter. He hadn't even told Golda about it. He didn't mention it to Surah either. What difference did it make, if Morty was dead now?

Somehow, Ben felt this was the easier part of the story. He could hardly speak when he reported how Golda had told him she did not want to retrieve Morty's body and insisted over and over that he was not her son. At the end he was sobbing again.

"She said that? He's not her son?"

Ben nodded. "I'm going to Liberty with this detective . . . his name is Hanrahan . . . and I will get his body and bring it back for burial in a Jewish cemetery. And we will sit shiva."

Cousin Surah patted his hand. "Do you need help with that? Retrieving the body. Finding a plot to bury him?" She was quiet for a minute. "Maybe Rabbi Levy could help. Just like with Esther."

Ben nodded. It was not lost on him the similarity here. The mother about to be buried in a pauper's grave. A Christian grave. And now her son had met the same fate. Ben took a cup of tea and a slice of bread, all he could swallow, and asked Cousin Surah if he could sleep at her house that night. He could not go home and see Golda now. Cousin Surah agreed, and Ben made plans to visit the rabbi first thing in the morning before he went to meet Detective Hanrahan. When it was time to go to bed, Ben lay on the sofa but could not close his eyes. Each time he did, he heard Golda's voice hammering in his head: "Not my son, not my son."

Rabbi Levy was happy to see Ben that morning, but not when he heard the story that Ben told him. This was a terrible outcome. The rabbi tried to comfort Ben and told him that when he brought the body back, he would help him bury his son near Esther's grave. Ben could barely speak. He thanked the rabbi, got up, and went to meet the detective.

Detective Hanrahan drove Ben to Liberty, and while Ben listened in perfect silence, he recited how they had discovered Morty's body almost two months after he had been murdered. It had been found in the bushes near Kiamesha Lake by a man walking his dog in the vicinity. He had gone to investigate an unusual odor and come upon the body. It had been impossible to identify because of the time it had been out in the sun, ravaged by insects and animals. Even his fingerprints were undecipherable, however the clothing and the contents of his pockets had helped with the identification. They were set to bury the body in a pauper's grave in the Christian cemetery, but Detective Hanrahan believed that he and Ben were in time to stop that from happening.

He was wrong. The body was already buried, and Ben had to get a judge to approve the exhumation. In the two days it took to arrange for the body to be exhumed, Ben walked around Liberty, trying to find out as much about Morty's life there as he could. He visited Mrs. Stein, the landlady, who had put his remaining possessions in the valise still in his room and was glad to return the items to Ben. She told him how much she liked Morty. "A very polite young man," she said.

Ben talked to the man in the candy store, who told him he thought Morty had gotten on a bus to go somewhere because he had seen him entering the bus terminal with a rucksack, and although Morty had told him he would be in later for cigarettes, he never came. "He told me a cock-and-bull story about leaving the rucksack for a friend . . . why would he do that? He could have left it with his landlady. I didn't believe him. I thought he'd hightailed it on the first bus he could get."

Ben met Albie, who told him about the guys who had taken Morty out of the sandwich shop that day in August. "But they let him go. I saw him walk past the window after a few minutes."

All of this made Ben question whether Morty really was dead, and he shared the information with Detective Hanrahan; he even told him about the note he had received stating that Morty was leaving Liberty and going into hiding.

"He must have been murdered right after he mailed that letter," Hanrahan said. "Because remember, we found his body."

Ben nodded. But he couldn't put his doubts to rest, and he mentioned them to the reporter from the *Daily News* who came to interview him about Morty's death. "I am not entirely sure that is my son, because the candy store owner told me he saw him go into the bus depot days before he was supposed to be murdered." He saw the reporter taking notes.

Still, the police had identified the body as Morty's. What else could Ben do but take the coffin with the remains they said were Morty's and go back to Brooklyn to bury him?

The article was published in the *Daily News* on the day Ben arrived back in Brooklyn after an absence of three days. It read:

Date: October 20, 1940

FATHER MOURNS SON, YET HOPES HE LIVES

FEINSTEIN, BURYING BODY IDENTIFIED AS SON, IS NOT SURE THE BODY OF MAN IS HIS SON

Benjamin Feinstein, mechanic, is about to begin a seven-day period of Orthodox Jewish mourning for his son, Morton Feinstein, although he is not certain his son is dead. He collected the body, said to be the son, when the police told him they had identified the body as Morton Feinstein. But when he arrived in Liberty, he found his son had already been buried in a Christian cemetery. The coffin was removed and transferred to Brooklyn, where it is to be buried tomorrow in a Jewish cematery. The coffin has not been opened. Feinstein hopes his son is still alive.

Morty Feinstein left Brooklyn Polytechnic College, where he was studying to be an engineer, six months ago, to take up racketeering and gambling in Liberty. Benjamin Feinstein has not seen him since June.

When Ben returned to Brooklyn, he put sheets over the mirrors in the bathroom and living room and even covered the ones in the bedrooms with a blue towel in preparation for shiva, which would take place after the funeral.

CHAPTER 33

GOLDA

Golda sat in the darkened living room on a hard-backed chair. She was picking at a loose thread on her skirt, worrying it back and forth, back and forth, trying to tear it without pulling it and making a hole in the material. But the thread was woven tightly, and the more she moved it back and forth, the greater was the puckering in the fabric.

She looked up at her husband but said nothing. Then she rose from the chair and went into the kitchen to put the kettle on for tea. Ben followed her and stood behind her, his face drawn, his eyes piercing. She turned to him.

He took a newspaper clipping from his pocket. The *Brooklyn Eagle*. "How could you say that?" He stared at her, pointed to the headline. "How could you say he wasn't your son? He was the best son there was."

Golda stared at the kettle; her shoulders slumped. "He was not my son. My son would not be a gangster."

Ben raised his voice. "He is your son. You were there at his birth. You are the only mother he ever had. You fed him, you clothed him, took him to school, made him study. You nursed him through the flu, even though our precious Isaac had passed and you were sick yourself. He loved you, tried his whole life to please you, always looking to you to see what you thought. Why did you not claim him as your own?"

"Because . . ." She hesitated and stopped speaking. She did not think she could say the words, speak what was going through her head, the jumble of thoughts, the pain. She bit her lip.

"Because what?"

Golda looked at Ben in surprise. All these years he had not

spoken to her this way. He wanted to know; she would tell him. "He threw away his life. He was going to make something of himself; we were so proud of him. We scrimped and saved for him to be an engineer, and he leaves school and follows his friend—that Rudy—into the world of gangs. For what did I stay and care for him? So he could be a gangster?"

"You don't know what you are talking about. He was never a gangster until I made him one." Ben turned his back and sat at the dining table.

Golda followed him out of the kitchen. "What? What do you mean you made him a gangster? How?"

Ben took a breath. "He did it to save me. Because of me, he got involved in that gang. He was a good son who tried to do his best, to make me whole with money." His voice broke. "I am the reason he is dead!"

Golda's mouth dropped open. What do you mean *he made you whole with his money*? What are you talking about? How are you the reason he is dead?"

Ben shook his head. "The money I owed for the rent on the two buildings. He got it from his friend . . . from Rudy . . . and then he had to work for him. It was my fault. My fault."

Golda turned paper white, stunned. "I didn't know."

"Where did you think I got the money from? I needed it to pay the rent or I would have lost the business. First I took from our savings . . . then I borrowed from the street. Then I couldn't pay that back, so he borrowed from that Rudy."

The kettle was boiling. The whistling sound pierced the air. Golda turned off the flame, and it stopped immediately. She did not know what to say. "I knew you took my embroidery money." She turned back to look at Ben. She had never told him this before.

Ben looked at her, his face red, then bowed his head. "It wasn't enough. Not your embroidery money, not his school money." His shoulders were shaking. She felt an urge to take him in her arms and pat his back to comfort him, but she was afraid that if she did, she would break inside, and all the barriers she had built would collapse. She wanted to say something, but she didn't know what.

She knew he was right. If Morty had gotten the money from Rudy, it had saved Ben. Otherwise, he might have been maimed or worse. Why had she not known that? Why hadn't Ben told her? Had she been so unyielding that he was not willing to show her his weakness? His needs? She was sick inside. She felt revulsion for herself. She turned away.

"You think you are the only one who was left without choice?" Ben said. "Because you stayed and married me—a man with a baby? I married twice because I had to. Esther because . . . because she and I had already been together. And then you. Again, because you had come here to help us, and I had a baby, and someone had to care for him. And we married. But I embraced the choice. Made it my own. Came to love you for everything you did."

She remembered how Cousin Surah had told her she did not have so many choices. How Rabbi Levy had said the same to her. She had made a choice but not embraced it until so much later. Had she never let Ben know she loved him? That she loved Morty? She staggered toward a chair and sat, mute. She wanted to touch him, to tell him how much she regretted.

Golda opened her mouth to speak, but Ben cut her off. "He was in Liberty because of me. Me." He repeated the story again. "I needed money to pay back loans I took from the street. The gangsters. He went to Rudy and begged him to help, and the price for help was that Morty had to work for Rudy. Which he did. And that ruined his chance to finish school."

Golda sat heavily on the sofa. She began to cry, and the words came out, punctuated by sobs. "He . . . did that . . . ? And I . . . didn't know? How . . . could you not tell me?"

Ben sighed. "I was so ashamed. So ashamed that I had to ask him for money. That he got the money that way. That I couldn't pay it back." They were silent. "At least we can give him a funeral, bury him properly, mourn him as we should."

Golda was weeping and couldn't speak. But she nodded, and Ben knew she would do what he asked.

Ben, Golda, and Sylvia buried Morty's body in the Jewish cemetery on Long Island. The trees were still gold and red with early November fall colors. The world was jeweled in the sunshine. All around them, the gray headstones lined up, some upright and newer, proclaiming the lineage of the dead, and others decrepit and crumbling, leaning helter-skelter, carved words illegible.

Golda had not been to the cemetery since they put the headstone on Esther's grave years before. Morty's grave was not next to hers but was close enough that Golda could see it. Morty's funeral was sparsely attended: Cousin Surah and her husband, Yaacov; Ben's old boss, Abe Frankel, and his children; a few friends; and Rabbi Levy. Ben looked around. Cemeteries were so peaceful, he thought. The graves were crowded together, but there were no flowers on the Jewish graves, just grass or ivy.

Golda took the rabbi aside and asked him if she was supposed to sit shiva for Morty. She knew the law. She was not Morty's mother or sister or daughter or wife. There was no obligation. But it was not forbidden, Rabbi Levy said, and he encouraged her to take her rightful place beside Ben, as Morty's mother. And in her heart, Golda finally had accepted him completely as her son. She was his mother in every way except legally. They had never done a legal adoption.

For the next week, the three of them—Ben, Golda, and Sylvia—sat on the wooden boxes provided by the funeral home whenever a visitor came to see them. They wore slippers on their feet, and their shirts had been ripped by the rabbi at the graveside as a sign of mourning. Their visitors sat on chairs. Ben answered all the questions the visitors asked and told them what he had discovered from the police. Golda sat quietly, barely speaking.

To Mr. and Mrs. Weissman from next door, Ben said, "They said they found the body, dead already two months. It was not able to be identified except by the clothes and wallet. They didn't open the casket for me. The police said later they would give me his wallet back."

To Cousin Surah he said, "There was a man I met from the store where I bought cigarettes up there. Bob something. He said he saw Morty going to the bus depot with a rucksack. Morty told him he was coming in for cigarettes later, but he never came. He was sure Morty took a bus out of town."

"Where would he have gone?" Cousin Surah asked. "Wouldn't he have written you?"

Ben shrugged. "I did get a note from him saying he was running away, but Detective Hanrahan said he was killed right after he mailed it."

Ben's partner, Abe, was silent at first; then he whispered, "Maybe it wasn't him?"

Ben shrugged. "But they said it was. And I told them what the store-man said. They didn't care."

To Mr. Aranov from the synagogue, he said, "They had buried the body already in a goyish cemetery. I took it out of there and buried him at Sons of Israel."

Mr. Aranov nodded. "Good you did that. At least it's a Jewish cemetery."

Golda listened to all of this but said little.

The week dragged on, and when it was over, the family went on with their lives . . . Golda and Ben to work and Sylvia to school. Life was gray, solemn, sad. Ben and Golda hardly talked. They had little more to say to one another that had not already been spoken.

CHAPTER 34

SYLVIA

After the week of mourning was over, Sylvia went into her bedroom, pulled open the bureau drawer with her socks, and took out the letter in the lavender envelope. She sat on her bed and held it in her hand, shaking, and wondered if she should open it or return it to Anna. Her address was on the left-hand corner of the envelope. She could go there, hand the envelope back to Anna, and tell her that Morty was dead. But maybe she already knew. It seemed that lots of people knew.

What could be so important that Anna would have come looking for Morty? She finally opened the letter, carefully peeling the glue away so she could glue it back, as if Morty would be coming and she could give it to him, and he wouldn't know she opened it.

Her hands shaking, she read the letter over and over, digesting the information, wondering what to do with it. Anna was pregnant with Morty's baby. She could not imagine going to see Anna and telling her that the baby she was carrying would be born without a father. She hoped Anna already knew. In the end, Sylvia tucked the letter away in her bureau, moving it to her underwear drawer, where it stayed.

It was summer again, late July 1941, and Sylvia once again stood in the cemetery beside her mother and father. The graves around her crowded one another, some grayed by exposure to the dirt and winds of Long Island, some pristine in their white marble. Morty had been buried almost nine months before, and today was the unveiling of his headstone. She stood before the small white stone that bore the words *Morton Feinstein, Beloved Son and Brother*, and his birth and death years, 1914–1940.

Sylvia, motionless, watched her father and nine other men recruited from other gravesites, men who wandered the lanes of the cemetery carrying worn black prayer books and wearing black hats. The men were for hire. They could be paid to fill a minyan of ten men so they could pray as a congregation. As women, Sylvia and Golda didn't count.

In her hand, Sylvia clutched a smooth stone that she had brought with her to leave on the headstone. *I was here*, the stone said. *I mourn you.* No flowers, no plants but green grass, and just rocks and pebbles.

Morton—Morty—lay in his grave. The words to "John Brown's Body" repeated in her head. She had learned the song in grammar school when they studied the Civil War. "John Brown's body lies a-moldering in his grave." Morton's body lay a-moldering in his grave. At least they had been told it was him. Sylvia didn't want to believe he was dead, so she preferred the other stories she had heard, the ones that cast doubt on his murder. But she had no reason to believe they were true. She wondered whether, in the plain pine box in which Morty had been buried, there were now only bones, a skeleton of his lean, handsome body.

The cemetery was quiet. Midweek. One funeral was taking place in the distance, a big gathering of mourners, all the men in a line waiting to shovel dirt on the coffin. At Morty's burial, there had been some friends, but today it was just Sylvia and her parents. Each time they had to recruit those rent-a-men.

Golda had not spoken at the funeral, only wept. And she didn't speak at the unveiling either. She was inconsolable, and Ben held her up through it all. Sylvia stood silently beside them.

Sylvia had loved Morty. He was her adored older brother. He had taken care of her in all kinds of ways. He'd made her laugh and bought her candies with the money he made working in a local grocery store. He'd played cards and checkers with her and taught her chess, although he rarely let her win—he said she had to learn to beat him fair and square. He'd helped her with her math homework because he was a whiz at math, able to run up sums in his head just by going down the column with his finger. He'd told her she was pretty, although when Sylvia looked in the mirror, she saw a slightly chubby adolescent with a few pimples scattered on her chin.

For as long as she lived, she would never forget his face, with his fine features, blue eyes, full red mouth, and cleft chin with the deep dimple. He had warm brown hair that always fell over his forehead so that when it grew too long, he had to flick his head back to keep it out of his eyes. He was so handsome that her best friend Frieda had a huge crush on Morty and called him "dishy."

Sylvia was full of feelings today, but she hadn't cried yet. Now, as she was flooded with memories, the tears came, and then the sobs. Her father put his arm around her, and she wept into his shoulder as they walked away toward the cemetery entrance.

Suddenly Sylvia stopped short. She was still clutching the smooth white pebble in her hand. She turned and ran back to the grave to place the stone atop the headstone. She would not want anyone to think that mourners had not been at Morty's grave.

It was a very long trip home from the cemetery. A bus from the Queens, Long Island, cemetery and then the subway to Brooklyn. Sylvia had a long time to think. After they had found out Morty was dead and reburied the body in the Jewish cemetery, Sylvia knew she should have told Anna. She should have looked up her telephone number, called her, and said, "He's dead. The police told us." Instead, she had let Anna go on thinking and hoping that Sylvia would deliver her lavender note to Morty and give him the shattering information that he was going to be a father.

But was he? How did she even know the baby was Morty's? Sylvia wondered. Just because Anna said it was? Sylvia had no one to ask. No one to check it out with. Rudy was dead. Morty's old friends Paulie and Davy knew only what everyone else knew. They had seen the newspaper articles about her parents. Everyone had seen them.

The baby had surely been born by now. She wondered what it was, and if they still lived in Ocean Hill. And Sylvia knew that if she could do it over again, she would have done it differently, gone to Anna and told her about Morty's death. Maybe Anna still didn't know Morty was dead. But maybe she had read those articles in the newspapers. All the guys on the street had heard about it; Anna probably knew them. She probably had heard. But still. Sylvia's head was swirling with thoughts. Back and forth she went. She did not know what to do.

She glanced at her mother and father. Golda leaned against the window. Papa sat still as stone, eyes closed. Every now and then his mouth moved silently. Was he praying? She closed her own eyes and leaned her head against his shoulder. The subway car rocked them through the underground, and the clacking of the rails crowded out her thoughts.

By the time they reached their station, Sylvia knew she would have to seek out Anna and find out whether she had really had a baby. She would fib a little and tell Anna that she had recently remembered the letter and opened it. That was why she was seeking her out now. Could she have kept the baby? She was a single woman, and her family were Italian Catholics. Sylvia knew that in Jewish families, an unmarried mother couldn't keep her baby. How would she raise it? Was it different in Italian families? And where would she be living now? She could see the neatly written home address in the top left corner of the envelope: 138 Hull Street, Ocean Hill, Brooklyn, New York. That was where she had been living then. She would have to start looking there.

When Sylvia looked for Anna DeMaio, she went alone on a hot summer day. She dressed carefully, wearing her second-best skirt and a clean white blouse. She took the subway to the Ocean Hill neighborhood, which was largely Italian, the way Brownsville was largely Jewish, and carefully checked the house addresses. When she found 138 Hull Street, she stood for a while gazing at the building.

It was a two-family house, like many of the houses on the street. The house was brick, with four steps leading to a porch where iron chairs waited for the occupants to come out and sit. There were two doors on the porch, each, Sylvia knew, leading to a separate apartment. Which one was Anna's? With a pounding heart, Sylvia walked up the stairs and read the names over the bells by the side of the doors. One said "P. DeMaio." The other said "T. DeMaio." Sylvia remembered Anna had said the phone number would be under P. DeMaio in the phone book. She pushed the bell.

She heard a clattering as someone came down the stairs and flung open the door. It was Anna. In her arms was a baby in a pink blanket. *So Anna kept her baby*, Sylvia thought. She tried to keep the surprise off her face. *How did she manage that?* She couldn't take her eyes off the pink blanket, a girl. *My niece.*

Anna stood and observed Sylvia for a long time. Sylvia's heart was pounding. She hadn't thought about what she would say to Anna when she first saw her. Now she was almost wordless. "I'm Sylvia . . ."

"I know who you are," Anna interrupted. "You're Morty's sister. The question is, why are you here?"

Sylvia felt her cheeks redden in embarrassment. She'd always hated how she blushed so easily. She took a deep breath. She was aware that Anna was blocking her way into the house. Was she not going to let Sylvia in? "I . . . I just opened the letter you gave me that day. I had forgotten about it, and when I read it, I wanted to make sure you knew about Morty . . . what happened to him."

"You mean that he died? Was killed?"

Sylvia nodded. She felt as if Anna was punching her in the gut. She focused her eyes on the baby, instead of staring at Anna.

"Yeah, well, I know about it," Anna said. Her voice was curt. She seemed to be observing Sylvia. "You might as well come in, now that you're here." She turned and silently led Sylvia into the hallway and up the stairs to her apartment. Sylvia followed nervously.

Anna's house was nice, Sylvia thought. She followed Anna and the baby through the parlor and dining room into the kitchen. The parlor was furnished with heavy mahogany furniture and a beautiful oriental rug. The dining room, wallpapered in embossed green velvet, had a large oak table and chairs and a sideboard that held crystal and bone china behind glass doors. In the kitchen was a big red Formica table with painted black chairs. A loaf of bread sat on a cutting board in the middle of the table, and glass salt and pepper shakers stood beside it. Sylvia thought it was like a house in the movies. The room was filled with a delicious smell of freshly baked cookies, which sat cooling on a plate on the table beside the bread.

They sat at the kitchen table, awkward at first. Sylvia wondered how to start the conversation.

Anna moved about the kitchen easily. "I just made some coffee. Would you like some?"

Sylvia nodded. "I'd love a cup."

Anna poured, placed the still warm cookies in front of Sylvia with a small pitcher of milk and a bowl of sugar, and sat across from her, holding the baby.

Sylvia began to tell her about Morty's death, but Anna cut her off. "I told you I already knew about it."

"When did you find out?"

"Well, I didn't know when I came to give you the letter." She stared hard at Sylvia. "Did you know then?"

Sylvia shook her head. "I found out about it two weeks later. And we were so shocked, so sad, I just forgot about you." Sylvia saw Anna's face relax. *She must have thought that I knew Morty was dead and didn't tell her. No wonder she seemed so mad.* Sylvia added quickly, "And I didn't know you were expecting. When was she born?"

"The end of April. She's almost four months."

Sylvia stuck her forefinger out, and the baby grabbed it. It felt wonderful, like the baby would never let her go. Sylvia laughed. "That feels good." She played with the baby's hand, waving it back and forth. "I wish I had known about her. But I didn't open your letter, so I didn't know."

"Yeah, well, I didn't know anything either. I didn't know Morty was dead until later. No one told me anything. But when I began to show pregnant, my uncle Mario told me. He had heard it on the street."

Sylvia looked at the baby. "She's beautiful. Can I hold her?"

Anna handed her the baby. "I told Morty not to get mixed up with that Rudy. He ruined his life," she said.

Sylvia could not think of anything to answer. Anna wasn't wrong. Rudy had ruined Morty's life. But he had also saved her father's. She wondered if Anna knew about that. Sylvia rocked the baby in her arms. "What's her name?"

"Lily."

Sylvia smiled. "Such a beautiful name." She wondered what her mother and father would say about this. Would they welcome this beautiful baby into the family as their grandchild? Would they refuse to acknowledge her? Sylvia knew there were Jewish parents who declared their children dead when they married non-Jewish people. They even sat shiva for them. But then, Morty was already dead. They had already sat shiva. *Families are often strange in the ways they behave*, she thought.

Sylvia looked into the dining room, where there was a sideboard that held photographs of dark-eyed, dark-haired men and women, gazing at the camera with serious expressions. Some held babies on their laps. It looked like a big family. Lily started to move, a bleat coming from her rosebud mouth. She opened her eyes. "She has blue eyes," Sylvia said, and looked at the photos. Most of the people in the pictures probably had brown eyes.

Anna nodded. "Yes. So did her father." Her voice was hard. She was not looking at Sylvia. Lily was fussing now. "I'll take her," Anna said, stretching out her arms. Sylvia handed Lily back to her mother.

Sylvia nodded to the photos. "Is that your family?"

"Yeah. In Sicily."

"We have pictures like that in our house too. Not from Sicily, of course. From Poland."

Anna looked confused. "I didn't know you're Polish. I thought you were Jews . . . Jewish."

"We are. Polish Jews."

Anna looked away. "I don't get all that. It seems so complicated. German Jews and Polish Jews and Russian Jews."

"In the end," Sylvia said, "the world just sees us as Jews."

There was a long silence. Anna looked at the floor. Sylvia looked at Lily. She was half-Jewish too. If she lived in Germany, she'd be considered completely Jewish. Sylvia wondered if Anna knew that. Sylvia felt awkward, like there was something unspoken between them. She wondered if Morty had felt that too. "Can I visit sometimes?" Sylvia asked.

Anna hesitated. "I guess so. You're her aunt."

Sylvia smiled. "Aunt Sylvia. Thank you for letting me see her. I'll come back again." In the long silence that followed, the question that Sylvia had wanted to ask from the moment she entered Anna's house was begging to come out. Was she being nosy? Sylvia stumbled over the words but said them anyway. "I know it's probably none of my business, but how did your family let you keep Lily? I think in mine, you would have had to place her . . . you know, for adoption or something." Sylvia found herself blushing.

Anna shrugged, licked her lips. "They weren't happy, I'll tell you that." Anna held the baby against her shoulder, patting her back. She walked to the kitchen window and stared outside for a long time. Sylvia wondered what she was looking at. "You know you're right. It's not your business. But here's the short version of the story. My uncle who owns the deli wanted me to marry a guy who worked for him. But surprise, surprise, this guy didn't want to marry me. He said he wasn't going to give his name to someone else's baby. I was very relieved because I sure didn't want to marry him.

"They couldn't talk me into giving the baby up for adoption. That I wouldn't do. And the truth is, my mother didn't want that and neither did my nonna. I'm all they have, and now my mother has a granddaughter and my nonna a great-granddaughter. I don't think the rest of the family wanted me to give Lily away either." Anna took a deep breath. "In the end we concocted a story to tell if anyone asked. That I was married, and my husband died in an accident. And guess what? So far no one asked. People in the neighborhood stare, but I just stare back."

Sylvia looked with admiration at Anna. She was standing proud, resolute. Sylvia could imagine her glaring at her nosy neighbors. She smiled at Anna. "I can see why Morty liked you. He always liked people with spunk."

Sylvia had finished her coffee and cookie and knew it was time to go, but before she left the house, she said, "I hate secrets. My parents don't know about you, or obviously about Lily. Would it be all right to tell them?"

Anna was quiet for a moment. "What do you think they would say?"

"I don't know. They would be shocked maybe." Sylvia thought about what she had learned of Morty's birth. "But maybe not." She remembered how innocent she had been when she realized that Morty had been born before Golda and Ben were married. Now, of course, she understood that her father and Morty's mother, Esther, had sex before they were married. Surely her father would understand how Lily was born. "I think maybe they'd be happy."

Anna shrugged. "It's up to you. They are Lily's grandparents, so . . ." Her voice drifted away.

When she left the house, Sylvia walked slowly back through the streets of Ocean Hill toward Brownsville. She thought she would love to come back to visit, to become friends with Anna, and to introduce her to Golda and Ben. It would be a connection to her brother. Maybe the only one she still had.

She thought about it for a week, then sat her parents down after dinner one night and said, "I have something important to tell you." Sylvia took a deep breath and said, "Before he went away to Liberty, Morty had a girlfriend. Her name is Anna DeMaio." She waited for a reaction from her parents. Golda blinked. Ben cocked his head.

"She was pregnant, but she hadn't told him. She gave me a letter to give to him when we all thought he was still alive. I didn't open it until much later . . . after the funeral. She had the baby in April, and I went to see her a week ago when the baby . . . Lily . . . was four months old." Still her parents were silent. "I thought you might want to meet them."

Golda shook her head. "Why would I?" She covered her mouth with her hands.

Ben spoke at the same time. "A baby? Morty's? You're sure?"

"Yes, Papa. She's beautiful. She looks just like him. Blue eyes. Will you come to meet them?"

"Yes," Ben said. "Of course."

Golda's eyes drifted to Ben's face. "A baby from an Italian shiksa? Not married?"

"Not too different from Esther. He probably would have married her if he knew."

Golda was silent. Then she nodded her head. "All right. I'll meet her."

Sylvia clapped her hands in joy. "The baby is so beautiful, Mama. You will love her. She looks so much like Morty. Blue, blue eyes. You could make her a dress, for a present. With embroidery."

Golda nodded slowly, thoughtfully. "Lily. Pretty name." Her voice was thick with tears. She reached out and touched Ben's hand. He took it in his and raised it to his mouth and kissed it. There was a small smile on his lips.

Golda didn't speak much more about it to Sylvia, but she made the baby dress of pale blue cotton, big enough so that Lily could wear it the next spring and summer. She sewed the top with intricate smocking, and on the collar, she embroidered white lilies in honor of the baby's name. She bought a baby teething rattle when Sylvia told her Lily was teething, and Ben bought her a soft Raggedy Ann doll.

CHAPTER 35

GOLDA

The first time Golda and Ben met with Anna, it was October, and they came to Prospect Park with all their presents. Anna was walking toward them with the baby carriage, along the paved pathways lined with green lawns; purple and gold asters crammed the fall flowerbeds. Golda was startled by Anna's beauty and had to keep herself from staring. *No wonder Morty fell in love with her. They must have made a beautiful couple.*

It had been awkward at first, but Lily, by that time a chubby, smiling six-month-old, had charmed them, going from one lap to the other on the park bench, chewing on her new teething rattle, and chortling with glee whenever Ben put the ragdoll near her face. Anna had been thrilled with the dress Golda made. She thanked her over and over again. They bought ice cream in the park, and when they left, they made plans to see each other again.

The second time they met was in early December, and the stores were festooned with Christmas decorations. Japan had just bombed Pearl Harbor, and now the US was at war. There was an air of excitement. For many of the men, this was their last Christmas before they became soldiers. It was too cold for the park, so they met in an Italian coffee shop and bakery in Ocean Hill. Lily didn't remember them, but she was happy to be cramming the creamy pastry in her mouth, and Golda and Ben were again delighted to spend time with Anna and Lily.

They had planned a third outing in January, but Lily had a cold, and then Golda did, and they all decided to wait to meet again when the weather was nicer. They still had not met Anna's mother, and they didn't know if Anna had told her she had already met Morty's parents.

Golda and Ben were very nervous about that. But now, they knew that they all had a piece of Morty, still with them, still alive.

CHAPTER 36

MORTY

When Morty got off the bus in Cincinnati that day in 1940, he had a little more than forty dollars in his pocket, and he was ravenous, not having eaten anything but a candy bar on the sixteen-hour bus trip. He needed three things: a room to sleep in, a shower, and a meal. Then he would get a job.

He asked at the bus terminal where there might be cheap rooms for rent and was directed to a neighborhood he could walk to, where he found a small hotel that rented rooms by the week, bath or shower included. After he had taken a room and showered, he walked down the block to the first restaurant he saw, a diner that had seen better days. He stepped inside, sat at the counter, and ordered their blue plate special: meatloaf, mashed potatoes, green beans, and two hot rolls. He ate without raising his head from his plate, shoveling the food into his mouth, wiping the gravy with the last of the rolls. He could just hear his mother saying, "Morton, your manners. You are eating like a hooligan!" But he couldn't stop himself, he was so hungry. Then he ordered a piece of apple pie and some coffee.

His stomach full, Morty looked at the counterman, a tall, skinny guy wearing a uniform splotched with grease and tomato sauce, and then behind him into the kitchen, where he saw dirty dishes piled up in the sink. There was a cook who was busy preparing the sandwiches and blue plates for a steady stream of customers.

He finished the pie and sipped his coffee, then asked, "Need any help here?"

"Dishwasher," the man said. One of his front teeth was missing.

"Twenty-five cents an hour, and your dinner's on us. You can start right now."

Morty got off his barstool, came behind the counter into the kitchen, and went to work. It took him five hours to wash and dry the dishes piled up alongside the sink. He put them away in stacks, which diminished as the cook used them, and the counterman, who served as a waiter too, carried them out to the diners. By the time the restaurant closed, he had earned $1.25, which he pocketed. After telling the counterman, whose name was Charlie, he would be back the next evening to work if they needed him, he walked the four blocks back to his room and crashed on his bed, sleeping like a dead man. Not once did he wonder what was going on in Liberty now that he was gone.

The next morning, he got up feeling better, dressed, and walked downtown, past restaurants and bars, many with HELP WANTED signs. People, climbing out of the Depression, were beginning to go out again, and business owners needed and wanted help.

He walked into a slick-looking restaurant and bar that reminded him of one he used to frequent in Liberty. Shiny mahogany wood on the bar, white cloths on the tables. He introduced himself and asked if he could learn how to mix drinks when they weren't busy, so he could bartend. He could tell the owner liked him, and he hired him to work that weekend as a trial. Morty accepted and went back to the diner for the next two nights, to get a free dinner and earn a little money with his hands plunged into greasy dishwater. On Thursday night he told Charlie that he had a weekend job as a bartender, but he continued working at the diner during the week. When he was proficient at bartending, he ended his dishwashing days forever. And that was how Morty began his new life in Cincinnati and his career as a bartender.

After about a month, he found a small apartment with a kitchen, and he began to explore the city, walking around the neighborhoods and finding short blocks with individual houses, so very different from the crowded apartments he was used to in New York. The weather was beautiful. Golden October, with the trees splashing color all up and down the streets. His life was quiet, and he liked it that way. Several times he was tempted to call Anna, but he knew she wouldn't want to hear from him, especially because he was running away from the law.

After Christmas and New Year's, in the dead of winter, Morty was still afraid to telephone anyone in New York who could give him away. He read the papers, looking for word of what was happening in Liberty or Brooklyn, but the Cincinnati papers were uninterested in what happened in small towns in New York State, and even in the New York City neighborhoods, and didn't report anything about them.

He had finally given up looking for news in the papers, but one day he decided to do some research in the public library. He knew the libraries had newspapers on microfilm. The librarian was helpful to him when he mentioned Murder, Inc., and found him several articles. A few were from the *New York Times*, following the arrest and conviction of Louis "Lepke" Buchalter, one of the heads of Murder, Inc. Another was from the March 29, 1940, issue of the *Iowa Telegraph-Herald*, which listed on their "Roll of Death" the names of the dead gangsters from 1930 to 1940. It also had a picture of famous gangsters. The one Morty immediately recognized was Abe Reles, called a vice president of Murder, Inc., who had turned state's evidence and was "singing" to William O'Dwyer, King County's district attorney, telling him everything he knew. Somehow this information helped convince Morty that if Abe Reles had become a snitch, no one would be looking for small potatoes like him.

Even so, although he continued to struggle with his strong desire to reach out to Anna and his family to let them know where he was, he forced himself to lie low. It wasn't safe. He could still be arrested for all the crimes that Patrick Hanrahan had mentioned: racketeering, illegal gambling, extortion. And then he also would remember Mickey Adler saying to him, "I know where your father's shop is," and that stopped his dreaming of home. He didn't want to bring gangsters into his parents' house. He remembered hearing terrible stories about how Abe Reles and the thugs in Murder, Inc., had dealt with men they thought had betrayed them.

He wondered if Adler had come up to Liberty with a few of his gang. Was Hanrahan waiting for him? Had there been a shootout? Morty wished he knew what had happened, but with no information, he felt he could not reach out to his family. So he went on with his life in Cincinnati, hiding in plain sight.

And he dreamed. The thought of Anna tormented him. Sometimes he imagined he saw her on the street, a tall woman with long black hair whose hips swung rhythmically as she walked. When he entered a restaurant, he was sure he smelled her perfume, and that sent him into a spin.

What would happen, he wondered, if he wrote her a letter with his current return address? *Cincinnati*, it would say. Who did she know in Cincinnati? How could a letter hurt? He lay on his bed, staring up at the ceiling. He wrote the letter in his head, going over and over what he would say. Then he sat up, went to the tiny table under the window, pulled out a piece of paper and a pen, and began to write. What the heck. He didn't have to mail it, but he had to get it out of his head and down on paper before he went nuts.

When it was finished, he sat back and read it. His heart was pounding, his fingers a little sweaty. He decided it was not a good idea, so he tucked the letter away with his socks and underwear, where it stayed in the drawer. And Morty built a life in Cincinnati.

He still wanted to be an engineer. He thought long and hard about it and realized that he could take the few courses he needed right there in Cincinnati at the College of Engineering and Applied Science. Figuring no one would be checking his school records, he sent off to Polytech for his transcript, applied to the University of Cincinnati, and was accepted. He only needed three classes to get his degree if they would credit everything he had taken at Polytech.

In January 1941 he began taking his last classes at night at the university. He also applied for a job at Getz Engineering, a new firm that had started five years earlier in Cincinnati. He was hired as an assistant in their civil engineering department, and by the summer he was working full time there. His life was taking shape, like a donut with a huge hole in the middle. School, work, his own apartment, and even the beginning of a social life surrounded the hole of his past, his family, and Anna.

Although he was afraid to get too close to the men he met at university, Morty was lonely. One of his classmates, Sam Heller, was a redheaded jokester who reminded him of Rudy. Sam was from the thriving Jewish community in Cincinnati, and he took a liking to Morty and asked him to Friday night dinner with his family.

The first time Morty came to dinner at Sam's house, he was awestruck. They lived in a large brick colonial on a street full of beautiful homes, lined with huge trees; he had to keep himself from staring with his mouth open.

"This is where you grew up?" he asked Sam.

"Yeah. We moved here when I was three. Both my sisters were born after we moved here. I guess you could say it's our family home." He hesitated a minute and then asked, "Where did you grow up?"

Morty thought about his family's cramped two-bedroom apartment. "A different world," he said. "An apartment house in Brooklyn." Then he added, "New York."

Sam laughed. "I'm not a rube. I know where Brooklyn is. But I've never been to New York. Someday I'm going."

"Yeah," Morty said. "When you do, I'll give you some pointers." He followed Sam into the house. To Morty it seemed like a mansion or a set from a movie. There was a large foyer with nothing in it but a round table under a chandelier. On one side was a dining room, and on the other side was the living room, where the family waited for Sam and Morty. After the introductions, the group moved to the dining room table, which was covered with a blinding white cloth and set with china and sparkling crystal wine glasses and water goblets. In the middle of the table was a small vase of flowers and a large braided challah with two silver candlesticks on either side, with long white tapers that were already lit. In Morty's eyes it all paid homage to Friday night dinner without the prayers for wine and bread, but it was more elegant than anything Morty had ever seen, except in the movies.

Morty looked down at his place setting. Two forks, a knife, two spoons, a large plate, a small plate. He wiped his sweaty palms on his trousers. He would have to watch what other people did so he wouldn't make any mistakes.

Dinner was presided over by Mr. Heller, a businessman who owned a luggage company, and Mrs. Heller, a beautifully dressed and coiffed woman who looked much younger than Golda, although she probably wasn't. Morty was half expecting a maid to serve dinner, but Mrs. Heller bustled in and out of the kitchen with her two teenage daughters, serving the soup and salad. Until the main course was served—a large roast chicken, carved at the table by Mr. Heller, with roast potatoes and green beans and carrots—the conversation was mostly about the weather and the girls' schoolwork. But once Mrs. Heller sat down with them to eat, the conversation centered on Morty. The Hellers were interested in Morty's background, and Morty found himself stuttering his answers.

It was always awkward for Morty when people asked him how he came to be in Cincinnati. The main story he told was that he was an only child whose mother had died when he was very young (not a lie) and that his father had passed away a year and a half ago, so he decided to try his luck in another city. He would embellish it from time to time with how difficult life was in Brooklyn. For the most part he was believed because none of the people he had met at school or at work were particularly interested in the details of his life or followed up with questions about his upbringing. But that night, Morty was pressed, politely, to answer all kinds of questions. He was not expecting this.

"Your father raised you alone? He never remarried?" Mr. Heller asked.

"Uh . . . no."

"My goodness, how did he raise you, without a mother?" Mrs. Heller asked.

Go with the truth, Morty told himself, *or as close to the truth as possible.* "My mother had a younger sister, and she stayed with us until she got married. That was right around the time I went to school, and she lived nearby, so I would go to her house after school. We managed."

"But then, poor boy, you lost your father too." Mrs. Heller had a lilting voice, with a slight Southern accent. "I'm so sorry."

"Thank you, Mrs. Heller. Do you mind if I ask you something?" Morty wanted to move the subject away from him. "I detect a slight lilt in your voice. Are you from the South?"

"Clever boy," Mrs. Heller said. "My people are from Charleston, South Carolina. My great-great-granddaddy came there as an itinerant peddler and stayed to start a store."

"Not just a store," Ivy, the older daughter, said. "It's a huge department store now. When we visit relatives, we can get anything we want for free."

"Don't brag, Ivy," Mr. Heller said. "It isn't polite." The girl blushed and looked down at her plate. Mr. Heller turned again to Morty. "And what did your father do before he passed on?"

"He was a mechanic," Morty said. "He owned a store where he fixed everything. He always wanted to be an engineer. That's probably why I'm in engineering school." He took a bite of his chicken, which was glazed with an apricot sauce. "This chicken is amazing, Mrs. Heller. You are a wonderful cook."

Mrs. Heller acknowledged the compliment, but then went on to inquire about other family members who might still be in New York, and wasn't he lonely without family, and what did his aunt who helped raise him think about his moving to Cincinnati? Morty stumbled and stuttered his answers. All this talk about family made him homesick. He wished he could tell them about his adorable, smart sister Sylvia. And brag about his mother's embroidery, some of which looked just like the rosebud design that ringed the china plates in pink and gold. But everything he said had to be hidden truths.

When the Hellers had run out of questions about his background, they inquired about Brooklyn and New York. Was it true there were Jewish gangs in Brooklyn? They read about the crime and the murders in the newspapers. Something called Murder, Inc., and the Jewish gangs who ran it. Had he ever heard of it?

Morty's heart pounded. Were the questions innocent? What were they trying to find out about his background? Again, he went with the truth. "Sure, I heard of them. I lived in Brownsville, you know. Once I even saw Abe Reles on the street when I was around fourteen years old. But I don't know much more than you do, reading the paper." He almost choked on his words.

The Hellers clucked about crime and how glad they were that they lived in Cincinnati. During dessert, they moved to Europe and the war there. What had happened in Germany, how the Nazis had marched into Poland in 1939, and the fate of all the millions of Jews in Europe. By that time Morty relaxed a little more, although he couldn't remember conversations like this at his own dinner table. His parents had focused on what was happening with their families who were trapped in the cities and towns overrun by the Nazis. He wondered if the Hellers knew anyone who was still in Europe, but he didn't want to ask.

The Hellers evidently liked him, because they invited him back often, and subsequent visits, to his relief, did not focus on him. He even spent the High Holidays with them in the Isaac Wise Synagogue, a large Reform synagogue. It was a beautiful building, looking like an ancient European church. Morty was very taken with the modern way people worshipped, so very different from the fusty Orthodox building he used to visit with his father. Men and women sat together, and there was an organ with music. It seemed almost like a church. He was awestruck. Morty's world was opening up. He was astonished at the different worlds people lived in outside of the crowded streets of Brooklyn.

In November 1941, there were stories in the papers, even in Cincinnati, featuring the death of Abe Reles when he fell or was pushed out of the window of the Half Moon Hotel, where he was waiting to testify against his old boss, Louis Lepke. Knowing that Reles was dead was a comfort to Morty. Maybe it would mean he could soon go home.

Then, barely a month later, on a December Sunday afternoon, while Morty was listening to a NY Giants football game on the radio, the program was interrupted mid-game by a newsflash that said simply that the Japanese had attacked the naval and air bases on the island of Oahu in Hawaii. If he hadn't been glued to the radio because of the football game, he might have missed it. But the next day, December eighth, Morty, along with more than eighty percent of Americans, listened to President Roosevelt's speech to Congress. The United States was at war with Japan. Four days later, in response to a declaration of war against the US by Germany, America declared war on Germany and Italy.

Morty, like many of his friends in Cincinnati, had registered for the draft the year before, when President Roosevelt signed a law requiring all men between the ages of twenty-one and thirty to do so. They all wondered if they should wait to be drafted or just go ahead and enlist in the army.

Morty wanted to join an army engineer combat battalion, so in January 1942, with his degree completed, Morty enlisted, and at the end of February he reported for basic training at Fort Benning, Georgia. Fnally, being in the army made Morty feel safe enough to write to Anna and his parents. He did not think anyone would look for him in the army.

Dear Anna,

This is a hard letter to write. Maybe you have forgotten me or married someone else. But I am in the army now, trying to make something of my life. I'm finishing my basic training and probably will be shipping out in a month or two, and I wanted to tell you what happened and why I disappeared.

You were right when you told me that there would be other gangs that came to Liberty, and I would have to choose between fighting them or getting out. The only way I figured I could get out was to run. I left Liberty on the first bus out and landed in

Cincinnati, Ohio, where I stayed until the war broke out, even fin-
ishing my engineering degree.

    I was afraid to contact you or my family because I thought the
gang or the police would find out where I was, and that would be
the end of me. It sounds stupid now. I wasn't so important that
anyone would waste time looking for me. I don't even think anyone
in the gangs knew I was seeing you—except Rudy—and he was
dead before I left Brooklyn.

    I'm sorry, Anna. Not a day went by that I didn't think of you,
dream of you. I know it's a lot to ask, but if you would write me at
least once and tell me how you are, it would mean a lot. I still love
you, and if you can find it in your heart to forgive me, I would be
the happiest man on earth.

    Morty

He wrote his army address on the letter, so, if she was inclined,
she could write back to him. He wasn't sure she would, but her letter
came just two weeks later. When he held it, his hand shook, and his
heart pounded. There, on the return address, he read "Anna DeMaio."
A wave of relief flooded him. She hadn't married anyone else. The
letter read:

    Dear Morty,

    I was shocked to get your letter. I thought you were dead. My
uncle Mario told me the Benjy Molino gang had taken over Liberty
from Mickey Adler, and there was a gang war there and in Brooklyn.
Mickey Adler was killed too. I heard you had been killed, and your
father went up and got your body to bury it in a Jewish cemetery.

    I can't believe you never thought to tell your family or me you
were okay. If you had, you would have found out you have a daugh-
ter. Her name is Lily, and she is ten months old.

    I don't know if I want to hear from you again, but I'm glad you
are alive.

    Anna

Morty put the letter down, a sinking feeling in his stomach. It was too much to take in all at once.

He had a daughter!

They thought he was dead.

Mickey Adler was dead too.

He imagined Sylvia, crying in her bed; his father, standing in the corner of the living room with a prayer book in his hand and praying for him, moving his body back and forth, his eyes closed. And his mother? Surely, she must be heartbroken too. He saw her sitting in her embroidery chair, her needle and thread in her hand, but unable to make a stitch.

His father had gone up to Liberty and taken his body back to bury it in a Jewish cemetery near Brooklyn. He felt sick to his stomach. The questions kept coming. Who was buried in the cemetery with his name on the grave? Who had told his family he was dead?

He had imagined that his family just thought he had run away, disappeared. That was what he had written to his father the day he left Liberty. Had he never received that letter?

How was he to know someone would report him dead? Was it that federal officer who had come to see him at the boarding house? Hanrahan. Was he the one who told them he was dead?

But why had the body been identified as him? He didn't get it at all. Those questions kept going round and round in his head.

And Anna. She was a mother. He was a father. What was Lily like? Did she look like him or did she look like Anna? At least Anna was glad he was alive. He thought for a minute and reread the letter. She didn't say that she never wanted to hear from him again. She said she didn't *know* if she wanted to hear from him again.

He would consider it an invitation. He would write to her again, after he wrote to his parents and Sylvia. He sat down and took out a pen and paper.

He wrote a letter to his parents. He apologized. He tried to explain himself but realized as he wrote that it wasn't coherent, didn't really make sense. Everything he said seemed foolish now. He sent a picture of himself in his army uniform so they could be sure it was him and that he was alive.

Then he wrote to Anna again, enclosing his picture to her as well. He was not sure this was the way he should approach her, but with an open heart, he wrote:

> Dearest Anna,
>
> Lily! I am overcome with happiness, and grief. I have missed almost the whole first year of our daughter's life. I pray that you let me back into your life so I can join you and Lily and make a life with you.
>
> I hope you will answer this letter, and please, please send me a photo of our daughter.
>
> All my love, and hope,
> Morty

Finally, he thought carefully and wrote a short letter to Sylvia. He took all three letters and mailed them.

CHAPTER 37

GOLDA

When Golda came home from work and picked up the mail that windy day in March 1942, two envelopes confused her. Who did she know in the armed forces? There was no name on the return address of either one, only the stamp of the US Military Postal Service. One was addressed to Mr. and Mrs. Ben Feinstein, the other to Sylvia. She carried the mail up to the apartment, put the letters on the table, and went into the kitchen to make herself some tea. She was reluctant to open the envelope addressed to her and Ben, though she didn't know why.

She took the teacup to the table, sat down, and examined the envelope. The handwriting looked like something she had seen before, and a thought came to her. She felt the skin prickle on the back of her neck. She shook her head. She would wait for Ben to come home to open it. She finished her tea and went into the kitchen to start supper. As she chopped the onions and set them into the frying pan, as she put the potatoes into the oven to bake, as she cut the carrots and put the small piece of liver into the frying pan, she glanced continuously at the table in the next room, looking at the envelope, at the handwriting. She kept hoping to hear the door open and Ben enter with the heavy steps of his characteristic walk. She wiped her hands on her apron, walked to the table again, lifted the letter, put it down, and went back to the kitchen. What was she afraid of? She didn't want to say out loud what she was thinking because it was so outlandish. She wanted Ben there when she opened the letter.

When he arrived and hung up his jacket, she walked to the table, stood there, and greeted him. "There's a letter," she said.

"Yes? From who?"

"I don't know. But it says the military." Suddenly something occurred to her. "You're too old to be called, aren't you?"

"Of course," he answered. He picked up the envelope, looked at it, looked at Golda, tore the envelope open, and pulled out the letter. A photograph spilled onto the table. Ben picked it up, looked at it, gasped, and stumbled to a chair. "Golda," he whispered. "It's him. Look, it's Morty." His hands shaking, he offered her the picture.

Golda sat beside him, and together they stared at the photo. There was Morty, tall, handsome, a grin on his face as he stared at them. "How can that be?" she asked.

Ben opened the letter and read it out loud:

Dear Mama, Papa, and Sylvia,

I don't know how to even start this letter. I just found out that you think I died. As you can see, I did not. I don't know how that body was ever identified as me or who it really is, but it isn't me.

You know after Rudy was killed, I had to go to Liberty. Well, I learned that a rival gang was coming up to the Catskills, and I was threatened, so I ran.

I got on a bus and wound up in Cincinnati. I was afraid to contact you then because I thought the gang was looking for me and they said if they found me, I'd be a dead man. I also was afraid that if the police found me, I could be arrested.

I didn't want you to have any information that would put you at risk. I never thought they would tell you I was dead. I am so sorry if you were sad. I heard you buried the body in a Jewish cemetery. I don't know who that body was, but it wasn't me.

In Cincinnati I waited tables, bartended, and eventually got a job with an engineering firm and went to the University of Cincinnati to finish up my engineering degree. And then when the war broke out, I signed up. A lot of times I thought about writing you or calling you, but I was afraid. So now I'm in basic training, and soon I'll be sent wherever they send me.

Please write me back. Tell me how you are. Say you forgive me.
Your son,
Morty

Ben's hands were shaking when he put the letter down. "He's alive. Alive. I always believed."

Golda's heart was thumping. Morty was alive. Their boy was alive. And a soldier. She did not know what to make of it all. What to think. She was stunned. She could see Ben was too.

But she knew that there had always been a part of him that hoped somehow that Morty was still alive. That man in Liberty had told him he had seen Morty at the bus stop. He had always hoped that there had been a mistake.

She shook her head. Suddenly she smelled the unmistakable odor of burning food and jumped up and went into the kitchen to check. Golda heard a key in the lock and knew Sylvia was home. The door opened, and Sylvia came in from her her classes at Brooklyn College. She looked at her father's face, drained white.

"What happened? What's the matter?"

Golda handed her the photograph.

"Oh, my God. That's Morty. Is he alive? Oh, my God. He's alive. He's so handsome."

"Read," Golda said. She handed Sylvia the open letter.

Sylvia read the letter and quickly sat down hard on a chair. "Mama, Papa, he's alive." She could barely contain her joy. She took a deep breath and reread the letter more slowly. "He doesn't say a word about Anna or Lily," she said. "I wonder if he knows about Lily."

Golda shook her head. "Maybe he wrote such a letter as this to Anna too." They all sat quietly thinking about the two times they had met with Anna and Lily and how Sylvia had brought them together. Now it seemed, with Morty alive, this would all have to be sorted out. Golda suddenly remembered the other letter that Morty had written to Sylvia, and she handed it to her. Sylvia tore it open and read it.

Dear Sylvia,

    I am so sorry for all the grief and trouble I caused. I hope when I get home, I can explain what happened and that you all forgive me. Hopefully you have read the letter I wrote to Mama and Papa. But I'm writing you separately to ask you for a very big favor.

    I don't know if you knew that I had a girlfriend, Anna DeMaio. She lives not far from us in Ocean Hill, on 138 Hull Street in a two-family house. I love her, Sylvia. I would have married her if things had worked out differently, and I am praying that it isn't too late.

    I wrote to her and she wrote back. We have a baby girl, Sylvia. Her name is Lily and she's ten months old. Would you go to see her? Would you write back to me, if Anna lets you see Lily, and tell me about her? Maybe you could even get a photograph.

    I'm sending you money to give her too. Here's the first install-ment. Oh, sister, I hope you can help me straighten out my life. I know I've screwed up badly.

    And I miss you too.

    Your loving brother,

    Morty

Sylvia put the letter down. "He did write to Anna. He knows about Lily, and he wants me to go to Anna, give her some money, beg her to write again." She gave the letter to her parents to read. "He has no idea I've been seeing her. I'm going to call her right away."

CHAPTER 38

SYLVIA

Sylvia planned to go to Anna's after her classes on Monday. It was a visit she had made often since that August day when she'd first gone to visit. Sylvia liked Anna, found her sharp and spunky, and admired the way she was making the best of a bad situation.

In all the times she'd been to Anna's house, she had only met Anna's mother once, and Anna had not told her that Sylvia was related to Lily's father. She had only introduced Sylvia as a friend. This afternoon, with the money in her purse and the Brownie camera in her book bag, she waited impatiently for Anna to answer the door.

Anna greeted her warmly, as she usually did, and Sylvia could hear Lily babbling away in her playpen upstairs. Sylvia followed Anna to her apartment.

Anna took Lily out of her playpen and put her into a highchair, where she gnawed on a Zwieback biscuit and babbled babytalk to Sylvia, who by now felt Lily knew her. Anna took a baked potato out of the oven and set it on the table to cool.

"Sit," Anna said to Sylvia. "There's a pot of coffee on the stove. I just made it."

"Thanks," Sylvia said. "I'd like that." When the coffee was poured and the decisions about milk and sugar made, Anna and Sylvia sat and looked at one another.

"Okay," Anna said at last. "I suppose you got a letter too?"

Sylvia nodded. "First my parents got one telling us that he was alive." Even as she said it, her heart skipped remembering the shock, the joy. No one had been angry. The happiness had overcome every other emotion. "And there was one for me too. Asking me to come to see you."

"Oh, yeah? What for?"

"Well, first of all, he doesn't know we've met." Sylvia laughed. "Or that we are friends." She looked at Lily sitting in the highchair and now banging her biscuit on the tray and saying, "Mama, Mama" over and over.

A small smile came and went on Anna's face. She nodded. "Go on."

In a rush Sylvia said, "He asked me to give you this money. And he said he'd send more." She reached into her bag and took out an envelope and put it on the table.

Anna closed her eyes and shook her head. "I don't need the money. You can see I don't need money, but I'll take it anyway. It's the least he can do." Her voice cracked, and Sylvia was afraid she would start to cry. The vocalizations from Lily were getting louder and louder. Anna got up and went to the refrigerator. She took out a baby bottle and put it in a potful of water to warm on the stove.

"I have to feed Lily. We can keep talking." Anna then took out some grated cheese and butter, cut open the baked potato, and mashed it with the butter, then drifted some parmesan cheese on it. From the silverware drawer she took out two small spoons. She gave one to Lily, who proceeded to bang it on the highchair tray, and with the other she took a small spoonful of potato and blew on it before offering it to Lily.

"I really loved him, you know," Anna said. She kept on feeding Lily, who opened her mouth like a little bird as each spoonful was offered.

Sylvia nodded. "He wrote me how much he loved you too," Sylvia said. "He said he would have married you if all the trouble hadn't happened. He wants to now."

Anna kept feeding Lily, and Sylvia sat silent. She didn't say anything but appeared to be thinking. When the mashed potato was finished, Anna put down the spoon and stood up. She took the bottle of milk from the pot, turned off the flame, and spilled two drops of the milk on her wrist to test the temperature. Then she handed the bottle to Lily, lifted her out of the highchair, and settled on the kitchen chair, cuddling Lily in her arms. Lily held her own bottle and sucked the nipple, all the while looking at Sylvia whenever she spoke.

Sylvia loved watching Anna doing all of the domestic things that mothers do with babies, and she was filled with admiration. She wondered what it had been like for her to go through the labor and delivery alone. Had she nursed the baby when she was first born? In all the times she had been with Anna, she had never asked her that.

"He asked me to take a picture of Lily. Is that okay?" Sylvia waited but Anna didn't answer. "Can I?" Sylvia reached down and took her Brownie camera out of her bag.

Anna sighed, a long breath out. "Sure. I guess so, seeing as you have the camera ready." There was a hint of a smile on her face. "He sent me a picture of him in uniform." She got up and went to the counter near the refrigerator and brought back her letter and the picture of Morty. It was the same one he had sent to his parents. "Handsome devil, isn't he?" she said to Sylvia. "Now let's take the picture of Lily." She took the bottle out of Lily's mouth, turned her to face Sylvia, and posed with her baby, mirror images of one another. Sylvia snapped several pictures and gave the camera to Anna to take one of Sylvia with the baby.

When Sylvia left Anna and Lily, it was four thirty. They'd talked for an hour, most of it about Lily and about Sylvia's studies at Brooklyn College. Just before she went home, she dropped the film for development at the camera store on Pitkin Avenue and then ran home to dinner.

The photographs were ready in five days. Sylvia picked them up and stood at the counter looking at them. Several of them were really good. Anna looked beautiful and serious. Lily, plump and dimply, was the quintessentially beautiful baby. There was one in particular that Sylvia loved, of her and Lily, and she was sure to include that one in the letter she wrote to her brother.

Dear Morty,

I did what you asked and went to see Anna and Lily. You can see from the photographs included in the envelope that she is a beautiful baby. And Anna is also beautiful.

We had a really nice visit.

Now I have to tell you something else that you don't know. I have been seeing Anna since Lily was four months old. Anna had given me a letter to give you before we were told you were dead. I had it in my drawer and had forgotten about it, not knowing where you were. After the unveiling of the headstone on your supposed grave, I opened the letter. It was telling you that she was expecting. I knew the baby would have been born already, so I went to see her.

We became friendly, Morty. And I even introduced her to Mama and Papa. They love Lily too. So there are no secrets anymore. I don't know whether she forgives you, Morty. She didn't say. But she didn't say no either. And she told me that she had loved you before. I told her you would have married her if things hadn't gotten so bad. I think you have a chance.

Do you get any time off after you finish your training and before they send you to the war? If you do, maybe you can come home and make amends . . . to Anna and to Mama and Papa.

Me—I forgive you already. I missed you so much, you don't have to do anything to make me love you again.

Sylvia

CHAPTER 39

MORTY

When Morty received Sylvia's letter, he could hardly hide his joy. He looked around to see who he could tell, but there was no one. His cohort in basic training was full of perfectly nice boys, none of whom Morty felt really close to. They were all ages: some of them were eighteen-year-olds who had signed up at the time of the declaration of war. Some of them were graduates of college, or even married men with children.

The men had been told that they would have two weeks off before they had to either report in New York before shipping out or go on to further specialized training. Morty had gotten his wish to be assigned to an engineering group and knew that after basic, he was going to Fort Belvoir in Virginia for training as an army engineer. But he wanted to go back to Brooklyn for his two-week furlough to visit his family and hopefully see Anna and Lily.

He wrote to Anna again. This time he poured his heart out and told her everything that had happened to him since he'd left her that day at the Red Apple Rest and put her on the bus to go back to Brooklyn. Even to him it sounded melodramatic . . . like a movie he had seen before, where the good guys struggled, were in danger, and finally won the day. He did not hear back from her, but he went on with his plans to return to Brooklyn as soon as his basic was finished. He wrote to his parents and to Anna to tell them when he would be coming. He didn't think it would be a good idea to surprise them.

The day he got on the bus to go home—it was even hard for him to say the word *home*, it had been so long since he had been there—was sunny and warm for early spring. The bus ride from Fort Benning,

Georgia, where he did his basic training, took over seventeen hours, and he got off the bus at Penn Station, exhausted and rumpled and famished. He took the subway into Brooklyn, walked the two blocks to his parents' apartment, and stood in front of the stoop looking up at the brick facade. The courtyard in the front of the building had broken concrete steps leading into the building. There was a patch of grass on the side of the building with a wooden bench on which two women were sitting. They looked curiously at him, and he was very aware of the fact that his uniform was not as sharp as it had been when he left the base. His hair was very short. One of the women seemed to recognize him, and she whispered something to her friend and then nodded her head at him. Since he didn't remember her name, he also nodded and then went into the building.

The smells were the same. He went up the stairs and stood before the apartment, his heart pounding. Finally, he knocked on the door.

They were expecting him. His mother was wearing a nice dress instead of her usual housedress. Sylvia hovered behind her, and he could tell that she was jumping out of her skin, wanting to run to him and hug him. His father stood behind Sylvia.

Morty's heart lurched. Ben looked so much older than he had when Morty left home. His hair was almost white. His face was lined, and he was a little hunched over, but he was beaming with joy, and when he came forward, they fell into each other's arms. His hug was hard, and Morty thought he was crying. Ben held him for a long time, whispering what Morty could only think was a prayer of thanks.

Morty then went to Golda, wondering how she would accept him. He reached down and put his arms around her. To his surprise and delight, she relaxed against his shoulder and patted his back. "Thank God, thank God," she whispered. "I only believe it now that I see you."

Sylvia could not contain herself anymore, and she rushed to him, hugging and kissing him and patting his cheek the way she used to when she was a little girl. When the kisses and hugs were over, Golda drew him into the parlor, and they sat, staring at one another. He felt awkward, unsure of what to say or how to express himself.

Several times one or another of them started to speak but were interrupted by another member of the family.

"Are you hungry?" Golda asked.

"Let's have a drink of schnapps."

"I can't believe how thin you are, and how handsome in your uniform."

"Frieda sends her love. She wants to come over and say hello."

When they had settled for a while, Morty felt he should be the one to speak and to tell them what had happened to him. He started with Rudy's lending him money to help Ben get out of debt. "You knew about that, didn't you, Mama?"

"I know now, but I didn't know then."

Morty nodded. "After Rudy was killed, they sent me to Liberty, New York, in the Catskills, to run their slot machine business. I didn't want to go, but I didn't think I had a choice. They were threatening me."

Morty spoke quickly and nonstop. He told them about his time in Liberty and how he had tried to get back to Brooklyn, but Mickey Adler wouldn't let him. He mentioned Detective Hanrahan and the Molino gang and how he had to leave Liberty and go into hiding. "I wrote you the day I left, Papa. Didn't you get my letter?"

"Yes," Ben said. "But they said you mailed it just before you were killed. That's what that Hanrahan said."

"Hanrahan? Was he the one who told you I died?"

"Yes, he came to the house. And he took me up to Liberty to get the body."

Morty shook his head. "All a mistake. I don't know why they identified the body as me. Did Hanrahan say how they identified me?"

"Your wallet was in the pocket. The keys to your car. And a leather jacket with your name sewn in it. That's what he said. The body was decomposed, so they couldn't even get any fingerprints."

Morty nodded. "I get it. I think the body must have been Jake

Gold. He's the guy who took it all from me." They sat in silence, thinking about this Jake Gold and what his family must think. Morty started to talk again. "I left Liberty and wound up in Cincinnati, and I was there until the war started. When I joined up, I realized it was time to get back in touch with you."

Then it was Ben and Golda's turn to fill Morty in on what had happened in Brooklyn and how Ben had gone to Liberty to retrieve his body. They did not mention the newspaper stories and how Golda had at first refused to take the body.

"Papa never believed that you were dead," Sylvia said. "And neither did I. At least I hoped. Me and Papa always believed."

There were long silences now that they had each told their stories. Morty took a breath. "Mama, Papa, I know you know about my girlfriend Anna. I have to try to see her and Lily if she'll see me."

Sylvia couldn't contain herself. "She will. She will. She's waiting for you. She said so. I saw her yesterday, and she said she knew you were coming, and you could come to her. There wasn't enough time for her to write to you, so she said I should tell you."

With his parents' blessings, Morty went down the street to the public telephone booth and called the number Sylvia gave him. When Anna picked up the receiver and he said, "Anna," the line went silent. "Anna?" he said again.

"Yes? Who is this?"

Morty was sure she knew it was him, but he allowed himself to wait a second and then whisper, "It's me. It's Morty." He heard the breath she drew on the phone, and he added, "Sylvia told me you would see me."

After a minute she said, "Yes, you can come. But if you want to see Lily, you should come now, otherwise she'll be sleeping."

"I'll be right there."

Morty ran to the avenue and grabbed a taxi. He didn't notice the changes on the street, the new stores, the way people were dressed, so intent was he on getting to Anna's house. When he rang the doorbell, he could hardly breathe.

Anna opened the door, holding a year-old Lily dressed in yellow Dr. Denton footie pajamas. Her black hair framed her face; she had the same eyes as her mother, violet blue with thick lashes. She looked at him with a solemn expression. Morty reached out to touch her hand, but she pulled back from him and turned her face away.

"Just give her a little time, and she'll get used to you."

Morty took a breath, encouraged by what Anna said. He followed her upstairs and into the living room. Anna sat on the sofa, pointed to a chair opposite, and put Lily on the floor between them. Morty wondered who should speak first. He stared at her. She was wearing a blue dress that made her eyes pop. "Thank you for seeing me," he said.

Anna laughed. It sounded a little bitter. "Like I had a choice?" She looked away, and he saw her fidgeting with her skirt.

Morty didn't think he could speak, so he knelt next to Lily, and the baby pulled herself up on his arm, standing unsteadily beside him. Morty held her hand to make sure she didn't fall; she let go of his hand, took a few steps alone, and then plopped down beside him.

"She walked," Anna shouted, clapping her hands. Lily laughed. "She just took her first steps. For you. For her father."

Morty was still on his knees, somehow in supplication to Anna and to Lily. He held out his hand to Anna.

"Sit next to me," she said, and she took his hand and waited.

Morty felt the words stick in his throat. His voice was scratchy when they came out. "I love you, Anna. Please forgive me. Please let me marry you and take care of you and our baby." The words he had been rehearsing came out in a rush now. "I'm going to be in a war. Anything can happen. I want to make sure you and Lily are taken care of. That she knows she has a father."

"She'll always know," Anna said. "I named you on her birth certificate as her father."

Morty felt his heart open. "Let's make everything legal then. Let's get married."

"I guess there really isn't anything else I can do," she said. Anna looked into his eyes, put his hand to her mouth, and kissed his fingers, and then, somehow, she was in his arms, and he was smothering her face with kisses, her eyes, her cheeks, her mouth. They reached down together and pulled Lily into their embrace, but she was having none of it and pushed away from them, crawling to a table where she pulled herself up, took a few steps forward, and fell again. Morty and Anna held each other, laughing and crying at their daughter, who was struggling to stand again. They crawled over to her and held her tight. They were still sitting there on the floor, still laughing and crying, when a voice interrupted them.

"Who is this?"

Morty swiveled his head toward the voice and jumped up from the floor so that he was standing and facing the door. Backlit by the hallway light was Anna's mother. Morty had met her once before, but she looked older now and less formidable. Her black hair was streaked with gray, and she stood with her hands on her hips, glaring at her daughter.

Anna jumped up too. She scooped Lily into her arms and said, "Mama, this is Lily's father, Morty Feinstein."

"Hello, Mrs. DeMaio," Morty said. He felt like bowing or saluting but thought that would be a bit much. Instead, he nodded his head.

Mrs. DeMaio made a sound in the back of her throat. "I thought you were dead."

"I know. That was a mix-up," Morty said. "I have to find out about that."

"Well, if you weren't dead, where have you been all this time?"

"Mama," Anna said, a plea in her voice. She held Lily close, as if getting support from her.

"It's okay," Morty said. "It's a reasonable question . . . I was in Cincinnati. Anna and I broke up last summer. She didn't like the work I was doing. And she was right. I was mixed up . . . involved with some bad characters. I had to leave where I was. I didn't think she wanted to see me again. I didn't know that she was pregnant." He rushed the words out. "When Pearl Harbor was bombed, I enlisted. And I'm shipping out soon. So, I got back in touch with Anna. And that's when

I found out we had this beautiful daughter, Lily." Morty turned and looked at Lily, who had put her head on her mother's breast and was sucking her two middle fingers.

"Give her to me," Mrs. DeMaio said. She held her arms out to Anna, who put Lily into them. "I'll put her to bed." She took the baby and was about to leave the room when she turned and said to Morty, "You better make this right." Then she left them alone.

Anna and Morty sat together on the sofa. "Don't mind her. She'll be all right once she gets used to the idea of me getting married to . . . to you."

Morty wondered if Anna had been about to say "married to a Jew," so he asked, "She remembers I'm Jewish, right? She asked me when I met her that time." Anna nodded. "Is that going to be a problem?"

"Not to me, Morty. Not to me. And my mother and my uncles will get used to it. My nonna doesn't care at all. She says she likes the Jewish shopkeepers on the avenue. Everything's changing now. They'll be okay with it eventually. They'll have to be."

Morty felt a weight lift from his shoulders. Anna and he spent the next hours talking and kissing and somehow filling in the happenings of the last year and a half, and by the time Anna's mother and uncle came back into the living room, bringing Anna's grandmother, they had made plans to get their license and get married.

There was one more thing weighing on Morty's mind. Detective Hanrahan. He was the one who had told Morty's parents that he was dead. He wondered if he should go to Hanrahan's office and turn himself in. On the one hand, if the police thought he was dead, he didn't have to worry about them looking for him for any of the so-called crimes Hanrahan had mentioned to him. On the other hand, Morty wasn't sure whether being legally dead in police records might be a problem for him later in life.

He mulled it over and decided that he just wouldn't deal with it right now. He had less than two weeks home with Anna and Lily and his family. Getting tangled up in police red tape now seemed crazy to him. *They think I'm dead. Let me stay dead to them. All the players in the Brooklyn mob are dead or in jail . . . Abe Reles, Mickey Adler, Rudy. Even Louis Lepke is in prison. I don't have to deal with it now. And I won't.*

Morty felt more settled having made that decision. He made up his mind not to think of it again. When he came back from the war— he paused in his thinking—if he came back from the war, he would straighten it all out. He decided to enjoy the week and a half he had left of his leave and then get on with his army life.

He and Anna spent every day together, but her mother would not let them sleep together at her house until they were married. Anna laughed at that. "It's a little like locking the barn door after the horse ran out!" Morty laughed too.

But then he said, "Maybe it's a little like a punishment for me, because I wasn't around when you were pregnant." So Morty asked Anna if she would go with him to a hotel room for the week, and they left Lily with Anna's mother, picking her up each day so that Morty could spend as much time as possible with her.

Morty loved Anna's nonna. She was a small woman, square and strong looking, with pure white hair and a wrinkled face like crushed velvet. Her blue eyes popped out and snapped when she smiled. She spoke English with a broad Italian accent that moved up and down melodically. Morty had never met any of his grandparents, so he loved sitting and talking to Nonna, who attempted to tell him stories about growing up in Sicily. Anna sat beside him and translated whatever he didn't understand.

"She likes you," Anna told Morty. "She says you'll make a good husband."

Morty laughed and hugged Anna. "She's right. I will."

At night, when they lay in their bed in the hotel room, Morty told Anna all his thoughts and dreams for them. He'd been having them ever since he'd received the letter telling him about Lily's birth. He told her how he hated himself for missing the joy of watching her bloom with her pregnancy. He asked her if she had nursed Lily, because he remembered watching Golda nurse his brother Isaac, who had died in the flu epidemic, and how beautiful his mouth was and how blissfully she looked at him. He was disappointed to find that Anna had not nursed Lily, but he did not say anything.

Anna told him that she'd had Lily baptized as a way of consoling her mother and nonna and uncles for having a baby out of wedlock. "And besides," she said, "I thought you were dead. And I'm a Catholic."

Morty said he understood completely. "When I come back from the war"—here his voice hitched with hesitation—"we can decide how to raise her. And if you want her to be Catholic, then I guess I'll be all right with it."

Morty told Anna about his days in Liberty, Detective Hanrahan, and the revolver that Mickey Adler had left in the car. "I gave it to the detective, and he said it had been used in a couple of murders. It didn't have my prints on it because I never touched it, but, as he said, I could have wiped them off. I know he thinks I'm dead. He was the one who told my family I was dead. But I'm not going to get in touch with him now. He thinks I'm dead, let me be dead to him." Morty looked at Anna out of the corner of his eye. He wondered what she thought.

"Of course, you shouldn't go in now. It's all water under the bridge. You'll get yourself all tangled up if you go in now."

Morty hugged her close. "I knew you would agree with me."

She laughed. "You mean you hoped I would agree with you."

They stayed up as late as they could, wanting to draw the two weeks out so they had more time together, and every night they fell asleep entangled in each other, exhausted, their eyes closing despite themselves.

They ate three times with each family, wanting to be fair to them so they had the same amount of time together. And then it was time for their wedding.

They planned to marry at city hall, like many of the soldiers and their girls, at the first appointment they could get, and that was four days before he had to leave for Virginia. Sylvia, Ben, and Golda were there, as well as Anna's mother, nonna, and uncles.

Morty knew that one of Anna's uncles was connected to the Italian gangs and the other ran a deli, but he had a hard time remembering which was which. He looked at Anna's uncles, trying to be casual. Had he seen them before? He'd caught a glimpse of her uncle Tony DeMaio, who owned the deli, twice several years ago. Morty remembered how Anna's uncle had come out of the deli looking for her one day when she had come out to meet Morty. He was a short man and thin, with curly black hair and a thin mustache. He had a ready smile that was very engaging. Her other uncle, Mario Amato, her mother's brother, was also short, but with a powerful physique and a muscular torso. He had curly black hair and a classically handsome Italian swarthiness, but he had a suspicious air about him, his eyes darting this way and that, as if trying to see what lurked behind every corner, every table, and every person. Both men wore suits, and both men held their fedoras in their hands.

It was the first time that Ben and Golda had met Anna's family, and it was civil but not warm. While they were waiting to go into city hall for the short wedding ceremony, Anna and Morty tried to fill in all the awkward silences with stories.

Anna was holding Lily, who wore the blue dress that Golda had made for her. Anna said, "Look, Ma, this dress was made by Morty's mother. She's like a painter with thread."

Mrs. DeMaio nodded her head. "It is beautiful," she admitted.

Golda nodded and said, "Thank you." Then she added, "If you like, I can make you a blouse or a scarf. And your mother too."

Mrs. DeMaio smiled and said, "That's very kind of you, but it isn't necessary."

"Ma!" Anna whispered to her. "That's not nice. She's a well-known dressmaker. People come to her from all over New York. I bet Nonna would love a scarf."

Mrs. DeMaio looked straight ahead and said nothing more. Golda, too, was quiet.

That afternoon, after the ceremony, Mrs. DeMaio and Anna's uncles were hosting a celebratory wedding luncheon. There was a big discussion between Ben and Golda beforehand about inviting their own friends.

"How can we not invite Cousin Surah? Or my partner, Abe? Or the Weissmans next door?" Ben had asked.

"We weren't asked to invite anyone," Golda said. "It's not our house, and it isn't our party. It would be rude to just assume."

Ben shook his head. "Are we ashamed of this wedding? Shouldn't we celebrate Morty's miracle? That he's alive? And our beautiful Lily."

"All right, all right," Golda said. "But not at their house. At our house. We'll have a party too."

And that was what was decided. Ben and Golda went to the DeMaio's party and invited Anna's mother, grandmother, and uncles to theirs. Morty and Anna did not argue with either family. They allowed their families to decide what to do.

Golda brought a beautiful home-baked pie to the DeMaio's party, and Anna's house was filled with her large Italian family. Even their parish priest was there. Anna had warned Morty that he would come. Since Lily had been baptized in the church, as far as the priest was concerned, Lily was Catholic. Morty didn't think he could really object after the fact, although he had not told his parents that Lily had been baptized. He wondered if they would care. He thought, *I can teach her about her Jewish background when I'm really in her life. And who knows when that will be, with me in the war.* It was not something he wanted to think about and certainly not anything he would mention to his parents.

Golda, Ben, and Sylvia were the only people connected to Morty at the DeMaio party. The food and wine were abundant, even with the new wartime restrictions. Anna told Morty that she had begged her mother not to bake a ham, which she had been planning on serving, but there were plenty of other meats that Morty knew his parents wouldn't eat. He was happy to see they took the cheeses and the breads and at least one pasta dish with vegetables. And each of them filled their dessert plates with pastries. He thought briefly how many little hiccups there were in this marriage of two different religions and cultures. But he pushed the thoughts aside and accepted all the toasts from each of Anna's relatives and was deliriously happy that he and

Anna were going to spend the next two nights at The Waldorf Astoria in Manhattan all by themselves.

Two nights later, Ben and Golda had their party, but rather than inviting people to a wedding party, they said they were celebrating Morty's miraculous return from the dead. They introduced Anna as his beautiful wife and Lily as their granddaughter, and the awkwardness of the baby being born before the wedding was not discussed. Anna's mother and uncles showed up for half an hour and then left. Golda and Ben were relieved and were able to celebrate Morty's return with their friends.

And just one day later, Morty had to leave for Virginia.

CHAPTER 40

GOLDA

The night before Morty left, Golda slept fitfully. She dreamed that her mother stood at the foot of her bed, giving her a message, repeating it over and over. Golda awoke, heart pounding, only understanding that her mother was insisting on a promise. She didn't know what the promise was. She went back to sleep, shaken and still unsure of what the message meant. When she awoke, she couldn't even remember that much. Only that her mother was insistent on something, but Golda did not know what it was.

The next day, Golda, Ben, Sylvia, Anna, and Lily all went with Morty to Penn Station, taking the subway train early enough in the morning that they could stop at Horn and Hardart's for lunch. Morty was dressed in his uniform and held his duffel bag between his legs on the subway. They sat together on the train, silent, each thinking their own thoughts, only speaking to one another when they wanted to say something about Lily.

Morty had to be on the train to Virginia at three o'clock. At breakfast that morning, Golda told Ben and Sylvia of her strange dream. "My mother was insisting I do something, but when I awoke, I couldn't remember what I was supposed to do. It was very upsetting."

"You don't believe that means anything, Mama?" Sylvia said.

"Maybe yes, maybe no. I haven't heard from her in a year. I don't know if she's alive or dead. Maybe she's gone, and she had something important to tell me."

"Do you believe in ghosts?"

Golda shrugged.

"Well, you don't know what she was saying, so if you don't remember, you don't remember."

Ben patted her shoulder. "If it's important, it will come back to you."

Golda nodded, hoping that she could shake the disquiet she felt.

The family got to the restaurant at noon and took a large table near a window. Morty went to the central desk, where a young woman took his dollar bills and gave out sleeves of nickels in exchange; the nickels could be used in the Automat machines. Morty came back to the table to distribute the coins. Then the family fanned out to get their sandwiches and coffee and pies. No one talked much at the restaurant either, except for Golda, who repeated her dream to the group, hoping the repetition would help her remember what her mother's message had been. Lily, who had taken a liking to Golda, sat on her lap babbling baby talk.

"She is like you were at that age," Golda said to Morty. "Chatter, chatter, chatter." Golda was smiling with delight at Lily, who had taken a cookie and was trying to feed it to Golda.

"Is she bothering you?" Anna asked. "I'll take her if she is."

"No, no. I love it. I love her." Golda hugged Lily, who laughed and patted her cheek.

There were other groups of families with soldiers at the restaurant, all of them going one place or another. Mostly everyone was eating quietly. Golda thought everything had been said and said again at home, and now the silence was pregnant with the many unspoken fears and worries about the unknown that lay ahead of them. She hoped none of them would cry when they finally said goodbye at the train station.

CHAPTER 41

MORTY

Morty looked at his family, at his parents and sister, his wife and daughter—saying the words *wife* and *daughter* still thrilled him—and he realized how lucky he was. Here they all were, together, despite the year and a half when he had been missing and afraid to contact them. Then he wondered if his luck would hold out long enough for him to survive this war and come home to them. Those were some of the unspoken words.

Morty polished off his roast beef sandwich and looked at his new wristwatch, a belated birthday gift from his parents. "We should leave," he said. Despite himself, even though he didn't want to leave his new wife and baby, he was excited to be going to Virginia for training as an army engineer. That training was two months long, he'd been told. He wasn't sure he'd have another furlough after that but thought he probably would be shipped out right after he finished his training.

The family left the restaurant, Morty carrying Lily in his right arm and holding Anna's hand with his left. Ben carried Morty's duffel bag. They walked the two blocks to the huge Penn Station, where they located the track number for the train to Virginia. They milled about by the gate, along with many other soldiers and their families, traveling to the same destination as Morty. It seemed Penn Station was full of soldiers from all over the country, all carrying duffel bags, ready to put the awkwardness of this last goodbye behind them. Families stood with their soldiers, some talking quietly, some standing silently, out of words, not knowing what to say now that the time for leaving had finally come.

It was two thirty, and there was suddenly a rush toward the gate, the men fearful of not finding a choice seat for the long trip to Virginia.

Morty handed Lily to Anna and hugged Sylvia first, whispering in her ear, "Thank you for being Anna's friend."

Sylvia hugged him back, hard. "Write," she said. "I'll write you every week."

"I promise I will," Morty said. Sylvia kissed him on both cheeks.

Then Morty stood before Ben, who also kissed both his cheeks and hugged him.

"I'm glad we aren't the kind of family where the men only shake hands and don't kiss and hug," Morty said.

Ben nodded. "That's like they do in England. We do like the Italians and the French." And he gave Morty another hug and kiss. Then he said, "You make me proud, Morton. And be safe. Promise."

Again, Morty promised, although he didn't know what he was promising to do.

Next came Golda, who held him close. She was crying. He felt the wetness of her tears on his cheek. "I love you, Mama," he said. "Thank you for everything you did for me." Golda couldn't speak. Her soft weeping had turned to sobbing. Golda clung to him until, finally, Morty pulled back, and she let him go.

Morty turned, picked up his duffel bag, and signaled for Anna to walk with him through the gate and down the ramp to the waiting train. Men were milling on the platform with parents, wives, and sweethearts. They shook their fathers' hands, kissed their mothers and wives.

Morty and Anna had said everything they had to say. They held Lily between them as they stood, arms around each other, waiting until the last minute to leave the warmth of their embrace. Morty was not sure if he would be able to let them go.

He thought he heard his name called, faintly, from the top of the ramp. "Morton. Morton." He looked and saw Golda running toward them. "Morteleh, Morteleh!" she called, using the name she had called him when he was a little boy, as she came closer to them. She stopped several feet away and walked slowly toward them. "I remember. I remember now what my mother said in my dream." As Golda came closer, her voice got quieter. "She said, 'Make him promise. Make him promise.' That was you, Morty. She wanted you to promise me."

"Promise what, Mama?"

"Come back to us, please. Promise me you will come back to us," she said as she reached him and hugged him one last time.

"I will, Mama," he said, and kissed her wet cheek. "I promise." He wondered if saying it could make it come true, so he added, "I promise I will come home."

Reading Group
Discussion Questions

1. When Golda arrives in New York, she faces the difficult choice to marry Ben or let Morty go to an orphanage. What other possibilities did she have, if any? What would you have done?

2. In what ways was Golda's marriage to Ben different from the arranged marriages that were common to young women at that time?

3. Ben recognizes the difficult choices that he and Golda had at the start of their union, but he declares that he "embraced" the choice and Golda did not. Is this true, and how did that play out in their family life?

4. Love comes up as a question several times in the book. What can we say about whether Golda ever loved Ben? What were her feelings about him? And how did Ben feel about Golda?

5. How was the love of Golda and Ben for one another the same or different from the feelings of Morty and Anna for one another?

6. Morty is eighteen years old before his parents tell him the true story of his birth and Golda's role. What difference would it have made to Morty if he had been told earlier? Would it have made a difference for Golda and Ben? Is this similar to a family's choice to tell children they were adopted?

7. Golda's ambivalence about her lost life opportunities and her feelings for Morty can sometimes make her a difficult character to like. How did you feel about her?

8. Ben and Golda were not religiously observant people, but they often spoke to Rabbi Levy. What role did he play in the family's

life? How was that different from the role that Cousin Surah played? Are there people like that in your life?

9. Morty's choice to help his father by going to Rudy put him on a dangerous path. Were there other ways he might have helped his father?

10. How do you feel about Morty's choice to run away to Cincinnati? Were there other ways he could have acted? Do you think he was right not to get in touch with his family or Anna?

11. What role does Sylvia play in the family, before and after Morty leaves New York?

ACKNOWLEDGMENTS

It is a well-established but not often talked about fact that many Jewish immigrant families had relatives who were involved with the violent gangs that ruled the Brooklyn streets in the first half of the twentieth century. For some of the poor and hungry boys who lived in crowded tenements and saw their parents work long hours for low wages, the glamorous and wealthy gangsters who owned the street corners became their role models for how to get rich with easy money. Not for them was the long slog of education and hard work that propelled most of their generation out of poverty. They joined the gangs, worked their way up the ranks of the organizations, and became criminals. Some of them were arrested and jailed, and some of them were found dead or disappeared.

As I listened to family stories when I was growing up, I vaguely remember hearing that my mother had a first cousin who was part of the nefarious Murder, Inc., the enforcement arm of the National Crime Syndicate, which ruled gambling, labor racketeering, bootlegging, moneylending, and all the other illegal activities of the time. But there was such shame attached to those activities that no one talked much about the details of his life, except that he was a college student who was a card shark. Then my daughter Ruth Kraut became an expert on researching our ancestry—looking up birth, death, and census data, scouring newspaper articles and graves in cemeteries.

Ruth came to me with two tantalizing articles in newspapers from those days that described our cousin's parents and their conflicting attitudes about accepting their murdered son's body. Should they bury it in a Jewish cemetery and sit shiva for him, or refuse the body and let it remain in a non-Jewish pauper's grave? The story intrigued me, and I embarked on the writer's journey of "what if . . ." And so evolved *Street*

Corner Dreams, my largely imagined novel of an immigrant family in Brooklyn during the time between the two world wars.

The characters in the book are completely fictional, except for the mention of real gangsters: Abe "Kid Twist" Reles, Meyer Lansky, Louis Lepke Buchalter, and Albert Anastasia. Any other gangsters, such as Mickey Adler and Georgie Lieber, are, again, fictional. I appreciate the opportunity to research the Jewish gangs in Rich Cohen's marvelous book *Tough Jews: Fathers, Sons, and Gangster Dreams*, in Michael Shnayerson's *Bugsy Siegel: The Dark Side of the American Dream*, and in Robert Rockaway's *But He Was Good to His Mother: The Lives and Crimes of Jewish Gangsters*. These books gave an unvarnished picture of the Jewish gangsters who murdered and stole and ran the rackets that ruled the streets of Brooklyn, New York, and other cities around the country. I would also like to thank Sullivan County Historian John Conway, whose article "The Body in the Berry Patch," (July 24, 2020) described the discovery of the body of my relative Abraham Finkelstein, known locally as Sol Gordon, a card shark. The article also describes the drama about the burial of his body, which I adapted for my book.

I began the book during the coronavirus pandemic in mid-2021 and completed it in December 2022. On the way, several people read pieces of the book and commented on drafts of it. I want to thank Virginia Weir, my friend and Zoom writing buddy, for listening to me read the scenes as they evolved from my imagination and then reading through the entire book. I am grateful to Nora Stonehill, Gail Reisin Goldstein, Ruth Kraut, Michael Appel, Joan Reinhardt Reiss, and my husband, Allen Kraut, for their close reading and comments on drafts of *Street Corner Dreams*.

Finally, I deeply appreciate all the editorial and production staff of She Writes Press, especially Shannon Green and Brooke Warner for their professionalism and guidance.

About the Author

photo credit: Allen Kraut

Florence Reiss Kraut is a native New Yorker, raised and educated in New York City. She holds a BA in English and a master's in social work, and she worked for thirty years as a clinician, a family therapist, and finally CEO of a family service agency before retiring to write and travel widely.

Her intense interest in family comes from growing up in a close family of twenty-six aunts and uncles and thirty-one first cousins where, listening to stories at kitchen table coffee klatches and family parties, she learned about the conflicts and mysteries of family life. These stories became the inspiration for many of the stories and essays written and published from the early years raising her three children throughout her career as a social worker. She has published stories for children and teens, romance stories for national magazines, literary stories, and personal essays. She has nine grandchildren.

How to Make a Life, her debut novel, was published by She Writes Press in October 2020. *Street Corner Dreams* is her second novel.

Learn more about Florence at www.florencereisskraut.com.

SELECTED TITLES FROM SHE WRITES PRESS

She Writes Press is an independent publishing company founded to serve women writers everywhere. Visit us at www.shewritespress.com.

Beyond the Ghetto Gates by Michelle Cameron. $16.95, 978-1-63152-850-7
When French troops occupy the Italian port city of Ancona, freeing the city's Jews from their repressive ghetto, two very different cultures collide—and a whirlwind of progressivism and brutal backlash is unleashed.

A Ritchie Boy by Linda Kass. $16.95, 978-1-63152-739-5
The true, inspiring World The inspiring World War II tale of Eli Stoff, a Jewish Austrian immigrant who triumphs over adversity and becomes a US Army intelligence officer, told as a cohesive linked collection of stories narrated by a variety of characters. Based on true events.

An Address in Amsterdam by Mary Dingee Fillmore. $16.95, 978-1-63152-133-1
After facing relentless danger and escalating raids for 18 months, Rachel Klein—a well-behaved young Jewish woman who transformed herself into a courier for the underground when the Nazis invaded her country—persuades her parents to hide with her in a dank basement, where much is revealed.

Even in Darkness by Barbara Stark-Nemon. $16.95, 978-1-63152-956-6
From privileged young German-Jewish woman to concentration camp refugee, Kläre Kohler navigates the horrors of war and—through unlikely sources—finds the strength, hope, and love she needs to survive.

Stitching a Life: An Immigration Story by Mary Helen Fein
$16.95, 978-1-63152-677-0
After sixteen-year-old Helen, a Jewish girl from Russia, comes alone across the Atlantic to the Lower East Side of New York in the year 1900, she devotes herself to bringing the rest of her family to safety and opportunity in the new world—and finds love along the way.

When It's Over by Barbara Ridley. $16.95, 978-1-63152-296-3
When World War II envelopes Europe, Lena Kulkova flees Czechoslovakia for the relative safety of England, leaving her Jewish family behind in Prague.